WINGS OF FIRE

WINGS OF FIRE

DARKNESS OF DRAGONS

by

TUI T. SUTHERLAND

SCHOLASTIC INC.

ISBN 978-1-338-31494-6

Text copyright © 2017 by Tui T. Sutherland. Map and border design © 2017 by Mike Schley. Dragon illustrations © 2017 by Joy Ang. All rights reserved. Published by Scholastic Inc., *Publishers since 1920*. SCHOLASTIC and associated logos are trademarks and/or registered trademarks of Scholastic Inc.

12 11 10 9   22 23

Printed in the U.S.A.   40

Originally published in hardcover by Scholastic Press, August 2017

This edition first printing, October 2018

Book design by Phil Falco

For Elliot and Jonah, my heroes and my heart, who make me happy every single day

With thanks to Robert Doar and Aayush Srivatsa for Typhoon and to Amy Doar for supporting Lifting Hands International

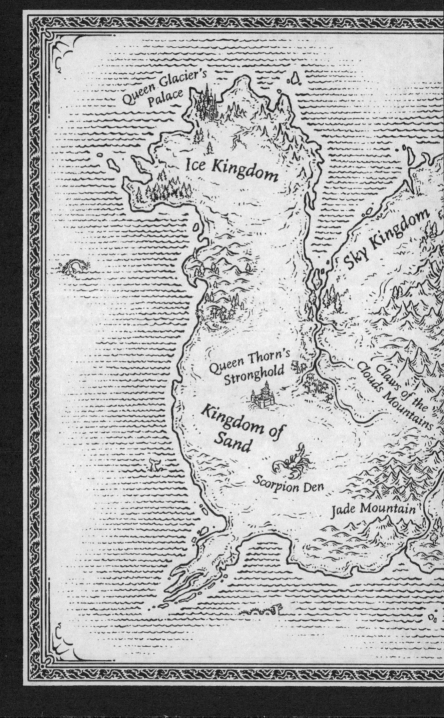

A GUIDE TO THE
DRAGONS

OF PYRRHIA

UPDATED AND EDITED BY
STARFLIGHT OF THE NIGHTWINGS

WELCOME TO THE JADE MOUNTAIN ACADEMY!

At this school, you will be learning side by side with dragons from all the other tribes, so we wanted to give you some basic information that may be useful as you get to know one another.

You have been assigned to a winglet with six other dragons; the winglet groups are listed on the following page.

Thank you for being a part of this school. You are the hope of Pyrrhia's future. You are the dragons who can bring lasting peace to this world.

WE WISH YOU ALL THE POWER OF WINGS OF FIRE!

JADE WINGLET

IceWing: Winter

MudWing: Umber

NightWing: Moonwatcher

RainWing: Kinkajou

SandWing: Qibli

SeaWing: Turtle

SkyWing: Carnelian

GOLD WINGLET

IceWing: Icicle

MudWing: Sora

NightWing: Bigtail

RainWing: Tamarin

SandWing: Onyx

SeaWing: Pike

SkyWing: Flame

SILVER WINGLET

IceWing: Changbai

MudWing: Sepia

NightWing: Fearless

RainWing: Boto

SandWing: Ostrich

SeaWing: Anemone

SkyWing: Thrush

COPPER WINGLET

IceWing: Alba

MudWing: Marsh

NightWing: Mindreader

RainWing: Coconut

SandWing: Pronghorn

SeaWing: Snail

SkyWing: Peregrine

QUARTZ WINGLET

IceWing: Ermine

MudWing: Newt

NightWing: Mightyclaws

RainWing: Siamang

SandWing: Arid

SeaWing: Barracuda

SkyWing: Garnet

SANDWINGS

Description: pale gold or white scales the color of desert sand; poisonous barbed tail; forked black tongues

Abilities: can survive a long time without water, poison enemies with the tips of their tails like scorpions, bury themselves for camouflage in the desert sand, breathe fire

Queen: since the end of the War of SandWing Succession, Queen Thorn

Students at Jade Mountain: Arid, Onyx, Ostrich, Pronghorn, Qibli

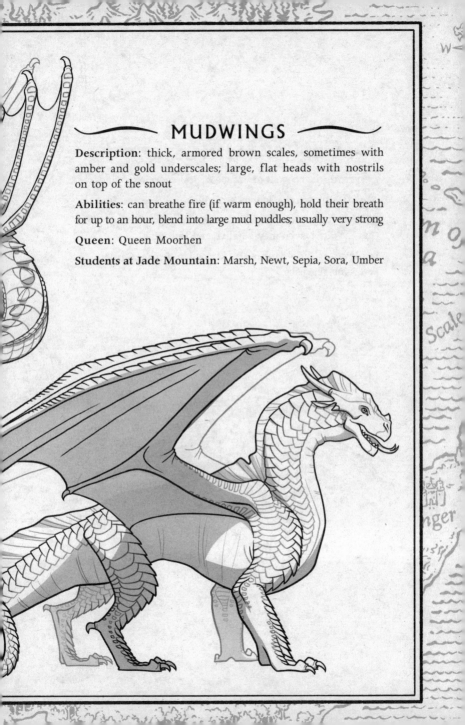

MUDWINGS

Description: thick, armored brown scales, sometimes with amber and gold underscales; large, flat heads with nostrils on top of the snout

Abilities: can breathe fire (if warm enough), hold their breath for up to an hour, blend into large mud puddles; usually very strong

Queen: Queen Moorhen

Students at Jade Mountain: Marsh, Newt, Sepia, Sora, Umber

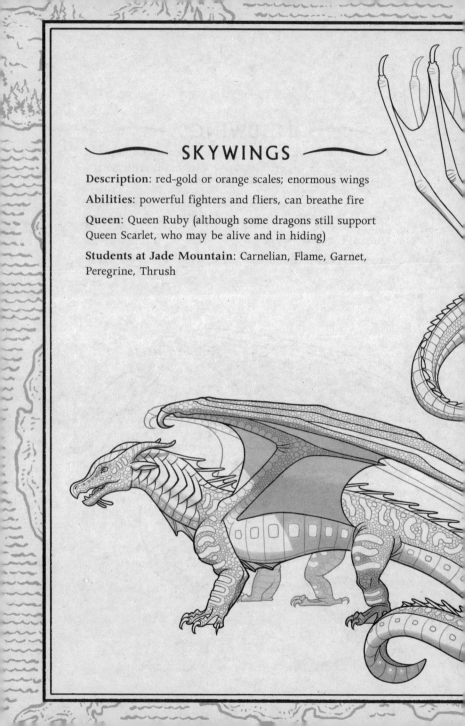

SKYWINGS

Description: red-gold or orange scales; enormous wings

Abilities: powerful fighters and fliers, can breathe fire

Queen: Queen Ruby (although some dragons still support Queen Scarlet, who may be alive and in hiding)

Students at Jade Mountain: Carnelian, Flame, Garnet, Peregrine, Thrush

SEAWINGS

Description: blue or green or aquamarine scales; webs between their claws; gills on their necks; glow-in-the-dark stripes on their tails/snouts/underbellies

Abilities: can breathe underwater, see in the dark, create huge waves with one splash of their powerful tails; excellent swimmers

Queen: Queen Coral

Students at Jade Mountain: Anemone, Barracuda, Pike, Snail, Turtle

ICEWINGS

Description: silvery scales like the moon or pale blue like ice; ridged claws to grip the ice; forked blue tongues; tails narrow to a whip-thin end

Abilities: can withstand subzero temperatures and bright light, exhale a deadly frostbreath

Queen: Queen Glacier

Students at Jade Mountain: Alba, Changbai, Ermine, Icicle, Winter

RAINWINGS

Description: scales constantly shift colors, usually bright like birds of paradise; prehensile tails

Abilities: can camouflage their scales to blend into their surroundings; shoot a deadly venom from their fangs

Queen: Queen Glory

Students at Jade Mountain: Boto, Coconut, Kinkajou, Siamang, Tamarin

NIGHTWINGS

Description: purplish-black scales and scattered silver scales on the underside of their wings, like a night sky full of stars; forked black tongues

Abilities: can breathe fire, disappear into dark shadows; once known for reading minds and foretelling the future, but no longer

Queen: Queen Glory (see recent scrolls on the NightWing Exodus and the RainWing Royal Challenge)

Students at Jade Mountain: Bigtail, Fearless, Mightyclaws, Mindreader, Moonwatcher

THE
JADE MOUNTAIN
PROPHECY

Beware the darkness of dragons,
Beware the stalker of dreams,
Beware the talons of power and fire,
Beware one who is not what she seems.

Something is coming to shake the earth,
Something is coming to scorch the ground.
Jade Mountain will fall beneath thunder and ice
Unless the lost city of night can be found.

PROLOGUE

Almost twenty-one years ago . . .

A dragon was fleeing across the dunes.

She didn't dare fly. The sun had just risen into the cloudless blue expanse overhead. Up there, she'd be as easy to spot as one of the dark, circling buzzards that seemed to be waiting for her to die.

But I'm not *going to die,* she thought fiercely. *Not today.*

She ran with her sand-colored wings outstretched, hoping to catch any stirrings of wind, but the air was still and hot down on the desert floor. Her scales were baking; her back had never been so hot; her body was a sack of fire-heated stones she had to drag along behind her. Her earrings felt like twin pieces of the sun blazing against her skull. Brief, dazed visions of roasted lizards drifted in and out of her head. Sometimes she was the one on the spit, turning above the fire; sometimes she had fallen in and was staring up at them as they rotated slowly overhead and the flames licked around her.

Was that the sound of wingbeats in the distance?

She threw herself down and burrowed until she was hidden. A few layers below the surface, she found a cooler swathe of sand, and she drove her scalded talons into it.

I left the dates out to dry for too long. They've all shriveled up. Quicksand will be so disappointed in me.

She blinked and blinked again, trying to shake off the hallucination without moving. Her old boss had been dead for years. She wasn't in the kitchens anymore. She was running for her life. She couldn't let the desert consume her mind right now.

The flickering shadows of two dragons swept past. She stayed still, buried, until the wingbeats were long gone.

And then she was up and running again.

It can't be much farther, she thought desperately. Of course, the journey never seemed this long when she flew. But she'd been running for half the night and surely the sun had risen hours ago. *What if I'm lost? Or what if she moved without telling me?* It had been almost a year since her last visit . . .

Something wavered on the blurry horizon — a hut? A tree? The dragon shifted course to aim for it, but as she got closer, it disappeared again.

A mirage.

I'm losing it. But I can't.

There's too much at stake.

She stopped, closed her eyes, and concentrated fiercely.

SandWings were naturally adapted to desert conditions — better at handling heat and a lack of water than other dragon tribes. But even SandWings weren't supposed to spend hours on the desert floor, running along the sand in the baking sun. They were supposed to get up and fly — to sweep from oasis to oasis on swift wings.

An oasis. She lives near that pool with the five palms. Maybe . . .

She strained her ears.

There — the faintest faraway sound of splashing, of a bucket plunging into water and coming out dripping.

She opened her eyes and ran toward it, determination in every muscle of her heavy body.

And finally there it was — the small hut by the pool, shaded by the five palm trees. She let out a cry of relief and stumbled, half sliding down the last dune and collapsing entirely into the water.

The door of the hut opened, and a sharp-eyed dragon emerged, wiping her claws on a small, sandy, dark green towel.

"Don't drink too much," she said acerbically. "If you're sick in my oasis, you're cleaning it up yourself."

"I know," said the fugitive, taking one more swallow and stopping reluctantly. She sat up, water streaming off her wings, and burst into tears. "Prickle, I'm in s-so much trouble."

"Oh, by the circle of snakes," her sister snapped, throwing the towel at her. "I told you to stay away from that prince. You should have left the palace with me when he first started mooning around the kitchens. I *knew* he'd get you killed sooner or later, and probably me too if I didn't clear out."

"Please help me," Palm begged. "You were right. Of course you were right. I'm sorry I didn't listen."

"Are the queen's guards chasing you right now?" Prickle said sharply. "Did you lead them to me? I will *not* be murdered for your mistakes." She glanced up at the sky and took a step back toward her door.

"No, wait!" Palm floundered out of the pool and threw herself at her sister's feet. "I was careful, I promise! I just need a place to hide for a few — even one day, just one day. Then I'll keep running and you'll never have to see me again, I swear."

Prickle stared down her nose at Palm, flicking her wingtips crossly. Side by side, the two dragons were clearly sisters from the same hatching, with similar patterns of light brown scales freckled across their paler yellow scales. But Palm was rounder, softer, a creature with access to the bread and date sugar cookies of the palace kitchens, while Prickle had the lean, weathered look of a dragon who'd been living on her own in the desert for two years.

"Please," Palm begged. "Can you help me?"

Prickle surveyed her coldly. Palm remembered the fight they'd had the first day Smolder stopped by the kitchen to compliment the camel stew. Prickle had seen the spark between them long before Palm realized that it was mutual. She'd thought it was innocent enough, having a crush on the handsome SandWing prince, and that Prickle was overreacting.

Until he came back . . . and then came back again . . . and then he invited her for a walk around the courtyards . . . and then they started meeting after dark and whispering about the future. Soon after that, Prickle moved out of the palace overnight, warning Palm to stay away from the royal family if she wanted to live.

"Fine," Prickle said abruptly. "You can stay for *one* night if you give me your earrings."

"What?" Palm reached up to touch the glowing fire opals in her ears. "These? But they were a gift from —"

"I know," said her sister. "They're much too expensive for you to afford on your wages. I'll get a whole lot of gold for them in the Scorpion Den."

My last connection to Smolder, Palm thought sadly.

"Hand them over," said Prickle, "or keep flying right now."

Palm knew her wings and talons couldn't make it another foot.

Her claws were shaking as she reached up,

unclasped the earrings, and dropped them into Prickle's palm.

It's not my last connection, she reminded herself. *I have something more important now.*

"Pretty," said her sister, examining the opals. "Maybe I'll keep them instead of selling them." She fastened them into her own ears, where they glittered smug little "I told you so" faces at Palm. "Now stop blubbering and tell me what happened."

"We tried to elope," Palm admitted. She wiped her eyes with the towel, leaving trails of sticky wet sand across her face.

Prickle let out a frustrated growl. "You have the brains of a sun-addled camel."

"I know," Palm sniffled. "But . . . we had to."

Prickle's gaze flashed over Palm's figure. "I take it back. Sun-addled camels at least still have a survival instinct." She turned and swept into the hut and Palm hurried after her.

It was blissfully cool inside compared to the scorching heat Palm had been running through for so long. A red curtain covered the only window, casting the room in shades of blood and rubies. Prickle stepped over to a low table, picked up a small mirror, and tilted her head to admire the earrings.

"You brought this on yourself," she pointed out self-righteously.

"But it isn't fair!" Palm burst out. "Why can't he fall in love? Why does his whole life have to be wasted just so his mother won't feel threatened? Other royal families aren't like this." She rubbed her eyes angrily. "Besides," she muttered, "it could be male, and then no one would even care about it."

Prickle rolled her eyes. "Finish your stupid story."

"We were supposed to meet by the caravan gate before midnight," Palm said. "We were going to go west, or maybe south, and find a small oasis where we could live in peace, just like you did."

"*I* didn't bring a prince or a secret potential heir to the throne into *my* hideout," her sister observed. She took down two bowls from a shelf and began rummaging in a sack. For food, Palm hoped.

"Well, the guards showed up before he did," Palm said, her wings drooping. "I don't know how they knew about me or our plans." She sat down in the corner, twisting the green towel between her claws.

"I have three guesses," Prickle growled, "and they all begin with B."

She was probably right. Palm had always felt the eyes of the three SandWing princesses on her — Burn's ferocious glare, Blister's malevolent scrutiny, even gossipy Blaze's watchful curiosity. Smolder tried to meet Palm in secret, but perhaps there was no such thing as a true secret in the palace.

Well . . . maybe one, she thought, touching her stomach.

"I was able to escape," she said. "They heard him coming and got distracted, and I bolted. But I know they're looking for me. Oasis won't let them stop until they find me."

"Smolder's probably already dead," Prickle said heartlessly. "You'll never be able to go back to the palace. If Oasis doesn't get you, one of her daughters will."

"I know," Palm said, her eyes filling with tears again. *Oh, Smolder, I'll miss you so much.*

"Shhh!" Prickle's head shot up. Her ears flicked toward the door of the hut. Her venomous tail lifted slowly, menacingly, over her head.

The two sisters waited in petrified silence for several long heartbeats.

"Are you sure you weren't followed?" Prickle whispered harshly.

"I'm sure!" Palm whispered back.

"Then what was —?" Prickle started, but her question was interrupted by the unmistakable *thump thump thump* of talons landing heavily on the sand outside.

"Oh moons," Palm whispered in terror. She shrank back against the wall as the door was flung open and two SandWing soldiers burst into the room.

"I knew it!" crowed the male soldier. "I told you I heard her sister had a place out here!"

The other soldier winced, and her eyes locked with Palm's.

She knew this dragon. *Agave — she's the little one who was so scared the first few days in the wingery.* Palm was only a year older, but she'd worried about the frightened dragonet. She'd shared her snacks and convinced Agave to play dragons and vipers until she calmed down.

But that was a long time ago. Agave was a full-grown soldier now, big-shouldered and long-clawed. She flicked her tail up and frowned at Palm.

"Yeah, you were right, Torch," she said. "Good thinking. All right, you prince-loving traitor, time to come with us."

She stepped forward and snapped a pair of shackles around Prickle's wrists.

Palm's gasp was drowned out by the snarl of outrage from her sister.

"I'm not Palm!" Prickle roared. "*She* is! I'm not stupid enough to sneak around with a sand snorter like Smolder! Take these off!"

"Nice try," Agave said, seizing Prickle's neck and slamming her back into the wall. The two bowls wobbled and one fell, spilling coconut milk into the sand.

"I'm *not*," Prickle wheezed. She clawed at Agave's talons. "Palm, *tell them*."

Palm couldn't find her voice. She couldn't breathe. Did Agave really think —?

"Are you sure about this?" asked the other soldier nervously. "They do look alike. But I would have guessed that the other one was Palm — I mean — it's hard to tell — but —"

"This one is Palm," said Agave calmly. "I knew her in the wingery. Besides, look at her earrings." She turned Prickle's head so the jewels glowed in the dim red light. "Those came from the prince, no doubt about it. I hear she's been wearing them around the palace."

"Oh, yes." The other guard exhaled with relief. "I heard that, too. Asking for trouble, flaunting a gift like that. You're right, that must be her."

"NO!" Prickle shrieked, trying to throw Agave off her. "They're not mine! She gave them to me! I'm not Palm!" The male soldier leaped forward and locked a heavy collar around Prickle's neck, attached to a chain, which he held while Agave shackled Prickle's back legs as well.

"*Palm*," Prickle screamed. "Don't let them do this to me!"

I should stop them, Palm thought in a panic. *She's my sister. I have to save her.*

But . . . I also have to save my dragonet.

If she admitted the truth and they took her back to the palace, the queen would find out quickly that she was with egg — and she would never let Smolder's dragonet live.

What can I do? How can I choose between my sister and my egg?

Palm stumbled to her feet as the soldiers began to drag Prickle to the door.

"Wh-what's going to happen to her?" Palm asked.

"Queen Oasis wants her locked in the deepest dungeon," said the male soldier. "Where no one will ever find her."

"As for you," Agave said, meeting her eyes at last, "you might be accused of helping her. I'd suggest you run."

Her gaze flickered slightly, down to the small scar on Palm's left wing — the one she got falling off the wingery roof.

She does know I'm me. She's trying to save me.

"Palm," Prickle growled. "Tell them the truth, or so help me I'll set the moons on fire and drop them on your head."

It's not just my *life that needs saving, though.*

I have to save my egg . . . I'm the only one who can.

"I'm sorry, Palm." She lifted her head and tilted it in exactly her sister's usual condescending way. "You brought this upon yourself."

"WHAT?" Prickle roared a blast of fire that Palm barely managed to duck. Flames caught and flared all around the hut: the small bed, the box beside it, the shelf, the bowls. The curtain blazed into a curling flag of red-white-gold.

The soldiers yanked Prickle out the door and Palm rushed out after them, coughing and blinking the smoke away. As her sight cleared, she saw them clamping iron around Prickle's snout. She wouldn't be breathing any more fire today — or shouting about her innocence. She'd have to fly back to the palace in livid silence.

And then someone there will recognize her, Palm thought. *They'll set her free. They'll think it was all a mistake.*

I hope. I hope Agave doesn't get in trouble.

She stood beside the oasis pool, watching the three dragons fly away, feeling the heat of the burning hut as it collapsed inward.

Prickle will never forgive me for this. But once the queen sees her, she'll know she's not me and let her go. And by then I'll be long gone.

Me and my dragonet.

This is the head start I needed.

She whirled to plunge herself into the pool, washing off the sand and taking huge gulps. She found two camelskin pouches hanging from one of the trees, filled them with water, and slung them across her chest.

Barely a minute later, she was flying. Up in the sky this time, south and east, toward the mountains. She'd hide in the forests and hills, maybe in the rainforest for a while — somewhere sheltered where she could have her egg in safety.

Then she'd keep moving. She'd keep her dragonet alive, and one day she'd tell her the truth about her heritage, and — if it was a girl — it felt like a girl — she'd teach her that the throne wasn't worth it. That it was better to hide and live. That she didn't need power or treasure. How to survive, that was all she needed to know.

Far below, sand whirled around something small, moving fast. Palm's heart gave a little nervous jump and she squinted down at it.

Scavengers — three of them, on horseback. Riding into the desert, toward the queen's palace.

That's odd, she thought. *Don't they know there are dragons out here?*

A moment later, she'd forgotten them again. Her mind was full of dreams of her dragonet.

I'm sorry you never got to meet her, Smolder, she thought sorrowfully. *But I remember the names we talked about, don't worry.*

If it is a girl — it feels like a girl — then I shall give her the name you chose and hide her away somewhere secret and safe.

She'll get the chance to be ordinary that you never had.

By the moons of Pyrrhia, I swear she will never have anything to do with thrones or queens or battles or crowns, for as long as we both shall live.

Ice Kingdom

Sky Kingdom

Queen Thorn's
Stronghold

Claws of the
Clouds Mountains

Kingdom of
Sand

Scorpion Den

Jade Mountain

PART ONE

STORM OF SANDS

CHAPTER 1

Qibli stood on one of the peaks of Jade Mountain, watching the group of seven dragons fly away to the west.

Although there were four small black NightWings flying in the group, he knew exactly which one was Moon. He'd flown with her all the way through the Sky Kingdom, to Possibility and back. He knew the way she held her wings to catch the changing winds. He recognized the way she tipped her head up to breathe in the sunlight.

If it were up to him, he'd spend every day of the rest of his life flying with her.

He certainly wouldn't watch her soar away with a dragon who might have evil plans and definitely had superpowers.

They all fall in behind Darkstalker, letting him take the lead, he noticed, *even though Darkstalker doesn't actually know the way to the NightWing village in the rainforest. They act like he's their leader because he acts like he's their leader.*

Maybe I should go after them. His wings twitched.

He knew he shouldn't — it would make Darkstalker suspicious of him, and Turtle would have a better chance of spying safely without Qibli there. But he couldn't bear this feeling, watching Moon fly away from him. Knowing that soon they'd be kingdoms apart.

He looked down at the small slate in his talons. He wished he could will a message into existence, although he knew Turtle was still flying and there was nothing to report yet. He wished the slates worked both ways, so he could send questions to Turtle; he'd already thought of five more things he wanted to ask.

The two SeaWings stood out among the black NightWings: near the back, the green, struggling form of Prince Turtle, and farther up, close behind Darkstalker, Princess Anemone, small and whitish-pinkish-blue-gray, doing flips in the sky.

Trying to show off for Darkstalker. She wants him to see that nothing frightens her. But I think she's really a bit nervous about leaving school against her mother's wishes. Nervous and thrilled. She's the sort who enjoys disobeying orders, because she's never had much chance to.

Which made it ironic and rather sad that she was so eager to follow Darkstalker. *I wonder what sort of spell he has on her — is it the same as the one he has on everyone else, or is it special to her?*

The sun flashed off Turtle's green scales as the dragons banked south. Qibli was worried for him, too. The SeaWing prince had cast a spell to make himself invisible to Darkstalker, but Qibli could think of a million ways for that to go wrong.

But I should stay out of the way. Turtle's the one with magic powers. He's the one who can save the day, if it needs saving. That's what special powers are for: making heroes.

If only they had let me have Darkstalker's scroll . . . if only Peril hadn't burned it. Then I'd have magic, too.

Then I could change the world. I could fix so many things, if only I had anything special or magic about me.

But he wasn't special and he certainly didn't have magic. In fact, he was a useless, spotted waste of scales, as his mother, brother, and sister had spent the first three years of his life reminding him.

He still heard them all the time, their voices in his head telling him how wretched he was. He tried to drown them out by concentrating on his life as an Outclaw, but the smallest thing could bring them crashing back in. Just the thought of how he'd lost the scroll — how he'd held infinite power for a moment, and then lost it forever — brought on a wave of memories of desert heat and scornful laughter.

The Scorpion Den, where Qibli grew up, was a cutthroat world of thieves, con artists, mercenaries, fences, thugs for hire, and assassins. But for really top-notch underhanded work of any kind, everyone knew there was one dragon in the city who outshone them all: Qibli's mother.

Her name was Cobra, daughter of a powerful crime lord. Her skills were legendary among certain circles. The three guests who'd died at Queen Scarlet's wedding years ago — everyone suspected one of Cobra's nefarious poisons, but no one could ever prove it. The two sisters of Queen Oasis who had vanished into the night — sure, it might have been the queen herself, but why get her talons dirty when she could afford someone like Cobra?

Rumor even had it that all three SandWing princesses had tried to commission her to kill the others during the War of SandWing Succession. According to the rumor, she'd refused them all on the grounds that an ongoing war was much more profitable for her.

Qibli had heard all the rumors about his mother. He knew that the biggest mystery in the Scorpion Den was why Cobra had bothered to have her three dragonets, and why she allowed them to live.

He'd heard the whispers as he stole pouches of gold coins from under the tables in the tavern down the street.

"She hates dragonets! How does she put up with three of them making noise and taking up space in her house all day?"

"Bah, she'll get sick of 'em sooner or later. They'll be lucky if they get a chance to make a run for it."

"Especially that scrawny one," the gossipers would say with incredulous chuckles. *The one with the freckled scales on his nose. The one who talks too much and notices too much and sneaks around behind her like a little trail of footprints. The one with the odd name.*

That was Qibli.

Everyone said Cobra hated her dragonets, and him most of all, but he didn't believe it.

Even when *she* said it, he didn't really believe it.

Not until the day she sold him.

Qibli remembered those first three years of his life with much more clarity than most young dragons.

He remembered the hot, musty smell of the carpets that hung from their walls and covered the floors, mingling with the scent of roasting coriander in the kitchen.

He remembered the time he found a bowl with a few drops of goat's milk left in it and licked it clean. He remembered the first time he stole something to feed himself — a runty, spotted persimmon that had fallen under a food cart — and how he hid in a fortune-teller's tent to eat it, knowing Rattlesnake or Sirocco would snatch it away if they saw it.

He remembered the roars of dragons coming to blows on the street outside, and how everyone would fly up to the courtyard walls to watch, and the buckets of sand that hung from every wall so that they could be poured over any fires the fighting dragons might set.

Most of all he remembered lying awake night after night, beside his snoring siblings, watching his mother on the other side of the room. Lit by a single lamp, she would sharpen her blades, mix poisons, study maps and blueprints, or dismember scorpions to study and extract their venom. Qibli would feel the tension shivering through his wings as he waited, night after night, for her to look his way.

One glance in his direction — one moment where her face would soften, where her love would slip through when she thought no one was looking. That was all he wanted. Just a tiny hint of that secret inner love that he was sure she felt.

But Cobra never looked up at her dragonets, not once in all the nights he watched her.

She never looked over during the day either, while Sirocco and Rattlesnake threw him into walls, trapped his tail in doors, or buried him in sand. His brother and sister realized a lot sooner than Qibli that Cobra didn't care at all what they did.

But Qibli kept trying. He got smarter and faster, hoping she would notice. He turned their traps back on them, learned to dodge and feint and trick them almost every time. Brute strength wouldn't work against two dragonets that were much bigger than him, so his cleverness was the only weapon he had to ensure that he got his fair share to eat.

He was convinced that eventually his mother would have to notice that he was good enough to be worth loving.

Qibli was three and a half years old when his salvation finally walked in.

It was an otherwise ordinary day, hot as blazes, and Cobra had ordered them out into the streets because she was expecting a client. (Her exact words were: "get your ugly snouts out of here and don't come back until dark, if you must come back at all." Qibli was choosing to find it hopeful that she'd been looking at Sirocco when she said "ugly snouts" and at him when she said "come back," like maybe she was subliminally revealing her true feelings. He came up with a lot of stories like this in his head.)

Other dragonets were always racing around the narrow alleyways that surrounded their house, scrapping and shouting and tussling over trinkets or prey. On that day, however, they weren't fighting. Instead, a crowd of grubby dragonets were gathered in a circle down one of the dead ends, jostling and shouting wagers at one another.

As Rattlesnake muscled her way to the front, Qibli caught a glimpse of fur and a small, quivering, whiskered nose between the talons and tails that blocked his view.

Qibli took a few steps back, then launched himself up to the window ledge on the second floor of a nearby lamp store. From there he could see down into the cleared patch of space where all the dragonets were focusing their attention. A large scrap of orangeish fur was circling a much smaller, gray bit of fur with a long tail.

"What's going on?" Rattlesnake demanded.

"Taking bets on how long the scritter lasts," one of the wiry orphans answered her, flicking a wing at the gray fur-ball. "Care to wager?" He was so covered in dirt and ashes that he looked half MudWing — which he easily might be. There were several hybrids in the Scorpion Den, since Blister wouldn't tolerate "cross-contamination" in her army and Burn hated them as well.

Qibli squinted and realized the little creature was a spiny mouse, slightly bigger than average. Its ears trembled with terror as it darted around, blocked in on all sides by enormous talons and sunbaked scales and fiery breath. The larger animal stalking it was a cat, which meant it must be the pet of someone important, or else it would have been eaten by now.

"Stupid game," Rattlesnake pronounced, tossing a scornful look at the two mammals. "I'd rather eat them than bet on them."

"Yeah, but those scritters are prickly on yer tongue," the other dragon observed. "'Sides, check out what the winner snags." He jerked his head at five coconuts arranged in a small pyramid next to the wall.

Five coconuts! Qibli would have been tempted to place a bet himself, if he'd had anything to wager.

He looked back along the alley toward his house. His mother loved coconut. It was one of the things she never shared with the dragonets, on the rare occasions when she managed to get one.

I may have nothing to wager, Qibli thought, *but maybe I can get one a different way.*

A few moments later, the cat had the spiny mouse cornered. It prowled a step closer . . . another step . . . the mouse was petrified with fear . . . the cat reached out one paw . . .

And a bucketful of sand cascaded over the cat's head, instantly burying it with a yowl of fury.

"Slasher!" roared one of the watching dragons. She surged forward and began digging frantically in the sand for her cat. "Who did that?"

Everyone was looking up now, but Qibli was already standing innocently in the crowd, casting bewildered looks at the sky. He took a sideways step, "accidentally" treading on the toes of a dragon he knew was prone to hysterics, and as he'd hoped, his mark started screaming melodramatically. Enough dragons jumped and surged around in the confusion that a gap opened up and the mouse darted out of the circle.

At the same time, Slasher the cat burst out of the sand, hissing and spitting furiously.

"Where'd it go?" shouted one of the dragons.

"Who won?" shouted another.

"Don't let the scritter escape!" bellowed a third.

"It went that way!" Qibli yelled, pointing out of the alley.

Dragons stampeded past him, and in the swift, roaring chaos, he managed to snatch one of the coconuts, tuck it under his wing, and hustle out along with the thundering crowd.

At the corner, everyone scattered, searching for the little creature. Qibli made his way casually toward his own house.

An adult SandWing was lingering outside, watching the gang of dragonets descend into finger-pointing and fighting. She gave him a speculative look as he approached.

"Morning," Qibli said, tipping his head toward her. He darted inside and scampered through into the back room where his mother always met with clients. He was in luck; whoever she was waiting for hadn't arrived yet. She crouched, alone, behind her table, studying a document with a scrawled sketch of a dragon's face on it.

He was also not in luck, because she was evidently in a terrible mood. Her head snapped up and she gave him an evil glare.

"Get out," she snarled.

"I brought you something," Qibli said quickly. He produced the coconut and held it out in his trembling talons. "I stole it for you."

Cobra rose to her feet, spreading her wings until she seemed to fill the entire room.

"You stole a coconut," she hissed. "And you brought it to me." She took a step toward him.

"Yes," he said proudly. "I know you like them, so —"

"Have I taught you *nothing* about survival?" she snarled. She smashed the coconut out of his talons and threw him into the wall. Qibli's head collided painfully with a torch sconce.

"*You* survive!" Cobra bellowed. "That's all you have to do! Nobody is ever going to take care of you! A dragon looks out for herself *and no one else*. You weak little worm, if you steal a coconut, *you keep it for yourself*."

She reached out to grab him again, but just then someone cleared their throat from the doorway.

Cobra whirled around, almost nicking Qibli with her venomous tail. Through his tears, Qibli recognized the dragon who'd been watching the fray outside. She angled her head to study him sideways for a moment.

"Am I interrupting something?" she asked.

"Just trying to teach my idiot son a lesson," Cobra hissed.

"About . . . what exactly?" asked the stranger.

Cobra folded her wings back. "He thinks about other dragons too much. It's going to get him killed one day."

"Interesting," said the other dragon. Her eyes flicked from Qibli to the coconut to Cobra, as if she were reading the story of what had just happened. "I happen to be looking for dragons who . . . work well with others, let's say. I'd like to take him off your talons."

"He's not for sale," said Cobra. Qibli glanced up at her. That sounded like she cared enough to want to keep him . . . except that she'd said it in her "opening negotiations" voice, not her "and that's final" voice. As though she was only bartering to get a better offer.

"Give him to me," said the other dragon, "and my Outclaws will stay out of your business."

Cobra's eyebrows arched. "Should I care what your little gang of ruffians does?"

"Yes. We will have full control of this city by the new year. If we're willing to leave you alone, that's an offer you should jump at." The dragon stepped past Cobra and beckoned to Qibli. "Come along, dragon who cares too much."

"I didn't say you could take him, Thorn," Cobra snapped.

"But I am taking him," Thorn answered calmly.

"Why would you want him?" Cobra tried. "He's useless. He's completely ordinary. He'll never do anything important."

"Ordinary dragons do important things all the time," said Thorn. "Or perhaps I just want him to steal *me* some coconuts. You don't need to worry about it, because you won't be seeing him again."

"Huh," Cobra snorted. "That would be an upside."

Qibli looked from one to the other in disbelief. His mother was about to back down — and he'd never seen her give in to anyone except his terrifying grandfather. Who was this strange dragon who wanted to steal him? Was Cobra . . . afraid of her?

"What about our business?" Cobra demanded, flicking one wing out to block Qibli's path.

"Have you found any of them?" Thorn asked, nodding at the sketch on Cobra's desk.

"No," Cobra answered. "Not a trace anywhere."

Thorn frowned. "Then keep looking. Same rate until you find them." She dropped a small, jingling sack into Cobra's claws and turned to Qibli again. "Time to go."

"But —" Qibli tried to protest. "My mother —"

"Doesn't want you here," finished Cobra. She was greedily digging about inside the sack.

Qibli blinked hard, trying to hold back his tears. His mother definitely wouldn't want to keep him if he cried.

The strange dragon crouched in front of him, and he realized for the first time how kind her eyes were.

"You will be safe with me," she said softly. "And wanted. And cared for."

"B-but," Qibli choked out, "I w-want my m-mother t-to —"

"To want you and care for you?" Thorn said, even more softly. "I know. I'm sorry she doesn't. But your life doesn't have to be like this. Come with me and you'll see."

She brushed his wing with hers and turned toward the door. Qibli took two steps after her, then looked back at his mother. Cobra was piling coins in careful stacks on her desk, but she felt his eyes on her and glanced up.

"Hoping for some last words of wisdom?" Cobra said scornfully. "Take care of yourself, lizard. You'll never amount to much, so don't go trying to be a hero, or you'll just get killed. And don't come crawling back here. How's that?"

Thorn put her wing around Qibli and steered him toward the door. Her jaw was tense, as if she was holding back a lot of things she wanted to say.

Qibli's home passed by him in a blur, and by the time he looked up, they were in unfamiliar streets, heading toward the other side of the city. There were palm trees here, staggered along the walls of the alleys or poking out of courtyards like curious snouts.

"Can I ask you something?" Thorn said.

He nodded.

"What did you do with the spiny mouse?"

He reached into the small pouch slung around his chest and drew out the small, trembling creature. Thorn stopped and watched him release it into a hole in one of the outer city walls.

"I figured you'd rescued it," she said.

"They're not really worth eating," he said, worried now. Should he have offered it to her? What did she want him to do? If he was going to belong to her now, he should start figuring out how to make her like him. Maybe he'd already failed.

"I agree," she said, thumping his shoulder in a friendly way. "I'd have let it go, too. It was clever, what you did. I was impressed with how you tricked everyone. Just the kind of smarts I'm looking for in my organization."

Qibli's heart was threatening to swell and burst right out of his chest. No one had ever praised him for anything. No one had ever noticed anything he'd ever done right.

She didn't do it intentionally, but in that moment, Thorn won Qibli's undying loyalty forever.

He'd thought she was the only dragon he'd ever care about that much — that he would spend his life fighting and dying for her and be happy doing so.

Until she sent him off to school and he met a dragon named Moonwatcher, and now everything felt different. He'd had a life plan: prove his loyalty, serve Thorn, be the best Outclaw possible. That life plan did not include thinking about a fascinating NightWing all the time.

Moon took up so much of his headspace. He caught himself watching her the way he used to watch Cobra, hoping for a glance that would hint she might love him back. He wanted to bring her new scrolls that would make her face light up. He wanted to make her soup when her visions gave her headaches and sing her silly songs to help her stop worrying. He wanted to fly beside her while she saved the world.

He most definitely did not want to watch her fly away, with no idea when she would ever come back.

Qibli saw a glimmer of silver farther down the mountain. It was Winter, gazing after the departing dragons with a soulfully tragic face.

Did I look like that, too, watching her leave?

Probably not. Winter has a much better snout for soulful tragedy than I do. Whenever Qibli tried to make heroic, dashing faces like Winter's in the mirror, it mostly looked like he was trying to suck bits of scorpion out of his teeth.

"Hey," he said, landing beside his friend. (He'd decided to fly with the label *friend*, although parts of him could acknowledge that it was a little optimistic.)

Winter jumped and gave him a sideways scowl. "Hrrmph," he said, clearing his throat. "Just uh . . . admiring the sunrise."

"Oh, yeah, me too," said Qibli. "Absolutely nothing else interesting happening out here. Nope. Excellent sunrise, that's it."

Winter transferred his scowl to the wings that were getting smaller and smaller in the distance. "Well," he said, "at least Darkstalker will take care of . . . uh, of them."

"Moon can take care of herself," Qibli pointed out.

"He'll get settled in the rainforest, make some friends, and then she'll come right back," Winter said, ignoring Qibli. "And we can all go back to normal. Except now we have a giant magic friend who can tell us the future. That'll be useful."

Qibli couldn't keep the worry off his face as he regarded Winter. He just didn't sound like the haughty, sharp-minded IceWing prince that Qibli had come to know.

Everyone else under Darkstalker's spell — if I'm right, and there is a spell — still sounds like themselves. They're less suspicious of him than they probably should be, but still normalish. Winter is acting like someone's wrapped his brain in walrus blubber.

"How can everything go back to normal?" Qibli asked. "Aren't you supposed to be dead? What happens when your queen finds out you've popped up back at school? Or your parents? Won't that be a little awkward for your brother, who supposedly killed you?"

Winter hesitated. "I . . . I'm not sure," he said. "My name must be gone from the rankings wall by now. I think if I choose to stay in exile, it shouldn't make any difference to my queen or my family. I'm as good as dead to them anyway." He paused again, then added in a lower voice, "I do worry about Hailstorm. I wasn't going to come back to school, but . . . " He trailed off.

But Moon was here, Qibli finished in his head, feeling imaginary claws sink into his heart. *And he'd risk anything to be with her.*

Qibli thought he would do the same, but he'd never been tested like Winter, sent through the cold darkness of betrayal and certain death. How could he ever think he'd be worthy of Moon, when she could choose someone like Winter?

Or at least, the real Winter — the one underneath the weird spell.

I have to get him back. For his sake and for hers. Once he's thinking for himself again, we can figure out what to do about Moon and Darkstalker.

I have to break Darkstalker's spell on him.

But how?

── CHAPTER 2 ──

Winter found Qibli in the prey center shortly after midday and poked him with his tail.

"Enough moping," he said. "We have class."

"I'm not MOPING," said Qibli, sitting up and throwing away the banana he'd been staring at for twenty minutes. "YOU'RE moping."

"I most certainly am not," said Winter. "IceWing princes never mope."

"Oh, I'm sorry," Qibli said. "I got the word wrong. You're BROODING."

"Well, that would be preferable." Winter drew back his wings and snorted a tiny cloud of ice particles. "But I'm not doing either. I'm going to history class, and so should you."

"History!" Qibli protested. "How can we possibly sit in a dark cave listening to Webs drone on about the ancient past? This *is* history, happening *right now*. We're in the middle of it, or we should be."

"Oh, really? What sort of history were *you* planning to make today?" Winter scoffed. "All the excitement has gone off to the rainforest. We're just the footnotes." He poked Qibli with his tail again. "Come on, or Tsunami will yell at us."

Qibli trailed through the tunnels after him, trying not to look as glum as he felt about the idea of being a footnote in someone else's heroic saga.

They found their way to the new history cave, several winding corridors away from the one that had been fire-bombed. This one had a skylight, but it was still too dark, damp, and chilly for Qibli. He missed the wide-open sunshine of the desert. He also wasn't a big fan of the fact that the cave only had one exit, or the way scrolls were piled in corners like inevitable kindling. Even though Sora was gone now, he couldn't help thinking of the last attack and what might have happened without Moon's prophetic warnings.

Tamarin, the injured RainWing, was already there when they arrived. She was circling the cave cautiously, tapping the walls with her talons and sniffing the air.

"Anything we should worry about?" Qibli asked her.

She shook her head. "Unless . . . do you smell smoke?" she asked.

"I don't," he said, inhaling deeply. "And SandWings have a pretty good sense of smell."

"So do I, normally," she said. "But I haven't been able to get the smell of smoke out of my nose since the explosion." Her wings twitched back and she reached out to touch the cave wall as if reassuring herself it was still there.

Qibli mentally flipped through what he knew about RainWing scales — when they weren't deliberately changed for camouflage or adornment, they reflected the dragon's emotions. Tamarin's today were a muted blue-gray with ripples of white, in between the bandages and scorch marks.

A little sad, Qibli guessed. *And Kinkajou turned white when she was attacked and knocked unconscious — so maybe that indicates pain?* "Are you all right?" he asked. "Do the burns hurt a lot?"

"Today they do," she said, wincing. "Mostly I'm worried about Kinkajou, though."

"Me too," Qibli admitted. He'd last seen their RainWing friend lying in a bed in the town of Possibility, far across the continent, unable to wake up. *That's one thing I could have done with Darkstalker's scroll. I would have healed her. I would have healed Tamarin, too, and all the soldiers who were hurt by the war.*

Oh, *why* hadn't his friends just let him have it? Then Darkstalker would still be under the mountain, Qibli would be fixing everyone's problems, Kinkajou would be awake, Tamarin would be able to see, and Moon would still be here where he could talk to her every day.

A SeaWing burst into the room, flapping his wings and staring around frantically. "Where is she?" he demanded. "Has anyone seen Princess Anemone?"

Pike. Qibli plucked the name from his memory of the winglet lists. *Clawmates with Bigtail — now dead — and Flame — now accused of trying to murder Stonemover. Pike is the SeaWing who's always defending Anemone and may be working for her mother, Queen Coral.*

"Um, yes," Winter answered him. He peered down his snout at Pike. "Anemone left for the rainforest with all the NightWings and their glorious leader early this morning."

"Did you literally just say 'glorious leader'?" Qibli asked.

"Do you literally not recognize sarcasm when you hear it?" Winter retorted.

Nearly everything Winter ever said sounded sarcastic, but Qibli thought he was developing a fairly good sense of when the IceWing was actually being sincere. And the intonation just then had been . . . troubling, to say the least.

"She *left*?" Pike cried. "Left *the school*?" He clutched his head.

"You couldn't have stopped her," Qibli said. "Don't blame yourself."

"I have to go after her," Pike said, turning in a circle. "But I don't know anything about the rainforest! Oh, Queen Coral is going to feed me to the sharks. The princess on her own! With no one to guard her!"

"Prince Turtle was with her," Winter pointed out.

"I don't find that reassuring," Pike snapped.

"I'm inclined to agree with you," Winter said, poking his nose back into his scroll.

"Turtle is great," Qibli argued. "He'll watch out for her." He didn't dare tell them that Turtle was invisible to Darkstalker. But surely that meant Turtle would be useful protection for his sister . . . didn't it?

"Besides," Tamarin added, "Anemone's an animus. She can guard herself better than anyone else could."

Perhaps, Qibli thought, *but it depends on what spells Darkstalker has cast on her.*

"I have to go after her," Pike said again. He spun toward the entrance and ran straight into their history teacher.

"Sit down, young dragon," Webs said, pleasantly but firmly. "It is time for our lesson."

"I have to go rescue the princess!" Pike cried.

"Fiddlesquids," Webs said, ushering him back into the cave. "You are a student. What you *have* to do is fill your mind with knowledge and wisdom."

Qibli sympathized completely with the frustrated look on Pike's face. He wanted to rip off the roof of the cavern with his claws and go flying after the other dragons, too.

"Since your two winglets are rather low on numbers at the moment, Silver Winglet will be joining us today," Webs went on. He flicked a beckoning wing at the hallway and four dragonets filed in.

"Rather low on numbers" is a generous way to describe us, Qibli thought ruefully. He and Winter were the only ones from Jade Winglet still at school, and Tamarin's Gold Winglet had been equally decimated by the explosion and Sora's attempted assassination of Icicle.

But wait — Qibli perked up. This meant he'd get to see Ostrich, the SandWing in Silver Winglet. She was the daughter of Queen Thorn's most trusted general, Six-Claws, and Qibli had promised to look out for her while they were at school.

He hadn't seen her yet since his return to Jade Mountain, although he'd gone looking the night before. Princess

Anemone had been the only one in the cave they shared. When he poked his snout in she was scattering jewelry around, clearly in such a bad temper that he hadn't dared stay to wait for Ostrich.

But the curious little SandWing wasn't among the dragonets settling into the classroom. Qibli checked his mental list — there was a big-shouldered MudWing named Sepia, a placid-looking RainWing named Boto who settled himself next to Tamarin, a haughty IceWing called Changbai who did *not* sit next to Winter, and a small-boned dusky orange SkyWing named Thrush, who took one of the front-row seats and gazed intently at the teacher.

Where is Ostrich? Qibli wondered. *She's usually so excited for her classes, no matter how boring they are. How did she escape this torture?*

"Now where were we?" Webs said in his maddeningly slow voice. "Ah yes, the five hundred years of transformation and resettling that followed the Scorching . . . "

Thrush raised one of his talons and spoke without waiting to be called on. "Can you teach us about Darkstalker today, please?"

"Yes!" Changbai agreed. "He doesn't seem anything like the dragon from our old stories. In that he did not immediately start murdering all of us."

"Three moons," said Boto, his claws turning lime green. "Is, uh . . . is he likely to do that?"

"Darkstalker," Webs grumbled. "Wrecking my lesson

plans. That's over three thousand years after the Scorching! We're not scheduled to get to that era for months."

"But we need to know about him *now*," Tamarin insisted.

"Because of the maybe murdering?" Boto said. "I think I agree yes, I would like to hear about that? Or more specifically about how not happening that is?"

"We can see with our eyes what kind of dragon Darkstalker is," Winter said scornfully. "I trust my own judgment better than any old history scroll."

"Says the dragon whose sister turned out to be a murderer," Sepia suddenly interjected.

Winter leaped to his feet and whirled toward her, his teeth bared. Qibli darted in between them, wings outstretched, ready to hold Winter back or help him fight, whichever turned out to be necessary.

"It was a MudWing who blew up the other cave, not my sister!" Winter flared.

"But she did it because of what *your* sister did," Sepia said stoutly.

"Winter, let's be fair," Qibli pointed out. "We just stopped Icicle from trying to murder Starflight and then Glory, so technically . . ."

"You're not helping, Qibli!" Winter growled at him.

"Now now now now now." Webs fretted, flapping his wings. "The war is behind us. That's the whole point of this place. No fighting allowed!"

Behind him, Qibli saw Sunny poke her head into the

classroom. She scanned the dragonets and frowned slightly, then disappeared again.

That was worrying.

"All right, all right, we can talk about Darkstalker," Webs said. "If you'll all sit down and shut up, I'll tell you what I know about him." He rolled up the scroll on his desk, muttering something like, "and I thought Tsunami was bad."

Winter subsided back into his seat, looking baleful.

"Darkstalker is the son of a NightWing named Foeslayer and an IceWing prince named Arctic," Webs rattled off. "He lived over two thousand years ago in the ancient NightWing kingdom, and he was the first animus dragon to hatch in the NightWing tribe — a gift he inherited from his father. But he rapidly became too dangerous to control, and he was plotting to assassinate the queen and steal her power when his friends Fathom and Clearsight conspired to stop him, stuffing him under a mountain and putting him to sleep forever."

"Clearly not forever," Changbai interrupted.

"Right," said Webs, a little flustered. "Until now. But he has emerged a changed dragon, humbled and unambitious, who only wants to use his powers for good. So, nothing to worry about; can we get back to our actual lesson?"

"Um," said Qibli, "wait. How exactly do we know he's humbled and unambitious now?"

"Because it's obvious," Winter said, rolling his eyes. "It's not like he immediately demanded to be made king of the NightWings or anything."

With impeccable comic timing, the slate in Qibli's pouch gave a little jump. He waited until no one was looking at him anymore, then pulled it out and hid it under his desk. He could see a message from Turtle appearing on the surface, agonizingly slowly.

DARKSTALKER WANTS TO BE NIGHTWING KING. NIGHTWINGS DECIDING WHAT THEY WANT.

Qibli nearly laughed, but he didn't want to draw attention to the slate.

And also, it was too terrifying to be funny.

Tell me more, Turtle, he pleaded silently. *What's happening? How are the NightWings reacting? What about Glory? And Moon . . . does Moon want him to be king? Is she still acting like herself?*

But nothing else appeared on the slate, and after a few minutes, Qibli had to accept that was Turtle's entire message. He sighed.

Darkstalker as king. I can see the logic. It's a choice between two difficult, unusual alternatives: to have a king or to be ruled by a RainWing. He knew several of the NightWings intensely disliked the idea of being ruled by Queen Glory. He'd seen it on their faces in the rainforest, even before Moon confirmed that she'd heard such grumblings in their minds.

No matter what Glory did, how hard she worked, how intelligently she solved their problems, or how fairly and kindly she treated them, some NightWings would never accept her, simply because she was a RainWing.

But what kind of king would Darkstalker be? Would he

be content with ruling his tribe? Did his ambitions stop there?

Qibli would have liked to believe they did, but the last words of Moon's prophecy kept repeating on a loop in his head.

Something is coming to shake the earth. (That was definitely Darkstalker, rising from his prison.)

Something is coming to scorch the ground. (He was pretty sure this was Darkstalker, too.)

Jade Mountain will fall beneath thunder and ice. (Why? When? How soon?)

Unless the lost city of night can be found.

He brooded on that last line for a moment. Darkstalker knew where the lost city was. Was there something there that could stop him? Something Fathom and Clearsight left behind, perhaps, in case their old friend/enemy ever emerged? That's what Qibli would have done if he were them — left some kind of backup plan. But how would anyone know what it was, or how to use it?

Sunny appeared in the doorway again. "Webs," she whispered. "I need to borrow Qibli."

Webs flicked his tail impatiently and Qibli leaped to his feet, just barely managing to keep the joy off his face.

"*Thank* you," he whispered to Sunny as he bounded out into the hallway. "Can you do that every time I have history? I mean, didn't you go through this exact same suffering when you were younger? How can you inflict it on other innocent souls?"

"Lessons with Webs were awesome," Sunny said sternly — or, at least, Qibli guessed that was her attempt at a stern face. "You be grateful you don't have to do battle training with Kestrel." Her expression shifted, worry lines creeping across her forehead. "Qibli — have you seen Ostrich today?"

"No," he said, instantly alert. "I haven't seen her since I got back to Jade Mountain."

"I had breakfast with her yesterday morning," Sunny said. "But when everything happened with my father and Flame — I forgot to check on her last night, and then today I haven't been able to find her anywhere."

Qibli's heart sank as Sunny rubbed her temples anxiously.

"I'm terribly afraid," she said, "that Ostrich is missing."

CHAPTER 3

Qibli helped Sunny search the entire mountain again. He studied the whole map in his mind, everything that was part of the school and everything that wasn't, all the corners where a small dragonet might hide or get lost or get stuck. He checked her favorite places — the music room, the library — and her least favorite places — the underground lakes, the slopes below Stonemover's cave that were littered with prey bones.

He even poked his head into Stonemover's cave itself, where he saw Flame trapped by the shackles Darkstalker had made, furiously struggling to get loose. Qibli had heard the story from Turtle, but he was still startled by Flame's smooth, perfectly healed snout, and by the flashing hatred in Flame's eyes. Against the wall, Stonemover was lying with his head averted and eyes closed. Qibli couldn't help thinking that trapping Flame in the same cave as the dragon he'd tried to murder was a worse punishment for the victim than it was for the attempted murderer.

But he didn't linger to dwell on that problem; he *had* to

find Ostrich. Her parents, Six-Claws and Kindle, trusted Qibli. Queen Thorn trusted him — she'd basically told him that the SandWings at the academy were his responsibility. And then he'd flown off and abandoned them! True, he'd been on a quest to help Moon and Winter, and of course he'd expected the students to be safe with Sunny. But still, he hadn't even stopped to worry about them at all.

Have I been thinking about Moon — about my new friends — too much, and not enough about Thorn and the rest of my tribe?

He'd beaten himself into a state of surging guilt by the time he met Sunny again, back at the cave where Ostrich and Anemone had been assigned to live together. It was hard to tell the young SandWing had ever been here. Like most dragons raised with the Outclaws, she was used to living sparely and compactly, in case they had to relocate suddenly or face a sandstorm or fend off a street gang invasion.

The SeaWing princess, on the other talon, clearly lived a very different life. The cave was covered in her mess, from piles of damp blankets to trails of wet moss to little fish bones scattered around, but more than all of that, there were the jewels and trinkets and treasures. Qibli guessed there was more wealth scattered casually around this cave than he'd ever personally have in his entire life.

He could see why it wouldn't make sense to take it all with her to the rainforest — but couldn't she have at least put it away in one of her giant wooden chests? Or found a better place to hide it all?

The glittering pink-and-gold tiara sticking out from under

one of the blankets — that was just *begging* to be stolen. A single one of those black pearl cluster earrings would fetch a price that could feed ten orphans for a month — and Anemone would probably just assume she'd lost it and not even care.

Dragons who treated treasure like this didn't *deserve* treasure like this.

Qibli sat down and wrapped his wings around himself, fighting back all his Outclaw instincts. He was very glad Moon wasn't there to read his mind and discover all the unworthy thoughts he was having.

Thorn had given her Outclaws strict instructions once she became queen. "We're not outside the law anymore," she'd said. "We *are* the law. Which means it's up to us to show how fair and just and righteous those in power can be. We won't be like the regimes that came before us. I know it'll be hard, but from now on, no more stealing, no more cheating, no more striking first or solving problems with our claws and venom. We all have to be better dragons now."

Argh, but wouldn't a good dragon take just *one* emerald necklace if it could pay for a real library for the Scorpion Den orphanages?

No no no. Qibli closed his eyes and took a deep breath. *Winter wouldn't have this problem. He wouldn't even be tempted by any of this. That's why he deserves Moon and I don't.*

"Three moons, what a disaster," Sunny said, stepping around him and surveying the room critically. "It looks like Princess Anemone hasn't quite gotten used to living without servants yet."

"The good news is, she hasn't managed to make Ostrich do her cleaning up for her," Qibli pointed out. He grinned. "It would be funny to see her try, though." Ostrich was one of the kinder, gentler souls among the Outclaws, but she had a streak of ferocity from her father and an iron core from her mother that made her impossible to push around. Qibli knew she would never bow to any royal — except Queen Thorn, of course.

They circled the room, looking for any clues that might hint at Ostrich's whereabouts. Her small corner of the room held almost nothing personal, other than a small sketch of her parents that was pinned to the wall beside her hammock.

Qibli was studying Six-Claws's face when he felt the slate twitch lightly again. He tugged it quickly out of the pouch and watched the new message appear.

THE NIGHTWINGS ARE GETTING A KING, Turtle wrote.

Qibli stared at the slate.

And stared at it some more.

But nothing else appeared.

Turtle! He growled softly. *Is that seriously all the information you think is worth reporting? WHAT HAPPENED?*

The slate stared placidly and blankly back at him.

What about Queen Glory? What about Moon? Are they all going to live in the rainforest together? Has he killed anyone or done anything dangerous or suspicious? Or is this the most peaceful transfer of power in Pyrrhian history? What's going on with the superpowers Darkstalker was handing out yesterday? Are you safe? How does Moon feel about this new king?

TURTLE, TELL ME ANYTHING.

"What's that?" Sunny interrupted his careening thoughts, coming up behind him and looking curiously at the little object in his talons.

"Nothing," he answered, tucking the obstinately uninformative slate back in his pouch. He wished he could tell Sunny the news about Darkstalker, but then he'd have to reveal Turtle's animus magic, which seemed not only unfair, but rather unsafe.

He had to focus on Ostrich. That was the only thing he could do anything about right now.

His gaze fell on a pair of rippling, beaten copper armbands, tossed carelessly on a pile of half-rolled scrolls.

"Aren't those the armbands Anemone enchanted to control the weather?" he asked Sunny.

She frowned slightly. "I think so."

I can't believe she just left them here. Such powerful magic, lying around abandoned? Anyone could get their claws on those and do all kinds of damage.

"Maybe you should take them," he suggested to Sunny. "So no one else does."

"I feel guilty about it, but I think you're right," she said. With a sigh, she gathered the armbands and slid them into her bag. Qibli watched them disappear with a small sting of envy.

Last night, he'd asked Turtle to make him an animus dragon. He'd taken his most secret wish and laid it at Turtle's feet, and then Turtle had stomped on it. Qibli understood why — another animus in the world meant more threats to the animus dragons who existed — but it still made him ache to think how close he was to all that power, and yet he would never have it. Instead he'd have to watch other dragons, like Turtle and Anemone, use their power on frivolous things they didn't even care about — weather-controlling wristbands and slates that only communicated in one direction — and he'd never get to do all the good he could have done with that power in his own talons.

With animus magic, I could find Ostrich easily.

"Let's ask the other SandWings when they last saw Ostrich," he suggested. And then, for the first time, he realized that Onyx — Tamarin's clawmate — should have been in history class as well.

But she hadn't been.

I'm such an idiot. How could I miss that?

"Where is the Gold Winglet supposed to be right now?" he asked Sunny.

"Herbs and Healing, with the Copper Winglet, I think," she said.

"Herbs and Healing?" he echoed, following her as she set off through the tunnels. "I don't think we ever had that class."

"We just added it a few days ago," Sunny said. "A couple of students asked for something like it — Tamarin and Peregrine especially."

Peregrine, Qibli thought, flicking through the information in his head. *SkyWing, Copper Winglet, clawmates with*

Pronghorn. He's the one who's deaf in one ear, from an explosion near his home during the war. Queen Ruby has devoted a lot of energy to taking care of those wounded in the war . . . I bet Peregrine is hoping to become a doctor so he can help.

The class was gathered in the healing center, watching Clay as he laid out bandages. A large blue-and-red drawing of a dragon was pinned to the wall behind him, illustrating where all the muscles were.

"Which muscle did you get all venomed and burned?" asked Pronghorn, poking at the drawing.

"This one here," Clay said, pointing to the drawing and then to the scar on his right thigh. "That's why I limp, because it was damaged where all these parts connect. But remember Peril saved my life by burning me here. Otherwise the venom would have spread and killed me pretty quickly." He traced his claw along the paths the viper venom would have gone throughout the figure in the drawing.

"Ooooooooooooooo," said a few of the dragonets.

Qibli studied the group of students. Onyx was not here either; the only members of the Gold Winglet in the class were Tamarin and Pike.

"Clay, can we borrow Pronghorn and Tamarin?" Sunny asked.

"Of course," Clay said, smiling down at her.

Qibli offered his wing to Tamarin, but she shook her head and found her own way into the hall. Pronghorn stood beside her, bouncing eagerly on his toes as he looked from Qibli to Sunny.

Pronghorn's family had been on Blaze's side during the war, hiding with her in a fortress in the cold tundra near the Ice Kingdom. So Qibli didn't know him all that well, but he liked Pronghorn's energy. Queen Thorn had chosen him for the academy because he'd sent her eight letters begging to be included, expressing his curiosity about the other tribes, and listing all the things he was excited to learn about.

"What is it?" he asked. "Can I help with something?"

"We're looking for Ostrich and Onyx," Qibli told him. "Have you seen them in the last couple of days?"

Pronghorn wrinkled his nose thoughtfully. "The last time I saw Ostrich was yesterday before lunch — she and Arid and I took some instruments to one of the upper caves to play with the sound of rain in the background. We invited Onyx, but she doesn't really like music."

"Doesn't like music!" Qibli echoed, startled. "Is she missing a soul? What else does she dislike — sunshine?"

"Me," Tamarin offered. "And most other dragons."

"Really?" Sunny said anxiously. "Oh, no, I had no idea. Is she hard to live with? Is she mean to you?"

"No, she's always nice to my face," said Tamarin. In the rose and purple lights of the hallway, it was hard to tell what color her scales were. "Most dragons don't realize how much I can figure out from their tone of voice, or the little huffs they make between sentences. She thinks because I can't see her, I won't be able to tell when she's rolling her eyes or making fun of someone. Sometimes she'll sneak in and out of our cave, because she doesn't want to have to talk to me, and she thinks I don't notice." She shrugged. "It's not personal, though. I think she doesn't particularly care about any dragons unless they can help her get what she wants."

"What does she want?" Qibli asked.

Tamarin shrugged again. "I don't know. But maybe she's gone to get it, because she didn't come back to our cave last night."

Qibli and Sunny both pricked up their ears. "She didn't?" Sunny asked.

"Whoa. Do you think Ostrich and Onyx left together?" Pronghorn asked. "Maybe to go back to the Kingdom of Sand?"

"Ostrich wouldn't leave without telling someone," Qibli said. "She wouldn't leave without telling *me*."

"Unless she was forced to . . ." Sunny said, trailing off. She twisted her front talons together, looking ill.

"You think someone took them?" Pronghorn asked keenly. "But why would someone kidnap Onyx and Ostrich?"

Qibli had no idea. He kept seeing Ostrich's face . . . the trusting look she always gave him.

I convinced her to stay at school. I told her I'd protect her. And then I left her here.

Whatever's happened to her — this is my fault.

CHAPTER 4

"Why can't we go *two days* without a crisis?" Tsunami demanded when they told her. "Why is this school a magnet for disaster?"

"Maybe it was a terrible idea all along," Sunny said, sinking into a pile of leaves in the corner of the library. She buried her face in her front talons. "Just like Blaze said it would be."

Starflight felt his way over to put one wing around her. "Blaze is literally the least intelligent royal dragon in the world," he said. "She *can't* be right, by definition. If she thinks this school is doomed, then it is definitely going to be wonderful."

Sunny gave him a rueful look. "Not if we keep losing all our students, it's not."

"I mean," Tsunami sputtered, "all we ask is that they sit in their classrooms and learn stuff. Is that so hard?"

"Well," Clay said, "it is a bit . . . I mean sometimes . . . it was for me," he mumbled quickly at her quelling look.

"And not go GALLIVANTING OFF on lunatic expeditions." She pointed significantly at Qibli. "I am talking about you. To be clear. And your whole troublemaking winglet."

"We were helping Winter!" Qibli protested. "And there's a prophecy!"

"No!" Tsunami shouted. She stuck her claws in her ears. "No prophecies, LA LA LA FATE IS STUPID."

"Well, at least we're all being adults about this," Starflight said.

"What?" Tsunami demanded, removing her claws.

"Nothing," he said innocently.

"I don't think Ostrich went gallivanting anywhere," Qibli said, pacing around the central desk. "She would have told me or Sunny if she needed to leave."

"Is there any chance Ostrich and Onyx went with Darkstalker and the others?" Starflight asked. "Maybe they were curious, like Turtle and Anemone?"

"No," Sunny said. "It sounds like they disappeared last night, before the NightWings left." She stood up decisively. "I'm going to try dreamvisiting them." She touched Qibli's shoulder with her wing and made him meet her eyes. "Don't you *dare* leave this mountain until I figure out where they are."

He nodded reluctantly.

"Until?" Tsunami cried as Sunny hurried out of the library. "What happened to *ever*? *Never* leave this mountain, that's what the rule should be!"

"Maybe we should send a message to Darkstalker," Clay suggested. "He could use his magic to help us find them."

The others agreed eagerly, while Qibli stared down at his feet. It didn't feel right to him that Darkstalker was already the first answer they were all reaching for . . . that Darkstalker seemed like the solution to all problems.

He reached up to touch his earring. This was his protection. This was the only thing that ensured his mind was his own. Turtle had enchanted it for him, using the words Qibli had planned out.

But Darkstalker had sensed Turtle casting this spell; that's how they'd learned that Darkstalker would know any time an animus dragon used his or her magic. So Turtle couldn't safely make any more protection spells, and if there was only going to be one, maybe someone else should have it. Maybe he should put the earring on Tsunami, or Sunny, or Starflight — on someone who could make a difference, if only they were seeing clearly.

Wait. There's someone who needs it even more than they do.

"I'll be back soon," he said, turning and hurrying out of the library. He ran down the tunnel to the sleeping caves and skidded into his room. Winter sat up on his ledge, looking irritated (but he always looked irritated).

"*Must* you tear about like a pack of elephant seals sliding downhill?" Winter demanded. "Some of us are trying to *read*. Like *civilized* dragons."

"That doesn't look like reading," Qibli said, pointing to the square of paper Winter was clearly drawing on.

Winter hid it quickly under his blanket, but not before Qibli glimpsed an outline of a dark face, with silver scales beside her eyes.

"Keep your scruffy, sand-covered nose out of my business," Winter said haughtily.

"Sure, but first you have to put on my earring," Qibli said, advancing toward him.

"I BEG your pardon," said Winter with a look of startled alarm. "No thank you! Absolutely not! Shoo!"

"Just for a minute," Qibli wheedled. He reached up to his ear.

"I said no!" Winter snapped. "You'll probably give me some weird SandWing disease, and besides, it would clash horribly with my scales!"

"I'm trying to help you!" Qibli said. "Stop being a beetle-brain and just put it on!"

He pounced on Winter and tried to pin him down, but Winter was a bit bigger and shockingly cold, and it was impossible to wrestle him and maneuver out his earring at the same time. Winter thwacked Qibli's head several times hard with his wings, threw the SandWing off his ledge, and bolted into the corridor.

"I'm getting my own cave for real this time!" he shouted. "I will not be forced to cohabitate with a deranged dragon!" Winter tore off up the tunnel before Qibli could stop him.

Qibli paused in the doorway, catching his breath. Curious faces poked out of other sleeping caves, goggling at him.

So. That went well.

He probably should have predicted that Winter would be a stubborn donkey for no reason.

He wondered what would happen to him if he did give the earring to someone else. It was unnerving to imagine willingly giving up his mind.

If only he'd had Turtle make two earrings at the same time. *If only I were smarter and less selfish. One for me, one for Winter. Double the earrings.*

He froze, struck by a sizzling lightning bolt of an idea.

Could it possibly work?

He darted down the tunnel to Turtle's nearly empty cave. Turtle's sleeping mat was on the floor of Qibli's room from the night before, but Umber's was still here.

Under Umber's mat was the satchel Turtle had left behind.

And inside that satchel were three pieces of curved wood that slotted together to make a bowl.

Qibli slid them into place, his talons trembling.

He put the bowl gently on the floor and reached up to remove his earring.

If this works, will Darkstalker sense it, like he sensed the original spell?

Qibli thought for a moment. *No. He can sense a new spell being cast by an animus. This is an animus-touched object being used, pretty much the way it always is. If Darkstalker's spell included an alert every time an animus-touched object is used, he'd be constantly barraged by dragons using dreamvisitors, Turtle's message slates, the palace and the tree of light and all the other spells in the Ice Kingdom . . . it would be too much to keep track of. So if we think it's safe to use the message slates, it should be safe to use this bowl.*

If it works at all.

Do it. Quick, don't think about it too much. Don't think yourself out of it. Blinking rapidly, he dropped the earring with a clatter into the smooth wooden curves.

Nothing happened. The earring lay there, warm and golden.

Qibli's wings drooped. *It must only work with food.* He sighed. *Of course it does. Turtle's spells are all like this. Very . . . specific.* He reached for the earring — and then remembered something.

There was a phrase — something Turtle said you had to say to make the bowl work.

He drew back his claws, thinking furiously.

"Do your magic!" he said to the bowl. "Be magic! Do a magical magic thing!" *Come on, Qibli, use that brain of yours.* "Double the stuff!" he tried. "Make yourself two! Twice the thing! Oh, that's it! Twice as much, twice as much!" He leaned forward excitedly.

Nothing happened. The bowl still contained one solitary earring.

Oh, come on! That had to work!

"Be more useful!" he shouted at the bowl.

"Are you yelling at dishware?" Peril asked, poking her head into the room.

"Just this one bowl," Qibli said grumpily. "Because it's the stupidest bowl in Pyrrhia."

Peril edged a little closer and peered at it. "Huh," she said. "Looks like a norm — nope!" she interrupted herself, seeing the look on his face. "You're right! Stupidest bowl I've ever seen! Can I join in? HEY, BOWL, YOUR SHAPE IS INANE! FOOD PROBABLY FALLS OUT OF YOU ALL THE TIME! I BET YOU DON'T EVEN STACK WELL IN CABINETS! YEAH, THAT'S RIGHT, YOU'RE THE WORST! Ooh, this is great. Let's do it every day! I feel much better."

"*I* don't," said Qibli (although honestly he did a little bit).

"Awww. Would it help if I set it on fire?" Peril offered sympathetically.

"No, no," Qibli said. "I mean, thank you, but I'm trying to make it *do* something. Turtle animus-touched it, but it's not *working*."

"Oh, aha," Peril said thoughtfully. "I know! Maybe if I set it on fire a *little* bit, that'll scare it into doing what you want!"

"Peril, it's a bowl. You can't scare it. It doesn't have feelings."

"As far as *you* know," she said. "*I* say it's looking awfully smug right now."

"I guess I'll have to think of something else," Qibli said with a sigh.

"Did you try asking it nicely?" Peril asked. "Turtle would say try asking it nicely. He's got a whole thing about how I'm terrible at that, or something. As if setting things on fire isn't always the most efficient way to get things done."

Asking it nicely . . .

Qibli picked up the bowl and realized that his talons were

trembling again. He took a deep breath, gazing down at the earring.

"Twice as much," he whispered. *"Please."*

There was a small popping sound in the air, and then, all at once, there were two identical earrings lying in the bowl.

"It worked!" Qibli yelled. "It worked! It actually worked!"

Peril peeked into the bowl, keeping her fiery scales as far away from it as she could. "Oh," she said in her "polite" voice. "Another earring! I see. Now your ears will match. That IS important. I always thought you looked very silly with only one."

"It's not for me," Qibli said. "And I do not! One earring is how all the Outclaws wear them!"

Does Moon think only one earring looks silly?

QIBLI, FOCUS.

He took out one of the earrings and hooked it back into his ear. Then he clasped the bowl and said firmly, "Twice as much, please." Another earring appeared. "Twice as much, please," he said again, and then there were four. "Twice as much, please. Twice as much, please. Twice as much, please." Four became eight, became sixteen, became thirty-two. *Enough for all the dragons in the school.* The bowl was nearly overflowing with enchanted earrings now, heavy as Thorn's crown in his claws.

Peril tipped her head to the side, watching the multiplying jewelry curiously. "OK, I can figure this out," she said. "Backups in case you lose your unfashionable ornament?

That's a lot of backups, though; you must have the attention span of a scavenger if you lose it that often. Maybe . . . a Qibli fan club and they all want one?"

Qibli was startled into a laugh. "I could never be that popular," he said. "Now a Winter fan club, that I can imagine."

"WHAT? WHY?" Peril said loudly. "He's —"

"Handsome, tortured, and heroic?" Qibli supplied. "Everyone loves dragons like that."

"*I* don't," said Peril, shaking her head. "I prefer dragons who are handsome, baffled, kind, and accidentally heroic. I mean, hypothetically, just *supposing* there were someone like that, I would maybe think they were pretty cool, is all I'm saying. Not that I'm thinking of anyone specific."

"Here, put one of these on." Qibli rolled an earring across the floor to her.

She poked at it gingerly. "This'll melt in a heartbeat on my ear."

"I thought so, but try it anyway?" Qibli asked.

"Actually, I have this new no-thanks policy about strange jewelry," Peril said. "Bad run-in with a necklace. But this wouldn't survive long enough to do anything to me anyway." She picked up the earring, and as soon as it touched her firescales, the earring melted into a blobby lump of gold around the amber teardrop. There was no way for her to wear it.

"I'm sorry, Peril," Qibli said. He could use the earrings to protect everyone else at Jade Mountain Academy, but not her.

"Well," she said, in a fairly delightful *pretending very hard to be sad* voice, "it is disappointing, because, boy, wow, so pretty, but I will just have to survive somehow anyway."

"It's enchanted," Qibli said. "Turtle put a spell on my earring to protect me from any spells Darkstalker might cast."

Peril did not react with the wild excitement he'd hoped for. "*Oh*," she said. "Darkstalker? Huh. Well, I'm sure that won't be necessary."

There's nothing I can do to convince her, as long as she's under his spell.

"I'm going to take these to Sunny," Qibli said. "Coming?"

Peril made a complicated face. "All right," she said.

It took Qibli a while to find the caves of the school founders; he'd never sought them out in their own rooms before. Sunny's was part sleeping cave, part office, with a bundle of blankets neatly tied away in the back corner. Three low tables arranged in a semicircle took up most of the room, scattered with paper, ink, small slates for announcements, and maps. There were two openings in the walls where the late afternoon sunlight spilled in and across the room, and the rest of the walls were covered in blue/white/gold SandWing tapestries, drawings of Thorn, and to-do lists with half the items crossed off.

Sunny was sitting in one of the shafts of sunshine, clasping a large blue sapphire in her front talons, with her eyes closed and her tail coiled around her feet.

Qibli hesitated in the doorway.

"What's she doing?" Peril asked in a whisper that just barely counted as a whisper.

"Looking for Ostrich and Onyx," he murmured back.

"SandWings?" Peril said. "Like the pair who flew off west yesterday?"

"What?" Qibli cried, whirling toward her. "You saw them leave?"

"Well, sure," Peril said. "I figured they were spooked by Darkstalker. I'm sure they'll be back once everyone calms the heck down."

"They were by themselves?" Qibli asked. "Just the two of them? Flying away?"

"Yup." Peril squinted at Sunny, who still hadn't opened her eyes.

"But then . . ." Qibli tried to puzzle this out. Ostrich had left willingly? Without telling anyone?

Unless it's not what it looks like.

We thought someone must have snuck in to kidnap them — but maybe there wasn't an outside kidnapper.

Maybe the kidnapper was right here at Jade Mountain.

Onyx could have said anything to make Ostrich go with her; Qibli could think of eight different threats off the top of his head that would have worked. The question was why. What could Onyx possibly want with a dragonet like Ostrich?

A path to her father, he guessed immediately. *Thorn's most trusted general. Whatever Onyx wants, she's hoping to use Six-Claws to get it.*

Which meant they must be on their way to Thorn's palace — and they had a day's lead on Qibli. He had to go after them! His queen was in danger! He had to leave right away!

He darted across the room and set the bowl at Sunny's feet.

"Sunny!" he cried. "Come back! Put on an earring! I have to go!"

Sunny opened her eyes, blinking in confusion. "What?" She looked around, slowly registering the mountain around her. "I was talking to Glory," she said. "She says Darkstalker has offered to become king of whichever NightWings want to follow him. I guess that'll make Glory's life a bit less complicated. Did you say put on an earring?"

"Glory doesn't care?" he asked, startled by this odd detail.

"Whoa," said Sunny, spotting the bowl in front of her. "That is . . . a lot of earrings just like yours."

"It's a long story," he said, "but I think Onyx has kidnapped Ostrich so she can use Six-Claws to get at Queen Thorn, so I have to leave now and you need to get everyone to wear these right away especially Winter all right good-bye."

He turned to dash out of the room, but Sunny grabbed one of his forearms in a steely grip.

"Qibli, *wait*," she said. "I have an idea where Ostrich is. But please explain this first." She waved her talons at the glowing gold-and-orange hill in the bowl.

Qibli blew out a frustrated breath. This was important, too, he knew that. Possibly the most important thing right now. But if anything happened to Ostrich or Thorn, he'd never forgive himself.

"These earrings are enchanted," he said, "to protect you from . . . evil spells." He wasn't sure she'd put it on if he told her the danger was Darkstalker.

"Oh, how nice," Sunny said a little dubiously. "Where did they come from?"

"One of the animus dragons left them for us," Qibli said, which he thought was a pretty inspired answer, really. It was true but avoided giving away Turtle's secret.

"Oh!" Sunny said. "You mean Darkstalker? Or was it Anemone? I hope Anemone didn't waste her soul on protection for us, although it is very thoughtful — earrings for the whole school, wow. Um, interesting choice to make them all look like yours."

"Please just put one on," Qibli begged.

"All right," Sunny said agreeably. To his delight, she picked up one of the earrings and slipped it right on.

He held his breath, watching her face.

"I don't see *whose* evil spells this is going to pro —" Sunny started to say. She stopped midsentence, staring at Qibli.

"Sunny?" he said.

"Qibli!" she cried.

"Um . . . yes?" he said.

"QIBLI!" she cried again, leaping to her feet. Her wings flared open in a glittering whirl. "A gigantic all-powerful possibly evil dragon just rose out of the ground and flew away with six of my students! SIX OF MY STUDENTS!"

"I know," he said. "Uh, don't panic?"

"Too late," Peril said, watching with bewildered amusement.

"Why did I let him do that?" she yelped. "I'm the worst school guardian of all time! Three moons, he took Turtle and Anemone! Queen Coral is going to have our heads!"

"What's all this hollering about?" Tsunami asked, bustling over from her cave next door.

"Why did TSUNAMI let him do that?" Sunny shouted. "We promised we wouldn't let Princess Anemone out of our sight! Tsunami, your sister just flew away with a total stranger!"

"Who, Darkstalker?" Tsunami said, tilting her head sideways. "He's not a stranger. He's your ancestor, remember? Charming, friendly, harmless? He said he's going to teach her about being an animus. She'll be back soon."

"Here, put this on." Qibli held out one of the earrings.

Tsunami snorted. "I have my own jewels, thank you."

"You need it," Sunny said. "Tsunami, trust me."

"I *dooooo* trust you," Tsunami said hesitantly as Qibli placed the earring in her palm. "About *most* things. But about *fashion* . . . I mean, it's not like you ever *wear* the gifts your mother sends you . . ." She shot a look at a small, locked chest next to Sunny's blankets.

"Just try it on for a minute," Qibli said impatiently. "Why are some dragons SO DIFFICULT."

Tsunami flicked her tongue out at him and stuck the earring on her ear. "There," she said. "Happy? What is this —" She stopped, blinking. "Why — why do I suddenly feel terrible?"

"Darkstalker has everyone under a spell," Qibli said in a rush. "He's enchanted everyone around him to — I'm not sure exactly — to trust him or believe him or like him, something like that."

"How did you know?" Sunny asked.

Because . . . it's what I would do, Qibli realized with a twinge of shame. That's why it had occurred to him so quickly. *It's one of the first spells I thought of. If I'd gotten Darkstalker's scroll — if I had all that power — first I'd protect my soul, next I'd cast spells to protect everyone I love, and then . . . I'd do a spell to make everyone like me. Even Winter . . . even my family.*

Would that be wrong? I wouldn't abuse it the way Darkstalker has. I wouldn't be tricking anyone into doing the things I want them to do. I just want other dragons to like me — and some of them won't, no matter how hard I try. I wouldn't be making their lives worse in any way.

But I know *it's wrong when Darkstalker does it.*

And yet I still wish I could do the same spell myself.

Rrrrrrrgh. He closed his eyes, trying to shut down the rushing tornado of thoughts going around in his head. Sunny was waiting for an answer.

"Because everyone was acting so odd," he said. "Especially Winter, but not just him. Everyone accepted Darkstalker as exactly what he says he is. And I thought, well, maybe we should give him a chance . . . but I wanted to be sure our minds were free to think it through for ourselves."

"Wow," Sunny said. She touched the dangling amber

teardrop in her earring. "I can't believe I completely missed it."

"You want to believe the best in every dragon anyway," Qibli said. "He probably didn't need to enchant you for you to give him a chance."

"A chance, maybe," Sunny said. "But six of my students? I'm horrified at myself."

"You got Anemone to make these for you?" Tsunami asked. "So she's wearing one, too? She's not under his spell?"

Qibli squirmed. "No," he said, wondering how to dance around the truth here. "I only had one, for myself . . . but today I figured out how to make more."

Tsunami and Sunny both looked puzzled.

"I'd rather not say any more than that," he admitted. "In case it puts someone else in danger."

"How do I know *this* earring isn't enchanted to mess with my head?" Tsunami demanded. "What if it's got a spell on it to make us *more* suspicious of Darkstalker than we should be? Or something else." She twitched her ear grumpily. "I don't like wearing animus-touched things. I don't trust them."

"Smart," Peril offered unexpectedly. "You shouldn't. They can have other spells hidden inside them."

"I'm *sure* this one doesn't," Qibli said. "I can tell you the exact words of the spell: *Enchant this earring to make the wearer immune to any spell Darkstalker has cast or will cast, whether past, present, or future.* That's all there is to it, I promise."

"Hmmph," Tsunami said, twitching her ear again.

"It sounds all right to me," Sunny said.

"Then Anemone needs one of those earrings," said Tsunami. "She's in more danger than anyone."

"Her and Father," said Sunny, then stopped with a stricken expression. "But I can't give one to Stonemover — Darkstalker saved his life with his magic. If I make him immune to all of Darkstalker's spells, it'll erase that one . . . and then Father will die."

"I'm not sure Flame will accept one either, even if it shows he's innocent," Qibli said. Sunny blinked at him. "I mean, I think Darkstalker might have enchanted Flame to kill Stonemover. It would make sense to get rid of any other animus dragons, considering what Fathom did to him."

Sunny covered her mouth with a small gasp. "But . . . he saved him," she said. "He didn't let Stonemover die."

"Maybe he changed his mind," said Qibli. "Or maybe it was a performance to make you trust him even more. Or maybe he needed an excuse to cast a spell on Stonemover — a control spell hidden inside a healing spell. Maybe all of those things."

"You have a very complicated brain," said Peril thoughtfully.

Darkstalker said something like that, too, Qibli remembered.

"He just doesn't seem that sinister to me," Peril added with a shrug.

"Because I can't take the spell off you," he pointed out. "Not yet, anyway. I'll figure out a way."

"We have to get one of these earrings to Glory, too," Sunny said, touching the bowl lightly with one of her wings. "If only we could convince all the NightWings to wear them."

"They won't, not if they know what it is," Qibli said. "It would mean giving up all the powers he's given them. None of them will agree to that." *But Moon . . . Moon should have one.*

"I could fly to the rainforest," he said. "Right now. I can take earrings to Glory and Moon . . ." He trailed off, remembering Ostrich.

"Someone else can go to the rainforest," Sunny said, putting one of her talons over his. "You have to go after Ostrich."

"I know," he said.

"I found her with the dreamvisitor, although she was too shaken to hear me. But I could see that there were dragons in black hoods all around her, and she kept dreaming about their leader — a really tall SandWing with a hooked snout and tattoos of dragon skulls all down his neck."

"Tattoos of dragon skulls," Qibli said slowly. "Like . . . lots of them?"

"Too many to count," Sunny answered. "The whole place gave me this dark, crowded, trapped feeling, and it had a smell I remember. I think she might be in the Scorpion Den."

Qibli rubbed his neck as though he could feel the stab of the tattoo needle on himself. "She is," he said. "And I know who has her."

They all turned to stare at him. "Who?" Tsunami asked.

He took a deep breath, trying to speak past the claws that were closing around his throat.

"My grandfather."

CHAPTER 5

"I'm going back to the Scorpion Den, Clay!" Qibli said. "The most dangerous city in Pyrrhia! To save one of your students! And this is all you have?"

"Sorry," said Clay. "I told you, it's not *exactly* a weapons cave."

"No. I would call that a weapons *box*," said Qibli, pacing in a circle around the box that sat in the middle of the stone floor. "With hardly anything in it."

"This is a school, you know," Clay pointed out. "Sunny and I thought perhaps an entire cave full of sharp objects might not be the best idea. We thought maybe, hey, something that locks instead."

"So to defend this entire school," Qibli said, "you've got . . . three knives, one sword, and a big stick. In a locked box."

"Hey, that stick is very heavy," Clay protested. "You wouldn't want to get whacked with that thing. Also, we have Tsunami! And now Peril. That's better than a couple of swords."

Qibli sat down and covered his face with his wings. "I can't face him with nothing." He felt as if his heart was trying to jitter its way down his arms and out through his claws. Breathing was much, much harder than it was supposed to be. "If I go to him with no weapons, I might as well cut my own throat and hang my corpse from the alley wall."

"Yeesh," said Clay. "Are we still talking about your grandfather?"

Qibli nodded. He didn't trust himself to stand up while the floor was doing the weird tilting thing it apparently had to do right now.

Qibli's first memory of his grandfather was of hundreds of eyes: the eyes of all the tattooed skulls staring at him with the same cold, calculating look his grandfather wore. The skulls were there to greet him the day he struggled out of his egg, and they returned, like malevolent clockwork, every three days — as they would have for the rest of his life if he hadn't been lifted out of his family.

A later memory: the hiss of snakes, their writhing scales covering the floor as he beat his wings to stay above them, while his grandfather timed how long Qibli and his siblings could last before collapsing. He remembered the sharp sting of the snakebites as less painful than the disapproval on his grandfather's face.

Vulture was a large, terrifying presence that loomed over every corner of Qibli's early life. Qibli was convinced that Grandfather would have killed off all three of Cobra's dragonets if it were up to him. This was Qibli's biggest clue that his mother really loved him — because, he reasoned, Cobra must be protecting them from Grandfather, risking his wrath to keep them alive. Which meant she must love Qibli in some way, after all, even if it was a deeply hidden way.

Qibli's plan for a long life boiled down to one essential element: never see Grandfather again.

But if Grandfather had Ostrich, there was no choice.

"You really have to be armed to visit your grandfather?" Clay said.

"Definitely. True when I was a dragonet, more true now. He never liked me," said Qibli, giving breathing another try. Nope. Still impossible. "I haven't gone back to see him since I joined the Outclaws. He made it clear he was pretty unhappy about that, though."

"Angry letters?" Clay asked sympathetically.

"Sort of," said Qibli. "More like a hundred dead rats. Spread out over a couple of years, and always in new unexpected places." *Like inside my blankets when I went to sleep at night. Buried and decaying in a vat of grain I was supposed to be guarding. Lying by the shores of the oasis pool with their throats slit.* He knew they must be from his grandfather, but he'd never told Thorn. He didn't want her to worry about him, or worse, try to do something about Qibli's grandfather that might get her killed.

"Do you have any poison?" he asked hopefully. "I could dip one of these knives into it and have a poisoned dagger! Oh, I'd feel a lot safer with a poisoned dagger. In a very sturdy sheath, I mean."

"Of course we don't have poison," Clay said. "Remember the whole 'this is a school' thing? Our plan is to teach these dragonets *peace*, not more violence. My training sessions are only about self-defense."

"That's all I want to do!" Qibli said. "Defend myself! With a poisoned dagger and a couple of swords and maybe some throwing stars and a mace would be nice."

"You don't need that stuff," said a gruff voice from the doorway. "You'll have me." Winter slouched handsomely against the cave wall, wearing one of his most heroic scowls.

"Oh, will I?" said Qibli.

"I'm coming with you," Winter said. "To rescue your little SandWing friend or whatever."

"*Really?*" said Qibli, genuinely surprised. "Why? Because you adore me and can't bear to see me leave?" *What's his real reason? Is he worried about the IceWings finding out he's still alive, so he's decided to get out of here? Or maybe Darkstalker has enchanted him to keep an eye on me, in addition to whatever other spells he has on Winter . . .*

"Because I owe you for helping me find Hailstorm," said Winter, "and if we're even, maybe you'll stop bothering me all the time. And also because it'll be funny to be the one annoying *your* tail for once."

"So, basically because you adore me," Qibli said with a grin.

"This is already backfiring," Winter muttered.

"Well, tragically," said Qibli, "I'm afraid you cannot come."

"I seem to recall saying something similar to you once," said Winter. "With equally unsuccessful results, just so you're prepared."

"No, you *really* can't," said Qibli. "I mean, I'm basically walking into a den of killer scorpions."

"I'm not afraid of the Scorpion Den," Winter said, bristling.

"I'm not talking about the city," said Qibli. "I'm talking about my family."

"They can't be as bad as mine," Winter said. He flicked a wing dismissively.

"Actually, they're exactly like yours," Qibli said, rubbing his eyes. "Except they don't bother pretending to be civil, they don't know which fork is for salad because in their minds all forks are for impaling their enemies, and they'll stab me from every direction at once, not just in the back."

"So you need me," said Winter. "Perfect. Ready when you are."

Qibli thought for a moment. If Winter was under some kind of Darkstalker-induced spying spell, there wasn't anything Qibli could do to stop him. Except . . .

"If I let you come with me," said Qibli brightly, "will you put on my earring?"

"Absolutely not," said Winter. His gaze fell on Clay's ear, where an earring exactly like Qibli's now glittered. Winter's frown went slightly deeper and more puzzled.

"Everyone's wearing them," Clay said cheerfully. He touched the amber teardrop so it wobbled for a moment. "Very fashionable."

"Qibli, *what* are you up to?" Winter demanded. "This is a startling new level of weird, even for you."

"Our animus friend enchanted them to protect us from evil spells," Qibli said, glancing sideways at Clay, who mercifully had not asked a ton of questions about where the earrings came from. "Come on, Winter, don't be a burrowing shrew. Just put one on and you'll understand. If I'm right, and you're under a spell right now, it'll release you. And if I'm wrong, you'll be exactly the same, but safe from any *future* spells, and isn't that a good thing?"

"I'm NOT UNDER A SPELL," Winter said. "And I don't want to be! I remember what Hailstorm's spell felt like and it was awful! You keep your enchanted geegaws away from me."

"*Geegaws*," Qibli echoed. "How can you call *me* weird and then use ancient old worm words like that?"

"I'm coming with you, and I'm not wearing any stupid earring," Winter said firmly. "I thought this was an emergency. Why are you still here?"

"I know, I know," Qibli said, clutching his head. "I have to go, I know I need to go *right now*, but facing my grandfather — I'm not ready. I don't know how to *get* ready. Did Sunny tell you about the tattoos?"

"No," Winter said in a bored voice.

"He has a dragon-skull tattoo for every dragon he's ever killed," said Qibli. "He's *covered* in them."

"Sounds a bit obvious." Winter yawned. "Why not just tattoo 'I'M TOTALLY MENACING' on his forehead."

Qibli laughed. He'd *never* ever laughed about his grandfather before. The tight claws digging into his lungs eased back slightly.

It would feel better to have an ally, even an enchanted, sarcastic one who pretends to hate me. And if I keep him close, I'll find a way to get that earring on him.

"All right, you can come," he said. "As long as you listen to me. Like, if I say, *Quick, dive into that barrel of scarab beetles!* you have to do it right away, no arguing."

"Oh, don't worry," Winter said. "I intend to be just as helpful and obedient as you were on *my* quest."

Qibli picked up one of the daggers. "I guess I'll take this one," he said to Clay. "If that's all right."

"Sure," Clay said with a shrug, reaching to close the box.

I wish I had something else. One dagger and a bowl that doubles anything you put into it. That's all I'm taking to face the king of the Scorpion Den underworld?

If only I had Darkstalker's scroll!

It was Winter's fault that Peril had burned the scroll. Winter was the one who'd refused to let Qibli have it; the one who'd turned a perfectly reasonable discussion into a fight, which Peril felt she had to stop by destroying Qibli's one chance at having magic.

But he couldn't be furious at Winter right now, not the way he wanted to be. As long as he was under Darkstalker's spell, Winter was basically not himself. Qibli had to give Winter back his mind.

And *then* he could be furious at him.

"Let's go," he said to Winter.

"*I've* been ready forever," Winter said with another yawn.

Qibli led the way through the school to the main hall, where Sunny, Starflight, and Peril were waiting for them. Night had fallen quickly outside and the cave was full of fluttering echoes, like the whispers of tiny dragon wings, as bats stirred and woke and took flight. Peril saw Clay enter the cave behind Qibli and gave a little sideways jump, then made a face like she jumped sideways all the time, no big deal, totally normal behavior, followed by an "is everyone looking at me? stop looking at me!" face.

(Qibli suspected he could spend hours tracking the emotions on Peril's face and never get bored.)

"Qibli, maybe I should give you my dreamvisitor," Sunny said, twisting her front talons together. "Oh, *why* didn't I keep the one we found on Flame? I can't believe I let Darkstalker just waltz off with it."

"Part of the spell," said Qibli. "You trusted him, so you didn't even think to worry about it."

"Hey, don't forget they were his originally!" Peril blurted.

"That's true," said Starflight, nodding. "He's the one who made the dreamvisitors, all those centuries ago."

Qibli tilted his head. "Oh. I wonder if that means they won't work for us anymore," he said to Sunny.

She opened her mouth, then closed it again with a startled look, reaching up to touch her earring. "Oh dear," she said. "I use it all the time! How am I supposed to check on you without it? Or communicate with Glory?"

"We'll have to think of something else," Qibli said. "But speaking of animus-touched objects, I was wondering . . . I was wondering if maybe I could borrow Anemone's weather bracelets." It would be a small piece of magic, but magic nonetheless, and he'd take any magic he could get right now. Any magic would be better than none.

Sunny hesitated, then glanced at Starflight and Clay. "What do you guys think?"

She doesn't trust me with them, Qibli thought with a crashing wave of anxiety. *She's like Turtle and Peril; she thinks I don't deserve magic, or that I'll do something terrible with it.*

But I wouldn't! his mind flared indignantly. *I'd be so careful! I'd think through everything that could go wrong before I did anything. And I have so many great ideas! I would have been the right dragon to take care of Darkstalker's scroll, I know I would have, no matter what Winter thinks.*

"Sounds all right to me," Clay said with a shrug.

"Unless we might need them to defend the school?" Starflight worried.

"You don't need magic bracelets," Qibli joked. "I've seen your secret weapon."

"Is it me?" Peril asked, throwing her wings open excitedly, which made Winter jump back with a hiss. "Am I the secret weapon? I'd be a great secret weapon!"

"Actually, I was talking about the very big stick in the weapons box," Qibli said, "but you're almost as scary."

Sunny dug into her bag and pulled out the bracelets. They glowed like captured lightning in the lamplight as she placed them carefully in Qibli's talons. "Be very careful with them," she said. "I don't know how they work. And please bring them back for Anemone once Ostrich is safe."

Qibli slipped the bracelets around his wrists; they looked like bands of fire against his pale yellow scales. These were not like Turtle's quiet, sidling, don't-look-at-me spell things. These bracelets shouted POWER POWER POWER and I DO AMAZING THINGS and ADORE ME and DID YOU NOTICE THE AMAZING THINGS I CAN DO? and STAND BACK WHILE I BRING THE LIGHTNING and P.S. YES I SAID LIGHTNING! COWER BEFORE ME, BORING NORMAL DRAGONS!

Real magic.

He wished he could wear them forever. *Maybe if I help save Anemone, she'll let me keep them.*

"They'd look better on me," Winter commented.

Qibli shot him a frown. He was not going to do this again; he was not going to let Winter start a fight that might convince Sunny to take them away.

"We'll see you soon," he said quickly to Sunny and the

others. "We'll get Ostrich and bring her right back." He glanced at Winter, then lowered his voice to whisper in Sunny's ear. "And you'll make sure Moon gets an earring? As soon as possible?"

"Tsunami is leaving with earrings for Glory, Moon, Turtle, and Anemone as soon as she's got them on the other SeaWings here," Sunny promised quietly. "I'll handle the rest of the students." She took Qibli's front talons in hers. "Thank you, Qibli. Good luck."

"You too."

"Gah, with the endless good-byes already," Winter grouched. "Let's GOOOOOOO." He stomped out of the cave and lifted into the night sky.

"I'll miss you, too!" Peril called after him.

"Wish we could take you with us," Qibli said, "buuuuut you would literally burn down the entire Scorpion Den the minute you touched anything. Not the most fireproof place, is what I'm saying."

"Dragons should really build more cities with ME in mind," Peril said. "Also rainforests and libraries. More fire-proof rainforests and libraries, that would be great."

It was time to go. Qibli knew it, and he couldn't put it off any longer . . . but it was almost more than he could bear, intentionally seeking out his grandfather. *His grand-father*, of all dragons. Couldn't he face Scarlet or Darkstalker or Blister or someone more generally evil instead? Did it have to be a dragon who very specifically hated and haunted him?

Think of Ostrich. Think of the oaths you swore to the Outclaws. Think of what Thorn would want you to do.

Think of what Moon would do.

Qibli waved good-bye to the watching dragons, spread his wings, and launched himself toward his darkling past, now become his uncertain future.

CHAPTER 6

During the night, as they flew, Qibli felt a twitch from the slate in his pouch. He breathed a small flame to read the message from Turtle.

KINKAJOU IS AWAKE AND FINE. PLEASE TELL TAMARIN. DARKSTALKER TAKING THE TRIBE TO THE OLD NIGHT KINGDOM IN THE MORNING.

And then a few moments later: EVERYONE DEFINITELY UNDER HIS SPELL EXCEPT KINKAJOU.

Kinkajou! Qibli did a delighted flip in the air. She was all right! Oh, he wished he was back at Jade Mountain so he could tell Sunny and Tamarin and see their faces.

"What are you flopping all over the sky about?" Winter asked from his left.

"Nothing," Qibli said, tucking the slate away. He wanted to let Winter know Kinkajou was fine — but as long as Winter was under Darkstalker's spells, he couldn't be trusted with any secret information, especially anything related to Turtle. "I'll tell you once you put on one of my earrings."

Winter pointed at him. "Peculiar. That's what you are." He powered his wings harder to fly on ahead.

But Qibli's elation began sliding toward dismay as the rest of the message sank in.

Darkstalker is taking the tribe away in the morning. What if he leaves before Tsunami gets there? Is Moon going with him? What if Tsunami misses her chance to give earrings to Moon and Anemone?

She'd have to follow them to the old Night Kingdom — if anyone was paying enough attention to notice where Darkstalker went. *I don't exactly love the idea of an all-powerful dragon and his army of brainwashed superpowered followers vanishing into the mist.*

But if someone is *paying attention, then we could go there, too, and save Jade Mountain from the prophecy.*

He worried and wondered about this for the rest of the night, as the mountains gave way to forest and then sandy dunes. It was just before dawn when they spotted the Scorpion Den splayed across the desert ahead of them.

Winter eyed it from above as they flew closer and the straggling alleys, tents, colorful carpet walls, fire pits, and ramshackle structures became visible.

"This place looks . . ." He struggled for words for a moment.

"Charming?" Qibli supplied. "Picturesque?"

"Unsanitary," Winter concluded.

"I'm sure you mean charming," Qibli said. "Thrilling? Untamed! Unconventional!"

Winter snorted. "Unkempt."

"Oh, yes, that's true," said Qibli. "We are definitely not kempt."

"So what's the plan?" Winter asked. "Wait until the cover of darkness, sneak over the wall, break into your grandfather's house, find Ostrich — why are you shaking your head?"

"There's no sneaking into my grandfather's place," Qibli said. "It's the most well-fortified structure in Pyrrhia."

"I highly doubt *anything* in *this* place could compare to the fortifications around Queen Glacier's palace," Winter said haughtily.

"And I mean in a deadly way," Qibli went on. "The whole thing is lined with mines and traps. One wrong step and your foot gets blown off. A different wrong step, and, hello, that's a lot of axes. Grandfather isn't interested in catching intruders and teaching them a lesson. He's interested in killing them before they even see his treasure."

Winter's eyebrows were arched high enough to reach his horns. "Really," he said. "Then what's *your* ingenious plan?"

Qibli grimaced. "Gather information first. Find out if he's changed in the last few years. Then . . ." He blew out a long breath. "Then I probably have to talk to him."

"Ah, I get it now," Winter said, nodding. "You're planning to annoy him so much he decides to throttle you, and while he's distracted with that, I rescue Ostrich. I'm in. Especially for the you-getting-throttled part."

"You think you're joking," said Qibli. "But that sounds pretty much exactly how this might go."

They swept down to one of the entrances to the town. Which was not even guarded, Qibli noticed indignantly. Clearly standards had fallen since Thorn and her Outclaws left to run the kingdom.

A sense of unease prickled along his scales. In his lifetime, there had always been two worlds in the Scorpion Den: the visible world, which Thorn ran with her ferocious strength and wisdom, and the underworld, which stayed out of her way and kept its more unsavory practices to a minimum as long as she was in charge.

But with her gone to the palace . . . who was keeping the underworld in check? Was anything keeping it below the surface anymore? Who had risen to take her place?

He had a terrible feeling he could guess exactly who.

They strolled right in the open gate, onto a street lined with stalls, many of which were still closed in the predawn light. Morning scents drifted from those that were open, the smell of roasting beetles and coffee wrestling with the many, many much less pleasant smells in the air.

"This place is the opposite of Queen Glacier's palace," Winter murmured, stepping delicately around a dirty SandWing who lay asleep, half in the gutter, his tail wrapped in grimy bandages and his wings tattered and marked with sores.

"The Outclaws wouldn't have left him like that," Qibli said.

"Left who?" Winter asked. Qibli squinted at him. He wondered if the IceWing prince even saw the homeless dragons underfoot, or if they just looked like inconvenient grime to him.

"You must have wounded soldiers, too," Qibli said. "Are they all perfectly taken care of in the Ice Kingdom?"

Winter twitched his nose uncomfortably. "I believe so," he said. "They're not in the palace, in any case. And they're certainly not . . . well . . ."

"In the *way*, like these are," Qibli mocked him, waving one wing at another huddled figure.

"That's not what I was going to say," Winter objected. "The Ice Kingdom is very CLEAN, that's all. We don't have anywhere like this." He jumped as a trio of small scuttling creatures darted across the street almost under his talons.

"As far as you know, Queen Glacier's nephew," Qibli pointed out.

"That's true," Winter said unexpectedly. "You're right. I didn't leave the palace much. There could be a lot I never saw."

Qibli glanced at him sidelong. Maybe Winter *had* changed, and not only from Darkstalker's spell. Maybe there was a reasonable, open-minded dragon in there just waiting to burst out.

He wanted to say something about palaces and queen's nephews and pristine lives — but then, out of the corner of his eye, Qibli caught a glimpse of shadows slinking after them.

"Never mind," he said, speeding up. He didn't need to draw any more attention to Winter's royal status; it was too obvious already. The silvery, immaculate prince stood out like a small iceberg would if it bounced down from the mountains and sailed through the cobblestone streets. The farther in they went, the more shadows seemed to be tailing them, and the more Qibli's unease grew. *Maybe it was a mistake to bring Winter.*

Strangers being watched was normal for the Scorpion Den. Being followed wasn't unusual either; the competition to prey on new visitors was always fierce.

Although I'm not a visitor, and they should recognize me, Qibli thought with a frown.

What felt strange was how long they were followed without any further action. No urchins accidentally rolled a ball under their feet to distract them. No cutpurses bumped against them as they went past. No one even tried to pick a fight to test how they'd react. No one approached them at all — the shadows did nothing but watch, and that *was* weird for the Scorpion Den.

They wound their way through the dusty streets to a neighborhood that Qibli had avoided for the last two years. Memories assaulted him as they turned each corner. The heavy sweet smell of incense burning. The flies incessantly buzzing the garbage for discarded bits of prey. The bright-sting cactus plants bristling in baked clay pots that hung from the windows. The carmine-red scrawls of paint on the stone walls, where rivals marked their territory and young dragonets imitated them boldly.

And then the archway, the black gate standing open, the courtyard beyond, where Qibli's brother and sister had nearly killed him a hundred times.

He hesitated as they reached the threshold. *I don't have to go in. Grandfather won't be here. He'd be in his own compound.*

But Mother . . .

After all these years, he'd really thought he didn't care anymore. But he found his talons taking him forward, straight into the sick, uncomfortable, hopeful, terrified headspace where he'd grown up.

Winter made a scoffing noise deep in his throat as they crossed the run-down courtyard, but Qibli couldn't stop to react to it. He pushed open the door that led inside and called "Mother?"

"Oh," said Winter. "You lived . . . here?" He gave the cracked pavestones a look as though he was even more disappointed in them.

I can't go inside, Qibli realized with a shudder. *I can't have those walls around me again.* The lingering smell of roasted coriander seeds brought back a rush of painful memories.

"Mother?" he called once more.

A heavy, drifting silence answered him, like the silence you'd find far under the dunes in the desert.

She's all right, he told himself. *She's one of the smartest and deadliest dragons in the Scorpion Den. Who could possibly get close enough to harm her?*

Grandfather, of course, but he wouldn't.

"Mother?" he tried one more time.

"She's not here," said a mocking voice behind him.

Winter and Qibli whirled around. Two dragons were perched on the top of the courtyard walls, one on either side of them. Their venomous tails coiled dangerously over the edge beside them, and their matching expressions were malevolently delighted.

"Hello, Sirocco," Qibli said, steeling his voice to sound calm. "Rattlesnake. Long time no see. You look . . ." *even crueler than you used to* . . . "older. Where is Mother?"

He noticed that in the years since he'd seen them, his brother and sister had acquired dragon-skull tattoos of their own — a trio marching down Sirocco's neck, five trailing from Rattlesnake's head like a long morbid earring. There was a small hope that these were only decorative, meant to imitate and flatter Grandfather, but Qibli was fairly sure that they represented exactly the same thing on his siblings as they did on his grandfather.

"Mother don't want to see you," said Sirocco in a rough, gravelly voice.

"But Grandfather does," Rattlesnake announced in a menacing singsong.

"Better come quick and easy," Sirocco growled. "He don't like to wait."

"Or you could put up a fight," Rattlesnake suggested. "Weeeeeeee don't mind." She flicked her forked tongue at Winter. "I like fighting shiny things."

"Ah, Grandfather," said Qibli, trying *so* hard not to feel like he was two years old all over again. Like he was about to be pounded into the dust, and all his cleverness couldn't save him. He glanced down at his wrists. *I have animus friends and magic bracelets. I'm not the same dragon they used to push around*. "How's he doing? Still a barrel of doom on four legs?"

"Come see for yourself," said Rattlesnake, flicking her tail pointedly at the gate to the alley.

Qibli caught the sideways frown Winter sent his way and shrugged. At least this would get them into Grandfather's compound, although he couldn't guarantee they'd ever come out again.

His brother and sister led the way down the street, with Qibli and Winter close behind.

"So where *is* Mother?" Qibli asked.

"Bit of a long story," said Sirocco.

"Let's just say she hasn't *exactly* been the same since you abandoned us," Rattlesnake hissed with a little smile.

"What does that mean?" Qibli asked. His brain went into hyperflight. *Mother regrets letting me go. I was right, she did love me after all,* swung straight into *Don't get your hopes up; maybe she was furious and has been waiting for me to come back so she can finally let Grandfather kill me,* which was bolstered by *Where did our shadows go; they must have been tailing us for Grandfather; he knew we were coming* shot directly on into *How did he know? Did Onyx guess I'd come after Ostrich? Was this all a setup?* followed directly by *How should I play this? Pretend like I've come back to rejoin the family? Surely they wouldn't believe me for a moment. What's the most clever way to save Ostrich and get out of this? (And will Mother notice if I'm really clever and then will she realize I'm more interesting than she ever thought I was?)*

"You'll see," sang Rattlesnake as they turned down an alley that suddenly turned left, then right, then appeared to end in a wall as high as six dragons. Sirocco pushed one of the bricks in, grabbed the revealed handle, and slid open the secret door to Grandfather's compound.

Thorn had never ventured here, nor sent her Outclaws; as long as Vulture stayed out of her business and let her run the city her way, she stayed away from him. So Thorn had never seen the vast wealth hidden behind that secret door — the sprawling palatial complex, the only marble anywhere near the Scorpion Den, the gold dripping from every surface.

Qibli had seen it a few times when he was younger, when he and his siblings were summoned to family meals on holidays. But it looked more ostentatious now — as if the gold and treasure had been plastered over with another five layers of gold and treasure. Or perhaps his time with Thorn had made him accustomed to more simple tastes. Now when he looked at the emerald-studded doors or the black diamond eyes of all the statues, what he saw was a tremendous waste of wealth that could have been used to make hundreds of dragons' lives better.

I probably wouldn't get in trouble with Thorn for stealing from here, he reflected. But if he was caught stealing from his grandfather, the punishment would be certain death.

As they walked through the garishly grandiose decor, Qibli could feel Winter's disapproval sticking out of him like giant prickly IceWing spikes. He hoped Winter could contain his sarcastic arrogance in front of Grandfather. He hoped he wasn't leading his friend into a trap. He hoped Vulture wouldn't dare harm a prince of the IceWings, if revealing that information would save Winter. (Vulture did not need to know he was a disgraced and banished and supposedly dead prince.)

Qibli kept himself alert for any signs of Onyx or Ostrich, but there were none. *She has to be here somewhere.*

They reached a pavilion where the floor and columns were inlaid with tiny turquoise, gold, and white tiles and the ceiling was covered in mirrors. Qibli could tell from the dragons lurking all around it that his grandfather would be here, even before he spotted Vulture's long neck, hooked snout, and dark eyes glittering from the dais in the center of the pavilion.

"Let me do all the talking," he whispered to Winter.

"That is how conversations with you usually work," Winter observed.

Vulture had added to his collection of dragon skull tattoos, so that by this point he looked rather like a leopard from a distance, pale yellow but stippled all over with black patches. He wore a black cape lined with gold and draped with gold chains all along his wings. His claws were dipped in gold leaf and enormous black-and-gold earrings shaped like spiders gleamed in his ears.

He didn't look up at Qibli and Winter as they approached. His eyes — and the eyes of the four dragons beside him — were fixed on a small wooden structure set up on the floor in front of him. It looked like a little maze. It *was* a little maze, Qibli realized, drawing closer. And inside were two scavengers, running in a panic from one dead end to another.

Uh-oh — Winter, don't react —

Winter drew in a sharp breath, then started forward. Qibli blocked him with his wings, but the noise was enough to make Vulture look up.

"Qibli," he said with the smuggest of smiles. "Just the dragon I've been waiting for."

CHAPTER 7

Vulture's eyes flicked over Qibli and Winter, assessing them at the speed of lightning, and then he returned his attention to the scavengers in the maze.

"Hold your tongues for a moment," he said. "I want to see who wins."

"Then what are you going to do with them?" Winter demanded.

Vulture slowly lifted his head to stare at Winter again. "Eat the loser," he answered. "And save the winner to try again tomorrow against a different one. I'm curious to see whether they can learn anything."

"They can!" Winter said. "They're very intelligent. Too intelligent to eat. Eating them would be cruel!"

"Winter, shhh," Qibli whispered.

"What a whimsical friend you've brought for my entertainment," Vulture said to Qibli. He turned back to Winter. "You're quite wrong. Everyone agrees they're no smarter than mice. If you were right, dragons would already know that, and no one would ever eat scavengers. And yet we eat them all the time, ergo, you must be mistaken."

"But —" Winter started.

"It's perfectly normal to feel like your pet must think the way you do," Vulture said, and the condescension was spread so thick that Qibli felt like rubbing his scales with sand to get clean. "It's happened to many dragons. The Camels' Rights Movement. Iguanas Are Dragons, Too. Save the Scavengers. World Walrus Fund. All very sweet, and very misguided. Save your energy for dragons, who can appreciate it."

"Stop arguing with him," Qibli hissed out of the side of his mouth. He'd seen this a million times, the way Vulture could grind down anyone who disagreed with him — or, if his opponent argued back for too long, the way Vulture was perfectly happy to win the most annoying arguments with casual violence.

"I'll pay you for them," Winter said quickly. The two scavengers had found each other and now one was trying to boost the other up to look over the walls. It certainly looked like intelligent behavior to Qibli. Much more intelligent behavior than what Winter was doing right now, that was for sure. "I'll buy them off you. I'm in the market for new pets, in fact."

"Oh, really, Prince Winter?" said Vulture, sitting back in his gilded chair. "And how exactly do you intend to pay me, when your family thinks you're dead and your royal funds have been cut off?"

In the silence that fell, Qibli tried to keep his breathing on track. He had already identified four possible escape routes, but none of them would work if he forgot to breathe.

Vulture waved at the scavengers and the maze. "Take them away," he said to a pair of dragons nearby. "My visitors have ruined my experiment for today anyway. We'll try again tomorrow." The dragons bowed, took either side of the board supporting the maze, and carried the scavengers out of the room while they were still trapped inside.

Winter watched them go with a dismayed expression, but Qibli couldn't pull his eyes away from Vulture's. How did Vulture know not only who Winter was, but his whole story? Had the news spread so quickly? Did he have spies in the IceWing tribe?

"So, Grandson," Vulture said commandingly. "I see that like many hundreds of SandWings across the kingdom, you've realized that Thorn is in no way qualified to be queen, and you've come to pledge your loyalty where it truly belongs."

War broke out inside Qibli's mind. *Play along! Find out what you can! Stay alive!* shouted one half, while the other roared, *No, no, no, never, I will NOT betray her.*

"Many hundreds of SandWings?" he echoed, buying time.

"Oh, yes," said Vulture. "Her erstwhile popularity, such as it was, is plummeting. Everyone agrees that she's been quite useless so far. Has the kingdom improved in any way? No one's life is any better, except of course for her own Outclaws, who are now rolling in treasure up there in the palace. I'm sure you saw that yourself. She pours wealth into the talons of those who bow and scrape to her, and she doesn't care a fig for anyone else."

No, Qibli thought fiercely, *that's what* you *do.*

"And these tragic bombings, tsk," Vulture said, reaching for a bowl of dates beside him. "Dragons are *dying* and she hasn't done *one thing* about it. She has no idea who's responsible. If she even cares. But *I* do. *I* have found the culprits! *I* am the only one who can protect our tribe."

"You know who's been setting off all the cactus fires?" Qibli asked.

"Of course I do." Vulture leaned toward one of his guards. "Summon our informative friend for me, will you?" The guard nodded and hurried away into the garden.

"It's really an outrage," Vulture said, sitting back. His spider earrings caught the light, reflecting it like a sharp knife in Qibli's eyes. "I mean, absolutely everyone is talking about how Thorn can't keep us safe." He chewed a talonful of dates noisily. "But *I* can."

"Really?" Qibli asked, battering back his rage. "How?"

"I have formed a private militia of my own," Vulture said smugly. He tapped his gold-tipped tail against a metal sheet hanging beside him, and an eerie, coppery noise rolled out across the garden like thunder.

From every shrubbery, from every shadow, from each corner and descending from the roofs and treetops came a wave of dragons. Black hoods covered their faces and gold medallions hung from their necks, emblazoned with the shape of a bird of prey — of a vulture, Qibli realized.

"We're the new law and order in this town, and soon in the whole kingdom," said Vulture. "I had them looking into these heartbreaking attacks and the dreadful mess Thorn has made of investigating. We discovered who's responsible and we'll bring them to justice."

As more hooded dragons slithered forward, Qibli's four possible escape routes became three, and then two, and both of those very questionable. *Who are all these dragons?* Qibli wondered. *How can there be so many who are willing to follow Grandfather and do his evil for him?*

Vulture spread his wings as though he were displaying a vast tray of new jewels. "I call them my Talons of Power," he said.

Beside Qibli, Winter made a choked noise. Qibli knew exactly what he was thinking.

The prophecy.

Beware the talons of power and fire.

I thought it was about an animus dragon — but what if it's about my grandfather's secret army?

"I always thought the Talons of Peace was too grand a name for that disorganized group of whiners," Vulture said. "I knew I could improve on both the concept and the reality. Ah, here we are."

The guard had returned, leading a dragon who was so heavily swathed in jewelry that it took a moment to see through it all to figure out which tribe he was from. Trails of gold chains encircled his neck, dangling from an elaborate ruby-encrusted headpiece that clashed with the rows of silver, emerald, and topaz earrings in each ear. Silver chain mail studded with sapphires covered his chest; golden silk veils wreathed his wings. He even had a tail band, which was an item of jewelry that had gone out of style centuries ago because they were hard to fly with. His was gold and shaped to look like dragon claws clutching every inch of his tail, each claw tipped with a sapphire.

Qibli had never seen a dragon look more ridiculous. He glanced sideways at Winter, whose expression suggested that his eyes might never recover.

But underneath all the glitter, the dragon's scales were simple mud-brown, and his snout was broad and flat.

A MudWing? Qibli thought, confused.

Vulture surveyed the walking, clanking pile of treasure for a moment with his jaw clenched. Qibli wondered if his grandfather was upset because the MudWing was being so obvious about the lavish bribe he must have gotten.

Or possibly Grandfather just doesn't like any other dragon to wear more gold than he does.

"How is your pavilion, Bog?" Vulture inquired with forced politeness.

"Much better than that prison cell," Bog answered cheer-fully, but very much as though he was reading back a line that had been written for him.

"I was hoping you could share your confession with our dear guests here," Vulture said, spreading one wing toward Qibli and Winter.

Bog's gaze tracked the movement and landed on them. He

jerked backward, nearly tripping over his chains and orna-
ments. An expression of horror surged across his face and
then he ducked his head, took a deep breath, and looked up
again, now placid and smiling.

What was that about? Qibli wondered.

"Of course, sir," he said. "The MudWings are the ones
who've been attacking cities throughout the Kingdom of
Sand. Queen Moorhen and the MudWings are responsible
for all of it."

Qibli stared at Bog, who was definitely avoiding his eyes.

No. I don't believe it. He's lying — but why?

"You see?" said Vulture. "Unlike Thorn, *I* investigated.
Unlike Thorn, *I* found out who is trying to hurt us.
And unlike Thorn, *I* can lead us to victory against this
enemy, along with my Talons of Power."

The MudWing nodded, his gold chains jangling.

Why is Bog doing this? Qibli wondered. *For treasure? How
did Vulture find a MudWing willing to betray his tribe this
way? A MudWing who's willing to lie to lead us into another
war . . . willing to see his tribemates die, just so he can have
another expensive ring on his claws?*

*He is lying — he must be lying. There's no reason for Queen
Moorhen to attack us. She wouldn't want more war.*

"See?" Vulture said condescendingly. "Now we know the
real truth, all thanks to me. And if we're going to defeat this
pervasive MudWing menace, we're going to need a strong
leader like me — not a corrupt, glory-seeking liar like Thorn.
You may go, Bog."

The MudWing scurried away as fast as he could clank, while Vulture stood up and swept toward Qibli in a cloud of heavily perfumed air. "I'm sure you agree with me, since you're here to work for us, right on time."

Qibli tamped down his rage. *Keep it together. Gather information.* "What exactly do you think I'm going to do?" he asked.

"First, tell me everything you know about Thorn, her palace, her guards, any weaknesses, everything a good little spy would have absorbed in your time with her. Next, teach my Talons any passwords they need to know to get close to the palace. And finally, return to the palace, and to our false queen, bearing a gift."

Qibli took a deep breath in and blew it out again, making sure his voice didn't shake with anger when he finally spoke. "Where is Ostrich?" he asked.

"Ostrich . . ." Vulture said reflectively. "Oh, the general's daughter. She's fine. Perfectly happy. She loves it here. Of all the places to be held captive, this is the best, obviously."

"I want to see her."

"And *I* want a new queen of the SandWings," said Vulture. "A true queen who will set up trade routes that make *me* richer and turn this town into the thriving metropolis it could be. I'm sure you can imagine how great that will be. All your old friends, your family, happy and wealthy and running the world. We'll kick out everyone who's not a SandWing and crack down on troublemakers. It'll be spectacular."

"A new queen of the SandWings?" Winter said skeptically. "Who? Blaze?"

Qibli had met Blaze, the only remaining daughter of Queen Oasis, and the only sister left alive after the War of SandWing Succession. Thorn had allowed her to keep living in the palace, as long as she didn't meddle in the kingdom's affairs. Blaze had agreed happily, thrilled to return to the desert warmth after years in the IceWing tundra border zone. All she cared about was keeping her scales polished and her gems sparkly. In Qibli's estimation, Blaze was silliness personified. She was the opposite of levelheaded, empathetic Thorn.

"No, no," said Vulture, wrinkling his nose. "Nobody wants Blaze. Have you really not heard the rumors, little dragons? The whole kingdom has been buzzing for months about a secret heir to the SandWing throne. One that nobody knew about until recently. A granddaughter who escaped the deadly claws of Queen Oasis and has been living in hiding since she hatched. A dragon, unlike Thorn, who has true royal blood in her veins —"

"Onyx," Qibli interrupted, the realization hitting him like snake fangs sinking into his neck.

Vulture snapped his mouth shut, thrown off the rhythm of his dramatic announcement.

"Of course she is — that's what she's been up to this whole time," Qibli said, his mind racing on ahead of his words. "Queen Oasis's granddaughter — but how? She could be the daughter of Blister or Burn, taken away by a trusted servant to be raised in secret. Except Blister would never let a possible threat to her leave her sight, and Burn didn't want anything to do with partners or eggs.

"Blaze has a lot of empty space between her ears, but she'd remember having a dragonet, if only because carrying it would have been a great aggravation to her. So she would have gone looking for it after the war, and she never did, so it can't be hers.

"Which leaves the royal sons, and of those, only one was rumored to have a love affair serious enough to warrant an attempted elopement. Except his true love was supposedly captured and killed by Queen Oasis shortly before the queen's own death — but if she wasn't, she could have escaped and hatched a dragonet who'd be just exactly Onyx's age.

"So Onyx could be lying, a false pretender to the throne, but it's equally likely to be true — meaning she's the daughter of Prince Smolder, the granddaughter of Queen Oasis, and directly in line for the SandWing throne."

There was a brief silence.

"Sometimes your brain makes *my* brain hurt," Winter observed.

"Well done," said Vulture. "I always suspected you were the smartest of Cobra's offspring."

Rattlesnake let out an injured growl and Sirocco stopped picking his claws for a moment to look at her and say, "What? I didn't do anything! What?"

"Now at last you can use that intelligence for a good cause," Vulture went on. "A righteous cause."

"No." Qibli straightened his neck and folded back his

wings. *I can't lie about this,* he realized. *I'm not a sneak. I won't betray Thorn, not even by pretending to.* "I'm loyal to Queen Thorn and always will be."

Vulture made a face. "You *think* you are," he said. "Because she stole you away and brainwashed you. You haven't thought for yourself in years. You do exactly what she tells you to and think whatever she tells you to think. You're not your own dragon, Grandson. Everyone knows her group is basically a cult. It's true; ask anyone. The whole kingdom has figured out that her Outclaws are blind followers. You don't want to be a blind follower, do you, Qibli? Don't you want to think for yourself?"

"I *am* thinking for myself," Qibli insisted, bristling.

"So think yourself back into your family," Vulture suggested in a deceptively friendly tone of voice. "You loved being one of us before Thorn snatched you away. She's fed you a lot of lies about us, hasn't she? Turning you against your own family, tsk. What kind of leader does such a thing? Don't you remember the puzzles we did together — the family dinners? The way I was grooming you to take over the business once you were older? Those were happy times."

Vulture's eyes reminded Qibli of the Eye of Onyx; not solid black, but black in loops all the way down, like looking into the longest, deepest hole in the world.

But Qibli was not going to let his grandfather's hypnotic eyes and confident attitude play tricks on him. He had Sirocco and Rattlesnake in his peripheral vision as a clear and present reminder of the torment he'd gone through every day before Thorn saved him.

"I did *not* love being part of this family," Qibli said firmly. "Give me Ostrich and let us go, and I will ask Queen Thorn to spare your life."

"Clever and stubborn," Vulture mused, slithering closer. "I knew you would be. You see, inferior grandchildren, this is why I was so unhappy with your mother when she lost him."

Rattlesnake hissed and shot Qibli a vengeful look.

"Who?" said Sirocco. "Us? What'd I do now?"

"But perhaps now that he's returned to us — if he has truly returned to us," said Vulture smoothly, "perhaps now it is finally time to release your mother from her punishment."

"Punishment?" Qibli's heart sank. *What has he done to her?*

It doesn't make sense. Punish her for getting rid of me? But I thought Grandfather never wanted us alive in the first place . . . did he?

"Where is she?" Qibli demanded.

"Let's go see," said Vulture, flicking out his wings. "Leave your scavenger-loving prince here." He started off down one of the garden paths without waiting to see if Qibli would follow.

Qibli hesitated, looking at Winter.

"I'll be fine," Winter said in a bored voice. He circled a spot on the cool marble of the pavilion and lay down, pretending to look sleepy and impassive. "Just don't forget we're here for Ostrich."

"All right," Qibli said. "Try not to get yourself set on fire while I'm gone."

"One time," Winter said icily. "*One time* I got myself set on fire."

Qibli hurried after his grandfather, who was already talking when Qibli caught up to him. The black cloak swirled out between his wings and around his tail, casting glinting gold reflections in the white marble walkway.

"I've always liked that word," Vulture was saying. "Oubliette. Ooooooooubliette. It sounds much friendlier than it is, like you should be able to eat it at parties. Do you know what an oubliette is?"

Qibli nodded, feeling as though his heart had sunk all the way into his stomach and was smashing big holes all through his insides.

I wish Moon were here. Everything is less awful when I'm with Moon.

I wonder, if she could read Vulture's mind, whether she'd still think that dragons are basically good inside.

She'd be brave enough to stand up to him. That's what I have to do, dig in my claws and keep standing, like she would.

"Here we are," Vulture said, stopping at a courtyard marked out by a circle of potted palms, all in giant clay pots painted gold. Qibli looked around for a moment in confusion. The courtyard was deserted, as far as he could tell. Then he remembered the word *oubliette* and looked down.

In the floor in the center of the circle of palms was a

trapdoor, just barely big enough to squeeze a medium-sized dragon through.

Qibli stepped over to it, his whole body swamped with dread.

Through the bars in the trapdoor, he could see down a long dark shaft — a hole that seemed bottomless at first, until his eyes adjusted and he could see a shapeless figure, and the glitter of eyes looking back up at him.

Too many eyes. From far below came a splash, and a low, ongoing hissing.

"Mother is down there?" Qibli said, disbelieving.

"Oh, yes," said Vulture. "Her and a few crocodiles, a number of snakes, probably a rat or seven if they haven't been eaten yet . . . I forget what else; we just throw down anything nasty we can find."

"Qibli," a hoarse voice called from the darkness.

"Mother," Qibli called back, gripping the bars fiercely. "Mother, I'm here. I'm getting you out, I promise." He whirled on Vulture. "You have to let her out of there."

"Well, that, my dear grandson," said Vulture, "depends entirely on what you do next."

— CHAPTER 8 —

It wasn't a prison, exactly, and it wasn't a dungeon — it certainly wasn't an oubliette — but Qibli had never felt more trapped than he did that day, waiting for his mother in his grandfather's observatory.

It was a beautiful little black marble building, actually, with a dome set up higher than all the other structures in the compound. Diamonds twinkled like stars everywhere, scattered throughout the walls and columns. Moon shapes were carved all around the outside of the building, from crescent to full, outlined with milky pale moonstones.

Inside, the floor was covered with large silk pillows in silver and black and soft dark blue carpets where dragons could lie down to look up at the sky. On two sides of the dome, telescopes pointed at one of the moons, and star charts lined the walls.

Under any other circumstances, Qibli would have adored this place. But here and now he found it unsettling, because he knew it was a re-creation of the old observatory in the SandWing palace — one that hadn't been used in years, since before the war. Which made him think of how long his grandfather had been alive, and how deeply entwined with the monarchy he had once been. It made him think of Queen Thorn, struggling to put the kingdom back together while a danger like Vulture and Onyx's conspiracy crept up on her.

And it made him think of Moon, who would love this room — a whole building designed for watching the moons, just like her name. He wished he could re-create it at Jade Mountain so dragons who would actually appreciate it could have access to it. He doubted that anyone used it very often here, where it was more of a status symbol than anything else.

Qibli paced around the perimeter of the dome as the sun crawled slowly across the sky. He could see it crawling if he looked up, because the dome was open at the top, but he refused to look up, because he knew there were six dragons in black hoods sitting up there, staring down at him and Winter.

There was only one message from Turtle, in the middle of the morning, and like all the others, it was breathtakingly uninformative: KINKAJOU, MOON, AND I FOLLOWING DARKSTALKER TO NIGHT KINGDOM. HOPEFULLY BACK AT SCHOOL SOON.

Qibli was in agony, wishing more than ever that he could be in two places at once. How many NightWings had gone with Darkstalker? Which way was the lost city of night? How was Moon; was the spell changing her? Had Tsunami reached them with the earrings and, if so, was Moon wearing one? Why didn't Turtle mention Tsunami at all? Was

Moon safe? What was she doing? What was she thinking? Had it only been a day and a half since he last saw her? Why did it feel like a million years?

He just wanted to be in the same room as her for a moment so he could breathe again. He just wanted to hear her voice and make her laugh and give her his heart; that was all.

He missed her.

His loyalty to Thorn and the Outclaws, his promise to Ostrich's parents, his ties to this family and what he owed his mother, all of that kept him here.

But he thought of Moon every waking moment.

So does he, he reminded himself, catching sight of Winter's face. *I think. I'm sure he does.*

Who is she thinking of?

Probably him.

"Has anyone ever told you that you are kind of an exhausting dragon to be around?" Winter asked from one of the silk cushions. "Are you even capable of sitting still?"

"Why is this taking so long?" Qibli asked. "Grandfather said he'd bring Mother and Ostrich to us hours ago. What if one of them is hurt and he doesn't want us to know? Or what if keeping us trapped here is what he really wants? To get me out of the way while he takes down Thorn?"

"Hmmm, yes," said Winter, "because before this *you* were the only thing stopping him. Never mind the other hundred loyal Outclaws or the palace guards or the entire SandWing army she commands."

"I wonder what the kingdom will think when they find

out Onyx is the granddaughter of Queen Oasis," Qibli said, trailing one wing along the wall. "Dragons love royal bloodlines."

"And if someone is setting off explosions in the king-dom —" Winter started.

"*Someone,*" Qibli said with a snort. "Someone is my grandfather."

Winter blinked and squinted at him. "You think Vulture is the one orchestrating the bombs? I thought he said he was investigating them."

"Of course," said Qibli. "Oldest trick in the book. Do something terrible in secret, make it look like your opponent can't protect their people, then sweep in and 'protect' them yourself. The worrying part is that he'll probably convince a lot of SandWings that we ought to go to war with the MudWings. But I'm *sure* it wasn't them, no matter what that strange treasure-lover said."

He held out his talons and studied Anemone's weather bracelets. "Maybe I should use these to get us out of here." Just the thought of wielding such magic made his claws tingle.

"What a well-thought-out plan," said Winter. "Please do make it rain so we can drown in here."

"Maybe a really big storm would be distracting," Qibli said. He flexed his talons optimistically.

"No, it would just be wet," Winter said. "I know you're excited about your magic toys, but try not to be absurd. Save them for when they can actually be useful."

The whoosh of wings made them both look up. Two dragons descended into the dome: Vulture and, right behind him, the long, thin shape of Qibli's mother.

Qibli caught his breath. Cobra was as beautiful and deadly looking as she'd been the day he left her. The oubliette hadn't taken away the dangerous glitter in her eyes.

But maybe it had changed the expression on her face when she looked at him. Maybe he was imagining things, but she looked a tiny bit less *out of my way, bug who needs squashing* and a tiny bit more *that's MY dragonet*.

The two dragons touched down on the floor and Cobra paced toward Qibli, flicking her tail barb slowly back and forth.

"You've finally come back to us," she said. "Took you long enough."

"I'm sorry — if I'd known you were being punished like that —" Qibli said. He hesitated. "Were you? This whole time? Because of me?"

"Because of her own mistake," said Vulture. "She knew I wanted heirs to my organization. I told her not to kill off or get rid of any of you. She knew there would be consequences to letting Thorn have you — of all dragons, that upstart nobody!"

Cobra nodded. "Yes. My mistake," she echoed.

Qibli's mind was reeling. He'd always thought Cobra was keeping them alive despite his grandfather's wishes — not because of them. His understanding of his own childhood wavered in front of him like a mirage in the desert.

"I'll go get the other one," Vulture said. "Give you two a chance to catch up." He took off into the sky again.

Cobra backed Qibli into the sunshine in the center of the dome and started examining him from horns to tail, as if he were a rented caravan and she was checking to see whether Thorn had damaged him.

"Hmm," she said, tapping the scar on his snout. "Clumsiness or war wound?"

"You gave that to me," he reminded her.

"Oh," she said skeptically. She tipped his head up and studied his eyes. "Well, you seem a bit stronger. Perhaps you'll be useful to your grandfather — maybe even more useful than you would have been if I'd kept you. Depending on how much you've stored in here." She tapped his skull once, then started brushing sand off his shoulders.

"There, that's a bit better." Cobra's gaze shifted to Winter. "Couldn't you have bathed before coming? You look a bit shabby next to this shiny creature."

I'm sure I do, Qibli thought, a thought that would not have bothered him anywhere else in the world, but here, under his mother's eyes, he felt keenly how unshiny he was, and he couldn't stop himself from thinking that Moon must see them the same way.

"Never mind," said Cobra, spreading one of her wings around him. Her breath smelled of coriander, just like it used to. "I'm glad you've returned."

Qibli's mother had never put a wing around him before. Brushing the sand off him; that was familiar — she'd done it every time Grandfather came to inspect them. But this light, protective touch came from nowhere.

Qibli couldn't stop himself from thinking, *She did miss me. She does love me.* And his talons felt as awkward and his heart as confused as if he were three years old all over again.

"Introduce me to your glittering companion," Cobra suggested.

"That's Winter," Qibli said, flicking his tail toward the IceWing. "I keep trying to get rid of him, but he follows me everywhere. Like that monkey who followed me home one day, remember?" He hesitated, remembering that he'd wanted to keep the monkey for a pet, but Cobra had decided to eat it instead.

Stay in the present. Don't get sucked into the past. He forced himself to focus on Winter, like a tether in a sandstorm that could lead him back to his true self. "It's pretty adorable. He's my biggest fan."

"Ha!" Winter barked. "Indeed! Ha ha ha! Don't believe a word he says! I can't stand him!"

"We'll probably end up married one day," Qibli said.

The only reply Winter made to this was a snort so vigorous he nearly knocked himself over.

Cobra arched her eyebrows. "Well, that would get your grandfather's attention," she said. "Marrying an IceWing."

She tapped her claws together, looking thoughtful, then added, "He's always been interested in a business alliance with that tribe."

Qibli blinked up at his mother. *Is she really taking me*

seriously? Or is she pretending to, for some reason? Or is she only making conversation while she actually thinks about something else, like being trapped in Grandfather's prison for years? Or does she truly mean it, that marrying an IceWing could be seen as advantageous to the family?

That wasn't the family Qibli remembered, with their fierce hostility to other tribes, but maybe things had changed. Maybe the peace had turned the other tribes from enemies into potential pots of gold.

"Are you going to help your grandfather?" Cobra asked abruptly, looking Qibli in the eyes.

He looked away first. "I can't. He wants to know all of Thorn's secrets, and I would never — I'm not that kind of dragon."

"I told him that," Cobra said. "I said you wouldn't . . . even for me. Even if it meant . . . well, it's not important."

"I'll find another way to help you," Qibli insisted. "Thorn will send her army to get you out of here, if I ask her to. I'm sure she will."

"I have a better idea," Cobra whispered. "You take me with you. We escape. Tonight."

Qibli studied her face, then looked up at the hulking shapes of the guards above them. "How?" he whispered back.

"I'm an assassin, remember? Between the two of us, I think we can outsmart my father."

Qibli thought for a minute, a billion thoughts cascading over one another. "All right." He stepped back from her. "But we're taking Ostrich, too."

Cobra's eyes narrowed to slits, but she nodded. "Shh," she said. "Here they come."

She was right; Vulture was descending again, this time with two other dragons: the rangy, black-diamond-studded form of Onyx, and beside her, tiny Ostrich.

"Qibli!" Ostrich cried. She flew across the dome to throw herself at him and he caught her, beaming. She was all right; she was uninjured. He hadn't failed Six-Claws and Kindle completely.

"Hey," he said, hugging her. "You had me kind of worried."

"Well, Onyx told me that Queen Thorn had sent her a message asking for us, and I thought, *whoa, that's kind of awesome*, but guess what, that turned out to be a LIE, Qibli! She was LYING to me! Why would she DO that?" Ostrich shot Onyx a resentful look. "And we were halfway to the palace when suddenly THIS guy showed up with, like, EIGHTY creepy dragons in hoods and they bossed us all here instead, although I was pretty sure Thorn wouldn't be here, and I was right, and then they said I couldn't leave, and finally I realized Onyx was actually WORKING with them, and then I was, like, ARRRGH NOOO, I'm a stupid HOSTAGE again, aren't I?"

She seized his front talons. "Qibli, I don't *like* being a hostage. Can we stab all these dragons in the face so no one will ever think I'd make a good hostage, like, ever again? And then maybe I need to eat all the camels in Pyrrhia to get really huge; I bet that would help, too. Super-Huge Ostrich:

Worst Hostage Ever. That is the look I would like to go for, please."

"We can definitely work on that," Qibli promised. "But you're all right?"

"Outraged but intact," Ostrich said proudly, and he could tell she'd been putting on a brave face, and that she'd been more scared than she'd ever admit, but that she was prepared to be strong and he could count on her.

"Delightful," Vulture interjected. "Now you have what you want. Let's discuss what I want."

"You mean what *I* want," Onyx said coldly. "The throne."

"Why don't you challenge Queen Thorn?" Qibli asked her. "If you're so sure the throne should be yours?"

"That was my original plan," said Onyx, shooting a glare at Vulture. "But *someone* told me I'd never make it all the way into the palace to issue my challenge. *Someone* convinced me my plan would work better if we delayed long enough to spread a bunch of rumors first. *Someone* thought it would be a great idea for me to go hide myself away at that idiotic pacifist school so I could find out more about the queen's daughter."

"Thorn's daughter? Sunny?" said Ostrich.

Something was happening outside. Qibli pricked his ears toward the roof of the dome. Some kind of commotion in the garden. One of the hooded guards flew off, probably to see what it was. Vulture had his head tilted toward the sky as well; his eyes met Qibli's and he grinned, as if to say, *See how alike we are? The only dragons who notice everything?*

"I thought she'd be another contender for the throne," Onyx went on, still talking about Sunny. She rolled her eyes and let out a small snort of flame. "But I've never met a less ambitious dragon. No interest in killing her mother at all. And so busy with that dratted school — I could never get close enough to learn anything useful.

"Finally I decided I'd had enough. The chaos of that giant NightWing arriving distracted everyone long enough for me to kidnap this little idiot, who would have been perfect leverage to get me through the gates and past her general father so I could kill Thorn in her sleep. But *no*. Apparently I have to wait *again* for some *other* convoluted plan to take shape."

"I know you're getting impatient," Vulture said soothingly. "But successful plans take a little time."

There was a crash and some muffled shouting outside. Now everyone looked up at the sky.

"What is it?" Vulture barked at the hooded figures.

"Someone tryin' to see you, sir," answered one of the Talons. "Won't take no for an answer. Already got a bit of 'is tail blown off charging the wall, but still comin' strong, bleedin' and everythin'."

"Great snakes," said Vulture calmly. "If he's that intent, let's have a look at him."

"Yes, sir," the guard said, ducking her head. She flew away and returned a few moments later, escorting a dragon along with three other Talons. Two of them had their hoods torn and tossed back, and the third had a long scratch on his side, but the newcomer was in far worse shape: bleeding from several wounds and with his tail ending in a bloody stump instead of a SandWing barb.

"Sir!" he cried as soon as he saw Vulture. "I have an urgent message for you! I'm not allowed to stop or rest or do anything else until I give it to you!" He collapsed on the marble floor as the guards dropped him in front of Vulture.

"Intriguing," said Vulture. "Go on."

"There's a new king of the NightWings," the dragon gasped, letting words spill out breathlessly. "A giant dragon, the biggest you've ever seen. He caught us in the rainforest and took the other four prisoner. But he sent me back to tell you it's not the right time to kill Queen Glory. He said he knows about your plan to replace Thorn and he'll help you if you help him. He said he'll be in touch soon and not to do anything until he sends instructions."

The last sentence whooshed out of the dragon in one garbled rush, and then at last he took a breath and closed his eyes and fell, unconscious, at Vulture's feet.

Qibli whirled toward Winter. This was proof! Proof that Darkstalker was working against their allies — that he couldn't be trusted. Surely Winter had to see him as he was now.

But the IceWing prince looked unaffected. He was watching Vulture with a politely curious expression, but he certainly didn't look as though an enormous revelation had just been dropped on his head.

Vulture, on the other talon, absolutely did. He stared down at the messenger, his tail lashing so his cloak shifted from side to side, rustling along the floor.

"A new . . . *king* of the NightWings?" he enunciated slowly.

"Must be that big guy I told you about," Onyx said with a shrug.

"But . . . *king*?" Vulture said again. "The NightWings agreed to this? Queen Glory just . . . handed them over? To a *king*?"

"Why would she want them?" Onyx demanded. "Bunch of lying grumblers. I'd give them away, too. Focus on my *own* tribe."

"Your tribe . . ." Vulture mused, and in a flash of insight, Qibli guessed what he was thinking.

If one tribe can have a king, why not another?

Why be the power behind the throne, when one could be the power on the throne?

Why bother installing Onyx . . . if perhaps the time has come for a SandWing king at last?

This was bad, bad, bad, bad, bad. Vulture scheming behind the scenes was terrible enough; Vulture openly trying to seize the throne for himself would be a new kind of threat to Queen Thorn. Especially if he was collaborating with Darkstalker to make it happen.

Qibli felt sick. *With Darkstalker's magic, they could kill Thorn anytime, from anywhere, with barely a thought.*

I have to get to her. I have to take her an earring, right now; I can't wait another moment.

"I'll take your gift to Queen Thorn," he blurted. "Like

you wanted me to. Whatever it is. I'll take it today, if you let Ostrich and Cobra come with me."

Vulture gave him a sideways smile, a smile that said *I see you seeing me.* "Oh, but that's not all I want," he said. "Remember? You're going to tell me all of Thorn's secrets first. Passwords. Secret stores of treasure. Closest allies. How to kill them all."

Ostrich gasped and shoved Qibli's shoulder. "You're not! You wouldn't!"

Vulture slid a blank scroll out of one of the racks under the star charts and unrolled it on the floor in front of Qibli. He weighed down the corners with pillows and a little ink pot. "You may get started now," he said. "Take your time. Apparently I'm waiting for . . . instructions." He made a little face at that word, just a small one, but Qibli noticed it and it gave him a tiny spark of hope that Darkstalker and Vulture wouldn't be the perfect collaborators they might think they would be.

"We could use that big NightWing's help," Onyx mused. "I mean, he's got magic. He can read minds. See the future. Useful stuff, if it's on our side."

"Indeed," Vulture said, spreading one wing toward the open dome. "Let's go discuss exactly how useful."

His Talons scooped up the unconscious messenger and they departed, leaving Qibli with Ostrich, Cobra, and Winter. *And the five guards still watching us,* he remembered.

"Don't you even think about it, Qibli," Ostrich

threatened, baring her teeth at him. "I will stop you. I will burn that scroll to ashes! Rawr!" A small burst of flames shot out of her mouth, setting one of the carpets on fire. Winter leaned over and exhaled frostbreath all over it to put it out.

"I'm going to get some sleep," Winter said to Qibli. "In the hopes that we'll only be here a short while longer."

"Good idea," Qibli said, nudging one of the blue cushions toward him. Winter dragged it into a far corner and stretched out across it. Soon his spikes were rattling softly as his chest rose and fell.

"I'm not going to tell Vulture anything," Qibli promised Ostrich quietly. "But if I don't do this, we need another way out of here."

"Pretend to start writing." Cobra brushed past him. "I'll look for weapons."

Ostrich's eyes lit up. "I have one!" she whispered. She huddled into Qibli's side, pretending to read what he was writing, and flicked her tail around to reveal that she'd been keeping her tail barb bent down, concealing something in the small fold. As she slipped it out, Qibli saw a thin line of blood where it had scratched her.

"I stole this from my guard," she hissed softly. She hid it quickly under a pillow and slid it over to Qibli.

It was a small round disk with a bladed edge around the outside, sharp and sinister-looking. Qibli had seen these in the market, in his mother's armory, and among the Outclaws, but he'd rarely practiced with any himself.

"A chakram," Cobra whispered, leaning over Qibli's

shoulder. "Be more specific here," she said loudly, for the guards' benefit, pointing to a spot on the scroll while she palmed the disk. "Your grandfather will want to know exactly how many advisors attend the queen's morning meeting."

Qibli glanced down at the scroll, where he had been filling space by writing: *There are lots of loyal Outclaws. So many loyal Outclaws. Lots and lots and lots and lots and lots of dragons who think Queen Thorn is awesome because she is.*

"I can take out one of the guards with this," Cobra whispered, "but that leaves the other four."

"I can make more chakrams if you distract the Talons," Qibli offered. He took the pieces of Turtle's bowl out of his bag, concealing them under one of the pillows, and slotted them together, then nodded at his mother.

"Has your handwriting gotten *worse* since you were a dragonet?" she spat, sounding scarily like the mother he remembered. She snatched the scroll out of his talons (dropping the chakram in the bowl as she did) and stormed around, glaring at it, until she was blocking him from view of the guards. "And your spelling is atrocious. What self-respecting SandWing can't spell *Capybara*? I swear you've gotten stupider since I sold you."

Qibli knew she was making a scene and didn't mean any of it. But it was still hard to quash the urge to defend himself (*I wasn't trying to write* capybara! *My spelling is fine! Other dragons know what I mean!*).

He leaned over the chakram in the bowl and whispered, "Twice as much, please. Twice as much, please. Twice as much, please." Eight scary-looking disks glittered in the bowl.

Ostrich goggled at the multiplying disks in the bowl, then up at Qibli.

"How did you *do* that?" she breathed, awestruck. "Are you magic?"

He shook his head ruefully. "Not me," he said. "Someone else." He checked the slate again, while he had a moment. Still blank. What was Turtle *doing*? Had something terrible happened to him? Or had he forgotten about Qibli, waiting anxiously for any news?

Ostrich tented one of her wings out a bit so Qibli could hide the bowl of weapons underneath.

"Try harder," Cobra spat, flinging the scroll down in front of Qibli again. "Remember your grandfather has very high standards. He wants every detail. Spelled CORRECTLY." She sat down behind Qibli again, every inch the looming, grammar-correcting mother the guards might expect to see.

"Most impressive," she whispered when Ostrich tipped her wing to reveal the chakrams. "Now we just wait for dark . . . and then, we escape."

— CHAPTER 9 —

Thwip — thunk!

Thwip — thunk!

Thwip — thunk!

Cobra threw three chakrams at once — two with her talons, one with her tail — and they struck three of the Talons perfectly in the throat, cutting off their vocal cords and killing them at the same time.

She seized the next two disks and threw them barely a second later, so the last two guards didn't even have time to turn around in confusion before all five were falling through the dome roof, their hoods fluttering like tent canopies as they fell.

Qibli stared up at the now-open sky, misted with the sparkling fog of galaxies. None of the moons were full tonight, which was lucky. They were lucky, too, that Vulture had not returned yet to examine the scroll and realize that Qibli was stalling. (Example: *And then there's the palace, which used to be Burn's stronghold, which is, whoa, so big, like, really big, like, just the biggest, definitely not an easy place to break into, I mean, with the walls . . . and the bigness . . .)* Perhaps the guards that had traded places with these guards at dusk had reported that Qibli was working diligently, and that had been enough for Vulture, for now.

He bent quickly to the fallen Talons and tugged off their hoods, handing one to Cobra and one to Ostrich and pulling another over his own head. Winter was hopeless; it was too obvious that he was a sparkly IceWing and in no way a Talon of Power. They would have to pretend he was a prisoner if they were stopped.

"Stay close to me," Cobra hissed. "Don't touch anything or step on anything if you can avoid it."

"Won't the traps and grounds be different from what you remember?" Qibli asked her. "If you've been imprisoned for so long?"

"I know my father's tricks," she said grimly. "I'll keep you safe."

Keep me safe. Protect me. Because she loves me.

Qibli shook himself and followed her to the roof, where they flattened themselves to slither along the outside, watching for more guards. Ostrich was close behind Qibli, with Winter taking up the end of the line.

The night air smelled of burned coconuts and Grandfather's perfumed oil, and of the oasis pool not too far away. Qibli could hear members of the Talons of Power toasting one another in the garden pavilions. The hood was heavy around his face, obstructing his peripheral vision; he wondered how the Talons could stand them.

They slipped down to the ground and hurried single file along one of the tiled paths, carefully stepping only where Cobra stepped, although Qibli thought the center of the garden should be safe to walk in, at least. It was the outskirts, where the walls were — where they were going — that were dangerous.

A small fortress loomed out of the dark ahead of them, bristling with long spikes. Qibli stopped, glancing around.

"This isn't the way to the outer wall," he whispered.

"I need to stop in here for a minute," Cobra whispered back, flicking one wing at the fortress.

"In *Grandfather's treasury*?" Qibli hissed. "Are you *insane*?"

"He has something that could ruin all our plans," Cobra growled. "I must take it from him, or everything we do is doomed to failure."

"But — of all the places definitely rigged to kill you," Qibli said, "this will do it in the most painful way."

She grinned, her teeth glittering in the dark. "I know where he hides his key."

"You mean, where he *hid* it," Qibli pointed out. "Years ago."

"This he won't have changed," she whispered. "Stay here. Stop worrying."

"No," Qibli said firmly. "Tell me what we're stealing. If you want us to trust you, you should be able to tell us that."

"Fine," she said, exasperated. "Ever heard of the Obsidian Mirror?"

"I have," said Winter, unexpectedly. "Legend says it gave

the NightWings the power to eavesdrop on any conversation happening anywhere in the world."

"Whoa," Qibli said, feeling that shimmer of envy he always felt anywhere near an animus-touched object. *You'd know everyone's secrets. You could hear what dragons are saying about you — although, would I want that? I don't think I would want that. But imagine the power to anticipate everyone's next move! It would be so easy to keep tabs on your enemies . . . or your long-lost grandson.* "That's how he knew everything about me and Winter," he said. "That's how he knew we were coming here."

"Exactly," said Cobra. "So we have to take it with us or else he'll always know where we are and what we're doing. Get it now, lizard?" she snapped at Qibli, then seemed to catch herself mid-snap. She closed her snout, took a deep breath through her nose, and said, "Sorry."

Sorry. Qibli was momentarily dazed. He wouldn't have guessed that his mother knew how to say that word. At least, not to one of her offspring.

"No, I'm sorry," he said. "You're right, we can't leave that in Vulture's talons."

She gave him a surprised look, as if she hadn't thought *he* knew the word *sorry* either.

"How did Vulture get the mirror?" Winter asked. "How long has he had it?"

"He must know so much about Thorn already," Qibli realized with a sense of mounting horror. "What does he think I can tell him that he hasn't already overheard?"

Cobra shrugged. "He hasn't had it long, I think," she said. "He found it, out in the desert, only a few months ago."

"Only a few months ago . . ." Qibli said thoughtfully.

She glanced at him. "I heard the guards talking about it, walking over my prison." Her wings folded back and she pulled the hood farther over her face. "Now stay here and stop chattering on. I'll be right back."

Before he could say another word, she sprinted toward the treasury, darting from bush to bush in the dark.

Qibli gestured Winter and Ostrich back into the shadows of a covert of trees. It was the best he could do while still staying on the path, and it felt horribly exposed. Talons of Power could come by at any moment. *Vulture* could saunter past at any moment.

Grandfather's been spying on the queen for months, Qibli thought. *Thorn will have to change all her passwords. Recode the secret message system, just in case. Change everything she's done, in case he's overheard it and can use it against her.* He rubbed his forehead, his brain starting to explode with all the implications.

Long minutes ticked by, and each one felt like a dagger Qibli was personally thrusting into his queen's heart. The Obsidian Mirror was a terrible thing for your enemies to have — but Darkstalker's power was even more dangerous. Thorn needed protection from Darkstalker *right now*, and he was just standing here in the dark, waiting for his mother.

Maybe we should go, he thought, crossing to the edge of the shadows so he could study the silent treasury. *But she's the one who can navigate us out of here. What if we just flew for it? Lifted off and tried to fly away as fast as we could? We'd be spotted but maybe they wouldn't be able to catch up to us. Maybe their arrows would miss.*

I can't risk Ostrich that way.

What if Mother doesn't come back? What if she's already lying dead on a pile of gems inside? Will we still be standing here when morning comes?

He turned back toward the others and had a small heart attack.

"Where's Winter?" he whispered, nudging Ostrich with his wing. She sat up and looked around with blurry confusion.

"I don't know," she said. "He was here a moment ago."

Qibli twisted in a frantic circle and spotted a white shape flitting through the pear orchard. He couldn't shout out to Winter without alerting the whole compound. Qibli growled softly.

"Stay here," he whispered to Ostrich. "Stay as hidden as you can. We'll be right back."

She nodded, folding back into the shadows.

Qibli hurried after the IceWing prince and realized that he was aiming for another small building in the center of the pear trees. This one was built low to the ground, with large windows on all sides; candlelight flickered in the dim interior. The outside was decorated with a turquoise-and-amber tile mosaic of snakes and lizards chasing one another endlessly.

Winter slowed down as he got closer, and then veered

around the building toward a shed that appeared to be a storehouse for food, judging from the smells Qibli could now identify coming from it. He smelled cinnamon and dates and coconut, smoked ham and a few live pigs as well, some kind of the fancy smelly cheese Vulture loved, lemons, scavengers, dried fish, live ducks . . .

Scavengers.

Arrrrgh, Winter, you obsessed ninny.

He caught up as Winter was tinkering with the lock on the shed door. Inside, a few of the animals had heard the scratching of his claws and were starting to stir in an understandably worried way. Qibli could hear feathers fluttering, pigs snorting, and the little stamp of tiny scavenger feet.

"Are you *serious*?" he said, and Winter jumped a mile, which was almost hilarious enough to make this side excursion worthwhile.

"Shhhhh!" Winter hissed.

"What are you thinking?" Qibli whispered.

"I'm thinking your horrifying grandfather is going to eat the poor little scavengers trapped in here," Winter whispered back. "Unless I save them."

"Right now?" Qibli asked. "In the middle of our own precarious escape?"

"Well, I'm not planning on coming back!" Winter said. He tugged on the lock again. "Hey, you're a street thug. Can you pick this lock for me?"

"An Outlaw is not the same thing as a criminal," Qibli

protested. "Oh, fine, move over." He studied the lock for a moment, then inserted his claw into the mechanism and wiggled it around until he heard a click.

"Now what?" he asked Winter as he nudged the door open. "We shove them in a bag and carry them off into the desert with us? I'm not sure if you've noticed this, but scavengers tend to get *very* noisy when they think a dragon is about to eat them. Or when dragons get anywhere near them, actually."

"We'll just let them out," Winter said, pacing past him into the dark interior. "They're smart enough to fend for themselves after that."

Qibli decided not to point out that they hadn't been smart enough not to get caught in the first place.

Winter crouched beside a large cage in the corner. Inside, three scavengers were huddled together by the back wall, squeaking. Two more poked their heads out of a little nest of straw and stared at Winter.

"Don't be afraid," Winter said softly. He unlatched the top of the cage, lifted it off, and set it aside, then took a few steps back and waited.

One of the scavengers from the straw immediately popped up and started clambering up the netting of the cage wall. A moment later, two of the others followed, squeaking busily at the two that hadn't moved yet.

"What's all this noise?" said a voice from outside. "Raiding the storehouse in the middle of the night? Is there a feast going on that I wasn't invited to?" A dragon stuck his head in the door, yawning hugely.

Qibli had him pinned to the floor before he realized it was Vulture's lying MudWing. He banged his elbow on the tail band and the chain mail tangled in his claws as he subdued the larger dragon. Winter flashed across the room to help, seizing the headdress to hold the dragon still.

"Don't shout," Qibli said as the MudWing opened his mouth. "We just want some answers. Tell us the truth and we won't hurt you."

"Ha!" said the MudWing with surprising bitterness in his voice.

"Who are you?" Winter demanded.

"Nobody," said the MudWing truculently. "Bog, just Bog, a regular MudWing, me."

"Why are you lying about Queen Moorhen ordering the cactus attacks?" Qibli asked.

"Not lying," said Bog. "All true. Definitely a MudWing plot."

"Where are your sibs?" Qibli pressed. "Are they traitors, too?"

"My what?" Bog said.

Qibli and Winter exchanged a glance. Sibs had come up during a class on MudWings at Jade Mountain. Qibli had heard about the idea before, but that lesson was the first time he'd learned in detail about how MudWings lived their lives alongside their siblings, creating families out of brothers and sisters rather than ever getting married or even knowing their parents.

"Um," Bog corrected himself. "Not here. Not traitors. Just me. I was captured by the Talons of Power and forced to reveal everything."

"I bet," said Winter. "Looks like they used the classic torture method of burying you in diamonds."

Qibli tried to shake off something that was snared around one of his claws and heard a clank from under the chain mail. He shoved a few of the links aside while Bog squirmed and spotted a pouch tied firmly under one of Bog's wings.

"Don't touch that!" Bog roared, suddenly slashing at Qibli's talons.

Qibli jerked back out of reach. Something had ignited a spark of recognition at last — the anger in this dragon's eyes, the pouch he protected with such violence.

"I know who this is," he said.

"You do?" said Winter. "When have you ever met a MudWing outside of school?"

"He wasn't a MudWing last time we saw him," Qibli said. "He was a NightWing calling himself Shapeshifter."

CHAPTER 10

"Shapeshifter?" said Winter with a hiss. "The one who was working with Scarlet?"

"You mean the one you robbed," Bog snarled. "Perhaps you remember beating me bloody in order to steal my scroll."

"Perhaps you remember putting our friend Kinkajou in a coma," Qibli snapped at him, sinking his claws into the brown scales. "What are you doing *here*, with my grandfather?"

"I didn't like the Mud Kingdom," Bog grumbled. "Too brown. Thought I'd try my luck in the Scorpion Den. Looking for treasure." He managed to flop one of his talons to a place where he could see it — and see the giant bejeweled rings on it. "Found it," he said with a smirk.

"But what kind of idiot would meddle in royal politics again, after last time?" Qibli demanded. "You could have gone anywhere and started over."

"I was *trying* to," Bog snorted. "Vulture approached me in the market and offered me a lot of treasure to tell people this MudWing story. What was I going to do, say no to treasure?"

"That would have been a good start," said Qibli.

"I'm confused about something," Winter said to Qibli. "How is he a MudWing now? Didn't we take away the scroll he was using to shapeshift?"

"Taking away the scroll meant he couldn't write any new spells," Qibli said. "But I'm guessing he had a little trove of spells already written — scraps of paper torn from the scroll that were enchanted to turn him into different dragons. Is that what's in here?" He poked the pouch and Bog snapped at his talons again.

"Haven't you ruined my life enough?" Bog snarled. "Aren't there any actual bad guys you could go harass?"

"I would love to have nothing to do with you," said Qibli, "but I can't as long as you're in the business of starting a MudWing-SandWing war."

Winter reached for the pouch, but as he leaned over Bog's head, the MudWing abruptly rammed his headdress into Winter's chin. At the same moment, he lashed his tail up and around and slammed the heavy gold band into Qibli's side, knocking Qibli off his back. Qibli scrabbled to keep his hold on the chain mail, but Bog ripped it off in a sudden, smooth motion, leaving Qibli with a talonful of limp silver links and sapphires.

Winter lunged for the MudWing again, but Bog seized something off the floor and held it out in front of him. "Stop right there," he snarled, "or I will bite this scavenger's head off."

Winter froze, his gaze fixed on the little creature in Bog's talons. It had evidently escaped the cage and made a run for the door, but Bog had caught it before it reached the threshold. It wriggled pitifully in his grip, the thatch of black fur on its head just visible over the MudWing's heavy rings.

"We can't let him go," Qibli said to Winter. "He keeps showing up. He's too dangerous."

"Put down the scavenger," Winter said to Bog.

"You get out of here and leave me alone," Bog growled. He whirled and bolted out the door. Qibli dashed after him, but the MudWing was halfway across the orchard already, running as fast as he could toward the sounds of a party at one of the far pavilions.

Qibli turned back in frustration. "We can't chase him," he said to Winter. "Or we'll end up right back in Vulture's claws. We have to get out of here *now*."

Winter was crouched beside a small shape in the grass — the scavenger that Bog had dropped as he fled. It scrambled to its feet and backed away from Winter, limping. One of the other scavengers darted out of the shed and waved a stick at Winter with some ferocious squeaking noises.

"I think you've done enough Champion of the Scavengers work for tonight," Qibli said, poking Winter in the side. "Come *on*."

They abandoned the scavengers and ran back through the trees to the spot where Qibli had left Ostrich. Cobra pushed through the bushes, grinning and streaked with dirt, as they came galloping up. A large black sack was thrown over her shoulder.

"That's what I call living," she crowed.

"We were seen," Qibli panted. "We have to go."

"Oh, wonderful," Cobra snapped, the triumphant look vanishing from her face. She darted off along another path. Qibli and the others raced after her, keeping their footfalls as silent as possible. He kept expecting to hear shouts of alarm and pounding talons as Bog raised the entire Talons of Power militia to find them. But nothing broke the stillness of the night.

"Stop!" Ostrich whispered, catching Qibli's wing. "Two dragons up ahead."

She was right; two hulking figures blocked the path in one of the courtyards, leaning over a fountain and splashing water onto their faces. Cobra skidded to a stop and plunged into the shrubbery beside the walkway.

"Shhh," Qibli said. He tugged Winter under an imposing statue of Vulture and spread his wings to hide him. Ostrich played along, pretending to measure him from wingtip to wingtip.

"Hmm," she said as the two figures came toward them. "Yes, I think we can manage an excellent tattoo of, uh, your face along here." She sketched out a shape with her claw on one of his wings. "And perhaps a pattern to match on the other side — diamonds are always popular, or snakes . . ."

"Skulls!" shouted one of the approaching dragons. "Th'only good tattoo izza skull!" He staggered sideways and the other dragon shoved him away from her with a hiss.

"Sirocco and Rattlesnake," Qibli muttered, staring fixedly down at his wings. He prayed that the hood would be enough of a disguise to hide him. His mother was very still, and he wondered if it was strange for her to see her other two children — who had, presumably, been working for Vulture the whole time she'd been imprisoned. Did she feel as if they'd betrayed her?

"Of course, there are always gem-embedding options," Ostrich said. "I hear they're painful, but such a statement."

"I want a ruby inna middle of my forehead!" Sirocco bellowed, lurching toward Ostrich. "Can you do that?" He tripped over his own tail and slammed down onto his snout, yelping in pain.

"You are such an embarrassment," Rattlesnake fumed. "That's why Grandfather thinks we're both stupid; because all he can see is you and your big empty head! Why aren't you on patrol?" she suddenly barked at Qibli and Ostrich. "Don't you know the compound is on lockdown tonight?"

"Yes," Ostrich stammered. "Just — on a break."

Rattlesnake swelled up so she looked twice her size. "On a break, *sir*," she said menacingly. "One day *I* will inherit *all* of this, both my brothers will be dead, and everyone will come crawling before me the way they crawl before Grandfather." She tossed her head and suddenly caught sight of Cobra in the shadows. A slight frown creased her forehead. "M-Mother? Aren't you —"

Cobra moved so fast that Qibli wouldn't have been able to

stop her, except that he knew what she would probably do and he'd been waiting for it. She had the disk out and ready to fly but he managed to knock her arm aside before she could throw it.

"You can't kill them!" he cried. "Mother! They're your children!"

"*You're* my only dragonet," she said coldly, reaching for another chakram.

"Qibli?" Rattlesnake gasped. She leaped backward and opened her mouth to yell for help.

Suddenly Winter was there, knocking her over, seizing her snout, and smacking her head into the tile. Almost at the same moment, Ostrich leapt at Sirocco, who was blinking in confusion. She landed on his back and threw her wings over his face.

"*No,*" Qibli said to Cobra. "They're awful, but they're still my brother and sister." He ran over to Ostrich, untying his hood. The black fabric worked just as well to muffle a dragon as it did to conceal one. Sirocco flailed around frantically at first, but soon he was bound and gagged behind the statue, tied up with a canopy stolen from a nearby pavilion. They dumped Rattlesnake next to him, unconscious and tied up as well.

"I thought your years as an Outclaw would have made you less soft," Cobra said to Qibli disapprovingly, staring down at her other two offspring.

"There's nothing weak about being compassionate," Qibli retorted.

"Can we fly now, before we run into any more of your loving family?" Winter asked.

Cobra beckoned and darted away, past the fountain, around another statue of Vulture, and to the edge of a stand of tall, bristling cacti. Beyond it, Qibli could see the outer wall of the compound, with the wide-open sky of stars beyond that.

"All right," said Cobra. "Stand back. This is going to be a little dramatic." She took a deep breath, then exhaled a whooshing ball of flame that engulfed the cacti.

Instantly several explosions went off inside the fire, as Vulture's traps all burst into action at once.

"What the —" cried Winter. "I thought the plan was stealth!"

"Stealth, and then flying really fast!" Cobra crowed. "See you at the palace!" She launched herself over the flames, beating her wings furiously.

Qibli couldn't hear anything beyond the crackle and roar of the fire, but he was sure Talons must be converging on them from all directions. He grabbed Ostrich and hauled her into the sky with him. "Don't look back!" he shouted to her as they swept over the wall. "Just keep flying!"

Winter's moon-pale shape soared up alongside him and together the three of them flew after Cobra, north to the palace of Queen Thorn.

CHAPTER 11

Qibli couldn't remember the last time he'd slept, but it didn't matter — the wind lifted him high over the dunes and his wings felt charged with lightning as he swept closer and closer to the SandWing palace and his queen.

Please let Thorn be safe, he prayed. *Please let Darkstalker be too busy with other things to have turned his thoughts to the SandWings yet.*

For the first hour there had been dragons behind them, chasing them, but they seemed to have given up and gone back to the Scorpion Den. Qibli wondered how his grandfather was reacting right now, and what Onyx might do next, and what kind of terrible retribution was coming.

He flexed his front talons and studied the weather bracelets in the moonlight. There had to be a way to use these to stop Vulture . . . if he could only figure out how to use them.

"We're almost there!" Ostrich called, doing a flip in the sky beside him.

Qibli looked up and saw the palace ahead. It still gave him a startling surge of fear and pride each time he saw it — like his first thought was always, instinctively, *Oh no! We're too close! Burn's going to catch us and kill us all!* and then he had to shift his brain over to *No, wait — we defeated her — she's gone, and that's OUR palace now, with the best queen of all time ruling the kingdom.*

The outer walls used to be lined with decapitated heads, in Burn's day, but those were all gone now, and the stone had been scraped and scrubbed and painted to remove all trace of the blood that used to drip there. Thorn was considering knocking down the gruesome walls altogether, the way she'd knocked down the weirdling tower, since they only served to remind everyone of Burn — but she had been too busy with other kingdom business to get that done in the few months she'd been queen.

Guards lined the top of the wall, the bristling shadows of their spears looking like IceWing tail spikes. Lamplight glowed in several of the windows.

Cobra slowed and circled back to fly next to him. "Outclaws first," she said with a toothy grin. She kept shifting the sack from one shoulder to the other as though it was heavy — or as though she was nervous.

"You'll be safer here than with Grandfather," Qibli told her.

"I'll be safe wherever you are," she said. Her eyes gleamed. "Perhaps we can take out Vulture and then you and I can rule the Scorpion Den. His whole compound and all that treasure would be ours."

"If I were given the Scorpion Den to rule, the first thing I would do is turn that compound into a home for orphans and wounded soldiers," Qibli said.

Cobra squinted at him, as if she couldn't tell whether he was joking or not. "Right," she said. "Of course. Me too."

Two of the guards on the walls flew out to meet them. Even by the dim light of the slender moons, Qibli recognized them both from their Outclaw days.

"Tawny! Parch!" he cried. "I have to see the queen immediately!"

The two guards swooped around them, waving to Ostrich and tucking their spears back into their holsters.

"Of course you do, Qibli," Parch said, laughing. "Let me guess — it's an emergency!"

"It *is*!" Qibli insisted, ruffled. "It's a danger you'd never even begin to imagine. I need to see her right now."

"She's in a meeting," Tawny reminded Parch. "A really important meeting with that cool hybrid dragon from Possibility, remember?"

"Yeah, but it's Qibli," Parch said agreeably. "She won't mind."

Qibli remembered that Parch was one of the Outclaws who'd had the most trouble adapting to the new rules and strictures of the palace. He still behaved like a renegade of the Scorpion Den when it came to things like a dress code or showing up for guard duty on time. But not out of malice — Parch just assumed nobody would ever get mad at him, considering how many times he'd nearly died to save the other Outclaws. And that was pretty much true, even if it was maddening to see him joke with Thorn like she was a regular dragon and not a queen at all.

But tonight Parch's disregard for the rules would work in Qibli's favor. "Yes," Qibli said, seizing one of Parch's arms. "She'll want to hear about this right away."

Parch shrugged at Tawny. "Sounds important."

Tawny rolled her eyes but waved them toward the palace. "All right, go ahead," she said.

"Wait for me by the Oasis monument in the courtyard," Qibli said to the others.

"I want to see Queen Thorn, too!" cried Ostrich.

"Seriously," said Winter. "Suddenly we're not invited inside?"

"Yeah," Cobra protested. "Why can't we come with you?"

"Because I need to explain you before Queen Thorn sees you," Qibli said patiently.

He watched them flap down toward the enormous white stone courtyard, muttering to themselves, and then he dove toward one of the gardens. If Queen Thorn was meeting with an important dragon, he knew exactly where she'd have that meeting — her favorite room in the palace.

It wasn't even a room, exactly; it was a tent made of flapping white fabric that Thorn had installed next to the largest palace pool, to remind her of her old Outclaw headquarters.

Qibli was right; he could hear the murmur of Thorn's voice as he approached the tent, although the wind and the trickle of water obscured her words. Pale yellow and pink lilies drifted across the pool, bumping into the petals of fat crimson flowers from the tree overhead.

"Queen Thorn!" he called from outside. "It's Qibli. May I enter?"

There was a pause, and then one of the walls was flung aside as Thorn peered out at him. "Qibli!" she cried, her face lighting up. "Maybe you can — no, wait — hang on." She sat up straight and looked stern. "Why aren't you in school, you ruffian?"

She's all right. Qibli nearly collapsed with relief. He was still a step ahead of Darkstalker's plans, at least for the Kingdom of Sand. It wasn't too late. He could protect her right now, before the giant NightWing started wiping out all the queens in Pyrrhia, or whatever he was going to do.

"I need you to put this on," he said, digging one of the earrings out of his bag. "Please. Right away. It's urgent, and then I can explain."

"Come on in," Thorn said, beckoning.

Inside, the tent was lit by the warm glow of oil lamps and smelled like cinnamon and cardamom tea. There were two other dragons with the queen, and one of them, Qibli realized with surprise, was Smolder, the brother of Burn, Blister, and Blaze.

Onyx's father, he realized with a shiver. *Does he have any idea she exists?*

The other dragon in the tent was a striking cobalt-blue color, shining like sapphires in the lamplight, with a white underbelly and dark black eyes. The spikes around his neck marked him as an IceWing, but he also had stripes under his wings that glowed phosphorescently in the semidarkness — like a SeaWing.

Tawny said there was a hybrid here, Qibli remembered. A SeaWing-IceWing hybrid apparently. He wondered how this dragon's parents had met and fallen in love, when their kingdoms were so far apart and probably at war at the time. There must be a story there.

"Qibli, this is Typhoon." Queen Thorn indicated the stranger, who nodded politely in Qibli's direction. "He's come with troubling news from Possibility."

"That's great," Qibli said in a rush. "I mean, not *great*, I'm sure whatever it is is terrible, but before we get to that, maybe just quick fling this earring on? And then everything else can go back to being top priority, you bet."

Smolder tried to hide his chuckling in his cup of tea, but not very successfully.

"This sounds rather suspicious," Thorn said, holding out her talon. Qibli put the earring in her palm with trembling claws and she lifted it up to study the light bending through the warm amber. "I'm guessing there's a spell on this," she said astutely. "The question is, is it a good spell or a bad spell? And the answer depends on whether *you're* under a spell, or possibly whether you have wrong information."

"It's a good spell," Qibli said desperately. "I promise. It'll protect you from something you really need protecting from, like, right now. Trust me."

"I do," said Thorn with calm certainty.

"Hang on," said Smolder, watching her lift it to her ear. "Do we all? Is this the smartest plan? Should we, um, vote or something?"

"I've been spoiling him by letting him express his opinion now and then," Thorn said to Qibli. She looked down her nose at Smolder. "I am the *queen*, you camel-chewing, snore-a-minute son of a toad."

"Oh, right," said Smolder. "Very dignified. Hard to argue with that kind of elegant turn of phrase."

Thorn laughed, pulled out the small ruby that was already in one ear, and stabbed the enchanted earring through. "Hmmm. I feel the same," she said to Smolder. "Have I been turned into a frog and just can't tell?"

"An extremely beautiful frog," Smolder promised. "One we're all still proud to call our queen."

"You are no help," Thorn said, waving her claws at him. "But I suppose I'll let you live, for today."

Qibli sank gratefully onto one of the large red pillows. His queen was safe. His most important mission was complete, and now he could feel his exhaustion setting in.

"You really are worried about something," Smolder said, studying him closely. Something darted under his feet and Qibli nearly jumped, thinking it was a wild animal — but it was only Smolder's pet scavenger, Flower. She clambered casually up Smolder's leg until she could sit on his shoulder and watch all the dragons.

I have to make sure Winter meets her, Qibli thought. *He could learn a lot from Smolder about taking care of scavengers.*

"I'll tell you everything later," he said to Thorn, pointedly looking only at her. Smolder was funny and interesting, but he wasn't an Outclaw, and he looked horribly like Blister, and he had done Burn's bidding all the way through the war, even including an attempt to imprison Thorn and Sunny so she could have them. Qibli was not prepared to trust him just yet.

"I'm sorry I interrupted you," he said to Typhoon.

"Quite all right," said Typhoon. "I would never want to get in the way of urgent accessorizing."

Smolder snorted a laugh, which was helpful, because Qibli hadn't been entirely sure if that was a joke. Typhoon had an excellent straight face.

"Tell Qibli what you told us," Thorn said to the unusual-looking dragon.

Typhoon leaned forward and Qibli noticed a snail-shell earring in his left ear. "All the IceWings in Possibility are sick," he said without preamble. "Three days ago, they were healthy and normal. There aren't very many IceWings living in the town yet, so we tend to stay close. And then all of a sudden, every single one of them started coughing blood."

A cold feeling ran down Qibli's spine, like an IceWing claw trailing along the ridge of his back.

Could be a normal plague. Cities get them all the time.

"You say you all stay close," Smolder observed. "So isn't it likely that one dragon got sick and infected everyone else?"

"It happened too fast for that," Typhoon said, shaking his head. "I've been studying medicine and disease for the last two years; I know how fevers like this usually spread. And no one is sick except the IceWings. This isn't normal."

"Why did you come to me, instead of Queen Glacier or Queen Coral?" Thorn asked.

"Because I think you're the smartest and most capable queen in Pyrrhia right now," Typhoon answered, looking her in the eye. "And to be honest, you were also the closest. My father is one of the most ill. If there's any chance of saving him, we need someone who can act fast."

"I have doctors I can send —" Thorn started.

"When exactly did the sickness hit?" Qibli interrupted. Thorn gave him a startled look, but she was still more Outclaw than queen, willing to give anyone a voice. Smolder, on the other talon, made a face as though he couldn't understand why Qibli was allowed to keep his head.

"The night before last," Typhoon answered. "Around midnight."

That was Darkstalker's first night of freedom.

Qibli remembered that Darkstalker had been away from Jade Mountain Academy for most of that night. What had he been doing?

Did he cast a spell to hurt the IceWings? Is he still looking for revenge, after thousands of years?

If so, how bad a spell is it? Is he trying to wipe out the entire tribe, or just weaken them?

"I know that look," said Thorn, watching him sharply. "You've figured something out."

"I think Typhoon is right," said Qibli.

"That's always nice to hear," said the blue dragon with a wry smile.

"This isn't a normal disease," Qibli went on.

"Less nice," Typhoon murmured ruefully.

"It's not a disease at all," Qibli said. "It's a spell. And I think I know who cast it — an animus dragon who hates the IceWings." A whole tribe under attack by such powerful magic. From a distance, and without even knowing that their enemy had arisen. They wouldn't even know this was an attack; it would just seem like an illness. Darkstalker would be able to deny that it had anything to do with him, and even unbewitched dragons might believe him.

"All IceWings?" Thorn said sharply. "You mean this could be happening in the Ice Kingdom, too, not just in Possibility?"

"I'd assume it is," said Qibli, flicking his tail.

But the world is different now than it was in Darkstalker's time. In his time, the IceWings would have all been in the Ice Kingdom, isolated, where a plague could wipe them out without anyone knowing until it was over. In this world — a world with Possibility in it, and the Talons of Peace, and hybrid dragons and soldiers from different tribes who fought alongside one another in the Great War — in this world, we can see the dying dragons.

We can see them, and we can save them. We can stop him.

He looked at the animus-touched bracelets on his wrists again, itching to use them against Darkstalker. He wanted to throw a lightning bolt into the NightWing's grinning face.

"We have to send someone to check on the Ice Kingdom," Thorn said, leaping to her feet.

"You can't," Smolder pointed out reasonably. "Any of our dragons would freeze to death or be shot down by the Great Ice Cliff."

"That's right." Thorn started to pace. "Queen Glacier warned me about the Ice Cliff." She whirled toward Typhoon. "Can you cross the Cliff safely?"

"Yes," he said. "Apparently half IceWing is IceWing enough."

But not enough to be hit by the plague? Qibli wondered, and his spinning brain answered itself: *Because Darkstalker is half IceWing, too. He must have left out hybrids, thinking there weren't enough of them to save the others . . . and so his descendants, like Sunny, would be safe.*

What about Winter? Why was he spared?

He thought of his IceWing friend standing outside in the palace courtyard with Ostrich and Cobra.

"Wait," he said, standing up quickly. "I know a faster way we can find out what's happening in the Ice Kingdom. But first, Queen Thorn — I need you to arrest my mother."

CHAPTER 12

"What is the meaning of this?" Cobra roared as four SandWing soldiers seized her wings and tail. They threw chains around her legs and efficiently snapped a metal cage around the end of her tail so she couldn't sting anyone with her venom.

"You are under arrest," Thorn announced, holding her flaming torch a little higher to examine Cobra's face. "For . . ." She gave Qibli a quizzical look.

"For lying to me," Qibli said, "and conspiring against the queen."

"Lying to you!" Cobra shouted. "What are you talking about?" She snapped her teeth at one of the soldiers and nearly managed to bite off his ear.

"You have not been imprisoned for the last two years," Qibli said, fighting to keep the tremor out of his voice. "I doubt you were even in that oubliette for a day before I arrived. Vulture knew I was coming and put you down there so I'd be willing to risk everything to save you."

"No," Cobra growled, struggling.

"Queen Thorn," said Qibli, "who's in charge of all your spies?"

"A dragon named Capybara," Thorn answered.

"That's what I thought," said Qibli. He turned to his mother. "You said the name Capybara when you were pretending to read my scroll of information for Vulture — but I hadn't written that name anywhere in it. You also mentioned Thorn's morning meetings with her most trusted advisors. You'd only know about those details if you'd been out of prison this whole time, spying on Thorn with the Obsidian Mirror, right alongside Grandfather."

"That's — that's ridiculous," Cobra sputtered. "A coincidence —"

"And when I went to our old house," Qibli went on, "I smelled roasted coriander seeds — the snack you always eat when you're preparing for an assassination. You'd been there only a day or so earlier, not gone for two years.

"That's also why we were able to escape so easily. Because this is what Vulture really wanted — for me to bring you, his top assassin, into Thorn's palace."

"Dung beetles," Cobra spat. "This is all wild speculation. You've always been a half-witted idiot with crazy ideas."

"Open that sack," Qibli said to the soldiers, flicking his tail at the bag Cobra had brought with her. "Carefully."

One of them gingerly undid the top and peered inside. She took out an oval of flat black glass and set it on the sand. That was followed by the remaining chakrams, a series of gradually pointier and scarier knives, a black hood, and a small glass vial with an emerald-green liquid inside. Last of all, the guard reached back into the bag and lifted out a fat, spiky dragonflame cactus.

That's what blew up the history cave, Qibli thought, feeling a creeping sense of horror at the sight of the prickly weapon. *That's what killed Carnelian and Bigtail.* He knew if it caught fire, it would explode and spray deadly sharp little seed pods in all directions.

Smolder took a step closer and squinted at it. "Your Majesty," he said.

"I know," said Thorn. "We've seen evidence of these at all the attack sites."

"Were you sent to blow up the palace?" Qibli asked his mother. He touched the vial lightly with the tip of his wing. "Or was your mission to poison the queen?"

Cobra's eyes narrowed. There was a beat of silence, and then she spat, "All right, Mr. Cleverclaws. You think you've got it all figured out. But did it ever occur to you that I might be betraying *him*? That he wouldn't have wanted me to take the Obsidian Mirror? That I might really want to destroy him and take over the Scorpion Den with you at my side?"

With you at my side. My only true dragonet.

Qibli forced bands of steel around his heart.

"Yes, I did think of that," he said to her, "but somehow, the idea that you're even untrustworthy to your own father didn't convince me to trust you more."

I wanted to, Mother. I've always wanted to. Vulture knew exactly how to mess with me.

But he underestimated how much I've learned from Queen Thorn — and how much stronger my friends have made me. He glanced at Winter, who was watching with an expression that said he'd had his doubts about Cobra, too.

"Take her to the dungeon," Thorn said to the guards. "Lock her in the cell next to the mad prisoner. They can keep each other company for a while."

Cobra shrieked with rage as they dragged her away, and Qibli tried not to imagine that alternate universe where he played along with her games and got to be her favorite for just a moment longer.

"Did you say the Obsidian Mirror?" Thorn said to him. "The one Sunny left in the desert and couldn't find again after the war?"

Qibli flicked his tail at the eerie oval that looked as if it was made of black glass. "Vulture's had it for the last several months."

"Well, that's . . . horrifying," said Thorn.

"I know, but now you can use it to check on Glacier," Qibli suggested.

Winter's head snapped up. "Glacier?" he said. "Why? What? Why do you need to spy on Queen Glacier?"

"We're not spying," Qibli said. He watched the mirror carefully as it was placed in Thorn's claws. "We think she's in trouble."

"What kind of trouble?" Winter hurried over and stared at the mirror. One of the moons was reflected in it, thin and sharp like a silver claw, with the torches' firelight crackling around the edges.

"Let's see if I can remember how Sunny described this," said the queen, closing her eyes and thinking for a moment. "Um." She held the mirror close to her mouth and whispered, "Queen Glacier of the IceWings," then squinted at it. After a moment of nothing happening, she nodded as if remembering something and breathed a plume of smoke across the dark surface.

The smoke curled into four separate tendrils, all in shades of pale blue and white. One, the largest, was in the center, with the other three clustered around it.

"She's getting worse," whispered one of the tendrils, making Qibli jump.

"She hasn't woken up since midday," whispered another.

"What do we do?" The third one twisted anxiously in little smoke-knots. "Narwhal is too sick to take charge and —" She broke off into a coughing spell that tore at Qibli's heart. He wished he could reach right into the mirror and hold her lungs together for her.

He looked up and saw a horrorstruck expression on Winter's face. Did he recognize one of the voices? Or — she'd mentioned someone called Narwhal. That had to be a member of the royal family . . . perhaps even Winter's father, Qibli guessed.

"Everyone's too sick to take charge," said the first in a small, sad voice.

"Should we send for help?" said the second, starting to cough as well. "Is anyone well enough to make it to the Kingdom of Sand?"

"Poor Glacier," Thorn said softly. "You were right, Qibli. It's hit all the IceWings in Pyrrhia."

"What is wrong with them?" Winter cried. "Why are they all sick? How did you know?" He whirled toward Qibli, then Queen Thorn. His tail spikes rattled frantically. "Is that supposed to be the queen?" He poked his claw at the still, solemn tendril of smoke in the center. "Queen Glacier is sick?"

"All the IceWings are," Qibli said. "I'm sorry, Winter, but —"

"I'm going to save them," Winter said fiercely. "I know what to do." He spread his wings and crouched to take flight.

Qibli barreled into him, knocking the IceWing prince to the ground.

"Hey!" Winter shouted.

"Help me!" Qibli yelled at the closest Outclaws. "Pin him down!"

"Don't you dare!" Winter roared at them with such commanding authority that for a moment they all hesitated. "Qibli, get off! I have to tell Darkstalker! He can save them!"

That's exactly what I can't let you do, Qibli thought. "Hold him down!" he shouted at the Outclaws again.

Three SandWings agreeably piled on, sitting on Winter's wings and tail so he couldn't go anywhere. Winter roared again with frustration.

"Qibli, I'm going to kill you for this!" he bellowed. "I

have to help my queen! Darkstalker's magic can save all of them!"

"You idiot!" Qibli shouted in his ear as Winter thrashed and kicked. "Darkstalker did this! He sent the plague to the IceWings! The war with your tribe isn't thousands of years ago to him — in his mind, it just happened. This is his revenge!"

One of Winter's serrated claws caught Qibli's side, leaving a long bloody scratch. Qibli jumped back with a yelp of pain, but Winter didn't seem to notice what he'd done. "You're wrong," he growled. "Darkstalker is a good, noble dragon! He's going to lead us all into a bright and wonderful future! And he can *save my tribe,* so *get off me and let me go find him!*"

"I don't think you're going to convince him," Thorn said to Qibli.

"I'm not," Qibli said. "I'm going to fix him." He drew another earring out of his bag and brandished it like a weapon.

"Three moons," said Typhoon. "You SandWings are a little intense about your jewelry."

"No!" Winter shouted as Qibli approached. "I said no! No spells!"

"You're already under a spell!" Qibli argued. "This will put your brain back the way it's supposed to be, Winter, I promise."

"You stay away from my brain!" Winter hissed. "I swear if you put that on me, I will hurt you."

"I *have* to," Qibli said. "When you're yourself again, you'll see that Darkstalker is behind this, and then I can help you save your tribe."

"You?" Winter snorted. "*You* don't have magic. You're *completely ordinary*. How could *you* save *anyone*?"

That cut deeper than Winter probably realized. Stung, Qibli yelled, "I *would* have magic and we wouldn't have *any* of these problems if you hadn't been a *complete slug* about Darkstalker's scroll!" He seized Winter's head and jabbed the earring at his ear.

Winter twisted out of his grasp and fired a blast of frost-breath that slammed right into Qibli's arm.

For a moment, the freezing pain shocked Qibli into paralysis. It hurt so much, so instantly, like his arm had been severed, and then, almost more frightening, his arm went numb and he couldn't feel anything anymore.

A second later, Thorn was there, seizing Winter's snout, holding it shut, and pinning down his head. She grabbed the earring from Qibli and thrust it briskly through one of the holes in Winter's right ear.

There was a long tense pause. Suddenly Winter went limp. His whole body collapsed to the ground under the SandWing soldiers, all the fight drained out of him.

"Get the doctors!" Queen Thorn was shouting, somewhere far away from Qibli. No, wait, she was still right in front of him — but the whole world was fading back, further and further, with hazy blackness marching in from all sides.

"I'm sorry, Qibli," she said, taking his talons gently to

examine the frostbitten scales on his arm. "I had no idea he'd do that. I thought he was your friend."

"He is," Qibli managed. Through the haze he saw Winter lift his head and look at Qibli wonderingly. "He's a good . . . a hero-ish guy . . . friend . . ." He felt the world pull away as the pain swept back in. "It was just a spell," he whispered.

"We'll fix it, Qibli, you hear me?" Thorn said. "They're bringing water and hot coals now. Don't you pass out, you sand snorter! Qibli! Your queen is giving you an order!"

"Earrings," Qibli said, or tried to say, or said too loud, he wasn't sure. "For all the IceWings, we have to . . ." and then everything faded to black.

── CHAPTER 13 ──

Qibli was on fire. He was buried in sand in the middle of the desert, the sun beating down on him, as dry branches snapped into flames all around him. His scales were melting, but he couldn't move a muscle or twitch a talon.

Wake up, wake up. Dragons are dying. Wake up, wake up, you have to save them.

He clawed his way out of the dream with excruciating slowness and finally opened his eyes to find Winter sitting beside him, staring glumly at his talons.

Qibli was pleased to see his earring glowing in Winter's ear. (Even if Winter was right and it did clash horribly with the IceWing's scales.) They were in a sunbaked brick room with light pouring in the windows and skylights. Qibli glanced down and saw that his arm was submerged in a cauldron of heated water. It still looked damaged here and there, but most of the scales had returned to their normal color, and he could feel all his talons again.

"All right. I'm ready," he said to Winter.

Winter snapped his head up and stared at him. "You're . . . ready for what?"

"Your heartfelt apology," said Qibli. "The tragic face is a good start, but I'm sure the speech is even better."

Winter scowled at him. "*My* apology? You're the one who attacked me! I was defend —" He stopped and took a deep breath. "Why must you make everything impossible?" he growled.

"Needs work," said Qibli. "But maybe it gets sappier as it goes along. Sorry, I'll shut up and listen attentively now." He put on his most sincere, thoughtful face.

"I *am* sorry," Winter said grumpily. "I can't believe I did that to you." He glanced at Qibli's arm, winced, and looked away quickly.

"Well, you know, evil spell," Qibli said, waving one of his wings as if he was clearing away smoke. "The important thing is that you can think clearly now. Do you feel better?"

"No," Winter huffed. "Because now I feel like an *idiot*. A friend-freezing, enchanted-moony-eyed idiot."

"Friend!" Qibli cried with delight. "You called me your friend! You DO adore me! Life goals: accomplished."

"I'm just saving syllables," Winter snapped. "'Friend' is faster to say than 'annoying clawmate.'" He hesitated. "I wish I *could* blame the spell," he said in a lower voice. "But I was so angry, and so afraid of any magic that would change me the way Hailstorm was changed . . ."

"Don't worry about it. It's sand in the wind," Qibli said.

"I'm going to kill Darkstalker," Winter said. "I promise you that. It'll be bloody and long-winded. He'll be sorry he started another war with the IceWings. He'll be sorry he messed with *my* mind. Rrrrrrrrgh, I knew he was evil — I mean, when my mind was my own, I knew it. I don't understand what Moon sees in him."

There was an uncomfortable beat while they both thought about Moon.

I wish I knew she was safe. Or what she's doing. I wish she could come tell me what to do. Qibli looked around for his pack, wondering if Turtle had finally sent an update.

"Maybe she's under a spell, too," Winter suggested.

"Maybe," Qibli said. "Although she trusted him even before he had his powers back, remember? Just from talking to him in her mind."

Winter growled softly.

"First things first," said Qibli. "Did Queen Thorn send protection earrings to the IceWings?"

"You said that before you passed out," Winter said. "But there were only two left in your bag. Typhoon agreed to take them and fly as fast as he could to Queen Glacier's palace."

"What?" Qibli sat up fast, spilling hot water over the sides of the cauldron his arm was in. "That's not enough! I can give him more!"

"He already left," Winter said, pushing Qibli's arm back under the water. "The minute we found the other earrings in your bag. I wanted to give him mine as well — but Queen

Thorn said she wasn't sure what I would do if I went back under Darkstalker's spell." He fiddled guiltily with the tassels of the rug Qibli was lying on.

"I agree with her. What time is it now?" Qibli asked.

"Late afternoon," said Winter. "The queen's healers gave you something to make you sleep longer."

"No, no, no, sleeping, arrrrrrgh," Qibli said, pulling his arm out of the cauldron and shaking water droplets off it. He rolled off the rug and hurried to the nearest shelf, where someone had left his pack.

While he slotted the parts of the bowl together, he checked the slate — but there were no new messages from Turtle. *It's been an awfully long time. Could I have missed one while I slept? I thought he said messages wouldn't disappear unless I erased them. But then what has he been doing for two days? Has Darkstalker caught him? Did Tsunami ever find them?*

Is Moon all right?

He dropped his own earring into the bowl and whispered, "Twice as much, please," hoarsely. Winter watched, openmouthed, as an identical earring popped into existence beside the first.

"Whoa. Are *you* secretly an animus dragon, too?" he asked.

"No," Qibli said ruefully. *Thanks to you,* whispered a bitter, dark side of his brain, which he hustled back into darkness as quickly as he could. "It turns out some of Turtle's spells aren't as useless as they look."

He put his own earring back on. "Get me a large sack," he

said to Winter. "And two dragons — one willing to fly to Possibility, and another that can make it to Queen Glacier's palace."

Winter hurried out of the room without arguing. By the time he returned, Qibli had made a pile of two hundred and fifty-six earrings and was starting again with eight. Thirty-two was the maximum the bowl could hold, so it was not as fast a process as it could have been with a larger bowl. (*Turtle,* Qibli thought disapprovingly, and then caught himself — poor Turtle had never guessed that his little food bowl would be used or needed for such a strange, urgent task.)

"Holy smoking vipers," Thorn said, coming into the room behind Winter, with another SandWing at her side. "Qibli, what in the world are you doing — no, I see what you're doing, so the question is how."

"Animus magic," Qibli said, holding out the bowl. "We have a friend who made this and the earrings. It means I can create more for all the IceWings. If I'm right, and the plague is sent by Darkstalker, it should cure them instantly."

Thorn watched him intently as he made more and more earrings. "Can't this animus friend just make a spell to stop Darkstalker completely? Perhaps instantly make everyone in Pyrrhia immune to his magic? Or send something to kill him? I thought animus magic could do that kind of thing."

"The magic can, but this particular dragon can't," Qibli answered. Poor Turtle, so afraid of everything — afraid of being discovered, afraid of making the wrong decision, afraid of killing. *That's a good thing, though. Better an animus who's afraid to kill than an animus who has no problem with it.*

"Are we entirely sure this animus is to be trusted?" Thorn asked. She picked up one of the earrings from the growing pile. "There's no hidden spell in these? How would we know if there was?"

Qibli took his earring off. "Look," he said. "I can take it on and off freely. I am still myself, with or without it. It just cleared my head of the spell that made me find Darkstalker so charming and trustworthy."

"But the spell on him —" Thorn said, pointing to Winter with her tail.

"Was different," Qibli said. "Targeted to make Winter worship him and agree with everything he said, I suspect."

Winter growled again and started pacing the width of the room.

The queen cupped the earring she held in her talons and squinted at the warm amber glow. Qibli wondered if she was thinking about how small it was, to protect against such a dangerous dragon. "Does Sunny have one?" she asked.

Qibli nodded. "Everyone at Jade Mountain should be wearing one now."

"Then I want them for the SandWings next, after the IceWings," she said. "I want one for every dragon in my kingdom." She thought for a moment. "And all the queens. You must have sent one to Glory, right?"

"Yes, but I don't know if she got it," Qibli answered.

"I'll check the Obsidian Mirror, but if we can't tell for sure, let's send another. I'll have a dragon go through the tunnel — three dragons, so the other two can go to Coral and Mudden."

"We're going to inflict Qibli's terrible fashion sense on this whole continent?" Winter asked, joking awkwardly.

"I'm afraid we have no choice," said Queen Thorn.

"I think you mean 'wow, what a lot of lucky, soon-to-be-stylish dragons,'" Qibli said. He glanced at the slowly growing pile of earrings. "Um . . . how many dragons would that be?"

"I don't know," she said. "Keep making them. This is my fastest messenger; she will take as many as she can carry to Possibility, for the IceWings there."

"And I'll take the rest to the Ice Kingdom," said Winter.

"Will they let you in?" Qibli asked in between "twice as much, please" whispers. "Will they trust you? Don't they think you're dead?"

"Yes — but if I'm there to save lives, surely . . ." Winter trailed off, as if he wasn't actually sure how his tribe would receive him, magic-plague cure or not.

"One of the IceWings in Possibility can take the rest of the earrings to the Ice Kingdom as soon as they're healed," Thorn ordered. "It's essentially on the way; we won't lose much time. You stay here and figure out how we're going to fight this demon dragon."

She turned and swept out of the room, muttering calculations under her breath.

Before long, the sack was full. The messenger seized it in her claws and soared out the window. They could see her pale scales flashing in the sky as she shot away toward Possibility.

I hope this works, Qibli prayed. *I hope I'm not sending false hopes to all these dragons.*

The day faded into evening, the golden light into deep purple dusk outside. Qibli kept making earrings. Winter brought him food and water and took over whispering to the bowl while Qibli wolfed down the meal and checked the slate again. *Turtle, WHERE ARE YOU?*

"I just had a horrible thought," Winter said as Qibli took the bowl back.

"No, thank you," Qibli answered. "I've got quite enough of my own."

Winter barreled on. "Darkstalker can see the future, remember? So if this works, mustn't he know by now that his plan to wipe out the IceWings will fail?"

Qibli felt that cold talon slide down his spine again. "Maybe the future doesn't completely change until the earrings get there — maybe we have a little time before he notices. But you're right, surely he will soon. I wonder if that will make him suspicious about who's working against him," he said. *Poor Turtle, exactly as he feared. But Turtle, I have to save these dragons. You'd do the same thing in my place, wouldn't you?*

There was a muffled boom somewhere not far enough away.

Winter and Qibli stared at each other, and for a panicked moment, Qibli thought, *It's Darkstalker; we brought him here just by talking about him; he's come to kill everyone and I don't have enough protection spells —*

And then there was another boom, and another, very close, that shook the bricks under their feet. Earrings slid and bounced off the pile, scattering between Qibli's claws.

He jumped to his feet, flinching slightly as he put weight on his wounded arm. He wanted to fly out there in a wild rush, but he couldn't lose the only items they had to fight Darkstalker. Quickly, he took apart the bowl and slipped it back in his bag, around his chest, along with several earrings, while Winter shoveled the rest of the earrings into more sacks and hid them among the jars and medical paraphernalia on the shelves.

They hurried out into the corridor and found themselves in a sea of running dragons. Qibli struggled against the tide for a moment, thinking the dragons were running away from whatever this attack was. But then he realized that most of them were Outclaws, and he knew these were the dragons who would run straight into the danger if it threatened Queen Thorn. He turned and ran with them. Winter's icy scales cast a chill over his tail and back as the IceWing ran close behind him.

They emerged onto one of the balconies that overlooked most of the palace. Qibli skidded to a stop with a gasp.

Smoke was pouring from a gash in one of the outer walls; more smoke rose from a hole in the roof of the treasury. It sounded as though dragons were fighting, but it was hard to see exactly what was going on. Qibli glanced up, wishing for brighter moons, and realized that much of the moonlight was blotted out by the wings of dragons filling the sky.

NightWings? he thought in confusion for a moment, but the firelight from the palace below reflected off pale scales like his own.

"It's not Darkstalker," he said to Winter. "It's the Talons of Power. It's my grandfather."

And as he said that, he recognized the nightmarish shape of Vulture rising triumphantly from the hole in the treasury roof, wreathed in smoke and holding aloft the Eye of Onyx.

— CHAPTER 14 —

"Friends!" Vulture roared. "SandWings! Talons of Power! Listen to me!"

He landed on the top of a dome that rose above many of the other palace buildings. Qibli wondered if Vulture knew what it was, and whether he'd deliberately chosen to give his speech with his claws on the mausoleum where the ashes of SandWing queens were kept.

Three of his minions circled him, breathing trails of flame that lit Vulture's face with a terrifying orange glow. The battling dragons pulled away from one another, looking up at him, and silence fell across the palace grounds.

"Have we really come to this?" Vulture said in his hypnotic voice. "SandWings fighting SandWings? So soon after the war that tore our tribe apart?" He swept his wings out to encompass all of them. "Look how divided we are! Do you know why we fight each other?"

Because you attacked the palace? Qibli thought, frowning.

"Because we are ruled by a false queen," Vulture boomed. "One who does not deserve this palace! She doesn't care about anyone but herself! She stole this throne to make herself rich! She's been letting SandWings die all over her kingdom without lifting a talon to save them. A *real* monarch would keep you safe. A *good* ruler would find the dragons responsible and protect you all! We need someone who will see the danger clearly! Our tribe is under attack, fellow SandWings!"

"Yes!" Qibli yelled. "By *you*!"

Vulture turned his dark, haunting eyes toward the balcony and Qibli had to tense every muscle in his body to keep from trembling.

"You see that? My grandson, once a loyal follower of Thorn, agrees with me," he said smoothly. "He knows *I* am the one who sees the danger and *I* am the one who can protect you all."

"That's not what I said!" Qibli shouted furiously.

"Because *I* have found the threat," Vulture announced, speaking right over Qibli. "I know who is attacking us, my fellow SandWings! It is the MudWings, and I have proof!"

Qibli felt the force of the gasp that went up around the crowd like a punch in his stomach.

"We caught one of the MudWing infiltrators and forced him to confess," said Vulture. "Then we took the last of his weapons and came here, knowing my Talons of Power were the only ones who could protect the kingdom." He brandished the Eye of Onyx like a bolt of lightning he was ready to hurl into the ground. "My friends, it is time for a new ruler of the SandWings!"

Where is Onyx? Qibli wondered. *Why is she letting Vulture do all the speechifying? He hasn't even mentioned her yet. Has he cut her out? Left her behind? Is he planning to take the throne for himself?* He glanced around, searching the crowds of dragons. *Or is she here — and if so, what is she up to?*

"Vulture." Queen Thorn's voice was calm but clear, carrying across the palace and into the desert beyond. "Enough."

Everyone turned to look for her.

The queen stood in the balcony of the Whispering Tower — a tall, thin tower that had been used by queens for hundreds of years to make speeches to her tribe. It was designed for perfect acoustics, so even dragons outside the palace would be able to hear her. Burn had never used it; she did not see the point of giving speeches, and she did not have a tribe unified enough to listen to her anyway.

"If you have illegally taken a MudWing into custody, I suggest you bring him here for questioning before spreading dangerous rumors. And if you have a serious challenger for the SandWing throne, let's take this to the dueling grounds."

"We don't need to duel," said Vulture. "*We* have the Eye of Onyx! The symbol of royal power!"

"It's much more than a symbol," Thorn said quietly, firmly. "It's animus-touched. And that is not the Eye of Onyx." She lifted off her necklace and held up a black sphere encircled by golden wings. "What you hold is a replica I keep in my treasury to fool thieves — and save their lives. This is the real Eye of Onyx."

Vulture narrowed his eyes at her, and even from a

distance, Qibli recognized the look his grandfather got when he was tricked — and ready for vengeance.

Please be careful, Thorn, he begged in his head.

"Why should we believe that's the real one?" Vulture demanded. His talons caressed the sphere he held as if it was an egg — but an egg that could hatch out unimaginable power instead of a dragonet.

"Because," she said, "the Eye of Onyx will kill anyone unworthy who tries to steal it and the throne." A small smile crossed her face. "And it hasn't killed me yet."

Vulture eyed the jewel in his claws suspiciously. Everyone could hear the implication in Thorn's words: *If that was the real Eye of Onyx, you would be dead.*

"Oh," Winter said quietly beside Qibli. "I bet that's where her name comes from. Onyx for the Eye of Onyx — a clue to her royal heritage."

Qibli was still frantically searching the SandWings in the sky and the ones that had spilled through the palace walls. She *had* to be here somewhere. And if he couldn't see her, she could be doing anything . . .

There!

It was only a flicker of movement, but it was enough to catch his attention — a twitch of a tail tip against the stone of the Whispering Tower, a hint of a dragon slowly slithering up beneath the queen.

"THORN!" Qibli shrieked, launching himself off the balcony toward her. "Look out! She's right below you!"

He dove toward the hidden dragon just as she reared up

into the moonlight. Her venomous tail plunged toward the queen's heart, and Qibli felt his own heart shudder and freeze.

Not Thorn. Not Thorn. Not Thorn.

But his warning had worked. Thorn was already spinning toward Onyx as she attacked. She smacked Onyx's tail out of the way with her own and shoved Onyx backward off the tower. Onyx's wings shot out to stop her fall, but before she could right herself, seven Outclaws were on her, including Qibli, seizing her limbs and tail and holding her in the air.

"Don't hurt her," Thorn ordered from above them. "Yet."

Qibli looked up at her in disbelief. "She just tried to kill you!" he protested.

Onyx snarled at him. "I'm only taking what's *mine*," she hissed. "*My* throne, *my* crown."

"If you really think it should be yours, then fight me for it like a true queen would," Thorn scoffed. "This crown will never fall to a sneaking, skulking shadow killer."

"Fine," Onyx spat, twisting free from one of the guards. "I am the granddaughter of Queen Oasis and the true heir to this throne. I challenge you."

Shocked murmurs ran through the crowd of watching dragons, but Thorn just grinned at Onyx.

"Anytime," said Thorn. "Let's take this to the palace stadium. That's where duels for the throne have always been fought — but maybe you already know that." She swept her wing toward the arena that took up a back corner of the palace grounds. Since Thorn had become queen, Qibli had only seen it used for games and moon festivals. He hadn't realized it had such a dark history.

How many queens have spilled their blood on those sands?

Is my queen going to be one of them?

"Release her," Thorn ordered, flicking her tail. She leaped aloft as the Outclaws reluctantly let go of Onyx.

"I'm taking my throne *right now*," Onyx growled, jabbing her tail at the dragons who had held her. "And then you will be the first ones I punish." She whirled in the air and dove toward the stadium, sending dragons scattering out of her flight path.

Qibli looked back at Vulture, who was rubbing his chin and studying the false Eye of Onyx.

He thought it would be enough to come and take it. He hoped that holding it would be enough to make him king. I bet he was going to cut out Onyx, if he could, after she killed Thorn for him.

But now, knowing the real stone might kill him . . . he's not going to take that risk. Not right now; not if he can throw Onyx into the fire first to see what happens.

If she wins, he thinks he can control her. He's cleverly surrounded her with dragons who are loyal to him first and foremost. She doesn't have an army of her own.

But she can't win.

I can't let her win.

Qibli felt a cold breeze sweep up behind him and turned in the air to see Winter. "What if the Eye chooses Onyx?" he blurted before the IceWing could speak. "It'll know that she's Smolder's daughter, won't it?"

Winter's expression said volumes more than any words he could have spoken. *He's sure that Onyx will win,* Qibli realized. *Of course he believes in the monarchy, in the line of succession and royal blood. That's how his family is defined, how his whole tribe is organized. He might even think Onyx should win,* Qibli realized with a surge of fury.

He turned away, unable to look at Winter's face a moment longer. They swept down toward the stadium in a whirling cloud of wings. Every dragon wanted to see what would happen. There were few left alive who could remember the last time the Eye of Onyx had been used in a proper challenge for the throne — although everyone remembered very clearly how it had killed Blister only a few months earlier in the palace courtyard.

The stadium was designed like an oval amphitheater, built of sandstone, with no roof. The benches rose like steps from the ground upward, and at the top, sturdy poles could be folded out to add more places for additional audience members to perch. The wall at the bottom still had barely faded paintings on it from the last moon festival — dark blue backgrounds covered with white and gold stars and circles.

Qibli managed to elbow his way to a seat in the front row, using his smaller size to slip under the wings of larger dragons. As he settled, drawing his tail safely under him, he saw a flurry of SandWings moving aside for Smolder and Blaze to land in the front row as well, not far away from him. They both looked confused and anxious.

Unlike Queen Scarlet's gladiator arena, this one had no royal box, no special platform for the royal family. Queen Thorn usually sat wing to wing with her subjects, singing and sharing shish kebobs and throwing coins at the best dancers just like everyone else.

But now she landed on the sand, briefly alone in that vast oval, and Qibli felt a terrible shudder of fear inside him. What would happen to the world without Thorn in it? What would happen to the SandWings? They *needed* her. She was the only queen who could heal the scars left by the war.

And she's my leader and my friend. She changed my life. If she hadn't saved me, who would I be?

Onyx landed heavily in front of Thorn, and his spasm of fear twisted tighter. Qibli had been thinking of Onyx as a fellow dragonet because she was a student at Jade Mountain Academy — but of course she was much older than the other students, almost twenty years old. Which made her around the same age as Thorn . . . but definitely bigger.

In the center of the far wall that ringed the oval there was an indentation, which Qibli had noticed before because it looked deliberate, and yet he'd never been able to figure out what it was for. Now its purpose became clear as Thorn set the Eye of Onyx into the hollow, where it fit perfectly.

Torches were being lit all around the stadium, so Qibli

wasn't sure if it was a trick of the light — but he could have sworn a crackle of blue energy zipped around the stone for a moment as Thorn lifted her talons away.

Onyx stepped closer to it, staring at the Eye hungrily.

"Are you sure you want to do this?" Thorn asked her. "What the Eye does . . . it's not a pleasant way to die."

Onyx scowled. "It won't kill me," she snapped. "I'm the true heir to the SandWing throne."

"You said you're a granddaughter of Queen Oasis . . ." Thorn prompted.

Onyx lifted her chin proudly. "My mother's name was Palm," she said. "My father is Prince Smolder."

Qibli leaned forward to see Smolder's reaction. *I should have warned him. I was so distracted with everything else.*

Smolder looked as though someone had driven cactus spikes under his claws. He blinked several times, then vaulted over the wall and ran across the sand toward the daughter he never knew he had.

She jumped back, scowling at him, and he stumbled to a stop in front of her.

"Palm's daughter?" he said, bracing himself to look down at her. "I didn't know she — she never told me. But if we'd had a daughter, we were going to name her —".

"Onyx," she answered. "That's me."

He took a step back, his wings sagging. "But Palm *died* — she died years ago. My mother killed her. It was rather a specialty of Mother's, killing dragons she didn't like."

"Not this one," said Onyx. "Palm escaped and had me.

She thought *you* were dead. Good job looking for us, though. Appreciate that."

"I would have if I'd known," he said fiercely. Behind him, Thorn reached out and brushed his wing lightly with hers. Smolder kept his gaze on Onyx, but his body seemed to react subconsciously, leaning toward Thorn so their wings stayed connected.

When did they start falling for each other? Qibli wondered. How had he missed it? He hadn't been away at school that long — but then, he hadn't seen as much of Thorn in the last few months as usual, with her royal duties keeping her busy. *Thorn and Smolder, really? I guess Sunny did tell her to go have some more eggs, so there would be heirs to the SandWing throne who actually want to be queen.*

But she'll have to survive this first.

And she might have to kill his daughter in front of him.

"Onyx, I have a suggestion," said Smolder, his usual half-mocking tone just failing to conceal a note of deeper sincerity. "How about *instead* of immediately risking death against our shiny new queen, you take a few days to get to know us first? Stay here at the palace. Tell me all about your life. See how incredibly boring the job of queen really is. Eat as much as you want. Hang out with me. I mean, wouldn't you rather get to know your father than expire in a ball of ancient crackly magic?"

"So give me the throne," Onyx said challengingly to Thorn. "We don't have to fight for it. I'd be happy to take it off your talons."

"I can't," Thorn said. "I couldn't give it to you even if I wanted to — which I don't, to be clear. But the Eye of Onyx must choose."

"We've been reading the legends about it," Smolder said. "An animus dragon named Jerboa created it for the queen of the SandWings thousands of years ago. It's been an essential — and deadly — part of the transition of power ever since."

"Yes, yes, Mother told me all about it," Onyx said impatiently. "She said it was the one thing that could prove I was royal, so she wanted me to stay far away from it." She rolled her eyes. "Let's get on with it. We fight until the Eye chooses the greater dragon, isn't that right?"

"Onyx," Smolder tried one last time. "Please."

"Sit down, you old lizard," Onyx snapped. "I'm not here for you. I'm here for my crown."

Qibli's heart started thumping painfully as Smolder bowed his head and turned back to his seat. Thorn and Onyx squared off, tails raised like scorpions, with the Eye glowering darkly in the wall beyond them.

I can't watch the Eye choose Onyx and kill Thorn. I can't just sit here and let that happen.

Maybe it will choose Thorn, argued another part of his brain. *Maybe it knows she's the better queen.*

How would it know that? Surely it'll sense royal blood versus common blood and that's all it needs to know.

Onyx let out a roar and leaped at Thorn, all claws and teeth and venom. Thorn ducked and rolled aside, delivering a blow to the back of Onyx's head as she whirled by. Onyx spat furiously and slashed at Thorn's wing. She just missed, but left bleeding claw marks along Thorn's side.

A new terrifying thought struck Qibli. *Darkstalker was offering to conspire with Vulture. What if he did something to the Eye? What if he used his magic from afar to make it choose Onyx?*

That's what I would do, he realized, digging his claws into the bench below him. *If I had Darkstalker's magic, I'd enchant the Eye to choose Thorn forever; I'd enchant it to protect her and destroy anyone who tried to steal her throne.*

But I don't have Darkstalker's magic. He slid a few inches away from Winter, hunching into his wings. *I have nothing to protect her wi —*

He paused, staring down at his wrists . . . and the glowing armbands there. If he could call a storm — maybe a lightning bolt to strike down Onyx, quick before the Eye attacked — he could end this fight with Thorn safe and sound.

The only way to fight magic is with more magic, right?

I have to do what I can.

Qibli sat back and raised his forearms. "Give me thunder," he whispered to the bracelets. "Give me rain."

He felt Winter twitch toward him, but he tented his wings around himself to shut Winter out. "Bring me a storm," he said in a low voice, closing his talons into fists.

A rush of wind swept across the arena, strong enough to buffet Thorn and Onyx nearly into the wall. With a howl it swooped away again, and everyone looked up to see dark clouds billowing up to cover the stars. The three moons were quickly swallowed.

"More," Qibli whispered, turning his wrists up toward the sky. "I want lightning."

His scales prickled under the bands, like sharp little teeth digging in. The wind rushed through again, fiercer this time, and the air crackled ominously around the arena.

"Qibli, you fool," Winter said, shaking his shoulder. "You don't know how to control those."

"I have to save Thorn," Qibli answered through gritted teeth. The bracelets were starting to hurt, as if they were constricting tighter and tighter. There was still no rain, but the wind was growing stronger than he'd ever felt it before, beating the clouds across the sky and shrieking around the walls and towers of the palace.

Down in the arena, Thorn and Onyx had stopped fighting. They were having trouble even staying upright as the wind tried to seize their wings and carry them away. Onyx took two clawing steps toward Thorn and stopped, coughing and choking on the sand that flew up into her face.

"SANDSTORM!" roared a dragon from one of the upper poles. She was looking out over the walls of the palace at the desert beyond. "SANDSTORM! HEADING THIS WAY!"

Oh no, Qibli thought. *That's not what I was trying to summon.* He'd seen bad sandstorms before; he knew they were not to be trifled with.

Another dragon tried to take to the air to see the storm, but the wind immediately caught him and whirled him away into the clouds, screaming. Qibli stared after him, stricken with horror.

"Everyone inside!" Thorn shouted. "Stay low and run! Get into the Great Hall! Close all the doors and windows!"

SandWings stampeded over the top of the stadium, clinging to the benches and walls with their talons and keeping their wings tucked in close. Blaze screamed louder than anyone and bolted, climbing over other dragons until she was one of the first ones racing through the gardens to the doors of the Great Hall.

"No!" Onyx cried. "I want to fight! I've been waiting for this my whole life!" She clawed forward another step, and then the wind picked her up and slammed her back into the far wall.

"Onyx, come on!" Smolder shouted, climbing into the arena. He ran over to his daughter, but the wind was building to another shrieking roar, so Qibli couldn't hear what they were yelling at each other.

"Can you stop it?" Winter asked, grabbing one of Qibli's wrists.

"I'm trying!" Qibli said. He sliced his arms downward as he'd seen Anemone do. "Stop this," he commanded them. "Enough. Stop the storm. Take it away. Bring back the sunshine! Stupid things, listen to me!"

"So we're running, then," Winter said.

Qibli glanced around and saw Thorn herding a group of palace dragonets to safety. Loyal Outclaw guards were gathered thick around her, keeping her safe in case Vulture or Onyx tried to assassinate her in the chaos. Qibli spotted the Eye of Onyx around her neck again.

At least she's still alive. Whatever happens next, I kept her alive that much longer. A sandstorm can't be worse than my queen lying dead in a ball of blue fire.

"Yup," he said to Winter. "Running."

They fled with everyone else, chased by the wind and sand. Wings jostled them and talons stepped on their claws as all the dragons in the palace ran for safety.

At the threshold of the Great Hall, Qibli risked a look back and saw the storm he had raised.

A thundering cloud of sand rose from the dunes up to the sky, spreading across the entire horizon and bearing down on the palace. It was a tidal wave of fury three times as high as the tallest palace tower.

And then Winter pushed him inside and doors began slamming shut all around them, as the SandWings locked themselves in and waited to be buried alive.

CHAPTER 15

The storm raged for hours, which was a long time to be packed into a room with over a hundred other dragons, even a room as big as the Great Hall. Blaze used one of the large curtains to make herself a hammock, hung from the tall ceiling, and proceeded to sleep through most of the storm. After a while, Thorn organized an expedition to the kitchens that brought back dried fruit, water, and bread for everyone, though all of it tasted a little gritty with sand.

Qibli spent most of the time worrying about the fact that Vulture, Smolder, and Onyx weren't in the Hall with everyone else. Where had they gone instead? Were they still alive?

He kept himself busy making more earrings in a sheltered corner where not too many dragons could see him and ask awkward questions. Ostrich and her father, Six-Claws, found him there halfway through the storm and volunteered to distribute earrings to all the dragons in the hall.

Qibli felt a little resentful about the fact that some of those dragons were Talons of Power, driven into hiding with the palace SandWings after attacking them. But even they needed magical protection — brainwashed Talons of Power would not be any improvement over the current version.

He also checked Turtle's slate every few minutes, and then again, and then again, more and more frequently.

Where *was* Turtle? Why had he disappeared for so long?

Had something terrible happened to him?

He didn't know how long it had been when he looked up to find Thorn standing over him, frowning slightly.

"Oh, hey," he said. Winter jabbed him with a pointy elbow and Qibli jumped. "I mean, hello, Your Majesty."

"I have the strangest feeling," said Thorn, "that you know something about this." She waved one of her wings at the rafters that were shaking in the wind.

"Um . . ." Qibli set his jaw and squared his shoulders. "Yes. That was me. I called the storm to save your life. I . . . didn't *quite* have a handle on how big it would turn out to be."

"More animus magic?" Thorn said, still frowning.

He held out his wrists to display the bracelets. "They're supposed to control the weather."

She tapped one claw against the copper. "I'm not sure *control* is the right word here."

"I'm sorry," said Qibli. "About the palace, I mean, and I hope everyone's all right. But I'm *not* sorry that you're safe. I was trying to protect you from the Eye."

Thorn's wings flicked up and down and she stared at him with raised eyebrows. "Protect me from the *Eye*? Didn't you trust it to choose me? Like it did before?"

"But Onyx is royalty," Qibli said. "And Darkstalker is on her side and I was afraid he'd done something to it . . . and plus she's *royalty*. I thought that's what the Eye would want."

She shook her head and lifted the Eye of Onyx necklace over her head to hold it in her talons. Qibli took an instinctive step back. It so clearly radiated power — and danger. Even if he hadn't seen it kill Blister, he'd be terrified of it. But since he had, it was hard not to remember the sinister dragon's silent, agonized thrashing, or the charred smell that was left after she exploded into black dust.

"I know it's scary," said Queen Thorn. "But I've been wearing it around my neck for months now, and I've come to trust it." She traced the wings gently with one claw. "It feels — *right* to me. Like it was crafted by an animus with wisdom and goodness in her heart. And all my research into it has confirmed that. The Eye doesn't choose the most royal or most dangerous dragon to be queen. It chooses the best queen available for the job."

She smiled down at it. "In fact, Smolder and I discovered a secret. The Eye has chosen commoners over royalty before. The current royal bloodline goes back to a dragon who grew up in a town a lot like the Scorpion Den — a dragon who got the throne basically by accident, because the Eye chose her to save the kingdom from a cruel and vicious princess." Thorn met Qibli's eyes. "The truth is, Oasis and her descendants — including Onyx — aren't any more royal than you or me. Except insofar as having power for hundreds of years *makes* you royal. But that's not what the Eye cares about."

"Really?" Qibli's mind was spinning. This was exactly what he thought animus magic *should* be used for — not personal power, but improving the world in ways that made entire tribes safer. Imagine if every tribe had an Eye of Onyx — something that ensured only wise and good queens were chosen. Wouldn't that mean Pyrrhia would always be at peace? So all dragons would be happier and well cared for?

"My theory is that Jerboa was playing a trick on her queen," said Thorn. "If she was ordered to make the Eye, perhaps the queen wanted something to keep herself in power. But instead Jerboa made this clever spell to pick good queens."

"I'm sorry," Qibli said. "I didn't realize. Of course it'll choose you, if that's the real spell."

"I think I am a good queen," Thorn said thoughtfully. "And I guess if I'm ever not, it should be comforting that there's a way for me to find out." She laughed. "It would be nice if I could bargain with it, though. Like, hey, Eye of Onyx, instead of blowing me up, could you just send me a note that's like, *Time to stop being queen, crazyclaws,* and then I could happily retire? If I had an animus of my own, I'd probably get them working on that."

Maybe I can get Turtle to do that for her, Qibli thought. *After we deal with Darkstalker. When we've averted the prophecy and everything is calm again.*

Thorn looked up toward the ceiling. "I think it's finally stopped," she said, and Qibli realized she was right — the wind had fallen silent at last.

"Let's go see what a mess you've made," Thorn said to

Qibli. "I don't suppose you brought an animus object that cleans up after you."

"Sorry," Qibli said ruefully.

The main doors of the hall were impossible to push open. They had to fly to one of the upper windows and open the shutters to discover that the palace was buried in a layer of sand three dragons deep, entirely blocking the doors and covering all the gardens. The sun sparkled cheerfully in the bright blue sky overhead.

"*Qibli*," Thorn grumbled. She scanned the palace — the towers and rooftops poking out of the ridiculous new dunes. Qibli realized that she must be worried about Smolder, although she was hiding it under her exasperation with him.

"I'll start looking for anyone who needs to be dug out," he offered and darted back inside to assemble a team.

They found dragons safely squirreled away all over the palace. It had been built to have a lot of places to safely hole up during a sandstorm, with reinforced shutters and strong doors. Some of them required digging to get to, but by the early hours of the morning, all the dragons in the palace seemed to be accounted for except for Smolder and Onyx . . . and there was no sign anywhere of Vulture.

Qibli took Winter, Ostrich, Six-Claws, and Tawny back to the giant sand pile that used to be the arena, the last place he'd seen Smolder.

Please let him be all right, Qibli prayed as they dug. Smolder might not be good enough for Queen Thorn, in his opinion, but if she liked him, that was all that mattered.

Please let him be all right. Please let us find him soon.

His shoulders ached. He wished Moon were there, digging beside him, with her never-giving-up face on.

"Any luck?" Thorn asked, landing on one of the perches that stuck out of the sand.

"Not yet, Your Majesty," Six-Claws answered.

Thorn wriggled her wings as though they itched. Qibli had noticed that she often did this when her closest friends called her "Your Majesty."

"You should try the Obsidian Mirror," he suggested.

"I know I should," she said, rubbing her snout. "It's buried in a very safe chest in a very safe hidden compartment in my bedroom, under a couple of tons of sand." She glanced back at a contingent of wings flurrying around the central palace building. "We're working on it."

Qibli sat up and studied the arena, shaking sand off his wings. What would he have done, if the storm had hit before he could get to the Great Hall? If he'd been standing right here, like Smolder and Onyx?

Smolder knows this palace better than anyone. He's lived here his whole life, all throughout the war while his sisters were away fighting one another. He survived Oasis and Burn. He must know every possible hiding hole, every safe place.

His eyes scanned the walls as his brain spun rapidly through possibilities.

I'd want to get underground, if I could. Somewhere fortified and secure . . .

Qibli looked down at his talons, then up at his queen. "Thorn!" he called. "Aren't the dungeons right below us?"

"Part of them," Thorn answered, wrinkling her nose. "This palace has a LOT of dungeons." She tipped her head. "What are you thinking?"

"Maybe the dungeon is connected to the arena somehow," Qibli said, pacing in a large circle. "So prisoners could be brought here to fight for the queen. Like in Scarlet's palace. It's possible, isn't it, that this arena was used that way a long time ago?"

"Horribly possible," Thorn agreed. "Good idea. You four, look for a way in from here. Qibli, come with me."

He followed her back to the upper windows of the Great Hall, then swooped down to the lower levels and out through the covered passageways that led to the kitchens, the throne room, and other parts of the palace. Drifts of sand lay across the floor in places where the windows hadn't been completely shuttered.

"Where's your guard?" Qibli asked, watching Thorn's tail whisk through one of these drifts, leaving a spray of sunlit sand motes in the air behind her.

"Digging out the palace, like everyone else," said Thorn. "I put all of Vulture's dragons who were still here to work as well, in exchange for amnesty and resettlement packages. Outclaws are watching them, but I think they'll turn out to be fine after we chat with them a little bit and get their heads on straight." She glanced back at Qibli. "It's hard to readjust after someone you trust has been lying to you for years. But hey, you turned out mostly normal, so I think there's hope for them."

"Mostly normal?" Qibli protested. "Three moons, I'm not sure which is worse, *mostly* or *normal*."

Thorn laughed. "Maybe normal is the wrong word. Generally acceptable? Reasonably fit for society? Solidly on the side of the not-so-murderous?"

"Stop, stop, this much flattery can't be good for me," Qibli said wryly.

She turned down a poorly lit, narrow passage that twisted and angled downward. Qibli stayed close, hopping down the occasional steps and keeping his wings away from the rough-scraped walls. Lanterns flickered from niches all the way down, casting jumpy little shadows around his claws. The air had an odd smell, like a trove of decayed lizards buried under a floorboard and forgotten about for years.

Thorn unlocked a series of gates on the way down, relocking them behind her. They passed a few guards, posted in pairs, who saluted to the queen and stayed in position, holding their weapons.

Finally a flight of stone stairs deposited them in an antechamber with four tunnels branching out from it. Thorn took a lantern from a low shelf by the stairs and breathed a small burst of flame to light it.

"I don't like coming down here," she admitted to Qibli. "Poor Smolder refuses to come with me — it's the one thing

I can't get him to do. I suspect his mother used to punish him by locking him down here overnight whenever he displeased her." She lifted her lantern to look down one of the tunnels. "If he had to take refuge down here because of the storm . . . I can't imagine how sick he must be feeling."

"We'll find him," Qibli promised. He pictured the palace in his head, mapping it over the turns they'd taken on the way down. "This one leads under the arena, I think — right?" He pointed to the darkest tunnel just as a strange gibbering wail erupted from it.

The sound sliced under Qibli's scales like freezing needles, terrifying him down to his bones. He leaped back from the passage and resisted the urge to run screaming up the steps back to the sunlight.

"What —" he said, picturing ghosts and furious spirits. "What —"

"That's the mad prisoner," Thorn said grimly. "She's been down here since the time of Queen Oasis." She brushed past him and set off down the passage.

Qibli scrambled to keep up so he could stay close to the light — and to Thorn's reassuring no-nonsense voice. "Mad?" he echoed.

"I wanted to release her, or at least talk to her," said Thorn, "but she attacks anyone who enters her cell or goes near her chains. She managed to stab two of my guards with her tail before we gave up. I think there were times during the war when she was forgotten for days and nearly starved.

Burn was not the most careful dragon with her prisoners. I'm sure she didn't even care what this one did to end up in here — there's no record of her crime anyway."

She waved one wing at the deserted cells they were passing. "The whole dungeon is almost empty now — I freed most of the dragons Burn had imprisoned, since their crimes all involved disloyalty to her. There's a jail in the courtyard barracks that's a lot more humane, for prisoners who we can try quickly."

Thorn sighed. "I *was* keeping those two NightWings here for Queen Glory, but somehow they escaped. Which is another argument for shutting this whole dungeon down and never using it again, if you ask me."

They turned a corner and Qibli saw the glow of firelight up ahead. In unspoken agreement, they both began to run, until they were close enough to see two dragons huddled by the wall at the end of the tunnel, outside the cells.

"Smolder!" Thorn called joyfully.

He lifted his head and grinned weakly at the sight of her. "About time, your royal sluggishness," he said.

"You didn't have to sit here and wait for me, you broiled snail," she pointed out, sliding her lantern into a niche across from the one that was lit. "You do have feet. You could have just come on upstairs instead of making us all worry about you. I mean, not that *I* was worried."

"Well, I was," Smolder said. He opened his wings and Thorn hugged him, pulling back quickly as though she didn't want to get too emotional in front of witnesses. On top of Smolder's head something like a little tuft of fur sat up and shook itself. It leaned into the light and Qibli realized it was Flower, yawning and stretching.

"But we couldn't leave," Smolder continued. "Onyx is hurt." He moved aside to reveal his daughter, curled into a sullen ball and breathing shallowly. One of her back feet looked as though it had been crushed by something heavy; it was an awful bloody mess, and she clearly couldn't walk — in fact, Qibli wasn't sure she'd ever walk on it again.

Thorn inhaled sharply. "We need to get you to a doctor," she said to Onyx.

"I know," Onyx spat. "I told *him* to go get one —"

"But I didn't want to leave her alone," Smolder interjected.

"Right." Onyx snorted. "More like he's a coward who's afraid of ghosts." She tried to shift her weight to sit up and froze, shuddering in pain.

Smolder lifted his wings. "Well, I haven't stayed alive this long by running *toward* the shrieking things in the dark." He made an "I am who I am" face.

The "thing in the dark" screamed again from somewhere very nearby, sending Qibli's heart pounding.

"That's just the mad prisoner," Thorn said to Smolder. "I told you about her. You couldn't remember what she was arrested for either."

"For LIES!" the dragon shrieked. "For my FACE NOT MY FACE I'M GOING TO KILL HER!"

Thorn sighed and took the lantern again, stepping back to

one of the cells they'd run past. Inside, a tortured-looking SandWing paced, clawing at the scales around her neck. Rusty chains stretched from her ankles to loops bolted into the floor. As the light illuminated her prison, she whirled around and threw herself at the bars, screaming.

"LET ME OUT SO I CAN KILL HER!"

"See, that just doesn't sound like a good idea," Thorn said. "Smolder, look, she's only a dragon. She probably wasn't mad when she got here, but more than twenty years in the dark will eat away at anyone's sanity."

"For LIES!" the dragon shrieked again. "I'M NOT HER! THE QUEEN NEVER CAME! NO ONE EVER CAME! NO ONE SEES ME! SHE STOLE MY FACE! SHE THREW MY FACE INTO THE FIRE! I'M *NOT HER!*"

"Wait," Onyx rasped. She dragged herself forward using her front talons, shoving Smolder off when he tried to help her. Her dark eyes squinted at the frantic prisoner.

"You can't possibly know her," Thorn said curiously. "She's been in here longer than you've been alive."

"She looks like my mother," Onyx said. "Who wasn't too emotionally stable herself, by the way. Lots of nightmares. Super paranoid. Would have kept me buried under a rock forever if she could have."

Smolder edged forward to take a closer look at the prisoner, too. She had her claws wrapped around the bars and her snout pressed between two of them, her eyes closed, as though she were trying to will herself free with the force of pure hatred.

"Does she look like Palm?" Thorn asked him.

"NOOOOOOOOOOO!" howled the prisoner.

Smolder sat back, lifting his talons to cover his snout with an expression of horror and dismay. "No," he said. "I mean — yes, but no, because this — I think this is Prickle."

"Who?" said Thorn.

"Aunt Prickle?" Onyx said, grimacing as another wave of pain seemed to grip her.

"Palm's sister," said Smolder. "Prickle, is that you? What are you *doing* here?"

"You," she snarled at him, clawing at her chains. A thin layer of clarity seemed to settle over her as she recognized him. "This is all your fault. Your earrings. Your fine words. Your *stupid dragonet*."

"That's me," said Onyx. "The stupid dragonet. Mother let the soldiers take Prickle, thinking she was Palm, so Mother could escape with me. She told me the whole story after her, like, nine thousandth nightmare about it. But she said they would have released Prickle within a day or two, once the queen realized the mistake."

"Except the queen died," said Smolder. "She must have died before seeing her. And then no one ever . . ." He trailed off.

"Wow," Qibli said faintly.

"I want to release you," Thorn said to Prickle through the bars. "But I'm a little worried about what you might do." She glanced sideways at Smolder.

Prickle hissed and turned her back, hunching her wings around herself.

"We'll come back and try again," Thorn said. "Now that we know who you are and what happened — we'll bring someone you can talk to. We'll get you back to the sunlight. I promise."

The only answer was a low growl.

"Hello?" called a bored voice. "If prisoners are being released, can I be next?"

"No, Cobra," Thorn called back. "And by the way, your father attacked without your help, failed to overthrow me, and left again."

Cobra chuckled somewhere in the dark. "You really think he would give up that easily?" she said. "You think he'll go back to his gilded compound and lie around eating scavengers peacefully for the rest of his life? Ha. Ha. Ha. Vulture will burn the kingdom to the ground before he gives up."

Thorn looked at Qibli and he nodded. He wished Cobra was wrong, but he knew it was true.

A grinding, scraping sound came from the wall at the end of the tunnel — the sound of the old door to the arena being dragged open from the outside. Sunlight tumbled in, chasing away the ominous gloom of the dungeon. Smolder turned toward it, relief scrawled all over his face.

Ostrich popped her head around the door. "I found it!" she chirped. "It was me!"

"You're very clever," Six-Claws rumbled affectionately behind her.

"Well done. Go get a doctor," Thorn ordered Ostrich,

striding over and shoving the door open another few inches. "Six-Claws, help me get Onyx out onto the sand."

Onyx hissed furiously as Six-Claws bent to lift her, but she kept her tail coiled safely away from him and Thorn as they carried her outside.

She won't be challenging Thorn again anytime soon, Qibli thought. *Maybe ever, if they can talk her out of it while she's recuperating.* He glanced at Smolder, who was hurrying after them. *That's . . . suspiciously lucky.*

In the chaos of the storm, anything could have happened.

Would Smolder deliberately injure his own daughter to stop her from fighting Thorn? To save Thorn's life, and her own?

He wasn't sure he wanted to know. Intentional harm or lucky accident — whichever it was, Thorn was safe and Onyx didn't have to die. The Eye could go back around Thorn's neck and she could continue to rule the kingdom in peace.

Unless Darkstalker comes for it. Until the next step of his plan, whatever it is.

"Bye, Qibli," Cobra's voice whispered from the dark. "I'm sure your grandfather will be seeing you soon."

Qibli shuddered and climbed out onto the arena sands. Winter reached down and caught his talons, hauling him up the last incline. The chill of his talons against Qibli's felt like a reminder of the cold, worried feeling inside of him.

Darkstalker and Vulture, working together. That could mean the end of Pyrrhia.

He reached for the slate in his pouch again, although he'd

almost lost hope that Turtle would ever send another message. Maybe he'd forgotten he had the slate, or that Qibli was out here waiting for news.

But this time there *was* a new message.

The message Qibli had been dreading ever since he watched Moon and Turtle fly away with Darkstalker.

It read:

> DARKSTALKER KNOWS ABOUT ME. TRAPPED IN THE
> NIGHTWING PALACE. HELP!

PART TWO

KING OF SHADOWS

CHAPTER 16

Winter turned the slate over a few times and then held it up to the sun, as if searching for a hidden message under the one that was there.

"That's it," Qibli said, spreading his talons. "That's all he wrote." He paced back across the tiles, coiled his tail around one of the outstretched wings of the pavilion roof, and stared out at the desert. The wind breezed cheerfully around him, as if it had nothing to do with the mess of sand covering the palace below. From up here, atop one of the tallest palace towers, Pyrrhia looked as if it stretched forever in all directions.

"This is bad," said Winter.

"DO YOU THINK SO?" Qibli shouted.

"There's no need to raise your voice at *me*," Winter said, ruffling up the spines around his neck. "*I'm* the one who's going to help you rescue him."

"I know, I know," Qibli said. He clenched his talons and tried to calm down. "Turtle's the one I really feel like yelling at."

"Turtle?" said Winter. "Isn't he the dragon in distress here?"

"Yes, but," said Qibli, "if you're going to send out a cry for help, shouldn't it be a USEFUL cry for help? With ANY information in it? Such as maybe for instance WHERE THE MOONSBLASTED CAMEL-LICKING NIGHT KINGDOM IS???"

"Ohhhhhh," Winter said, looking at the message again. "You're right. He doesn't mention that."

"How are we supposed to rescue him?" Qibli cried, flinging his front claws in the air. "When we can't even find him? Why hasn't he sent me a message in three days? Just 'hey, off to the Night Kingdom, toodles!' and then 'OH NO ACK I'M TRAPPED IN THE NIGHT KINGDOM' and nothing in between! Rrrrrrrrgh." He buried his face in his talons.

And nothing about Moon. Is she all right? What does she think about Darkstalker trapping Turtle? Does this mean she's in trouble, too?

He took a deep breath and looked up at Winter again. As frustrated as he was, he had to admit to himself that he really didn't know what Turtle had been going through, or how awful the last few days might have been for him. Most likely there hadn't been any time to write a message. And now Turtle was living his worst nightmare.

"Poor Turtle," he said. "He must be terrified."

"What do you think Darkstalker will do to him?" Winter asked. "I mean . . . he did promise Moon that he wouldn't hurt any of her friends."

"Sure, but I have a feeling Darkstalker knows a lot of ways to wriggle around his promises," Qibli said. "Like, it's not *hurting* Turtle to gently throw him in a NightWing dungeon. It's not *hurting* you to put a brainwashing spell on you. It wouldn't be *hurting* Kinkajou if he cast a spell like the one on Hailstorm, turning her into an entirely different dragon. See what I mean?"

"He knows how to play tricks with words," Winter said, nodding. "Kind of like you."

"What?! No! But *evil*," Qibli protested. "So *nothing* like me."

"Right," Winter said unconvincingly. "Oh, look, she's found it." He pointed at the shape of Queen Thorn flying toward them.

Qibli beat back the suspicion that Winter was trying to change the subject. He stood up and waved, and Thorn swooped down to drop the Obsidian Mirror in his talons.

"Thank you," he said as she landed beside him.

"I hope you find your friend," she said. "Do you need an army? 'Cause guess what, I have an army now. Like, a big one. They're pretty awesome."

"But the NightWing army has superpowers," Winter pointed out darkly.

"And Darkstalker will see us coming if we arrive with an army," Qibli said. "That's the kind of thing that would show up bright and clear in his visions of the future. I don't want to get any SandWings killed." He balanced the mirror on his front talons. "I'm hoping Winter and I won't look like much of a threat to him. I mean, we're no threat at all right now, since we can't even *find* him."

"I'm not sure this will help," Thorn said, nodding at the mirror. "You can't see the dragons you're spying on — there aren't any details about where they are. They'd have to say something helpful."

"I know," Qibli said. "Cross your claws for me."

He breathed smoke across the smooth black surface and whispered: "Moonwatcher."

Winter gave him a sharp sideways look. "Moon?" he said. "Not Turtle, or Darkstalker?"

"I'll try them next," Qibli said. He'd chosen her instinctively. He really needed to know Moon was all right.

The smoke coiled immediately into one small black spiral and a slightly smaller twist of blue-pink-yellow-red, which was flurrying wildly around the first one.

"Bet I know who that is," Qibli said, just as Moon's voice said, "Kinkajou, *please* calm down."

"Kinkajou's all right?" Winter said, his eyes lighting up.

Qibli nodded and shushed him.

"*Me* calm down?" Kinkajou cried. "You need to *un*-calm down! You need to ramp all the way up to *freaking out* right now!"

"About what?" Moon protested. "How can I freak out when you won't tell me why?"

"I can't tell you!" Kinkajou yelped. "Aaaarrrrrgh! Because you don't have skyfire, so if I tell you, Darkstalker might read it in your mind, and then he'll know I told you and

ALL KINDS OF TERRIBLE THINGS MIGHT HAPPEN. AAAAAAARRRGH!"

"Oh my goodness, Kinkajou," Moon said. "Whatever it is, I'm sure it's not the end of the world."

"Except that it totally is! It is probably the actual literal end of the world. I have to go back to Jade Mountain," Kinkajou said abruptly. "Will you come with me?"

"Right now?" Moon hesitated. "Darkstalker asked me to stay until tomorrow at least — he said he wants to introduce me to someone. Can we leave after that?"

Kinkajou's curl of smoke turned several different colors, finally settling on an interesting mix of pea green and smoky red. "Fine," she said. "I'll do some detective work until then. Stealth mode! That's me!" All the colors vanished, leaving barely a whisper of pale smoke behind.

"Just be careful," Moon said. "Remember, Darkstalker is paranoid for a reason, considering what happened to him."

"Which he brought upon himself," Kinkajou observed. "By being completely evil."

"Kinkajou —"

"Don't you argue with me," Kinkajou said. "Just tell me when you're ready to get out of here." Her barely visible smoke whirled away, leaving Moon's wisp alone on the mirror.

"I can't believe Kinkajou is making more sense than Moon right now," Winter said, rubbing his forehead.

"I hope she's all right," Qibli said. "Darkstalker could figure out Kinkajou isn't under his spell any moment." He frowned. "But I don't understand how Moon is still enchanted. Didn't Tsunami ever catch up with them? She should have given Moon an earring days ago."

"Maybe we should look for her, too," Thorn suggested.

"Let's check on Turtle first," said Qibli. For a moment he gazed at the tiny trail of smoke that was as close as he could get to Moon right now, and then he breathed the mirror clear again and called up Turtle.

Turtle's smoke was dark green and somehow radiated sadness, as much as a wisp of smoke could do that. It was coiled miserably in the middle of the mirror. Qibli couldn't tell if he was asleep or just sad — the only sound the smoke made was an occasional deep sigh.

"At least he's alive," Thorn said hopefully.

"Probably in a cell," Winter guessed. "No one to talk to."

I hope this isn't our fault somehow, Qibli worried. *Like if something I did changed the future, which led Darkstalker to figure out that another animus must be working against him . . . oh, Turtle, I'm sorry.*

That wasn't giving them any information, so Qibli finally tried Darkstalker, although even saying Darkstalker's name gave Qibli the creepy feeling that the ancient dragon would somehow hear him and know he was being spied on.

Darkstalker's spire of smoke was taller than anyone else's and it moved slowly but purposefully across the obsidian.

"Hello," his voice rumbled, and Qibli saw Winter take an involuntary step back — as if he, too, feared the NightWing might be looking back at them.

"Hello," Darkstalker said again. "Oh, very nice work clearing the weeds. Smart thinking. We should get these gardens going again so we can feed ourselves. You haven't received a gift yet, have you? I could give you the power to sprout every seed you plant — some kind of master gardener skill. Wouldn't that be useful?"

"Um," said a small dark purple wisp that had unfurled beside his. "I mean, yes, very useful, sir, thank you. But I was thinking something more like seeing the future . . . I guess I've always thought seeing the future would be cool."

"Hmmm," said Darkstalker. "I suppose it is. But you don't really need to, since *I* can see the future, and one seer in the tribe is really quite enough. Whereas we could use lots of gardeners . . . well, you think it over and we'll talk again soon."

"Wait," said the other dragon. "Sorry, sir, you're right, I'd love the power you described. I'm ready for it now."

"If you're sure . . ." Darkstalker paused heavily.

"I'm sure! I'm sure."

"Yikes," said Thorn, leaning forward as Darkstalker muttered something. "It's that easy? You want a superpower, here, done?"

"It's that easy," Qibli said, curling in his claws. That could have been *him* handing out powers to make dragon lives better, if he had Darkstalker's scroll.

They listened for a while longer, but Darkstalker seemed to be strolling through the streets of his kingdom, visiting his subjects. And no one he spoke with said anything like,

"Boy, this island half a day's flight due west of the Scorpion Den is pretty neat" or "Who would ever have guessed there was a whole kingdom buried under the mountains and accessible by a tunnel at the foot of Scarlet's palace?" (Both of which were among Qibli's numerous theories for where the ancient kingdom might be.)

No one dropped any clues at all; the only thing Qibli picked up on that might have been useful was the background noise of the wind, as if it was whistling through deep ravines. (So, not underground, then.)

"I think there's only one thing we can do," he said at last.

"What's that?" Winter asked.

"Go back to Jade Mountain." Qibli blew away Darkstalker's smoke with a little more vigor than was really necessary. "We know Kinkajou and Moon will hopefully be there in a day or two. Or maybe Sunny and Clay can help us." He shook his head. "I hate leaving them all wherever they are, though. I want to get to Turtle *right now*." *And to Moon and Kinkajou, who are in danger every second.*

"Last one," Winter said, pointing to the mirror. "Try Tsunami."

"She's probably back at the academy," Qibli said with a sigh. Most likely she'd arrived at the rainforest after everyone had left, and they were too far ahead for her to figure out where they'd gone. But he whispered her name to the mirror and breathed out smoke.

It seemed to take a moment, coiling back and forth and

around before settling into a blue spiral in the center, which immediately started yelling.

"I SAID WHO ARE YOU?" shouted Tsunami's voice. "You coward! Show yourself! What do you want with me?" She took a deep breath, as if listening for a response, then roared again. "LET ME OUT OF HERE! My friends are heroes, you know! YOU'LL BE SORRY FOR THIS!"

Thorn's eyes met Qibli's, both of them shocked into silence.

Tsunami wasn't safely back at Jade Mountain after all.

The great warrior of the Five Dragonets, one of the best and most ferocious dragons Qibli knew, was somebody's prisoner.

— CHAPTER 17 —

"Tsunami's a prisoner?" Queen Thorn said disbelievingly.

"But whose?" said Qibli. "And how? *Tsunami?* Of all dragons — how? And why? And who?"

"Darkstalker, right?" said Winter. "Who else could it be? He must have had a vision of her coming with the earrings, snuck off, captured her, and stuck her somewhere."

"But Tsunami doesn't seem to know who her captor is," Qibli pointed out. "Even if she was blindfolded or drugged, she'd have some clue just from his size, wouldn't she?" He closed his eyes, trying to think. Who else could have Tsunami? Who would dare grab the famous warrior of the five prophecy dragonets? What did they want with her?

Darkstalker did make the most sense . . . but it didn't *feel* like the right answer to him.

"Now we really have to go back to Jade Mountain," Winter said, standing up. "They must be worried sick about her. And we'll need their help to find her and rescue Turtle anyway."

"I'll check on Glory and the other queens," said Thorn. She took the Obsidian Mirror back from Qibli, clearing its surface. "And I'll start distributing all those earrings you made. Thank you, Qibli."

"I don't know if it's enough," he said. "Maybe I should leave you the bowl . . ."

"There are earrings all over my palace right now," she said. "Between them and your sand I'm surprised I can see any of my royal things. Trust me, it'll be enough for the time being. I'll keep the Obsidian Mirror, but you might need the bowl."

"We should give it an imposing name, too," he said. "The Inscrutable Bowl of Infinite Stew, or something."

Thorn wrapped her wings around Qibli and hugged him tightly. "Go keep saving the world," she whispered in his ear. "I always knew you would."

"Me?" he said as she let go. "Really?"

"Yes," she said. "Well, unless you screw up and bury it all in sand first." She tapped one of his bracelets. "No more storms, Qibli."

"Right," he said. "Absolutely." He nodded. "Unless it's an emergency."

"No!" she said. "Use your brain, not someone else's unreliable magic. Or I will hunt you down and bury *you* in a sand dune."

"Yes, boss," he said, grinning at her.

But he thought about it as they flew south toward Jade Mountain; he thought about magic and power and who had which and what you were supposed to do to fight bad guys when you had neither. Surely it was better to create an accidental sandstorm here and there, if it was all in the name of stopping villainy? He needed that magic, any magic at all, to even the balance — not that balance was even possible when it came to Darkstalker.

What else could he do? How else could Qibli fight, or rescue Turtle? *Ordinary* rang in his head. *Small. Insignificant. Useless.*

One scruffy street dragon against the most powerful dragon in history and all the minions he'd given superpowers to?

Winter's flashing silver scales crossed his peripheral vision and he glanced over at his friend.

One scruffy street dragon and one exiled prince. Plus a fierce little rainbow, if we can get to her before Darkstalker does.

Qibli's wings were tiring by the time they flew past the Scorpion Den, but he didn't want to stop until they reached Jade Mountain. The sight of the sprawling den gave him more of a shiver than ever as he wondered where Vulture had gone. *To Darkstalker, or back to his compound?*

"What's that?" Winter said suddenly. He pointed to a shape crouched by one of the small desert pools, barely big enough to count as an oasis. They flew closer and saw that it was a dragon drinking the water — but not a SandWing; the coloring was more of a gray-blue-pink . . . odd but familiar . . .

"It's Anemone!" Qibli gasped. "I thought she was with Darkstalker! What's she doing all the way out here?"

"We should stay away from her," Winter said, banking sharply up to a higher air current. "She practically threw herself into Darkstalker's web. She's more loyal to him than anyone."

"Or deeply enchanted," Qibli pointed out. "She needs to be freed from him as badly as you did."

"Have you forgotten that she's an animus?" Winter argued. "And your hideous earrings only protect us from Darkstalker's spells, right? She could tangle us right back up, or do something worse. It would be idiocy in the extreme to go anywhere near her."

"I think she needs our help," Qibli said stubbornly. "She's alone in the desert — maybe she ran away from him."

"Or maybe Darkstalker sent her this way for one of his sinister plans," said Winter. "Qibli! Stop! What are you doing? Get back here, you absurdly irrational dragon!"

Qibli ignored him, swooping down toward the SeaWing princess. He understood Winter's points, but he was *sure* Anemone needed help and that it was important to free her from Darkstalker if they could. In addition, she was a promising link to Darkstalker and the Night Kingdom. He just had to hope he could charm Anemone into putting on an earring.

He wheeled around to approach her from the front so he wouldn't startle her. She looked up at the sound of his wingbeats and, to his surprise, her whole face lit up.

Does she actually know who I am? Is Winter right — did Darkstalker send her looking for me?

"Wow," Qibli said, landing with a splash in the shallow water beside her. "It's not every day a SeaWing princess looks so happy to see me." He couldn't help grinning back at her. Dragons who smiled at him, dragons who seemed to actually like him — he could never resist them.

But Anemone didn't say anything. Instead she sat up, waved her front talons in the air, and frantically pointed at her snout.

"Something's wrong," Qibli realized out loud. "Is it — wait." He stepped closer, staring at something she held in a death grip with her claws. "Is that Turtle's stick?" He'd only seen it once, briefly, when Turtle had been rearranging things in his pouch before he left for the rainforest with Moon and Darkstalker. But he knew the importance of the stick Turtle had enchanted to hide him from Darkstalker. And this one Anemone was holding had the same aura to it — a don't-notice-me-but-I'm-everything aura.

Anemone's wings drooped and she nodded miserably.

"So that's what happened," Qibli said. "That's how Darkstalker knows about Turtle? Because you have his hiding stick. Did you take it from him?"

Her head snapped up and she scowled at Qibli.

"Why can't you talk?" Qibli walked slowly around her. Her silver neckband — the one that was supposed to protect her soul — was missing. And she was covered in scratches, as though she'd been in a fight very recently. Had she fought Turtle to take his stick? Had Turtle cast a spell to stop her from speaking?

It was sort of hard to imagine Turtle fighting anyone. Or coming up with a useful spell on his own. *Sorry, Turtle,* Qibli thought with a wince. He wished he could stop himself from having thoughts like that about Turtle, who was a good dragon at heart. It wasn't Turtle's fault that the universe had given him magic instead of Qibli, or that he was sort of terrible at using it.

Anemone let out a frustrated growl, splashing her tail in the water. She pointed to her mouth again, then used the stick to write in the sand in big wobbly letters: *Darkstalker spell.*

"Oh!" Qibli said. "We can fix that! Anemone, look!" He had taken a few earrings from Thorn's stockpile; now he dug in his bag and pulled one out. "Just put this on. It'll cancel any spells that Darkstalker has put on you, and protect you from any in the future."

Anemone reached for it hesitantly, but paused, studying him.

"It's safe, I promise," he said. If she had Turtle's stick, she must know by now that her brother was an animus. He hoped anyway — he didn't want to be the one breaking that news to her. "Turtle enchanted it. He made one for me, see?" Qibli pointed to his own ear. "I asked him to protect me from Darkstalker's magic. That's all it does, I swear."

The look of hope on her face was heartbreaking — which was a strange feeling to have for the SeaWing princess, who had always been kind of a brat to everyone.

She took the earring delicately between two claws and

stared into the amber for a moment. Qibli felt his heart jumping nervously as she lifted it and affixed it to her ear.

Her blue eyes were as big as full moons. "Did it work?" she said, and then gasped, clapping her talons to her snout.

"Looks like it," Qibli said, beaming.

"I can talk!" she shouted. "I'm free! Let's go kill that evil son of a slug!"

"Whoa, hang on, hang on," Qibli said, catching one of her wings before she could take off. "Tell us what happened! All we know is that Turtle's been captured by Darkstalker."

"Us?" Anemone echoed. She looked up at the sky and spotted Winter.

Qibli waved to him to come down and Winter reluctantly descended, looking wary and disgruntled. As he did, Anemone leaned over and grabbed one of Qibli's forearms.

"Hey!" she said. "These are MY bracelets!"

"Oh, right," he said. "Sorry — um. We needed them and you just . . . left them behind, so . . . we thought you wouldn't mind."

"Well, you can give them right back," she said, flicking her claws demandingly at him.

He felt a twinge of outraged possessiveness. *Why should I give them to her? She left them at school; she didn't even care about them until she saw I had them! She has plenty of magic, but this is all I have.*

"I want to keep them," he said. "I mean, for now. Until we

deal with Darkstalker. Please?" He gave her a charming grin. "In exchange for my very fashionable earring?"

"That earring looks even worse on her than it does on me," Winter announced, splashing toward them.

"Doubtful," said Anemone. "*I* can pull anything off." She tossed her head. "Besides, I'd wear a necklace of dragonbite vipers if it meant I was free of Darkstalker's spells." Her large blue eyes narrowed at Qibli for a moment, as if she was looking at him through a jeweler's glass, examining all his flaws. "Fine," she said finally. "You can keep the weather bracelets, FOR NOW."

"Thank you," Qibli said.

"So what happened?" Winter asked. "What are you doing all the way out here?"

"And why did Darkstalker enchant you to stop talking?" Qibli asked.

"He did worse than that," Anemone admitted. "He enchanted me to obey his every command."

"Like the spell on his father," Winter said, shuddering. "You're lucky you're still alive."

"*Oh*. Turtle *gave* you his stick, didn't he?" Qibli realized. "To protect you from that spell. Once you were erased from Darkstalker's mind, he couldn't control you anymore — or at least, he could, but only if he somehow remembered you were there."

"Wow," said Winter.

"Yeah." Anemone drew the stick in toward her heart. "I

know, I know, it was super brave of him, but can we save the mushy stuff for after we kill Darkstalker?"

"You could kill him right now, can't you?" said Winter. "We can end this right here! One spell from you and zap, he's dead."

Anemone shook her head with a little snarl. "I would, believe me. But he told me none of my spells will ever work on him. He's protected himself against my magic — the same way these protect against his, I guess." She touched the earring in her ear.

"And you couldn't cast any other magic — like freeing yourself — because he can sense animus spells being cast," Qibli said. "You're in the same current as Turtle was. You don't want to do anything that will make him notice you."

"Yes, I do!" Anemone said ferociously. "I want to make him notice me by stabbing him in the eyeball!"

"I am suddenly seeing the family resemblance between you and Tsunami," Winter remarked.

"Who is also in danger," Qibli said to Anemone. "Someone has her prisoner, but we don't know who."

"Um, of course we do!" Anemone cried. "It must be Darkstalker! He hates all SeaWings because of Fathom; especially my family, because we're descended from him." She jumped into the air, nearly whacking them both in the face with her tail. "Now we have to rescue my brother *and* my sister! You can tell me as we go — let's talk and fly, talk and fly, slowpokes!"

"Where are we going?" Winter asked, stepping back as Qibli jumped aloft with the princess.

"To the lost city of night!" Anemone said.

"To fulfill the prophecy!" Qibli said gleefully. "To save the world!"

"To kill Darkstalker!" Anemone cried. "Hooray!"

— CHAPTER 18 —

Winter argued with them all the way to the Night Kingdom, across the miles and miles of desert they flew over, heading southwest.

"Listen, this is all very enthusiastic," he said. "But Darkstalker is literally impossible to kill. Invulnerability spells! Immortality! And he can see the future! He must know we're on our way right now."

"Not me," Anemone said, holding out the stick. "He can't see ME in his future. So *I'm* the one who gets to kill him."

"She's got a point," Qibli said. "You and me, we're just going to see Moon and Kinkajou. Got that, Winter? Keep it in your head. That is our goal. We're not going to alter the future in any way that would threaten Darkstalker. We're just going to find our friends." *And give them protective earrings,* he thought hopefully. *I'm coming, Moon. I'll be with you soon.*

"But you *can't* kill Darkstalker," Winter said again. "No ordinary method of killing will work on him, and your magic is useless against him."

"So let's start by rescuing Turtle," Qibli said. "And hopefully Tsunami, if she's there, too. Maybe Turtle's magic will still work on Darkstalker."

"Not a chance," said Winter.

"Your positive attitude is my favorite thing about you," Qibli said to him.

"And *your* long-term planning is *my* favorite thing about you," Winter snapped back. "Why can't we have a plan? Just once?"

"If you have too much of a plan, it'll show up in Darkstalker's view of the future," Anemone observed.

"See, so it's actually better to wing it," said Qibli. "Ha ha, dragon pun, *wing it*. I'm hilarious." He did a little flip in the air. His heart was soaring as high as his wings. They had an animus on their side now — one who was hidden *and* safe from Darkstalker's magic. They had a guide to the Kingdom of Night and they'd be there soon. And he was flying toward Moon at last. Everything felt possible, even defeating Darkstalker.

"I really think we should go to Jade Mountain first," Winter protested. "We should tell the other prophecy dragonets, in case something happens to us."

"No," Anemone said bossily. "The more time we give Darkstalker to see us coming, the more prepared he'll be to stop us."

"When did you start to see him clearly?" Qibli asked.

"Turtle cast a spell to take all of Darkstalker's spells off me," she said. "We were in the middle of a fight, so I didn't really realize what I was feeling at first. But when I was able to stop and think . . . I could see that he wasn't the wonderful all-knowing mentor I'd been looking for. I saw that I'd done some kind of awful things to try to make him like me."

She looked down at the dunes flashing by below them, and then she told them everything that had happened — how Darkstalker had won over most of the NightWing tribe in the rainforest; how they'd agreed to follow him to the old kingdom; how she'd cast a spell to wake up Kinkajou —

"That was you?" Qibli interrupted. "You healed her?"

Anemone hesitated. "Yes," she said awkwardly. "It was Turtle's idea. I guess he couldn't do it without Darkstalker noticing. But . . ."

"But what?" Qibli asked.

"Nothing," Anemone said. "She's doing great. Safest dragon in Pyrrhia. Darkstalker won't hurt a scale on her head because she's Moon's best friend." She lifted her chin haughtily. Qibli let a few moments of silence pass. He had a feeling there was something Anemone didn't want to tell them.

"All right," she said finally. "Here's the thing. I kind of . . . had a fight with Moon, and Darkstalker kicked me out."

"A fight with Moon?" Winter said sharply. "What did you do to her?"

"Is she all right?" Qibli asked.

"She's FIIIIIIINE," Anemone growled. "Everyone is SO OBSESSED with her for NO REASON. It was only a little bitty spell, but Darkstalker totally freaked out and sent me home to kill my mother."

"WHAT?" Qibli cried.

"Stop interrupting and listen," said the princess. She told them about the fight — how Darkstalker was always worrying about Moon and listening to her and caring about her instead of Anemone, so Anemone tried to do a *little* spell that would make him care about Anemone more. But it backfired, and so she'd gone to the Kingdom of the Sea to get a weapon that would kill Queen Coral — "But I didn't," she said quickly, seeing the looks on their faces.

"I don't even know if it was me who really wanted to kill her, or if Darkstalker enchanted me to want to, somehow," she said. "I mean, I grew up thinking I would have to, you know? And I was so angry by then . . . it just felt like the right thing to do. But Turtle stopped me."

She described a flat-out animus fight on a beach, spells exploding all around them. (*That's what tipped Darkstalker off*, Qibli thought, *not anything I did . . . or not just what I did; maybe both together, the spells and then the future changing when we saved the IceWings.*)

And then she told them how Darkstalker had summoned them back into his throne room, cast his obedience spell on Anemone, threatened Kinkajou, and uncovered Turtle — but how Turtle had thrown her his stick at the last moment, casting its hiding spell around her instead of him.

"He told me to look for you," she said to Qibli. "So I ran away, as fast as I could. I don't know what happened to

Turtle after that." She scrunched up her snout as though she was having a lot of feelings she didn't particularly want to deal with.

"He's still alive," Qibli told her. "We know he's in a cell or something like that. I'm sure he's all right. I don't think Darkstalker would kill him if he could find a way to use him instead."

Winter had been flying in an odd pattern for a few minutes, sweeping away and above them as if he was surveying the land below. Now he pulled up on Anemone's left, frowning in his brooding aristocratic way.

"Princess," he said, "where exactly are you taking us?"

"The old Night Kingdom is south of those mountains," she said, pointing to a range of tall peaks in the near distance.

"On the Talon Peninsula?" Qibli asked, picturing the map of Pyrrhia in his head. "But — it's so small. There's no way a whole tribe could have lived there." That was one of the theories he'd had and dismissed, studying the map with Moon while they were in Possibility together.

"It used to be bigger," Anemone said with a shrug. "Earthquakes, avalanches, tidal waves, something something blah blah blah. Darkstalker was a little melodramatic about it, to be honest, like *Roar where did my kingdom goooooooo*, but like, what did he expect? I mean, he's been gone for thousands of years. Of course it's different. Anyway, the tribe is small enough to live there just fine for now, and he was already muttering about pulling rocks out of the sea and rebuilding the whole place with his magic." She made a grumpy huffing sound with her nose. "I was supposed to help him, but I'm CERTAINLY NOT GOING TO NOW."

Qibli suddenly realized that Winter had fallen behind them. He paused in the air and turned, hovering, to face his friend. "Winter? Everything all right?"

"I can't go there," Winter said.

"Why not?" Qibli asked, startled.

"It's cursed." Winter waved a talon at the sharp-edged shapes of the mountains. "No IceWing has ever returned from those mountains alive. They're a legend as old as Darkstalker in our tribe."

"With a poetically ominous-sounding name, I bet," said Qibli. "Peaks of Doom? Mountain Range of Certain Death?"

Winter frowned at him. "We call them Darkstalker's Teeth," he said with immense dignity.

"Seriously?" Qibli cried. "SERIOUSLY? A mountain range called Darkstalker's Teeth, and you never thought maybe the old Night Kingdom was on the other side?"

"It's not like I think about it very often!" Winter objected. "And no, honestly, we all assumed he went around cursing random parts of Pyrrhia as traps for IceWings to fall into."

"What are we waiting for?" Anemone demanded, flying back to them.

"Winter thinks the mountains are going to eat him," Qibli answered.

"I DO NOT," Winter protested. "But I do think they're going to kill me, yes."

"Um, a whole horde of dragons just flew over them a few days ago." Anemone flicked her tail at the evening sky, dimming to purple. "And *they're* all fine."

"Because *they're* not IceWings," Winter pointed out.

"The mountains only eat IceWings," Qibli explained with a straight face.

"STOP THAT," Winter hissed at him. "It's a REAL CURSE."

"If it's real, then it's not a curse, it's a spell," Qibli said practically. "And if it's a spell, then Darkstalker cast it, in which case the earring will protect you."

Winter touched his ear doubtfully. One piece of jewelry against centuries of nightmare stories . . . Qibli could practically see Winter's courage trying to stamp out his childhood fears.

"You'll make it through," he said. "Remember, Moon is on the other side."

He knew that would work, because it was working for him.

Winter gave him a puzzled look, as though he would never understand Qibli. "Yes," he said. "All right. Let's fly."

"Fiiiiiiiiiiiiiiiiiiiiiiiiiiiiiiiinally," Anemone grouched, wheeling about in the sky.

As they flew through the shadowy peaks, with darkness stretching long thin claws around them, Qibli did sort of wish Winter had kept his ghost stories to himself. But nothing reached out to grab them; no ancient spells dragged them screaming into the perilous ravines below.

And at last they flew up behind a towering palace and saw the ruins of the Night Kingdom — now dotted with flickers of firelight, as though Darkstalker had spread his wings out to welcome his new tribe and each flame was one of the starlike scales against the black.

She's here. She's close. Qibli's heart thumped painfully.

"So, King of Winging It," Winter asked. "Are we sneaking in, or do we knock on the front door?"

"We can go in through the room he offered me," Anemone suggested. "No one will be in there, since it's dusty and *dreadful* and unfit for dragon occupation, let alone a princess." She swept huffily up the walls of the palace to a dark balcony.

Qibli and Winter followed as she hopped off the balcony rail and crunched through debris into the deserted room beyond. As Qibli had expected, it was nine times the size of any room he'd ever lived in, even at Thorn's palace. He breathed out a small flame so he could look around. True, it was a little run-down now, but he could imagine how beautiful it must have been all those centuries ago. It looked as though it even once had a running fountain, over in the corner.

His fire reflected off something on the floor next to the tiled fountain pool. He picked his way carefully over to it in the dark and then breathed out again to find it.

He'd expected some kind of treasure, but it turned out to be a strange-looking little contraption, like a telescope with an hourglass attached — but an odd hourglass, with black sand on one side and white sand on the other. He picked it up and studied it in the moonlight. Was this some kind of advanced machine the NightWings had built and then lost all knowledge of over the last two thousand years? What did it do?

"Hey, fire-breather," Winter said gruffly. "Do something useful and light this for us." He shoved a torch under Qibli's nose.

Qibli was too absorbed in the little machine to make a crack about royal IceWing manners. He absentmindedly lit the torch and then peered through the miniature telescope at Winter. It seemed to work like a regular telescope, but then what was the hourglass for? Oddly, when he tipped the whole thing upside down, nothing happened to the sand inside the hourglass. One side held white sand, the other black, and although they shifted around inside their bulbs, the grains of sand never drifted to the other side or mingled together. Maybe it was broken.

"Strange," Qibli said.

"You mean boring," Anemone said with a yawn. The princess seemed to be listing slightly to the side, and he remembered that she was younger than him and his friends.

"When was the last time you slept?" Qibli asked her, tucking the telescope-hourglass object into his bag so he could study it later.

"I . . . can't remember?" she said.

"Do that first," he said, handing Winter the torch

and nudging her toward a blanket that had been left inside the door.

"No!" she whispered loudly. "I want to go kill Darkstalker!"

"And rescue Turtle," he prompted her.

"Right," she said. "I'm very busy. I don't have time to —" She stumbled over the blanket and flopped onto it. "Maybe just a little nap." She sighed as her eyes closed and she curled into a ball.

"Don't go anywhere without us," Qibli whispered in her ear.

She mumbled something that sounded like "Go sit on a reef."

"Right," said Winter. "She'll definitely be gone when we get back."

"Have a little faith in your fellow royal," Qibli said with a grin. "Ready to explore?"

Winter nodded, and they crept out into the hallway. The palace was massive and imposing, but they could hear music coming from somewhere, so they followed that until it grew louder and they saw lights glowing up ahead.

The corridor they were in turned out to lead to a long colonnade encircling and overlooking a courtyard, which, at present, was full of dragons mingling and chatting, feasting and dancing. All around the courtyard, like sentinel ghosts from the distant past, were statues of dragons in black marble in various heroic poses, all of them with diamonds for eyes.

Four NightWings were in one corner playing instruments Qibli had never seen before. It was silvery cheerful music but without the driving excitement of any drums. The smell of food wafted up from long tables around the courtyard — fried bananas and roasted sweet potatoes and wild boar; all taken from the rainforest, Qibli guessed.

Winter and Qibli crept forward, staying low, until they spotted Darkstalker, sprawled across an unmistakable throne, wearing a spiky crown on his head.

Qibli hadn't seen Darkstalker in days, and in his mind, the ancient NightWing had grown bigger and scarier and more menacing every minute. It startled him to see how normal Darkstalker looked in reality — bigger than everyone else, yes, but not cackling with power or dripping with blood or glaring dangerously down at his cowering subjects. He looked friendly, at peace, even a little bored. His tail flicked occasionally in time to the music, and he kept glancing around the courtyard like a host who'd invited all the wrong dragons to his party.

Qibli searched the crowd intently, but he couldn't see Moon or Kinkajou anywhere.

"Is it time yet, Your Majesty?" called a tall, bony NightWing from the center of the crowd.

All faces immediately turned toward Darkstalker as though he were the sun. Qibli hoped he didn't look like that at Thorn. There was loyalty and then there was . . . this, this other thing, something more desperate and grasping.

The NightWings had nothing for so long, he thought, remembering the brief glimpse he'd had of the volcanic island where they'd lived for the last two thousand years.

They lost their homes, their status, their powers. They want Darkstalker to give them back everything they think they should have. They want power to be dropped on them magically, because they think they deserve it.

He inhaled sharply. *But . . . isn't that what I want, too?*

"All right," Darkstalker said, waving at the musicians, who all dropped their instruments and leaned forward in the eager silence that followed. "You're all very lucky. Once again I have found a way to hand out ten gifts tonight."

NightWings clasped one another's talons and whispered excitedly.

"Although," Darkstalker went on in a cautionary tone, "again, in order to make that work, I had to prepare the gifts ahead of time. So these can't be individually chosen, I'm afraid. These are for dragons who can be happy with whatever they're given." He stood up and beckoned, and a bristling female dragon came striding out of the shadows carrying a basket of silver bracelets. She plunked it down next to Darkstalker and gave him a rebellious face.

"Thank you, Fierceteeth," he said politely. "Let's see, is our guest here . . . ? Oh, yes, there you are. Come watch; I think you'll be impressed by this."

Qibli somehow knew in his bones who it would be, and yet he still felt a pit opening in his stomach as he saw his grandfather slither forward to stand beside Darkstalker.

"Who's that?" Fierceteeth asked. "What's a SandWing doing in our secret kingdom?"

"It doesn't have to be secret anymore," Darkstalker pointed out. "We can have normal allies and trade routes now. And this SandWing may be our hope for a truly loyal and helpful ally to the north. Which we'll need when the IceWings decide to unfairly attack us, as my visions say they might. Welcome, Vulture."

Vulture's eyes were avidly scanning the courtyard — cataloging Darkstalker's wealth in his head, Qibli guessed. He ducked lower, unable to avoid the feeling that Vulture's obsidian gaze would snatch him up no matter how well hidden he was.

"These bracelets," Darkstalker announced, "like the ones last night, bestow the powers of superstrength and invulnerability on anyone who wears them. Pretty exciting, don't you think? Now who wants one?"

"Me!" shouted several dragons in the crowd. "ME! ME!" At least twenty of them started pushing forward, clawing their way to the front.

The other NightWings fell back to leave a space for the combatants, watching with laughter or cheers or hisses. Darkstalker watched, too, a small smile curving the arch of his mouth, as his subjects began brutally fighting at his feet. Eventually the ground was littered with defeated, groaning challengers, and only ten dragons were left standing. They were still bleeding and gasping for breath as they staggered forward to the basket.

But once the bracelets snapped around their wrists, each

one stood taller, his or her wounds healed. A new surge of power seemed to ripple through their muscles.

Together, they threw their wings back and bowed to Darkstalker.

Qibli's eyes met Winter's, and he saw his worst fears reflected in the IceWing's pale blue eyes.

Darkstalker was preparing for war with the IceWings . . . and creating an army of super soldiers to kill them with.

CHAPTER 19

Qibli couldn't watch this anymore. He couldn't stand seeing Vulture this close to Darkstalker, the two of them chuckling together like best friends plotting to tear apart the world.

"Let's check the gardens for Moon," he whispered to Winter. On a night as clear as this, he had a feeling she would be outside under the stars.

"I want to watch him a bit longer," Winter said, flicking his tail at Darkstalker. "In case he says anything else about fighting the IceWings."

Qibli hesitated. He didn't want to leave Winter alone — but he felt something tugging him toward Moon, like he was a broken vase and she was the piece that would fit him all back together. "All right," he whispered. He slipped away from the balcony edge. "Meet you back in Anemone's room?"

Winter nodded absently. His breath had left small traces of frost on the stonework of the railing.

Qibli followed the breeze he could feel wafting through the corridors until he reached a grand staircase that swept down into the terraces of gardens. At least, he could tell that there used to be orderly terraces around the levels of the palace, but the plants had rioted in the last several centuries. Vines and ivy had wrapped their way around the stonework a hundred times over, and it was hard to tell where the gardens were supposed to begin and end anymore.

He stopped for a moment, looking up at the moons, and then suddenly he got a strong, horrible creeping feeling along his spine . . . like someone was staring at him from one of the shadows . . . like he was being watched.

He was definitely being watched.

He vaulted quickly over the railing and into a large, leafy bush. Acidly fragrant flowers assaulted his nose as he tried to calm his breathing.

He couldn't see anyone. No NightWing guards appeared, no super soldiers with enhanced sight or whatever other magical abilities Darkstalker might have thrown around.

The staircase was silent. The shadows were still.

And yet he was sure. Something had been watching him. Something that could still be out there, waiting. Some*one*, he corrected himself. *There's no such thing as ghosts. There are no vengeful spirits haunting this palace. I am not hiding from a phantom.*

In these ruins, though, it was all too easy to imagine something unearthly whispering through the crumbling halls.

Qibli crept through the greenery as soundlessly as he could, keeping close to the wall where the vegetation would hide him. The prickling feeling in his scales slowly subsided, and he breathed a sigh of relief when he finally reached a spot out of sight of the staircase.

He rounded the corner and collided head-on with a very sturdy bit of empty space.

Empty space that yelped with joy and tackled him as he staggered back dizzily.

"Qibli!" cried the empty space. "You're here! You're really here! SHHHHH!"

A pair of invisible talons closed around his snout and he felt the flutter of wings around his face for a long moment.

"All right, he's still there," she whispered, "but keep it down, would you?"

The talons retreated as Qibli muffled a laugh. "Kinkajou?" he whispered. "I hope?"

"Oh, yes, it's me!" she said softly. An outline of her wings and face shimmered into view briefly before her scales shifted back to camouflage. "I'm investigating a *suspicious character.*"

Suddenly her talons wrapped around his mouth again. "Shh, he just turned around!"

"Mm mmsbmms chmmmr?" Qibli inquired.

She tipped his head toward a half-tumbled tower that rose out of a swarm of ivy by the edge of the terrace. He spotted a dragon snooping around the base of the tower, picking up anything that glinted.

"I was on a mission," Kinkajou whispered, "exploring the palace, just like that intrepid detective in the scrolls Moon was helping me copy back at school. And then I saw the weirdest thing — a *MudWing*. Here, in the old Night Kingdom! Just sauntering around the palace like it was his own personal swamp!"

Qibli stared alertly at the distant dragon. *A MudWing. It has to be Bog. He must have come with Vulture.*

"So I followed him," she said, "very stealthily, it was awesome, you'd be so impressed, and then he went into a room and closed the door. And I stood there thinking about ways to keep spying on him, but then the door opened and out came a NightWing. Well, that's not so weird, right? So I waited until the NightWing was halfway down the hall and then I zipped into the room because he'd left the door open and guess what? The MudWing was gone. I guess out the window? But I couldn't see him anywhere. So I figured I'd follow his friend over there. He's kind of a big honking NightWing, I have to say. And a little boring; all he's done is steal little crumbs of treasure wherever he can find them."

Yup. Bog. Or rather, in this form, Shapeshifter.

He tapped her claws and she let go of his snout. "Kinkajou," he whispered, "don't freak out. But I'm pretty sure that's the dragon who attacked you in the Sky Kingdom."

Little splashes of startled orange appeared in the air as Kinkajou's scales reacted. "No way," she whispered. "The one who can change shapes? Peril's dad?"

Oh, right. Qibli had actually managed to forget that part of it. "Turtle told you about him?"

"He sure did," she said fiercely. "I owe that guy a few broken bones and a coma."

"We were hoping he'd disappear forever after we took Darkstalker's scroll away from him," Qibli whispered. "But now he's working for my sinister grandfather and pretending to be a MudWing. We need to take away his shapeshifting spells."

"On it," said Kinkajou.

Qibli pounced at the empty air and managed to catch her tail before she darted away. "Not by yourself!" he said. "He's enchanted this shape to have extra strength and super-hot fire or something. Maybe invulnerable scales, too. We do *not* want to get in a fight with this version of him, if we can help it."

"Awww," Kinkajou said. "Can't I just spit a *little* venom in his face?"

"I think your stealth mode is what we need here," Qibli said. "Sorry. Face full of venom can be Plan B."

"All right, fine. So I sneak up and grab — what am I grabbing?"

"He carries his transformation spells inside pieces of jewelry in a brown leather pouch. Last time I saw him, it was tied under one of his wings, so it won't be easy to get. And then he'll also be wearing something containing his NightWing spell." He squinted at the moonlit dragon. "The good news is he's wearing a lot less jewelry now than he was before. But it could be anything — I see an earring, three bracelets, a ring, and a couple of necklaces on him."

"It's the earring," Kinkajou said confidently. "He was wearing all that other stuff when he was a MudWing. The earring is what's new."

Qibli tried to give the empty air a skeptical expression.

"I was being a detective!" she said. "I was being super observant! I mean, OK, I missed the part about how he was actually the exact same dragon, but I did notice the matching treasure. I just thought the MudWing had handed over all his jewelry for some reason. It's not like that makes *less* sense than 'he shapeshifted into a whole other tribe of dragon.'"

"The earring," Qibli murmured. "All right, all I can think of is I distract him and you try to lift the pouch. We might not be able to get the earring, but at least he'll be stuck with only one form instead of seven."

"You distracting him doesn't sound very safe," Kinkajou pointed out.

"I'll be fine. We have a solid Plan B, right?" He grinned and had the unique experience of sensing that the air was grinning back at him.

Shapeshifter had found something in the ruins of the tower and was exhaling little bits of flame so he could peer at it. Qibli let the branches crackle under his feet as he approached, and the NightWing whirled around. His face contorted angrily.

"You again!" he snarled.

"I come in peace," Qibli said quickly, spreading his wings. "I just want to talk."

"That would be wise," said Shapeshifter. "This form could snap your neck as easily as breathing if you come any closer."

Oh, Kinkajou, please be so careful.

"Sure, all right," Qibli said. "I'll stay right here. I just wanted to ask whether you're ever planning to see Peril again."

"Why should I?" Shapeshifter snorted. "She betrayed me. She turned me in to Queen Ruby and then she helped you all steal my scroll."

"To be fair," Qibli said, "you really kind of betrayed her first."

"But she betrayed me more!" he complained. "Besides, she doesn't want to see me again either."

"I don't know about that," Qibli said. "I told her I ran into you in the Kingdom of Sand, and she asked me to give you something, if I saw you again."

"Yeah, right." Shapeshifter took a step toward him, squinting. "What is it?"

"Just an earring," Qibli said. He held out one of the amber and gold earrings, shiny and warm on his palm. "It's not as fancy as your other treasure, I know. But Peril felt bad about what happened. She wanted you to have something that would make you think of her."

He forced himself to keep breathing normally. Shapeshifter stomped another few steps closer and studied the earring with an avaricious gleam in his eye.

"Kind of small," he muttered. "Not very sparkly." He frowned at Qibli. "Looks like yours."

"I bought them both at the same shop in Possibility," he said. "She couldn't touch it herself, obviously, or it would melt. But she said to get one just like mine."

"Hmph. Seems like a pathetic peace offering, after what

she did." Shapeshifter grumbled softly to himself for a long, anxiety-inducing moment. But the lure of treasure, any treasure, was too strong for Peril's father to resist. He snatched the earring out of Qibli's talons and immediately put it on.

"Tell her I don't forgive her, though," he snapped. "Tell her this isn't over and I still — I — hey, what's happening?!" He flared his wings, which had rippled suddenly from black to lime green, and Qibli saw a blur of movement in the air as his pouch was quickly sliced away and vanished behind Kinkajou's back.

"NO!" Chameleon roared, now fully transformed back into his real self, who was much scrawnier and less intimidating than any of his false shapes. "This was a trick! You lying SandWing!" He reached up to the earring, but Qibli lunged forward and seized his talons.

"I'm sorry!" he shouted over the thunder of Chameleon beating his wings around Qibli's head. "Peril let you keep your shapes because a part of her still loves you, even after what you did to her. But we can't trust you with them!"

Chameleon let out a yell and Qibli looked up to see that the silver earring was gone from his other ear.

Nice work, Kinkajou.

"You can't do this to me!" Chameleon hissed, snapping his jaws at Qibli's face. "I'm nothing without my shapes! You can't leave me as a useless RainWing! Where am I supposed to go?"

"Go back to the rainforest," Qibli suggested. "Queen Glory is very fair. She'll take care of you."

"I would NEVER —" Chameleon started, and then a chunk of stone from the tower above them came toppling down and cracked him on the head. Chameleon's eyes rolled up and he slumped to the ground, unconscious.

Qibli blinked down at him, then up at the tower. "Whoa," he said. "That was —"

"Awesome?" Kinkajou finished, popping into view on the tower. "I thought so." She bounded down from the ruins and landed beside him, beaming.

"You were perfect," he said.

"I still think he deserves a face full of venom," she said, "but yeah, that wasn't bad. You were perfect, too. I mean, I'm not quite sure what you did, but it was very impressive."

He hugged her. "It's so great to see you awake," he said. "I was so, so worried about you."

"Pshaw. Me? I'm too tough to be taken out by a superstrong shapeshifting traitorface," Kinkajou said brightly. Her scales had turned the most startling shade of lemon yellow splashed with pink. "Plus, I can't die, because I'm, like, Queen Glory's best friend and she needs me. And Moon needs me to keep her head on straight! And we have to stop Darkstalker! And rescue Turtle!"

"I know," he said. "We will. Do you want to hang on to those?" He pointed to the pouch of shapeshifting jewelry. "Or we could destroy them now. When Chameleon wakes up, he might come looking for them."

"Then I'm definitely keeping them," she said, twisting around to tie it under her wing the same way he'd had it. "I am absolutely up for having a heated discussion with this dragon, anytime he'd like to try me."

He smiled at her. "So what heroic feat should we perform next?"

"I'm still working on finding out where Turtle is being held," she said. "You should go find Moon and convince her to leave with us as soon as possible. Do you think you can do that?"

Qibli's heart thumped as if it was flipping over. "Where is she?" he asked.

"Down there." Kinkajou pointed to the square far below the palace. Qibli saw a torch flickering — and a figure carrying that torch who slipped into the vast building across from the palace.

It's Moon. She's right there right there right there.

"Go on, sort her out," Kinkajou said, and her eyes were mischievous like she'd read exactly what she expected to on his face. "I'll see you soon." She let her scales shimmer back into the colors of the background.

That tugging was taking over Qibli's heart again, and a moment later he was soaring down toward the square, his wings skimming the tops of the wild palace trees.

CHAPTER 20

There were four large structures forming the sides of the plaza, including the palace. This particular one had tall columns across the front that were carved to look like scrolls, holding up the roof. In the moonlight Qibli could see that letters were etched into each column, but the moons weren't bright enough for him to read any of the writing. One of the columns had cracks all around the base and another column had broken in half and toppled over. But for such an old building, it seemed more intact than a lot of the others.

The doorway yawned emptily — whatever door had once been here had either rotted away or been taken for some other purpose. More writing was carved into the lintel: something about knowledge and flames and darkness, as far as Qibli could tell. He stepped cautiously inside, hoping there weren't other, less friendly NightWings lurking in the shadows.

The glow of firelight was coming from one of the rooms off the central hall. As Qibli tiptoed up to peek in, he realized suddenly what this building was, and then he felt like rather an idiot for not guessing sooner.

It was a library.

The biggest library in the world, most likely, if every room was like the one that was lit up. The walls in here were lined with slots for scrolls from floor to ceiling, and the ceiling was pretty far overhead. A vast wooden table filled the center of the room, so large it couldn't have fit through the doors.

Most of the slots were empty — but up by the ceiling, a dragon was flying from one to another, pulling out the few scrolls that were left. She was humming quietly to herself, and the light gleamed off the silver teardrop scales by her eyes.

It is *her.*

Qibli felt as if he could breathe again, for the first time in days. He listened to the song she was humming for a moment, and then he stepped over to the table and began lightly drumming on it with his claws, in rhythm with her music.

It took her a moment to notice, but finally she whirled around, looked down, and saw him.

The expression of joy that flared across her face nearly made his heart burst. He wanted to make her smile like that every day. He wanted to feel like this forever — like a dragon who was welcomed and missed (and maybe something else he didn't dare put into words).

"No way!" she cried.

"Always a way," he answered, smiling back at her.

"Qibli!" She stuck the torch into a holder near her and soared down, landing in a run that threw her into his wings.

He caught her, laughing (and not crying *not crying*). "You're real," he blurted. "I was starting to feel like I'd imagined you." Inside the dome of his wings, her talons took his, and she leaned against him, a mystery of cool scales and strong muscles and beating heart. He bent his head toward her, letting hope wash over him.

"How are you *here*?" she asked.

"Well," he said, "I figured, check every library in Pyrrhia and you'll run into Moon eventually."

She laughed and looked up at him, her eyes shining. "Isn't this place amazing? Wouldn't you live here forever if you could?"

No, Qibli thought, *in these cold halls, away from the sun and the sky? Only if you asked me to.* And then he thought, *Would Winter say yes? Doesn't that make him the better dragon?*

"Come see," Moon said, tugging him toward the shelves. She led him around in a whirl of excitement, describing the old classification system, the archives, the collections each room used to hold, and the giant index scrolls that used to contain the entire catalog of books in the NightWing library.

"The tribe took as much as they could, but they left so much behind," she said. "And we have to be so careful, I mean, scrolls are *not* supposed to last two thousand years — some of these are just fragments or dust — but some are beautifully preserved. We've started copying the most important ones, quick before they fall apart. There's so much *history* here," she said dreamily.

"I haven't seen you this excited since . . . the library in Possibility," he joked.

"That one was great, too!" she said. "Especially because it had scrolls from all the tribes — do you remember we even found that really old RainWing scroll?"

Of course Qibli remembered. He remembered that Moon had shrieked loud enough to bring a stern SkyWing librarian bustling over to grump about how hopping up and down was not allowed in the library.

"This much excitement about scrolls is strictly forbidden," he said in an imitation of the SkyWing's pinched voice.

And he remembered this, too: the way Moon collapsed against him in giggles after the librarian left, exactly as she was doing now.

"Why would you be a librarian if you don't get excited about scrolls?" she cried. "I will never understand some dragons."

"I wish *I* could find them this exciting," he admitted, a little nervously.

She tilted her chin up to look at him, then reached up to touch his face. "Not everyone has to be a scrollworm. For you, other dragons are like scrolls — you love meeting new ones and trying to read them. You're always thinking about how other dragons think and what they're like on the inside. That's what . . . I mean, that's one of the interesting things about you." She pulled back suddenly and looked down. "Sorry. I know you don't like hearing about what I overheard in your thoughts."

"I don't mind anymore," he said, catching her talon. "I mean, if *you* don't mind what a mess it is in there." *Or the mean thoughts I have sometimes. If she has looked all the way into me and still wants to be my friend . . . maybe I'm . . . maybe I'm actually worth something.*

"Least messy brain I've ever met," she said, smiling and squeezing his claws.

She doesn't seem enchanted at all. She seems exactly like herself. But we haven't talked about Darkstalker yet . . .

Moon whacked his side with her wing. "You're distracting me with library talk," she said. "How did you really get here?"

I shouldn't tell her about Anemone, he realized. *Just in case.* He didn't want to lie to her — but he had to, at least for now, for Anemone's safety.

"You're not going to believe it," he said. "Winter remembered that the IceWings call those mountains out there 'Darkstalker's Teeth.' So we thought, huh, maybe the 'lost city of night' is on the other side. And here you all are."

"That's why I'm here!" she said. "I mean, in the library. I'm still trying to figure out the prophecy. We found the lost city of night . . . so now what? Is Jade Mountain saved? Or is there something here we're supposed to get or read or figure out . . . maybe something that Fathom or Clearsight left behind? But I can't find anything about what happened to his friends afterward."

Qibli tilted his head at her. It was a relief to discover she was still worried about the prophecy. (And kind of cool that she'd had the same thought he did, that maybe Fathom or Clearsight had left something for them.) He'd expected that Darkstalker's bewitching would make her think everything was absolutely fine, like everyone else did.

"I can help you look," he said. "But I, um — I have kind of a weird request first."

"Everything about my life has been weird since school started," she said. "Give it your best shot."

The amber teardrop of the earring glowed like a captured ball of fire, reflecting the light of the torch up above them. Qibli cupped it in his talons for a moment, wishing he could add more armor to the spell for her, and then he held it out for her to see.

Moon blinked at the earring, then at him. "Matching earrings?" she said curiously. "Is this a SandWing thing? Are we — um, does this mean —"

"They're enchanted," he said quickly, before she misunderstood any further. "There's a protection spell on both of them — all of them — there are others."

"Oh," she said. Did she seem disappointed? Or relieved? Maybe in brighter light he would have been able to tell. "What kind of spell?"

"I asked Turtle to make me immune to any spell Darkstalker casts," Qibli confessed. "It protects me from his magic — and this one can protect you."

Now she definitely looked sad. "I hope I don't need that," she said, but she lifted the earring out of his claws. "He promised not to cast any spells on me. I want to trust him."

"Even if you trust him, isn't it better to be safe, just in case?" Qibli asked. "It's like the skyfire. We trust you, but you gave it to us anyway so our thoughts would be private. He might cast a spell accidentally — or think he's trying to help, but it's something you don't actually want. You know?"

"I do." She touched the amber gently with one claw, then reached up and put the earring on.

Just like that. He'd expected more arguments — he'd worried that Darkstalker's spells on her would be so strong they'd repel any effort to fight them. But there she was now, safe, with a tiny sun on her ear. Qibli smiled.

"It's a weird feeling, right?" he said. "Doesn't everything feel different? Like the air around you was full of smoke and now it's all blowing away and everything is clear?"

She gave him a funny look. "No," she said slowly. "I don't feel any different." She glanced around the library and shook her head. "I really don't think I had any Darkstalker spells on me, Qibli. I've been confused since he came out and I'm still the same amount of confused now. He's a complicated dragon. I know that. But I don't think he's evil, I really don't. He's my friend."

Qibli stared at her in astonishment. It sank in slowly. *She's not bewitched. She genuinely likes him.*

His understanding of Darkstalker shifted around, like a puzzle box clicking into a new configuration.

Because he genuinely likes her. I bet he wanted to have one dragon in the world who likes him for real — not because of a spell. She's important to him.

They're really friends.

But she doesn't know everything he's done.

Can I tell her? Is it safe? Darkstalker can still read her mind. Anything I tell her, he'll find it there. The spell on Winter — threatening Kinkajou, imprisoning Turtle — the plague killing the IceWings — his alliance with Vulture. Will it put her in danger if he realizes she knows about all of that?

I need to find skyfire for her. Then I can tell her everything.

He shivered suddenly with a realization. *As soon as he sees her, he'll know about the earrings, too.*

"Don't worry, Qibli," Moon said. "We're together now. We can figure out the prophecy and save Jade Mountain. I'm sure of it." She clasped his talons, her face lighting up. "Oh, and the best thing ever happened! Kinkajou's awake! She's all right, Qibli!"

"I know," he said. "That's awesome. And Winter's here, too."

He watched her face intently for a reaction, but she just looked happy. Happier than she'd been to see him? Or the same? Did she feel anything more for either of them? He couldn't tell.

"Our winglet," she said with a smile. "Now we just need Turtle." The smile faded from her face. "I haven't seen him for days. There was a — a problem with Anemone."

"I know about that, too," he said.

"You do?" she said. "How —"

A soft thump from outside interrupted her. They both

turned toward the door, and Qibli heard talonsteps slowly approaching through the central hall. He reached out to twine his tail around Moon's (carefully, carefully, the way SandWings always had to because of their venom barbs). He remembered the crawling feeling of being watched by something in the palace.

But it was no ghost who poked his head into the room.

It was Darkstalker.

"There you are," he said cheerfully to Moon. "That party was SO boring without you. Don't worry, I get it, you don't like parties like that. Clearsight didn't love them either." He transferred his smile to Qibli, looking thoroughly unsurprised to see him. "Welcome to the Night Kingdom, Qibli. I was wondering when you'd show up. I didn't think you'd be able to wait very long before coming to find Moon." Darkstalker winked, and Qibli wondered if he looked as flustered as Moon did.

"This is a really cool library," Qibli said quickly, spreading his wings to indicate the vast space around them. "So . . . am I supposed to call you Your Majesty now?"

Darkstalker shrugged. "You're not one of my subjects, so it's up to you." He wriggled his shoulders slightly. "King Darkstalker. It's weird how it kind of feels exactly right and kind of doesn't fit."

And then he froze suddenly, with his ears pricked as if he was listening to something. A small frown crossed his face. He stepped forward and ducked his head way down to peer at Moon.

"New earring," he said flatly. He shot a sideways glance at the one in Qibli's ear.

He knows, Qibli thought with a twist of fear in his heart.

"Don't be sad," Moon said, meeting Darkstalker's eyes. "You know it's just a precaution. You'd do the same thing, if our situations were reversed. Wouldn't you?"

"Hmmmm," said Darkstalker. "It just . . . reminds me of a bracelet I made for someone once. Because she didn't trust me. Which, turns out, should have been the other way around."

"You promised not to put any spells on me or my friends," Moon reminded him. "So these shouldn't make any difference." She tapped the earring with her claw.

"I promised your friends would always be safe," Darkstalker corrected her. "What if you get attacked and I need to heal you, like I healed Stonemover? What if Qibli gets kidnapped and I can't get him back for you? And all the beautiful magic I've made. No more dreamvisiting? I was going to fly you to one of the moons — dragons standing on an actual moon, can you imagine?"

"Let's see what happens," Moon said, kindly but firmly.

Darkstalker swiveled his head to focus on Qibli. His gaze was intense, and yet Qibli got the impression that Darkstalker was looking *through* him as well — like he could see all the Qiblis that had ever existed and all the ones that might ever be.

He's checking my future.

Qibli didn't know if it would do any good, but he bent all his willpower toward imagining the future he wanted most — and a future that would alarm Darkstalker the least. A future where Qibli was a loyal advisor to Queen Thorn, living in the SandWing palace. With Moon. She appeared in his vision without him realizing it at first. He was imagining walking the palace grounds, and there she was beside him, brushing his wing, and they were flying over the desert, laughing, and they had a suite of their own that she filled with scrolls . . .

He couldn't delude himself that Darkstalker would really find this idyllic dream in Qibli's actual future. But hopefully he'd see only Qibli trying to help Thorn and nothing about Qibli trying to stop Darkstalker's plans.

He wished he knew more about how future-seeing worked.

Unexpectedly, Darkstalker chuckled. He dipped his head to Qibli as if he'd just eaten a particularly delicious goat that Qibli had caught for him.

"Well, do what you feel you have to do," Darkstalker said to Moon, sounding much more cheerful. "Can you come outside for a moment? I want you to meet someone."

He turned and padded away, swinging his tail back and forth to some music in his head.

That was the most ominous thing I've seen him do yet, Qibli thought. *What did he see in my future? Why did it make him stop worrying?*

Moon gave Qibli an amused shrug, like, *well, that went better than I'd hoped.* She flew up to get her torch and they went out through the central room, through the arched doorway, and into the moonlit square.

Darkstalker had paused by one of the scroll-like columns, as if he'd been arrested by the sight of something ahead of him. The expression on his face . . . the closest Qibli could get to describing it was the way Winter looked at Moon sometimes.

A beautiful black dragon was walking through the toppled statues and overgrown weeds of the square. Her wings reached out to brush across the stones, as if she needed to touch them to believe they were real.

She looked up and saw them, and saw Darkstalker, and Qibli thought, *OK,* that *is what seeing someone you love looks like.*

"Moon, Qibli," Darkstalker rumbled. "I'd like you to meet Clearsight."

— CHAPTER 21 —

Moon reacted first, while Qibli was still trying to fit Darkstalker's words into something that had meaning and reality. He could hear music playing from the distant palace, eerie and remote, like it was actually coming from the stars.

"Clearsight?" Moon said in a startled voice. *"Clearsight?* Like . . . the Clearsight from two thousand years ago?"

"My Clearsight, yes," said Darkstalker. He reached out one of his talons and the NightWing came forward to take it, smiling at him. A gust of wind swept down from the mountain peaks, blew through the square, paused for a moment, and then diverged around the two dragons as if it didn't dare disturb them.

"That's . . . not possible . . . how is that possible?" Moon took a step closer, blinking at the new dragon.

How could it be possible? Qibli's mind began hypothesizing. *Maybe he enchanted her to be immortal, too, all those centuries ago. Which seems like something he would do — but then where has she been all this time? Lurking around the ruins? Waiting for him to return? Is she the presence I felt watching me earlier?*

Or perhaps it wasn't Darkstalker; maybe Fathom did something to keep her alive . . . or to bring her back to life if Darkstalker ever returned! That would be an interesting plan. Maybe she's what we were supposed to find in the lost city of night — the only dragon who has ever been able to stop Darkstalker.

He studied her hopefully. Was this the meaning of the prophecy, revealed at last?

Hmmm. She doesn't exactly look like she's planning to stop him from doing anything right now. She looks more like she'd happily set the world on fire if he asked her to.

"It's nice to meet you, Moon," Clearsight said sweetly. "Darkstalker's been telling me all about you and how you helped set him free."

"That's not exactly —" Moon hesitated. "How are you alive right now?" she asked.

"Why wouldn't I be?" Clearsight blinked large dark eyes at Moon.

"How she's alive isn't important," said Darkstalker, who looked as though he'd found literally all the treasure in Pyrrhia. "What's important is that she's here now. She can rule the tribe with me. We're getting married tomorrow."

"That's right," said Clearsight with a dreamy expression.

Darkstalker doesn't look surprised, Qibli realized abruptly. *Even if he had a vision of this — shouldn't he still be surprised to find his long-lost love here? This should be a miracle.*

Not to mention she's the one who betrayed him and trapped him under that mountain. He should be surprised and mad at her.

Instead he looks . . . triumphant?

"Married?" echoed Moon. "After everything that happened with . . . the bracelet and . . . the murder . . . ?"

"All forgiven," said Darkstalker, looking at Clearsight fondly.

There was a pause while Clearsight gazed affectionately back at him.

"And you?" Qibli prompted her. "You forgive him, too?"

"For what?" she asked.

"Darkstalker?" Moon said incredulously. "What —"

"I mean yes, of course," said Clearsight. "I forgive him, too."

Moon and Clearsight regarded each other with mutual confusion for a moment.

"Your visions of the future are legendary," Moon said slowly. "I'd love to learn how you do it — how you can send your sight down each possible path and study all the futures at once."

"Oh," Clearsight said, flicking one of her wings at a moth flying by. "You know, I'm not really interested in studying the future anymore. I'd rather live in the present."

Moon wrinkled her snout at Clearsight. "Seriously? You?"

"She's a little different after two thousand years, that's all," Darkstalker said hurriedly. "This is better, though. She always worried about the future too much. Now she won't worry and we can just be happy and everything will be fine." He nudged one of her wings with his and she nodded, smiling.

"But — I still — how —" Moon started.

"Enough questions. Clearsight is tired," Darkstalker announced. "I'm going to show her around our palace and find her a royal suite of her own. Please join us for breakfast in the morning. We're all going to be great friends. You can come too, Qibli." He ducked his head at Moon and Qibli, then put one wing around Clearsight to steer her back across the square. She waved brightly to them, and a moment later, the two black dragons were soaring up to the palace together.

"Nope," Moon said to Qibli as soon as they were gone. "Nope. No no no. This is not happening. WHAT IS HAPPENING?"

"Very weird things," he agreed.

"More than weird! Clearsight is suddenly back from the dead? With the personality of a sun-dried tomato?"

"Maybe she was always like that?" he said. "We don't know."

"*I* know!" Moon protested. "I've been reading everything I can find about her. I found papers she wrote in school and stories written about her by a friend named Listener. Clearsight was brilliant, maybe the most brilliant NightWing who ever lived. No one's ever been able to navigate multiple futures in their visions the way she did." She flapped her wings at the looming palace. "That's why Darkstalker loved her. He wouldn't love someone like *that*."

"Maybe she's just waking up," Qibli tried. "Or maybe

she's manipulating him to change the future. I was thinking she might be the heart of the prophecy — the one we're supposed to find in the lost city of night."

Moon twisted her front talons together, thinking. "That might make sense," she said finally. "If she can warn us about something so we can stop it. But she didn't even want to *talk* about the future or her prophecy gift." She shivered, and Qibli sidled closer to give her the warmth of his scales. "I'm just worried," she admitted. "Something about this worries me. I mean everything. *Everything* about this is *super weird*. Why wouldn't he tell us where she came from?"

Qibli could imagine a few reasons, but all of them would only worry Moon more.

"I should get back to Winter," he realized out loud. "He'll be wondering why I've been gone so long."

"Yes," Moon said, flaring her wings. (*Don't be selfish, Qibli — you wanted to make her smile. If taking her to Winter would make her happy, isn't that what you want?*) "I'll get Kinkajou and we can all brainstorm about the prophecy. And maybe you can talk her off whatever moon she's on; she won't tell me what's wrong."

A dozen new anxieties stampeded across Qibli's mind. He *did* want to talk to Kinkajou about what had happened to Turtle — but he couldn't do that in front of Moon. He also couldn't take Moon to Anemone's room, because Anemone was there. Darkstalker wouldn't be able to hear any thoughts Moon had about the SeaWing princess, but to explain why she was there, they'd have to tell Moon about Turtle's imprisonment, and THAT would show up in her thoughts.

Arrrrrrgh, mind readers.

"I'll get Winter and come to you," he suggested. "How will we find you?"

"I'll mark our balcony," she said. "You'll know it's ours."

"All right," he said, spreading his wings. "See you soon."

"Qibli," she said, and he stopped short of launching, turning to her with his momentum instead.

Her smile was all the moons and the sun together, warm as gold coins on desert sand. "I'm really glad you're here," she said. "And I think our matching earrings are pretty cool."

"Me too," he said with an answering grin.

It was strange, he reflected as he flew back to the castle, how it could feel like the world was falling apart and yet he could still be happier than he'd ever been before.

Except . . . there was Winter.

Winter, who also loved Moon. Who became his best self around her. Winter, Qibli's friend.

Save the world first. Sort out complicated feelings later.

When he reached the balcony — which took a few moments, finding the correct one — Anemone was still asleep, curled in the blanket and breathing peacefully. Winter was pacing the length of the room, twitching his spiky tail back and forth.

"You've been gone a long time," he said to Qibli.

"I found her," Qibli said softly, glancing at Anemone. "Come with me."

They flew out from the palace and banked around so Qibli could scan the balconies. "Listen," he said to Winter as they wheeled about in the sky, "be careful what you say to Moon, all right? She doesn't have skyfire of her own. Darkstalker can read her mind as easily as a scroll. So I haven't told her about Turtle or the IceWings or anything else. She thinks we're just here to figure out the prophecy, and it has to stay that way until we can find a way to shield her thoughts. Do you understand?"

"I hardly think I need a lecture on discretion from *you*," Winter said.

Qibli spotted movement on one of the balconies — wings unfurling and then incandescent patterns spilling across them, like the glow-in-the-dark stripes on a SeaWing, but spiraling across her scales.

"Kinkajou," he said, nudging Winter.

They dove for the balcony. As they got closer, Kinkajou saw them and waved excitedly. Qibli adjusted his trajectory and speed so he could swoop right into her, catching her in his front talons and tumbling her backward into the room in a giant hug. She erupted in giggles as they slid and crashed into a pile of cushions.

"Ack, sorry!" he said, helping her up.

"Are you kidding? I wish everyone said hi to me that way!" she said, shaking out her wings.

Qibli turned toward Winter and Moon and immediately wished he hadn't.

They were just . . . *looking* at each other. But Winter had a way of looking that any tragic hero would die for. His face was full of such tortured longing that even Qibli wanted to go wrap his heart in furs to protect it.

That's what I should have done, he thought sadly. *I should have tried to put how I feel in my eyes like that, instead of joking around like her goofy friend.*

Why would she ever choose me when she could have that?

And how can I even fight for her, knowing what it would do to Winter if I won?

"I can't believe you two are here!" Kinkajou chirped, breaking the spell. She bounded over and gave Winter a hug as well. "Oh, BRRRR, I forgot how cold you are," she said, jumping away from him and whacking herself with her wings.

"I'm very relieved to see you're fully recovered," Winter said to her.

"I know, it's awesome," she said. "Anemone totally healed me, except it's also *not* awesome because she also —"

"And you," Winter said to Moon, smiling. He reached out to touch the earring in her ear. "Although we can all agree these are hideous, at least you're free now."

"I don't think they're hideous!" Kinkajou interjected. "Hey, wait a second. Why does everyone have a matching earring except me? Is this some kind of secret club thing? Can I be in it? Why aren't I in it already?"

Moon's smile had faded and she was giving Winter a concerned look. "What do you mean, I'm 'free'?"

"Of Darkstalker's evil spells," Winter said. "You see what he's really like now." He paused. "Don't you?"

"I wasn't under any evil spells," she said, taking a step back from him. "He's just my friend."

"Your friend?" Winter exploded. "What is wrong with you?" He backed away from her, lashing his tail until it knocked over an antique-looking vase on a side table. Kinkajou jumped to catch it but missed. The porcelain shattered at her feet, scattering white petals and pointed shards in a spreading puddle of water around her claws. Kinkajou looked down at it with a helpless expression.

Winter didn't seem to notice. "How can you even consider being friends with someone who's completely evil?" he shouted at Moon.

"He's not evil!" Moon flared before Qibli could step between them. "I think he's really trying to do the right thing! He just does it differently than we would sometimes. Why are you so mad? I thought you said you would give him a chance!"

Her front talons suddenly flew up to her snout as if she'd been struck by lightning. She turned to Qibli with an anguished expression. "Oh no. He wasn't —"

"Brainwashed?" Winter said fiercely. "Bewitched? Did I have my mind taken over by your 'friend,' is that what you're wondering? The answer is yes. This dragon you like so much used his magic on me, Moon!"

"You knew right away," she said to Qibli. "But Darkstalker promised —"

"He only promised we'd all be safe, remember?" Qibli said. "Hey, he probably thought everyone would be safer if Winter was enchanted to like him, instead of trying to start fights all over the place. I mean, if *I* had a spell that would make Winter like me —"

This was the wrong thing to say, he realized immediately. Winter whirled toward him, hissing.

"Don't you trivialize this!" Winter growled. "Don't act like what he did is normal or acceptable. He was trying to make me *adore* him. Against my will! Changing my thoughts and my feelings like I'm just a character in the story he's writing about himself. Like nobody else is real except him. If that's something you would seriously do, SandWing, then we can never, *never* be friends."

Qibli opened and closed his mouth. Even when he'd been at his most worried about Winter, there had still been a small part of him that thought the basic idea of Darkstalker's spell was all right. A spell that could make everyone like him — would that be so terrible? He hadn't thought of it as something completely selfish.

"You're right," he said quietly. "I'm sorry."

Winter turned to Moon as if he was ready for her apology, too. She met his gaze for a moment, then folded her wings and crouched beside Kinkajou, helping her pick up the broken pieces of the vase.

"Don't move," she said to the RainWing. "You'll cut your feet."

"I pretty much think he's evil, too," said Kinkajou. "I'm sorry, Moon." She rested one of her wings lightly on her friend's back.

Moon looked up at her, then over her shoulder at Qibli. "But I've seen good in him," she said. "And I've heard it in his thoughts. He has this vision of a peaceful future where everyone in Pyrrhia is safe and happy . . . he wants to make sure it happens. I believe that's what he really wants."

"Tell me something," Winter said harshly. "Are there any IceWings in this blissful future?"

She blinked at him, uncomprehending. "Of course there are."

"Winter," Qibli said in a warning voice.

"No, there aren't!" Winter snapped. "Because he just sent a magic plague to kill every single one of them!"

"Winter!" Qibli cried. "What did we just talk about? Did you really not understand me? You can't tell her stuff like that!"

"What?" Moon started to stand up and let out a yelp as one of the vase shards stabbed her palm. A line of blood welled up, bright red against the black scales.

"She has to know," Winter insisted as Qibli grabbed one of the dark green blankets from the closest bed and ripped off a swathe. "She has to understand how dangerous he is."

Qibli crossed to Moon, took her talon gently in his, and wrapped the bit of cloth around the wound. This was the side of Winter he didn't like — the angry, self-righteous side. It was the only thing that made him wonder if Winter was good enough for Moon. How could he yell at her the way he did, if he really loved her?

"I do want to know," Moon said, touching her snout to the top of Qibli's head. "I want to know everything."

"But it puts everyone in danger," Qibli said anxiously. He tied the bit of blanket together so it would stay and met Moon's eyes. "You don't have skyfire. I don't know where to find more. Darkstalker already knows about the earrings from your thoughts — now he'll know we know about the IceWing plague, too. I don't know what that'll make him do."

Her talon was trembling between his. "So it's true? He really did that? An IceWing plague?"

"Yes," said Winter. "A spell that would kill every IceWing in Pyrrhia."

"Except Winter. Or any hybrids. And I guess we don't have confirmation that it was him," Qibli said, trying to be honest. Winter shot him a glare. "But we're pretty sure."

"I feel sick," Moon said, sitting down and pressing her talons to her eyes.

"We have to do something!" Kinkajou said. "Can't we save them? We have to make him stop the spell — or find another animus who can!"

"It's all right," Qibli said. "We think we've stopped it. If it was a spell from Darkstalker, they should be cured now." He tugged away one of Moon's talons from her face so she could see him smile. "We sent them hundreds of my hideous earrings."

"So the entire IceWing tribe is in the secret club?" Kinkajou said. "Huh. I don't get it, but I'm still offended."

"They're protection spells," Qibli explained. "They make us immune to Darkstalker's spells. You can have one, but I think Turtle already made you immune, didn't he?"

"That's true," she said.

"I don't know what to do now," Qibli said. "Moon, I think we have to get you away from here before Darkstalker sees you again."

"That won't be necessary," said a voice from the window. "*I* have skyfire."

CHAPTER 22

Princess Anemone stepped regally through the doorway from the balcony, delicately avoiding the puddle of water from the broken vase. She had a new makeshift pouch tied securely to her chest, which Qibli guessed must have the enchanted stick inside.

"Anemone!" Kinkajou snarled in the most un-RainWing-like voice Qibli had ever heard her use. She arched her back, turning an ominous dark red.

"Calm down, fruit eater," Anemone said snottily. "I'm not here to hurt Moon. I'm here to help." She turned over her wrist and poked around under the silver-and-sapphire bracelet she was wearing. A moment later, a small, glittering black rock popped out and rolled into her talon.

"Turtle gave me this right before Darkstalker summoned us back here," Anemone said, holding it up. "But as long as I have Turtle's stick, Darkstalker can't read my mind anyway. So I guess Moon can have it." She tossed it to Moon, who caught it awkwardly between her good talon and her injured talon. "There. Now we're even."

"I'm still *really* mad at you," Kinkajou said to Anemone. "You know why."

Anemone arched her eyebrows at the angry RainWing. "I do?"

"Wait, Turtle's stick?" Moon echoed. "Why do you have it? What do you mean, Darkstalker summoned you back here?"

"It's . . . kind of a long story," Qibli said. "But now you can hear it, as long as you hold on to that skyfire and don't let Darkstalker know what you know."

"Make it snappy, though," said Anemone. "I'm ready to go rescue my brother."

Qibli hurried through it as fast as he could — the slate with the messages from Turtle, his trip to the Kingdom of Sand and what he'd discovered about Vulture, Typhoon, and the news about the IceWings. Anemone told her part, about the fight with Turtle and the scene in Darkstalker's throne room, and finally Kinkajou told them the end — about how Darkstalker had decided to put Turtle in his dungeon and then enchanted Kinkajou to forget everything she'd seen in the throne room.

"Except of course it didn't work," she concluded, "because brave noble handsome Turtle protected me. And if I sound a little strange about it, that's because this SEA VIPER over here put a LOVE SPELL ON ME." She bared her teeth at Anemone.

"Oh, you know about that?" Anemone said. "I can't believe he told you! Turtle is such a doofus."

"He's a HERO! With a REALLY KIND HEART! And I CAN'T EVEN TELL IF I REALLY THINK THAT because of YOU. I am so mad at you I could *drown* you in venom!"

Anemone edged away from her. "Ahem, if you do that, I won't be able to rescue him," she said. "And I'm his only hope."

"No, *I'm* his only hope!" Kinkajou flared. "Darkstalker can't see me in his future either! He thinks I'm completely insignificant. So *I'm* going to save Turtle."

"Are you all right?" Qibli asked Moon, who hadn't spoken in a long time.

"Just thinking about what to do," she said, wrapping another strip of blanket around her talon. "Anemone, can you take the spell off Kinkajou?"

"I guess, probably," Anemone said in an annoyed voice. "But I can't right now because if I cast any new animus spells, Darkstalker will know it, and we've already had one horrible hidden animus unveiling. Or, I mean, she could drop her rock from Turtle and maybe the spell would go away, but that's the same rock with all the other spells on it, so she probably needs to hang on to that."

Kinkajou growled at her.

"Well, at least you know how I feel," Winter said to Kinkajou. "Unlike these two." He waved one of his wings at Qibli and Moon.

"I feel lied to," Moon said sharply. "I feel like there's a whole side of Darkstalker he's been hiding from me. I'm just not sure what we're going to do about it."

"Well, *I'm* going to get Turtle," Anemone said, sailing toward the door.

"No, *I'm* going to get Turtle!" Kinkajou cried. She ran after the princess and threw herself in front of the door. "Why should any of us trust you? You've been using your magic so much you probably don't have any soul left!"

Anemone stiffened, her wings snapping back.

"I think you should both go," Moon said. "It sounds like you're the only ones who can, at least safely, without Darkstalker realizing what's happening. And you might need each other's help."

"I would eat my tail before I accepted any help from *her*," Kinkajou said, scowling at Anemone.

"*I* don't mind if she tags along," Anemone said with a little flick of her wings. "But I think we should go now, before Darkstalker changes his mind and decides to get rid of Turtle."

Kinkajou let out a little squeak of fury. "You just try to keep up with me!" Her scales abruptly switched to camouflage and she vanished against the backdrop of the wall. The air around the door blurred as her camouflaged talons opened it and she whisked out into the hall.

Anemone rolled her eyes. "So mature. Like *you* know where the dungeon is." She stomped out after Kinkajou.

"Look for Tsunami while you're down there!" Qibli called as the door swung closed. "Yeah, that's definitely going to go well."

He realized awkwardly that he and Moon and Winter

were alone. *Do they wish I would leave? So they can finish fighting and forgive each other with a big romantic scene?*

Winter didn't look as though he was feeling very romantic. He paced the length of the room, winding between the two beds, the chests on the floor, and the little side tables piled with scrolls.

"Please don't break anything else," Moon said to him. "Qibli, come with me."

"Me?" he said. "Where are we going?"

"To talk to Darkstalker. You stay here," she said to Winter.

"What? No!" Winter said. "That's a terrible idea!"

"See, that's why you're staying here," she said, going to the door. "Qibli?"

Qibli gave Winter an apologetic shrug and hurried after her.

"He could kill you!" Winter protested. "Or he could take your earring and cast a spell to make you kill us! You have no idea what he's capable of, Moon."

"I do now," she said. "But he won't kill me. There are some true things about him, and that's one of them."

"You still think you can trust him, after all the evidence," Winter said wearily. "At least let me come with you to protect you."

"I'm afraid you'll 'protect' me by attacking him as soon as you see him," she said. "Trust me, stay here, and think about the prophecy. We'll be back soon." She held the door open for Qibli.

Winter flung himself down on one of the beds, his face an

icy mask that hid his feelings. He didn't meet Qibli's eyes or respond to his wave good-bye.

Qibli waited until they were at the other end of the corridor before he said quietly to Moon, "I have to admit, I don't *not* think this is a terrible idea."

"Talking to Darkstalker?" Moon said. "It's the right thing to do. I want to see what he says when he's confronted with his lies. And I want to hear how he's justified the IceWing plague to himself. I think I'm one of the few dragons left he'll at least try to be honest with — I mean, about himself and his reasons for what he does — unless I'm completely delusional about our friendship. But I think he wants me to agree with him so he can feel like he's doing the right thing."

"I think that's true," said Qibli. "But if you *don't* agree with him, I'm not sure how long you'll stay his favorite dragon."

"The other thing is," Moon said, "I'm hoping this will distract him long enough for Kinkajou to get Turtle out of the dungeons. If he's arguing with me, he won't be studying the future and seeing it change."

She froze suddenly midstep and crumpled forward, clutching her head. Her wings pressed close around her like a scarab shell.

"Moon, what's wrong?" Qibli crouched beside her, stretching one wing over her back. "What's happening?"

She didn't answer for a long moment, and then she grimaced and sat up, rubbing the spot on her forehead between her horns. "Speaking of visions of the future," she said.

"What did you see?" he asked.

"The same thing as always." She sighed. "Lightning flashing, an avalanche crushing dragons, Jade Mountain cracking and falling. Everybody dying. I've been having it a lot in the last few days, awake or asleep. With the words of the prophecy repeating over and over again."

"Does that mean it's going to happen soon?" Qibli asked.

"All I know is it means we definitely haven't stopped it yet," she said. "Even though we found the lost city. That's something else I want to talk to Darkstalker about. I worry *he* might be the thing that destroys Jade Mountain, but I don't understand how or why."

They were walking again now, down yet another black marble corridor. Qibli wondered if Moon had already memorized the layout of this confusing place.

"His room is just up here," she said, picking up the pace.

But when they knocked on the door, nobody answered.

"I hope he's not in the dungeon," Qibli whispered.

"Let's check the throne room," she said. "He's got natural NightWing tendencies — he prefers to stay up all night and sleep during the day, if he sleeps at all. Maybe he's working on something."

The throne room was also empty, as was the courtyard where the feast had been held earlier that night. They kept walking through the quiet palace and Qibli, oddly, felt his hope returning. There was something about being alongside Moon — it reminded him of the days they had spent, just the two of them, in Possibility, looking for clues about the old Night Kingdom and waiting for Kinkajou to get better or Winter to return. They'd walked the streets together then, too; they'd tossed ideas back and forth and studied maps and taken turns reading to their unconscious friend.

Being with Moon felt to him like a concentrated version of being an Outclaw — like being on a team with someone who really cared about you, who worked with you and made your own brain work better.

Finally they heard a voice coming from one of the smaller council rooms on the top floor of the palace. They crept toward it, listening. It was Darkstalker.

"No, no, no," he said. "That's not *right*. Back up." They heard his claws scraping the marble and the slither of tails on the cold stone. "Start over. All memories intact up to the day before she took off the earrings."

"Hey, you," said Clearsight's voice. "Have you seen Fathom anywhere?"

"Stop," said Darkstalker. "That's worse."

They were close enough to peek into the room now. It was empty except for Darkstalker and Clearsight, with a wall of open windows overlooking the city below. A scroll was laid out on the floor; Darkstalker stepped over to it and made a note in green ink. Clearsight stood watching him with a patient expression.

"The memories are the tricky part," Darkstalker said, half to himself. "But no memories at all is useless. OK." He went over to Clearsight and placed one talon on the top of her head. "Be Clearsight with all her memories up until the day after she met me. But with no powers. Completely in love with me. No worries about the future at all."

She closed her eyes for a moment, then opened them again and smiled at him adoringly. "Whoa, are we in the palace? How did we get here? By all the moons, what happened to you?" she asked, blinking at his size. She went on without waiting for a response. "You know what's weird? My visions don't seem to be working. Isn't that funny? It's very relaxing. Maybe we should go to the beach today." She glanced out one of the windows. "Hmm. There seems to be something wrong with the city. Did you notice? Oh, well, I'm sure it's nothing."

"Clearsight," said Darkstalker. "Will you marry me? I'm going to rule the NightWings and I want you to be my queen."

She laughed. "You can't rule the NightWings. We have a queen, remember? Her name is Vigilance. But sure, I'll marry you. If it makes any difference to the future, I can't tell! Such a weird feeling!"

"Rrrrrgh," Darkstalker growled. "Freeze."

Clearsight stopped moving, frozen in the middle of a laugh.

"Maybe it's not the memories," Darkstalker said, leaving a smudge of green ink on his face as he tapped his snout thoughtfully. "Maybe . . . maybe your power was one of the things I loved about you. Even if it was spectacularly annoying sometimes." He sighed. "Fine, be Clearsight, with all her memories and an understanding of what's happening now, but only able to see the good futures, where everything turns out perfectly. Unfreeze."

Clearsight didn't move for a moment. She stared out the window, reaching toward the ruins visible below.

"Darkstalker," she whispered. "What happened?"

"It doesn't matter!" he said. "It's all in the past. We're together now. We can be happy."

"Ruling the NightWings?" she said disbelievingly. "After everything you did, they —"

"Stop," said Darkstalker, and she froze again.

"This is awful," Moon whispered to Qibli.

"I don't even understand," Qibli whispered back. "It's like she's not real. He's — he's rewriting her, over and over again."

"She isn't real," Moon agreed, "or at least, she's not really Clearsight. He must have . . . *made* her somehow."

"Be Clearsight," Darkstalker said, now visibly frustrated, "exactly as I knew her but without any nagging or *worrying* or *pessimism* or telling me what to do and what's wrong with me all the time! By all the shining moons!" He seized the scroll and ripped it into shreds. "Go on, be her!"

"Oh, poor Darkstalker," Clearsight said soothingly. "Don't you fret so much, darling. You're just perfect. You'll be a wonderful king."

"Why isn't this working?" Darkstalker said to her. "Why does being with you feel so wrong and weird?" He slumped to the floor and buried his face in his talons. "I really *miss* you, Clearsight."

"I'm right here," she said gently.

"Not you. Freeze." She stopped with one wing around him. "The real you," he said miserably to the floor. "What am I doing all this for, if I never get to be with you again?"

"That's the dragon I see," Moon whispered to Qibli. "Underneath the other dragon."

"You're right," Qibli said to her. "Underneath the brainwashing genocidal murderer is a very lonely brainwashing genocidal murderer."

"All right, I know, I get it," she said. "But this is the right time to talk to him. Stay close?"

"I'll be right here," he said, brushing her wing with his. "I'll always be close, if you need me."

She took a deep breath and stepped into the room.

CHAPTER 23

Darkstalker looked up and started violently at the sight of Moon.

"What are you doing here?" he said. "Why didn't I hear you coming?" He touched his head for a moment, then gave her a searching look. "Are you all right? I can't reach you."

"I'm using skyfire," Moon said.

"Skyfire? Protection spells?" he said, looking genuinely wounded. "Moon, aren't we friends?"

"I thought so," she said. "But then I found out you've been lying to me and doing some really terrible things."

He raised his front claws to his forehead again. "All the futures are wavering, Moon. The futures where we're not friends — those aren't good futures for anyone." His eyes drifted to the side, as if he was watching a path unfold. "Something is happening. Something very bad."

Turtle escaping? Qibli thought worriedly. *Is he seeing the ripples from that?*

"This dragon isn't real," Moon said, pulling his attention back to her. She pointed at Clearsight. "I don't know how you made her, but I know she's not the real Clearsight. At first I was worried you'd really brought her back from the dead somehow."

"No." Darkstalker sighed, regarding the silent, enchanted dragon. "Rumor has it that's the one thing an animus dragon can't do. I'd probably need her bones to try anyway. I mean, not that I would," he added, catching Moon's expression. "Because creepy? Right. Creepy."

"But that's why she feels wrong to you, Darkstalker," Moon said. "Because *this* is wrong, this . . . experimenting with other dragons. Trying to create a perfect dragon for yourself. Trying to change someone to be exactly what you think you want. That's not love."

"I do love Clearsight!" Darkstalker insisted.

"Right, and this isn't her," Moon said. "You loved the real her even when she fought with you, because she was always completely herself." She spread one of her wings toward the false Clearsight. "Not the version of her you tried to create. Let her go, Darkstalker. Whatever this is — whatever you enchanted to turn into Clearsight — turn it back."

It's not what*ever*, Qibli guessed with a bolt of inspiration and horror. *It's* who*ever. There's someone else under there.*

Darkstalker looked at Moon for a while, thinking.

He doesn't want her to know it's another dragon. He knows how she'd react.

"All right, I will," he said finally. "If you promise to stay my friend. Always."

Moon picked up a torn piece of the scroll and started folding it carefully between her claws. "I don't know if I can promise that," she said. She looked him in the eyes. "Not if it's true about what you've done to the IceWings."

"What *I've* done?" he said. "What do you — *that's it.*" His voice abruptly dropped into a low hiss. "That's the change. I see it. It's the IceWings. They're — my spells aren't working on them anymore." He whirled furiously toward the window. "Who did this? What idiot — Moon, can't you feel it?"

"A vision?" she said.

"Yes!" he said. "*Your* vision! It's drawing closer — can't you tell how soon it is?"

"I have it all the time," she said. "Every day now."

"I thought I'd stopped it for you! But somebody ruined my plans." Darkstalker pounced on the other half of the ripped scroll and picked up the bottle of green ink. "Tell me what the IceWings are doing right at this moment," he said, upending the bottle over the paper. Green ink poured out, but instead of splashing into a blobby puddle, it spread and shifted into letters that scrawled across the scroll.

"Queen Glacier is dead," Darkstalker read aloud.

Qibli stifled a gasp. *Oh no.* They hadn't been fast enough with the earrings. Winter was going to be devastated.

"The new queen of the IceWings is her daughter, Snowfall," Darkstalker read on. "She has declared war on the NightWings after learning that the Darkstalker has returned and that he was responsible for the plague decimating their tribe. The entire IceWing army is on the move, planning to wipe out the NightWings for good." He snarled angrily.

"So you *did* try to kill them all," Moon said.

"Because I knew otherwise they'd come kill us!" he cried. "There are a lot more IceWings than NightWings right now, in case you hadn't heard. And they hate us. They're going to wipe out our whole tribe, and it's all because of your interfering friends."

"No, it's because of you!" Moon said spiritedly. "The IceWings and NightWings were at peace! Queen Glory and Queen Glacier had worked out a truce, finally, after all those centuries of hatred. We were starting over. But of course they're going to fight back after what you did!"

"They would have come for us anyway," Darkstalker insisted. "As soon as they heard I was alive. That's what your vision was always about — the coming war between the NightWings and IceWings. That's what I was trying to save us from."

"By murdering an entire tribe?" she said. "Darkstalker, you really don't see how fundamentally horrible that is?"

"They started it," he growled. He turned back to the scroll, lashing his tail. "Tell me where the IceWing army is now."

Moon tipped her head to read the new letters that rearranged themselves on the page. "On their way to Jade Mountain," she read. "To demand answers about where Darkstalker and the NightWings are. Oh no." She pressed her front talons together. *"Jade Mountain will fall — the prophecy —"*

"It's too late to stop it now," Darkstalker said. "We have to go fight them, or else they'll come here and destroy the new home we're building."

"Maybe they won't," Moon said desperately. "Qibli told me they're afraid of the mountains on the northern border. Maybe they won't want to come through them."

Darkstalker stopped, looking at her with glittering eyes. "That's right," he said. "My spell to protect the border. That was a stroke of genius. It did an excellent job of protecting our kingdom from invading ice dragons. Well, guess what? IT'S COMPLETELY USELESS NOW." He stabbed a claw violently into the scroll. "Thanks to whatever cleverclaws made the IceWings safe from all my spells. Now the whole tribe can come pouring through to wipe us out!"

He shook his head. "No. We won't just wait for them to come destroy us. We're NightWings! The greatest tribe in Pyrrhia! We're taking this fight to them."

He whirled toward Clearsight. "Go back to the dragon you were, with no memory of the spells I put on you," he barked.

She smiled and nodded pleasantly, and then a moment later, sleek, beautiful Clearsight was gone, and in her place stood the thin and scowling shape of Fierceteeth. She glanced around the room, scowling more deeply in confusion.

Yikes, Qibli thought.

"You —" Moon pointed at Fierceteeth, aghast. "She — you —"

"Gather all the NightWings who can fight," Darkstalker

said to Fierceteeth. "The very young and the sick can stay here safely. The rest should meet me in the Great Diamond as soon as possible."

"The Great Diamond?" Fierceteeth said snippily.

"The plaza below the palace," said Darkstalker, waving one talon out the window. "Go on, fly as fast as you can. And don't annoy me again."

"But what for? What do I tell them?" Fierceteeth demanded.

Darkstalker's face looked carved from stone. "Tell them we're going to war."

CHAPTER 24

Qibli and Moon ran through the palace, flying down the levels, leaping over staircases on their way back to Moon's room. Qibli had a stitch in his side, and Moon's wound was bleeding again, leaving little smears of blood behind them, but neither of them stopped.

"I'm guessing that wasn't exactly how you hoped it would go," Qibli said.

"Well," Moon answered, "at least now he's definitely going to be too busy to worry about Turtle escaping."

"Can we get a message to Jade Mountain?" Qibli asked, panting for breath. "To Sunny?" He shook his head, answering himself. "I can't think of a way. We have to get there ourselves, as fast as we can."

"And we have to break the news to Winter," Moon said with an agonized wince.

"I can do that," Qibli volunteered. "I can tell him. You don't have to."

"No, I'll do it. You go look for Kinkajou and Turtle," she said, skidding to a stop outside her door.

"Where are the dungeons?" he asked.

She lifted her wings in a hopeless shrug. "I'm guessing . . . down?"

"I could end up running around this huge palace for the rest of the night," he pointed out. "Is there anyone we can safely ask?"

"Yes!" Moon said. "I mean, no, but there's a scroll with the architectural plans of the palace — I was looking at it in the palace library earlier today. It'll still be out on the table. Up those stairs, second door on your right." She pointed at the closest flight of stairs.

Qibli hesitated. "I don't want to leave you here. I — I don't want Winter to yell at you again."

"I've heard it all in his thoughts," she said, "and worse in other dragons'. I can handle it."

"Does it make you hate everyone?" he blurted. "Knowing what we're really thinking?"

She tilted her head to the side. "No, Qibli. Just the opposite," she said, catching one of his talons. "It helps me see what's really going on inside everyone. It's why I believe every dragon has good in them." She squeezed his claws. "Some have so much kindness inside, it gives me hope for the world."

Does she mean me? he thought wonderingly. *Is that what she found in me?*

"Find Kinkajou," she said. "Get back here as quick as you can."

He raced up the stairs and found the palace library

immediately. It was only one room, but a very big one, and more than one of the tables had a scroll unrolled on it. It didn't take him long to find the one with the blueprints, though. He fumbled to roll through it, leaving a little tear in the paper with his claws by accident.

There were three floors of dungeons at the very bottom of the palace, it turned out, which seemed a bit excessive to Qibli until he tried imagining what else Darkstalker might do with prisoners if he ran out of room to jail them. He studied the little sketches of stairs carefully and figured out that there must be an entrance to the dungeons right next to the royal throne room.

The back of his neck started to prickle, as if his scales were shifting uneasily. That haunted feeling rolled over him slowly, like curling wet fog.

He whirled around.

And to his surprise, someone was actually there.

"Hello," said the strange NightWing. She stared at him for a moment. "I can't figure out who you are." She took a step closer, studying him with eyes that were neither friendly nor entirely unfriendly. Her face was hard to read.

"Just . . . a friend," said Qibli. "Of . . . Moonwatcher's."

"Moonwatcher," she said as if she were tasting the name on her forked tongue. "I see. Are you a friend to Darkstalker?"

The pause was tense, laden with danger, but Qibli wasn't sure in which direction.

"Moon is his friend," he said at length. "I would say I have some concerns."

She flicked her tail. "Such as? Be honest, please."

"I kind of have to be somewhere," he said, taking a step backward toward the door.

"Then be honest and brief," she suggested, in a tone that wasn't open to argument.

"All right," he said. "Such as the fact that he killed his father; the fact that his seer girlfriend thought he was so dangerous he had to be hidden under a mountain for eternity; he can enchant dragons to do anything he tells them to, or turn them into other dragons entirely if he wants; the fact that he just tried to kill the entire IceWing tribe with magic; and the fact that he's so charming and sincere that smart dragons tend to like him even when they're not enchanted to. Also, I'm not sure there's anyone who can stop him." He kept edging toward the door as he spoke, putting more space between him and the stranger. "I'm not sure there's anyone he cares about enough that he'd listen to them — or anyone who's willing to try."

"I see," she said. "Compelling. One last question. Why was there an angry SeaWing chasing after him?"

This arrested Qibli midstep. "Tsunami?" he said. "Are *you* the one who stopped her? Where is she?"

"I understand Darkstalker has had some trouble with angry SeaWings before," she said. "This one was . . . very shouty. Not terrific at answering polite questions. Confining her seemed like a sensible precaution."

"Where?" Qibli asked. "Is she here? At the palace?"

"No," said the NightWing. "I left her in a convenient cave

in the rainforest while I assessed her threat level. Upon reflection, I would like to let her go," she added thoughtfully. "But she's made some very specific threats. One might call them alarmingly detailed."

"If you tell me where to find her, I'll let her out and make sure she understands it was your idea. I can talk her out of any revenge, I promise."

"That would be very helpful," she said. She held out a scrap of folded paper. When Qibli unfolded it, he found a sketchy map of the rainforest with a little X marked about halfway between the mountains and the RainWing village.

"Is that why you approached me?" he asked, studying the map for a moment before looking up. "Because you guessed I'd — oh."

The NightWing had vanished.

Which was weird, since Qibli was standing in front of the door. He peeked under the closest table, glanced around the vast room, and realized there must be another exit at the far end.

Still wondering what had just happened, he hurried to the throne room and searched the corridors around it until he found an appropriately sinister-looking iron door, coated with rust. It wasn't guarded, which surprised him.

Maybe the guards are in the Great Diamond, listening to Darkstalker call for war.

Or maybe he chose not to post any here because he didn't want Moon to notice them and ask who was in the dungeon.

Three heavy iron bolts studded the edge of the door, sealing it in place. He threw them back one by one, then seized the handle and pulled as hard as he could. With an outraged, grating shriek, the door swung open.

On the other side was darkness; he could see a few stairs going down, but the rest vanished beyond the edge of the light. He blinked, letting his eyes adjust for a moment, and then something slammed into his chest.

He stumbled backward, feeling wings smack him in the face but unable to see anything of his attacker.

"Ow!" he yelled. "Please be an excited RainWing and not something scarier!"

"Oh, sorry!" said Kinkajou's voice. She popped into view, disguised as a NightWing in black and silver scales. It was *very* weird to see Kinkajou's face on a NightWing. Qibli wasn't sure any NightWing in history had ever smiled so much.

"We've been stuck in there for ages," Kinkajou said. "All because SOMEONE refused to stay outside the door and make sure it didn't get locked again."

"Yes," said Anemone's irate voice. The princess poked her head around the door and peeked up and down the hall. "And that SOMEONE is you."

"No, it isn't!" Kinkajou yelled. "It's you! I was talking about you!"

"I got that," Qibli reassured her.

"All right, it's safe to come out," Anemone said over her shoulder.

"I can see more of the hallway than she can and *I* say it's safe to come out!" Kinkajou said quickly.

Anemone rolled her eyes elaborately and ascended into the corridor, tucking herself behind the open door. Behind her, slow and blinking, came Turtle.

He looked older and more tired than he had the last time Qibli had seen him. There were tiny little dried trickles of blood all over him — his face, his neck, his sides, his wings, his tail. For a moment Qibli was afraid Darkstalker had tortured him, but then he remembered the fight with Anemone (and he noticed how Anemone was having trouble looking at Turtle).

"You got my message," he said to Qibli in a wavering voice, his eyes brightening.

"Of course I did," Qibli said, feeling immensely guilty for how much he'd complained about Turtle's communication skills. "We came right away." He stepped forward and wrapped his wings around Turtle.

"Anemone says you made her safe from Darkstalker's spells," Turtle said. "Thank you."

"No, *you* did that," Qibli said, pulling back and grabbing Turtle's shoulders. "You're a hero, Turtle! You saved her and Queen Thorn and everyone at Jade Mountain and the whole IceWing tribe!"

Turtle squinted at him. "Um . . . I'm pretty sure I'd remember that."

"It's true!" Qibli pointed to his ear and then Anemone's. "Look familiar? The spell you used to protect me — it's the same one protecting her. And Sunny and Clay and Starflight and Winter and Moon and all the IceWings. *Your* spell. Darkstalker sent a plague to kill the entire IceWing tribe and *your* spell saved them."

"What?" said Turtle, looking dizzy. "It did?"

"Told you you were a hero," Kinkajou said proudly. She scrunched her snout and rubbed her face with her talons. "Arrrrrgh, I think I'm making a stupid love spell face. ANEMONE."

"Pretty sure your face always looks that stupid, KINKAJOU," the princess snarked back.

"All right, stop it," Qibli said, grabbing Kinkajou before she could tackle Anemone. "I have bad news. Those IceWings Turtle saved? They're *pretty* mad about what Darkstalker tried to do. They're on their way to Jade Mountain, looking for a fight, and Darkstalker is about to lead the NightWings there to give them one."

"Over Jade Mountain?" Kinkajou cried. "Like —"

"Yes. Just like in Moon's vision," Qibli said.

"But we found the lost city of night!" Kinkajou said frantically. "That should have stopped the prophecy!"

"Well, it hasn't yet," said Qibli. "But maybe if we can get to Jade Mountain first, we can do something. With your magic or your magic, if we have to," he said to Anemone and Turtle.

Turtle's wings drooped. "I don't have any magic anymore," he said. "Darkstalker took it away from me."

"Oh, Turtle," Kinkajou said sympathetically. She reached

over and twined her tail around his, then shot a glare at Anemone as if to say *I'd be doing this even without your spell.*

Qibli was horrified. To have animus magic and then *lose* it must be the worst thing that could happen to someone. Maybe even worse than never having animus magic at all.

Like holding a scroll with infinite power in your talons, and then watching it burn to ashes a moment later.

"The earring should fix that," he said quickly. "It'll remove any spells Darkstalker ever put on you. You'll be an animus again." He dug in his pouch, realizing he was almost out of earrings and needed to make more.

"I'm not sure I deserve to be," Turtle said sadly.

"Well, that's irrelevant," Anemone barked. "We're fixing you whether you like it or mope about it."

"She's right," Qibli said. "Sorry, but we need all the animus magic we can get on our side if we're going to defeat Darkstalker." He held out the earring and Turtle took it, his eyes wide and a little blurry, like he was holding back tears.

"Except none of our magic will work on him," Anemone pointed out. "So don't get too excited. Are we going to stand around feeling sorry for each other all day, or can we go to Jade Mountain now?"

"Oh, very compassionate," Kinkajou said to her. "It's so comforting to think you might be running a kingdom one day."

"Come on, this way," Qibli said. They saw no NightWings as they ran through the palace. It was eerily deserted, as if the tribe had vanished again. But when Qibli glanced out one of the windows, he saw the Great Diamond below swarming with black wings and flickering torches. The tribe wasn't going to run away this time. They were going to fight, and dragons were going to die.

He had the map of the palace clear in his head, so it didn't take long to lead the others back through the winding halls and stairs to Moon's room, where Winter looked about ready to explode.

"Hello, nice to see you, glad you're safe, let's go let's go," Winter said, herding them toward the window with his wings. He was the first one to leap into the sky, and then the others followed, one by one. They soared toward the mountains, catching the strange twisting currents of the wind and beating their wings as fast as they could.

Beware the darkness of dragons.

The prophecy ran through Qibli's mind like a drumbeat, pounding darkly alongside his heart.

Something is coming to shake the earth.

Moon's vision was about to come true.

Jade Mountain will fall beneath thunder and ice.

And he had no idea how to stop it.

Ice Kingdom

Sky Kingdom

Queen Thorn's
Stronghold

Claws of the
Clouds Mountains

Kingdom of
Sand

Scorpion Den

Jade Mountain

PART THREE

THE LIGHT OF DRAGONS

── CHAPTER 25 ──

Invisible paintbrushes streaked pink and orange clouds across the horizon ahead of them, and soon the sun rose, a ball of fire that shone brightly in Qibli's eyes. He was glad to be a SandWing, built for long flights across the desert without stopping and able to go days on very little food (*when did I last eat?*).

He could see Kinkajou, Anemone, and Turtle struggling, although none of them complained (not even Anemone, which was surprising). RainWings were not long-distance fliers or accustomed to deprivation; they usually swung and hopped from branch to branch in a rainforest always full of food. And SeaWings preferred to alternate swimming and flying when they had to travel a long distance; not only that, but Anemone and Turtle had both traveled all the way across the continent only a few days ago, with almost no time to recover since.

As an IceWing, Winter could handle the length of the flight, but the heat of the desert clearly wore on him. Still, he clenched his jaw and flew with grim determination, no doubt driven by the danger his tribe was in.

Only Moon flew as swiftly and surely as Qibli, but he watched her carefully and saw the agony that twisted across her face from time to time — the visions hitting like a tree smashing over her head. Once the pain looked so bad that her wings faltered, and he dove underneath her to catch her if she fell. But she righted herself and flew onward, shooting him a rueful "thank you" look.

The long flight gave Qibli a lot of time to think — and think and think.

We have magic, if we can figure out how to use it. Darkstalker's going to discover Turtle is free soon enough; Turtle should start using his magic before Darkstalker thinks of another way to stop him.

But how? What's the best spell?

Could we enchant the two tribes to agree to a peace treaty? But would it be right to magically compel them? Is that any better than bewitching dragons to like you, or Anemone's love spell, or Darkstalker's manipulation?

And there would be nothing to stop Darkstalker from breaking the treaty whenever he wants.

I wonder if Turtle and Anemone could craft a spell to protect Jade Mountain . . . like some kind of shield around it. I wonder if that would stop it from falling. It wouldn't save the IceWings or the NightWings, though.

How many dragons are going to die today?

Around and around went his mind, chasing the same questions.

We should evacuate Jade Mountain as soon as we get there, to be safe. The other dragonets in the school — they should be moved to safety. The rainforest is closest — or Queen Moorhen's palace.

But they were only halfway to Jade Mountain when a wing of black dragons suddenly flashed past them — at least fifteen dragons, flying at twice the pace of the fastest SkyWing. Three of them were carrying something white, perhaps pieces of a scroll or cloth; Qibli didn't get a good look. A few threw the dragonets smirks of triumph as they whisked by.

"No!" shouted Winter, pounding his wings to try and catch them. But it was no use — they vanished into the distance with frightening speed. *The super speed that Darkstalker gave them.* Qibli lashed his tail with frustration.

They didn't talk about it, saving their energy for flight, but Qibli felt new fear creeping through the group after that. What other powers had Darkstalker handed out in preparation for war? How many invulnerable, super-strong dragons were on their way to kill IceWings right now?

What if he had given someone else animus magic? The earrings wouldn't protect anyone from a new animus. But Qibli couldn't imagine Darkstalker doing that. He didn't trust other animus dragons. He wouldn't want there to be more of them in the world — each one was a threat to his absolute power.

Soon after they reached the edge of the Claws of the Clouds mountain range and were flying over the foothills, two of the swift NightWings came tearing back from the mountains and swept past them again, this time without even a glance at the breathless dragonets.

Gone to update Darkstalker on the situation — how many IceWings, whether they have weapons, where they are. That must be useful, scouts as fast as that . . . although I'm sure Darkstalker has magical ways to get all the same answers. This way, though, his subjects feel useful. He's been careful to feed their vanity so they'll love him all the more.

Qibli finally sighted Jade Mountain ahead of them in the late afternoon. At first glance it looked peaceful, the two peaks crowned with golden sunlight and long streaks of puffy clouds above it like dragon smoke.

But as they got closer they saw flashes in the sky, like light bouncing off bright snow — the white and pale blue wings of IceWings swooping around the mountain. Qibli focused his sharp eyes on a nearby peak that was dusted with snow — and realized it wasn't snow. Those were more IceWings, hundreds of them, gathering into formations, ready to surge into battle.

He saw no sign of the NightWing scouts, which was worrying.

Down on the wide ledge that formed the main entrance of the school, he spotted three large IceWings, bristling with spikes and righteous anger. Facing off against them, blocking the way into the school, were Sunny, Clay, Starflight, and

Peril. All of them, even Clay and Peril, looked small next to the tallest towering ice dragon.

A moment later, Winter saw them, too, and let out a hiss.

"Friends of yours?" Qibli asked. "No, worse . . . relatives?"

"My father, Narwhal," Winter said, pointing to the biggest of the dragons. "My cousin, Snowfall, the new queen. And you remember my brother, Hailstorm." He sighed a long breath in and out through his nose.

"They think Sunny and Starflight know where the new Night Kingdom is," said Moon.

"Can you hear their thoughts?" Qibli asked.

She shook her head. "The skyfire blocks my mind reading when I'm holding it. But I can tell from the way they're shouting at them."

That would have been Qibli's guess as well. Narwhal and Snowfall radiated fury, snapping their wings out and rattling their tail spikes as they roared. Hailstorm stood a step behind Narwhal, frowning stiffly, like a dragon in a play trying to be the most serious and menacing character.

As they got closer, they could hear the dragons' voices echoing off the cliffs around them.

"How could you let a monster like that loose on the world and then stop paying attention?" Narwhal bellowed.

"Our entire tribe nearly died and it would have been your fault," Snowfall snarled.

"We didn't let him loose," Sunny cried. "He enchanted us, same as you."

"And we've been trying to figure out what to do ever

since the spell was broken," Starflight added nervously, edging a little closer to Sunny's warmth. Qibli guessed that even without his sight, Starflight must have been able to feel the cold glares the three IceWings were sending his way.

"That's quite simple. All you have to do is tell us where he is." Snowfall bared her teeth.

"We really don't know!" Clay said helplessly. "I don't know how many times we can say it."

"But we wouldn't tell you anyway!" Peril spoke up fiercely. "We can SEE that giant army behind you, you know."

"This is a centuries-old war," Narwhal hissed. "You would do well to stay out of it."

"Fine by us!" snapped Peril. "So go away, then!"

"No, please don't go attack the NightWings!" Sunny said passionately. "They're all under his spell, don't you see? It's not the tribe who tried to hurt you — it's just Darkstalker. We'll find a way to stop him, but IceWings and NightWings killing each other isn't the answer."

"Twenty IceWings died of that plague, including our queen," said Snowfall. "They started this. They're going to pay for it."

"I don't know why you're here yelling at us!" Peril jumped in again. "It was a Jade Mountain student who sent those earrings to save you all. Without Jade Mountain, you'd *all* be dead, so, you're welcome very much."

"Without Jade Mountain, the Darkstalker would still be buried deep under the earth, where he should be," Narwhal growled.

"That's —" Peril hesitated, and they were close enough now for Qibli to see the heartbreaking look that swept across her face. She glanced down at her talons and covered them with her wings.

Clay reached out and rested one of his wings over hers, wincing a little as her firescales touched him.

"Please give us time to find another way," Sunny pleaded. "Let us try to deal with Darkstalker without killing any more dragons."

"It's too late," said Winter as they all landed on the ledge between the IceWings and the Jade Mountain dragons. He bowed solemnly to his family. "Father. Cousin. Hailstorm."

They stared back at him, thunderstruck.

"What — but —" Narwhal turned around to look at Hailstorm, as though expecting that his other son might have vanished. Hailstorm's expression was petrified and trapped and anguished and a tiny bit relieved as well, if Qibli was reading him right.

"You're *dead*," Snowfall exclaimed. Her tail twitched back and forth in bewilderment. "You totally *died*."

Winter spread his wings. "Not totally, I'm afraid."

"This is awkward," said Qibli. "But we don't have time for epic family sagas right now. The NightWing army is on its way here."

He might as well have lit a dragonflame cactus in the middle of the gathering.

"WHAT?" Narwhal and Snowfall roared simultaneously.

"Oh no," Sunny cried, turning toward the school as if she wanted to wrap her wings around it.

"Great!" said Peril. "Now you can go be idiots at each other and leave the rest of us alone!"

Starflight skittered back a few steps toward the entrance, paused, and crouched, gripping the stone with his claws as though he was preparing to hold his ground in a strong wind.

"How much time do we have?" asked Clay. "Enough time to get the IceWing army away from here?"

"We're not going anywhere," Snowfall declared. "We're ready to fight them!"

"Enough time to evacuate the school?" Sunny asked, taking a step closer and looking Qibli in the eyes.

"I hope —" he started, but before he could finish, three NightWings burst from the trees, shot through the air with their claws outstretched, and attacked the new queen of the IceWings.

— CHAPTER 26 —

Snowfall shrieked and everyone on the ledge leaped forward —
but the closest dragon to her was Narwhal. He struck one
of the NightWings full force, killing her with a single blow,
but the other two were only a moment behind, and now he
was between them and their prey. As he twisted to confront
them, they caught his throat in their slashing talons.

"Father!" Hailstorm and Winter screamed.

Hailstorm reached him first, throwing off one of the
NightWings and smashing his spiked tail into the other.
Winter grabbed for the one he'd flung aside, but the black
dragon flashed out of his reach with his unnatural speed and
sliced his claws along Hailstorm's side.

Hailstorm roared with pain and now Clay was there, too,
dragging one of the NightWings back by his tail, and Qibli
darted forward to leap on the other one's back, but suddenly
three more NightWings plummeted from the rocks above the
cave opening, all aiming for the young IceWing queen.

"Stop it!" Moon shouted at them, trying to throw herself

in their way. "Smokeseer! Eclipse! Don't do this! We don't want a war!"

They swerved around her as if she were a rock in a stream; only one stopped for a moment to yell, "*They* want this war! We're defending ourselves and you should be fighting alongside us, traitor!"

Snowfall shrieked again, this time shooting a blast of frostbreath that hit one of the attacking NightWings in the face so hard it knocked him backward. He crashed to the ground and scrabbled at his snout frantically as ice spread across his nose and eyes.

Frostbreath was everywhere now as Snowfall, Winter, and Hailstorm all fought back. A slick of ice spread across the back of the dragon below Qibli's talons, the chill hitting his claws just as he lost his grip and fell off. He hit the ground with a hard thump and leaped to his feet again, ramming his shoulder into another NightWing. Through the mess of frostbreath and fire and scales he saw Moon frantically trying to pull her tribemates back, but they shook her off as though she was a clinging spiderweb.

He heard Kinkajou overhead shouting something about using her venom on everyone. He caught a glimpse of Anemone backing into the school, calling to Turtle. A black tail smashed Qibli back into a silvery-blue wing; freezing, serrated claws stamped down on one of his feet. He heard a roar of pain that sounded like Clay. He tried to fight his way toward Moon or Winter, but they were both lost in the melee of surging scales on the blood-slick stone.

And then one of the NightWings screamed at a higher register than everyone else and a wall of heat swamped over Qibli. He staggered back, covering his eyes, as the screaming black dragon turned into a mass of flames from wings to tail.

"Who's next?" Peril shouted, storming through the fire with her wings spread wide and her tail lashing. "Who else hurt Clay?"

The remaining NightWings fell back, hissing, to one side of the ledge. IceWings were diving down from every direction now, some of them holding long icicle spears, but they wheeled about in the air at the sight of the burning dragon.

"I'm all right, Peril," Clay said, trying to stand before he collapsed forward over a deep bite wound in one of his forelegs.

Peril darted to his side and glared around at the watching dragons. "You all stop fighting and talk this out like Sunny says, or I will SET EVERY SINGLE ONE OF YOU ON FIRE, STARTING WITH YOUR EYEBALLS." She threw Clay's wing over her back and lifted him; Sunny ran forward to support his other side as the three of them hobbled toward the school. Starflight leaned toward them as they passed, and Sunny said something to him that made him nod and sit down again.

Qibli looked up at the warring tribes, all of them briefly unified in their fear of Peril. Would it work? Could she terrify them into bargaining for peace?

But then, rolling in from the west, he saw a cloud that was not a cloud — it was a roaring tide of black scales and flashing claws. It was the NightWing army, with Darkstalker at their head, and they were not here for peace.

The IceWings saw them, too, and rose up from the mountain peaks like a snowstorm whirling backward, up into the sky. On the ledge, Snowfall growled something at Winter and shouted, "Fly! Fly!" at Hailstorm as she leaped into the air. She soared up into the midst of her army as the NightWings and the IceWings crashed into each other in a chorus of roars and screams and furious wingbeats.

Hailstorm paused for a moment over the body of his father. Narwhal lay in a pool of blue IceWing blood, which spread and dripped into crevices and across the rocks, mingling with dark red NightWing blood in ghastly violet puddles. Winter joined his brother, and in silence they rested their front talons on their father's head and closed his staring blue eyes.

"Would you fight alongside us?" Hailstorm said to Winter. "Even after . . . what we did to you?"

"You're my tribe," Winter said to him. "You're my family."

"But, Winter —" Moon tried, reaching for him.

"I'm sorry," he said to her, and then the two IceWings were aloft, racing toward the battle.

Qibli looked around, feeling as though he'd been run over by a herd of dragon-sized camels. One NightWing corpse lay next to Narwhal's; the other dead NightWing was a charred heap of ashes. Overhead, the IceWings outnumbered the NightWings five to one — but he could see some NightWings fighting with the strength of ten IceWings, smashing dragons into cliffsides with their tails and ripping others apart with brute force. He saw IceWings forming lines to create a wall of deadly frostbreath — and he saw some NightWings fly right through it, their scales invulnerable to harm, laughing as they sank their claws into the ice dragons.

"What do we do?" Kinkajou asked, landing just outside the puddles of blood. Her scales had turned dark green — on the RainWing spectrum for fear, Qibli thought from his observations — but shot through with deep purple (determination? he hadn't seen enough of that color on them to be sure). "How do we stop them?"

Turtle limped up beside her, his wings dragging tiredly behind him.

"I don't know," Moon said helplessly. She stared up at the fighting, dying dragons. "They wouldn't listen to me when it was only a few of them — I'll never get through to the whole army."

"What about just Darkstalker?" Qibli suggested. "You're the only dragon he ever will listen to. Could you talk to him?"

Her eyes shifted to the epicenter of the battle, where the enormous figure of Darkstalker was lashing out ferociously. Spears bounced off his side; frostbreath slid away with no effect; claws and teeth and the sharpest of spiked tails left no mark. He couldn't use his magic against them, with every IceWing in the tribe wearing Qibli's earrings, but he could still kill them face-to-face easily. He was untouchable, invincible, and every IceWing he caught in his talons dropped away from him, dead.

"I can try," said Moon. She braced herself to fly.

"No, don't, please don't," Qibli said, catching her and wrapping a wing around her. "If you go up there, you'll be just another NightWing, and I'm afraid you won't make it to Darkstalker before an IceWing kills you."

Maybe even Winter, if he's fighting too hard to see what he's doing — and that would kill him, and me, along with you.

"Don't I have to try?" Moon asked. "My head — the vision." She squeezed her eyes shut and folded into herself. "We have to get the students out — and Sunny, and Clay, and everyone else — before Jade Mountain falls."

Qibli glanced over his shoulder and saw Starflight still sitting determinedly at the cave entrance, trembling but there. Beside him was Fatespeaker, looking equally determined, as though they would both fight anyone before they let them near their students, even dragons from their own tribe.

"It's not going to fall. I'll come up with another plan," he said. His eyes searched the mountain for ideas. The peaks were glimmering oddly in the sunset and he realized they were covered with frost and ice, collateral damage from the IceWings swooping around them. As he stared at them, a NightWing was flung into the cliff wall of one of the peaks with such force that a crack shivered out in the rock from where she struck.

If I had magic, what would I do? If I had Darkstalker's scroll or Anemone's power, I could stop this, I know I could. What would be the right spell? A few possibilities flashed through his head, and he whirled toward Turtle.

"Uh-oh," said Turtle, seeing Qibli's face. "I mean, um, yes, whatever it is. Ready. To do it. That's me."

"Where's Anemone?" Qibli asked.

"Here," she said, emerging from the cave with her tail dragging. "I'm sorry I ran away. That was a lot of fighting at once." She hunched her wings with embarrassment.

"It's all right," Turtle said kindly. "Mother would want you to be safe, and jumping into an IceWing-NightWing war is the opposite of safe."

"No one will be safe until Darkstalker is dead," she answered, tipping her head up with a dangerous gleam in her eye.

"Your spells won't work on him," Qibli said to both of them, "but maybe we can do something else with your magic."

Turtle twitched nervously. "Like what?" he asked. "I mean, I'm in. But what do we do?"

"Something to stop the fighting," Moon said.

"But won't Darkstalker notice if Turtle does magic?" Kinkajou asked, reaching out to brush wings with him. "And what about Turtle's soul? A spell big enough to stop a war — that can't be good for him."

"That's up to you, Turtle," Qibli said. "The earring will keep you safe from Darkstalker's spells, but he's dangerous in other ways, too. And we all care about keeping your soul safe, so if you're worried about it at all, you don't have to do any of this."

"I want to do *something*," Turtle said firmly, setting his jaw. "Just tell me what."

"Well — what if we put an invisible wall between the IceWings and the NightWings?" Qibli suggested. "Something that won't let any attacks through."

"There's nowhere to put one at this point," Moon said, pointing to the melee in the sky. "They're all over the place."

Anemone flicked her tail. "Anything we do, Darkstalker will find a way around it."

"How about a message?" Qibli climbed onto one of the rocks, trying to scrape the blood off his talons. "A telepathic message to all the NightWings that seems to come from Darkstalker, telling them to retreat? They'd believe he could do that, wouldn't they?"

"Let's try it," said Turtle. "I'll do it."

"No, I'll do the message," Anemone said. "I can sound way more like Darkstalker than you can. You just stand next to me so he thinks it's coming from you when he feels the magic happening."

"Right, you're right," he said, nodding. He fidgeted in an awkward circle, searching the ground, and finally picked up a scrap of moss that had been clawed off one of the closest rocks during the fight. "Here, you can use this," he suggested.

Anemone wrinkled her nose at it. "A pile of dirt?" she said. "Doesn't anyone have any jewelry or something I could enchant instead?"

"It only needs to last long enough to work once," Qibli said. "Nothing fancy."

"Fine." Anemone clasped it between her talons, shuddering theatrically at how damp it was, and closed her eyes. Turtle sat down beside her with an anxious expression.

Moon climbed up beside Qibli and twined her tail around his. He could feel her heartbeat through her scales as they leaned into each other, watching the battle overhead.

"Please let this work," Moon prayed softly. "Please stop fighting."

Qibli saw Fearless, one of the dragonets from school, darting through the battle, slamming dragons aside with her tail. He remembered she was the first dragon to be gifted with superstrength by Darkstalker, and he saw with dismay that she was using it to cut a swathe through the IceWings. She threw a pale blue dragon into Jade Mountain with a crack that echoed off the peaks and sent a small avalanche tumbling down into a crevasse.

Then Fearless turned and lunged at a silver dragon who looked as young as she was, a skillful fighter with blue scales freckling her snout — but Winter shot across her path before Fearless reached her, spraying frostbreath on Fearless's wing. The NightWing let out an agonized roar and crash-landed on the nearest stretch of mountain, where she dragged herself into the shelter of a small cave.

Elsewhere in the sky, Hailstorm was struggling with two NightWings who were dive-bombing him, flames blazing from their mouths. Qibli glanced uneasily back at Anemone. She looked as though she was concentrating as hard as she could.

Moon grabbed one of his talons, inhaling sharply, and he looked up again. Winter had flown up beside Hailstorm and they were trying to drive off the NightWings together, fighting back to back.

Suddenly the NightWings darted away, shaking their heads slightly with confused expressions. They looked at one another, then over at Darkstalker — whose head snapped up. Darkstalker threw four IceWings aside and slammed his tail into the cliffside of another mountain. A rain of boulders fell around him and he deftly caught the largest one.

Without even a pause, he whirled in the same motion and flung the enormous rock with all his strength — straight at Turtle and Anemone.

"No!" Qibli shouted, leaping to his feet.

He was too slow. He felt the wind of its passage as it shot past him like a plummeting comet and he heard the impact as it smashed into the SeaWings.

Moon screamed.

One of the NightWings was whispering in Darkstalker's ear now. Darkstalker lifted his snout and yelled, "It's a trick, NightWings! Hold the line! Don't be fooled!"

The NightWings surged forward again with vicious new energy. But Qibli barely noticed; he crouched beside the boulder with Moon, trying frantically to dig under it or push it aside or anything useful.

Did I just get them both killed? he thought in a rising panic.

Finally he and Moon got their talons underneath the rock

and heaved up together. It clunked aside with an ear-rattling scrape, and Qibli saw Turtle lying underneath, his wings spread to cover Anemone.

"Turtle?" he cried. "Are you dead?"

"No," Turtle said in a raspy full-of-rock-dust voice. "I'm all right. Anemone?"

"I'm fine!" she called from under him. "Except that I have a great galumphing brother on top of me! Get off already, kelp-breath."

"But how?" Moon asked. "That rock was heavy enough to kill you. I really thought —" She took a breath, fighting back tears.

"I kind of accidentally made my scales invulnerable a couple of days ago," Turtle said, stretching out his wings and standing up. "When somebody *else* tried to drop a rock on me." He winced; apparently something could still hurt.

"Well, you're welcome," Anemone said to him. "Anyway, so much for that plan," she said to Qibli. "If we do any other spells, they better work, because he'll notice us and kill us super quick and probably more effectively this time."

Qibli's head was pounding. What else could they do? Was there anything that wouldn't put Anemone and Turtle in danger? They needed new magic, magic that could compete with Darkstalker's.

The setting sun flashed into his eyes, reflecting off the copper around his wrists.

The weather bracelets.

The only magic he had.

It had been a disaster last time, at the SandWing palace —
but what other choice was there? If he could call a big
enough storm, surely that would stop the battle. A well-
placed lightning bolt might even knock out Darkstalker, if
they were lucky.

He took a deep breath and raised his talons toward
the sky.

CHAPTER 27

A savage gust of wind whipped down from the north, scattering dragons right and left.

"What are you doing?" Moon whispered.

"Calling a storm," Qibli answered. "A big one." The air felt as if it was crackling around his claws. He felt stronger this time, more sure. He could sense heavy clouds in the distance, to the north. He just had to reach for them and pull them over Jade Mountain. They would come looming down, a third army crashing the war.

Then the rain would fall and the lightning would flash and thunder would roll over the battle and the dragons would all . . .

The dragons would . . .

His gaze fixed on the sky, he felt more than saw Moon crumpling beside him, her talons clutching her head as she cried out with pain. A flash of white and orange in his peripheral vision was Kinkajou darting forward to catch her friend, shouting "Moon! Moon, are you all right?"

Thunder.

Jade Mountain will fall beneath thunder and ice.

No oh no oh no . . .

It's ME.

He jerked his talons back in toward his chest, dread surging through him.

I'm the one who brings the thunder. If I do this, I make Jade Mountain fall.

The sky was already darkening, early evening stars blotted out by the incoming clouds. Qibli stumbled backward off the rock. *Go back!* he thought desperately at the storm. *Go away! I don't want you! I didn't mean it!*

He clawed at the bracelets, stabbing the tiny clasp over and over again until one snapped open and clanked to the ground, and then the other.

"Tell the storm to go away," he cried, shoving the bracelets at Anemone. "Make it leave! Quick!"

"Why?" she asked. "I think a storm is a good idea." She caught the bracelets, blinking at the panic on his face.

"No!" he shouted over the rising wind. "The storm is the thunder in the prophecy! That's what brings down the mountain!" He pointed to the trembling peaks overhead, the ice, the cracks, the avalanches ready to fall on the turn of a dagger. "Can you stop it?"

The SeaWing princess nodded, finally understanding. She slid the bracelets onto her own wrists and curled her claws in, murmuring to herself.

Qibli ran over to Starflight and Fatespeaker. "We have to

get the students out!" he called. "I'm worried about the mountain!"

"Isn't it safer inside than trying to fly through a war?" Fatespeaker shouted. Her claws dug into the ground as the wind tried to batter her off the ledge.

"Not right now," Qibli said, shielding them with his wings so they could hear each other. "Is there another way out, on the other side of the mountain?"

"Through Stonemover's cave," Starflight suggested.

"Flame is still in there," Fatespeaker reminded him. "Trapped. Angry."

"And possibly doomed unless we get him out," Qibli said. He tipped an earring out of his pouch and pressed it into Starflight's talons. "Offer him this. Tell him it'll free him from Darkstalker's spells, including the stone cuffs. That means his face will go back to the way it was. But if Darkstalker cast any secret spells on his mind, he'll be freed from those as well. That's a trade I would gladly take."

He hesitated. "I don't know how to free Stonemover from the wall, though," he said. "I think he has to choose that for himself, if he wants to escape."

Starflight spread one wing instinctively toward Fatespeaker and she lifted hers to rest underneath it so she could lead him into the school.

"You'll get to safety, too?" Starflight said to Qibli. "You and the others?"

"Especially the SeaWing princess," Fatespeaker said with

a slight eye roll. "We'll be in all sorts of trouble if a single one of her scales is harmed."

"Don't worry about us," Qibli said.

Starflight let out a small laugh. "You make that quite impossible," he said.

"Oh, and take this, just in case," Qibli said, giving Starflight the map from the strange NightWing in the palace library. "This is where Tsunami is — she's a prisoner in the rainforest. She's safe, but she needs rescuing. And tell her no revenge! Her captor sent us to let her out."

"Rescuing Tsunami? That'll be fun," Fatespeaker said.

Qibli watched the two of them run into the mountain. Fear shivered along his spine and out to the tips of his wings. He hoped everyone would get to safety. He hoped the school would survive. After everything that had already happened here, if it all ended in an avalanche and devastation, what hope would there ever be for a school like this again? Would any of the tribes be willing to send their dragonets to a second grand experiment? Wouldn't they blame Sunny and Clay and the others, no matter who survived . . . or didn't?

He dashed back to Moon and Kinkajou, who were huddled together with Turtle against the fat raindrops that were starting to fall. Anemone stood beside them, waving her talons at the clouds.

Moon looked up at him, the wind whipping her wings and tail back. She had a really odd expression on her face, as if the agony of the prophecy vision had suddenly popped and meerkats had come cartwheeling out of the cracked mountain instead of death.

"What is it?" Qibli asked her. "What happened?"

"I don't know," she said. "I caught a glimpse of a new vision, I think, but a strange one." She shook her head. "It was a dragon, someone I've never seen before."

"What was he doing? Joining the battle? Was he a SandWing?" Qibli narrowed his eyes at the sky, wondering if Vulture was up there somewhere . . . or if not, where he was and what evil he was plotting.

"No, he was — he was picking strawberries," Moon said.

Qibli stared at her for a moment.

"Evil strawberries?" he asked finally.

"I don't think so," she said with a hint of a smile. "I know, it was strange. Probably not worth mentioning."

But he knew it must have felt important to her. He'd spend more time puzzling over it later . . . if they had a later.

"I think we should move away from Jade Mountain," he said. "Just in case."

"No need," Anemone said, tossing her head triumphantly. "I'm winning. Off you go, storm clouds." She flicked her wings at the sky.

She was right. The raindrops were slowing and the wind was dying down. Glimmers of starlight were visible through the thinning clouds. The sun was almost down now, rendering many of the NightWings impossible to see, but Qibli could still make out the vast shape of Darkstalker, lifting his head to scent the air.

Does he sense the storm retreating? Does he know I stopped myself from using the bracelets? Did he know that was part of the prophecy?

Is that what he saw in my future in the library — me bringing down Jade Mountain? Is that what he wanted me to do?

He didn't think I'd be able to stop myself. He also didn't know Anemone would be here.

"We still have to stop the fighting," Moon said. She reached into the pouch around her neck and drew out the skyfire. The rock looked more than ever like a piece of a fallen star, winking enigmatically in her talons. "If I put this down, I can reach Darkstalker's mind. I'll try to talk him into ending the battle." She sighed. "It seems kind of fitting that this started with us talking in our minds, and maybe that's how it'll end, too."

"But there are so many dragons here," Qibli said, catching her talon and closing her claws around the rock. "Angry dragons, violent dragons, injured and dying dragons. Won't it be overwhelming? Won't it hurt you, to have all their minds flooding into yours right now?"

"Maybe," she said, "but it's what I have to do." She tugged herself out of his grip and carefully placed the skyfire on top of the jagged tooth of a boulder beside her.

Qibli could see the tension whiplashing through her muscles as the thoughts of hundreds of warring dragons clashed and clawed at one another inside her head. Moon slowly sank to the ground, her wings spreading around her like a carpet of fallen leaves, her palms pressed against her eyes.

I hope she comes out of this still thinking there's good in other dragons.

I wonder if she's right, or if she sees us that way because that's how she is.

I wonder if those dragons up there would fight like this if they could read each other's minds. If everyone could feel what she's feeling — if they understood all the other dragons around them — would they still be able to kill each other?

A tremor shivered through his wings.

What if that's the way to peace?

What if the way to change other dragons isn't a spell that forces them to like you or makes them do what you want?

What if it's opening them up to other minds and letting them decide for themselves?

"I have an idea," he said to Turtle, who jumped slightly.

"Oh, good," said Turtle. "Because I don't have any, apart from stand here and try not to die."

"It's another spell," Qibli said. "One that Darkstalker won't be able to counteract, I hope, at least not right away."

"We want the IceWings to win, don't we?" Anemone interjected. "What if we give all of THEM superstrength! That would make it fair, at least."

"No, no," Qibli said. "We don't want to make the war worse. We want to end it, for good, forever, with no more dragons dying." He put one talon on Turtle's shoulder. "Can you do one more spell?"

"Yes," Turtle said solidly. "Or more. Whatever you need."

"No," Anemone jumped in. "I should do it. Darkstalker

can't see me in his future. He won't see it coming if I'm the one to cast it." She shot a look at Turtle and then down at her feet. "Besides, there's still hope for Turtle's soul. We shouldn't waste it."

Qibli cleared the leaves from a patch of dirt with his tail. He used his claw to write out the spell, erasing and rewriting it until it was the way he wanted it.

While he was working on it, Turtle bumped his shoulder against Anemone's and ducked his head to meet her eyes.

"It's not too late for your soul," he said to her. "You're here now, with us. You're on the right side, doing the right thing. You're not evil."

"Maybe a tiny bit evil," Kinkajou muttered.

"I'm here because I want to destroy Darkstalker," Anemone said. "That doesn't exactly make me the most heroic dragon in the world. Come on, sea snail, aren't you done yet?" she said to Qibli.

He nodded down at the spell. "That's it," he said. "I think. I hope it'll work."

"Can we trust her?" Kinkajou asked. "What if she randomly decides to make all the IceWings fall in love with Winter or something?"

"You are so ungrateful," Anemone said huffily. "I was just trying to do something nice for my brother because of his enormous crush on you. I was *trying* to make your love lives a little happier. And all I get for it is whine whine whine."

"You don't get to decide who I'm in love with!" Kinkajou cried, her scales rippling scarlet and lavender.

"Could we have this fight later?" Qibli asked.

"Yes, pipe down," Anemone said to Kinkajou, who bared her teeth furiously. "I'm saving the world right now. Although this spell is super weird, SandWing."

"Just do it, please, Anemone, or let me," said Turtle.

"I need a thing to enchant," she said.

Qibli felt in his pouch and took out his library card from school. "Here, might as well use this," he said.

Anemone held it up gingerly in one talon and leaned over to read what Qibli had written in the dirt.

"I enchant this object to connect the minds of all the dragons in the battle overhead for the space of a hundred dragon heartbeats," she said aloud, "so that they feel what every other dragon is feeling as completely as they feel their own emotions, and know exactly whose feelings they're experiencing. When that time is up, they will return to normal, and at that moment I enchant this object to instantly transport all the IceWings to the main palace of the Ice Kingdom and all the NightWings to the Great Diamond in the Night Kingdom, safe and unharmed."

Anemone's eyes flicked up to her brother for a moment. "And while we're at it," she added, "I also enchant this object to take the love spell off Kinkajou, so she can feel whatever incredibly special feelings she wants to feel about absolutely anyone and stops annoying me about it."

Turtle gave her a wordless, grateful smile. Kinkajou just looked startled.

Qibli tipped his head back to watch the fighting dragons.

Something was rippling through them. It took a few moments to sink in, but he could see the attacks faltering, the claws pulling back, the confusion on every face.

He felt Moon rise to her feet beside him, her expression suddenly clear and peaceful. She took a breath and words spilled out of her, just like the time she'd spoken the Jade Mountain prophecy, but spinning and tumbling faster and free like cactus blossoms in the wind.

"I see her dragonets, waiting in fear back in the Night Kingdom. I feel her terror that she'll never see them again. She's fighting to protect them. She thinks I want to kill them and she has to kill me first.

"I see his mother, dying of the plague that Darkstalker sent. He loved her as much as I loved my mother. He wants to stop us before we kill any more of his family.

"I see years of hunger and fear; I see a volcano seething with danger; I see the endless struggle for survival and the constant worry that his beloved tribe would die out forever. I see hope arrive in the form of a dragon who promises everything, who promises all the glory and power the tribe used to have in a place of safety and beauty. I see him fighting to protect it because he needs that hope.

"I see her in an IceWing nursery, listening to the ancient tales of Darkstalker and the NightWings with wide, frightened eyes. I see her nightmares, I hear the stories that run through the tribe about how many IceWings Darkstalker killed even after his supposed death. I see her study the scrolls about NightWings, wondering when they will take the animus gift they stole, break through the Great Ice Cliff, and wipe out the entire IceWing tribe because they hate them and have always hated them.

"But you hated us first.

"You hated us first.

"You want to kill us all.

"You want to kill us all.

"I'm afraid of you.

"I'm afraid of you.

"I'm afraid, and that is why I fight."

Silence fell. The hundred heartbeats were up.

The NightWings and IceWings faced one another for a long moment.

And then they all vanished from the sky.

— CHAPTER 28 —

"They're gone," Kinkajou said wonderingly.

"Oops," said Turtle, scanning the sky. "I think we might have zapped Winter back to the Ice Kingdom along with everyone else."

"Are they gone for good?" Kinkajou asked. "Or will they come flying right back? Did we end the war, or just postpone it?"

"If I understood their thoughts correctly," said Moon, "I think those dragons will have a hard time killing one another from now on."

"We did it," Qibli breathed.

"*You* did it," said Moon. She turned toward him with shining eyes.

"He certainly did," said Darkstalker, swooping down out of the sky. He seized Qibli in his talons with startling speed and shot away on his enormous wings.

"Qibli!" Moon shouted.

It happened too fast for Qibli to react. Massive claws dug into his chest, holding him just tightly enough to let him know that with the slightest bit more pressure, he'd be dead. His wings were pinned to his back in an uncomfortable twisted position; he could tell if he struggled too much he might sprain one of them. His tail swung free, but he knew that stabbing Darkstalker's invulnerable scales with his venom barb would be useless. He could see the ground rushing by far below him, or if he craned his neck around he could see the line of icy white scales under Darkstalker's beating black wings.

Where is he taking me? Why not just kill me?

Darkstalker was huge, but carrying an entire dragonet in his talons still had to be exhausting for him. He wouldn't be able to go far — Qibli hoped.

Sure enough, it wasn't long before Darkstalker banked suddenly and dove. Qibli's eyes stung in the rush of wind. The earth seemed to be hurtling up toward him and he wondered if this was how he was going to die: smashed into the dirt by a vengeful monster from the past.

Then he saw a gaping maw ahead: a mouth studded with rocks and drooling splintered trees. The crevasse gouged out a piece of mountain and went too deep to see the bottom, at least from Qibli's dizzy, spinning point of view.

Apparently he would see the bottom, though. Darkstalker plummeted straight into the fissure and down, spiraling as the walls narrowed in around them. Qibli's suppressed claustrophobia rushed over him. Dying in a dark cave, where the sun and wind would never touch his scales again, was a recurring nightmare of his.

Is he taking me somewhere to kill me out of sight? So Moon doesn't have to see it?

The light had faded to a small line overhead when Darkstalker slowed and dropped Qibli the last short distance to the ground at the bottom of the gorge. The stone was smooth and cold under Qibli's talons as he stood up shakily.

Darkstalker sat on an outcropping just above him, blocking the route to the sky. He plucked a stone from the cliff wall and conjured it into a compact ball of flames, setting it spinning beside him like a haunted imitation of the sun. The glow illuminated a cramped crawl space behind Qibli, barely large enough for a dragon the size of Darkstalker to turn around if he squashed his wings in and stood on his own tail as he did it.

All around Qibli were claw marks in the stone, hundreds upon hundreds of scratches, some of them firm and bold, others tiny and slanted to fit in around the others. A discarded scrap of rusty metal wires lay near the opening, frayed and looped around a trio of misty white gemstones.

His tail brushed something the size of a tooth. When Qibli bent to pick it up, it turned out to be a mouse skull rubbed almost smooth as velvet.

"One thing I like about you," Darkstalker said conversationally, "is that I don't have to waste a lot of time on tedious explanations. I drop you somewhere and your brain goes clickity-click and a moment later, you know where we are and we can get on with the interesting bits."

"This is the cave Clearsight left you in," Qibli said. "Where you were buried for thousands of years. That's the broken bracelet." He nudged the fragment of wires — such a small, fragile thing to hold back such a powerful danger. Qibli lifted a claw to touch one of the scratches. "And these are the number of days you were awake down here before Peril set you free."

Darkstalker flicked his tail at the skull in Qibli's talons. "And that leftover from my only dinner was also my only friend in the world, until I heard Moon's thoughts overhead and realized another mind reader was finally nearby."

"Did you bring me down here to make me feel sorry for you?" Qibli asked incredulously.

Darkstalker's mouth quirked into a small half smile. "Well, that empathy spell of yours was so effective on my subjects," he said. "I figured it couldn't hurt for you and I to understand each other a little better."

"It wasn't my spell," Qibli said, tracing the tiny eyeholes of the mouse skull.

"Let's be serious." Darkstalker nudged the floating sun a little closer to him. "That was *your* spell. You lack the magic, but you have the ideas."

Qibli didn't answer.

"You have the brains to be a great animus dragon, but Turtle has the power instead," Darkstalker observed. "I know that's frustrating for you."

There was a pause.

"I've noticed something," Darkstalker said a little more quietly. "You're just like me, Qibli. Maybe even as smart as me; certainly smarter than everyone else. You have big ideas and lots of them, not just one or two in a lifetime like some dragons. You want to change things — all the things that are wrong with the world. You know you could do it, if you had the chance."

"I'm *not* like you," Qibli interrupted. "I'm not a murderer."

"Oh, but you would be, under the right conditions," Darkstalker said, waving this off. "To protect your queen, to save your tribe, or if it would make Moon love you."

"That's not true," said Qibli. "She wouldn't love a murderer."

"Sure she would." Darkstalker looked amused. "You don't think she would love a dragon who had to kill someone in order to save Kinkajou — just for one example? Or what if you figure out how to kill me?" The amusement faded from his face. "Wouldn't she still love you then?"

"Do I figure out how to kill you, in the future?" Qibli asked, avoiding Darkstalker's question and the other questions that spiraled out of it, inside him. "Is that why you brought me here, to stop that from happening?"

Darkstalker chuckled. "No, no. There's no future in which I die. That's impossible. But there are futures where I go about my business peacefully, and there are futures where certain clever gnats continue to annoy me for an interminable length of time."

"Something to aspire to," said Qibli. "Annoying, clever gnat-ness."

Darkstalker pointed a talon at him. "There's one crucial

difference between us," he went on. "You want to be loved *so desperately*. I think it lies underneath everything you do. *Will this make that dragon like me better? What should I do now to turn all these dragons into friends? If I can convince this cold, standoffish IceWing to like me, surely that'll prove that I'm a dragon worth liking.*"

"Excuse me," Qibli said. "*I'm* not the one who literally enchanted the entire world to like me. That was you, if you've forgotten."

"But I got the idea from you," Darkstalker said, now immensely amused. "Your first day at Jade Mountain. *Oh, if only I could magically make everyone like me!* Don't you remember? That comes from the holes in your heart that your family never bothered to fill. My first thought was, *how tremendously sad. What a tragic well of need that dragon is.* And then I thought, *but my, that* would *be a useful spell.* How easy life would be if everyone liked and trusted me. No one scheming against me, sending assassins to kill me, or getting irrationally upset over perfectly harmless enchantments." He frowned, as though a part of him was locked in an endless argument with someone long gone.

"Clearsight and Fathom liked you," Qibli said. "As I understand it, they loved you. But they still risked everything to stop you, because they saw how dangerous you are."

Darkstalker snorted. "They couldn't think big," he said. "Not like you and me, Qibli. They couldn't imagine all the wonderful things we could do with our magic. They would have been content with small, meaningless lives — clearly that's what they chose; look how they vanished from history after I was gone. They didn't want to take the hard steps to get to the best futures."

He leaned toward Qibli. "But *you* can imagine it. You know what you would do with unlimited power — you've thought about it enough. Your big secret dream: to be an animus." He scratched a talonful of pebbles into his claws and they started to bounce and bubble like boiling water. One by one they turned into gemstones: tiny opals and emeralds and amethysts and tiger eyes leaping and dancing together. Qibli couldn't pull his eyes away from them.

"So what if you could be?" Darkstalker asked in a low rumble. "What if I made you an animus, too?"

Qibli's talons felt as if they were drifting away from him, suddenly as unreal as the rest of this situation. "You would never do that," he said. *Even Turtle, my actual friend, refused to do that for me.*

"I would, actually." Darkstalker plucked a ruby from the spinning galaxy of gemstones and scrutinized it. "Because I can see that if I do, it leads to the best future — for you, for me, for Moon, for all of Pyrrhia."

For you? Qibli wondered. *Wouldn't I use my magic against you, in these hypothetical futures?*

"No, this is a trick," he said out loud. "You're trying to trick me into taking off my protective spell, and then you'll enchant me."

"That would be a reasonable worry," said Darkstalker, "except that I am about ten times as strong as you and right now I could literally rip that earring off your ear anytime I wanted to."

That was quite true, Qibli realized uncomfortably. He felt smaller than the dead mouse.

"So I don't need to orchestrate an elaborate trick." Darkstalker twitched his wings, set the ruby in its own constellation, and nudged an agate over to orbit it. "But you're right, there is a condition to this offer. I'll give you unlimited animus magic, in exchange for a tiny spell that says you can never do me any harm. That seems quite fair to me, though. My hope, of course, is that you won't *want* to do me any harm once we are allies."

Never do him any harm, Qibli thought. *There would be ways around that. This might be a trick, but I can turn it back on him once I have that magic. I could outsmart him if I was an animus.*

If I say yes . . . I could stop Darkstalker and *get all the magic I've ever wanted.*

"Let me tell you about the best future," Darkstalker said dreamily. "You'll adore it. Everyone loves us. We share the continent and rule all the tribes with benevolent wisdom — you and Moon, me and Clearsight, once I get her right. Our dragonets play together in the palaces of Pyrrhia. There's no more war. There's no more sickness, thanks to us. No more sadness or worry, no more hunger, no more starving dragonets scrabbling for food in back alleys. No more terrible parents, because we can fix them. You could make your mother a dragon who loves you. I could have healed the scars on my father's soul. I know that's what I should have done, to make him a father that Whiteout and I could love." He bowed his head for a moment.

Qibli didn't want to give him ideas, but he had to ask. "But you could do all that by yourself. So why would you share your power with me when you could simply kill me right now?"

"Because I don't *just* want power, Qibli," Darkstalker said a little impatiently. "That's what so many dragons get wrong about me. Even Clearsight thought that way, toward the end." He selected a pair of perfect diamonds from his treasure cloud and set them spinning on their own axis with the ruby. "I also want to make the world a better place. I want to have real friends I care about. I want my happily ever after."

"You think I could be your real friend?" Qibli asked.

"You're funny and not boring," said Darkstalker. "You can keep up with my conversation, unlike pretty much all my subjects except Moon. You have ideas that I haven't already had myself, which is fascinating and rare. I like to be surprised — I mean, unless the surprise involves betrayal and involuntary comas, of course. Yes, I think we'd get along really well."

Qibli wondered about that. Was Darkstalker right? Were there really futures where they were friends, even co-rulers?

"And you'd be a good influence on me!" Darkstalker said charmingly. "I can see that, too. You steer me through some pretty rough times and save a lot of dragons from my mistakes. We all end up on much better paths if we're friends. I mean, consider my alternatives. If you're not my friend, Moon won't be either, and then who do I have? This lizard?"

He snapped his claws and with a startling popping sound, Vulture suddenly materialized in the air beside him.

Qibli's grandfather let out a yell of surprise. "Where am I?" he shouted. "What did you do?" He craned his neck to look up at the speck of sky far above them. His talons pressed against the sheer rock walls, and Qibli knew the SandWing claustrophobia was snaring him, too.

And yet, even though he could see Vulture's fear, Qibli's heart still tried to make a run for it. He felt it galloping wildly around his chest like a terrified chinchilla. He couldn't stop himself from crouching, trying to make himself smaller until perhaps he'd be invisible, and then Vulture wouldn't be able to hurt him. He wouldn't be able to worm inside Qibli's ears and make him doubt everything that was real.

"Enchant this dragon to obey my every command," Darkstalker said offhandedly. He tapped Vulture on the forehead. "Stop talking and stay where you are."

Vulture's eyes bulged as he tried to snap something furious and failed. His talons touched down on a small bump of stone and he teetered there, unable to fly away.

"I can't believe you're so terrified of this salamander," Darkstalker said to Qibli with a chuckle. "He's so *easy* to manipulate, even without magic. Thin scales, loves treasure, lies about everything until he doesn't even know what's true, not that he cares. He's a dragon made of paper who has never been happy one day in his life."

Qibli took in a lungful of air, trying to see his grandfather that way. It was hard, with those black eyes attempting to spear him in the gut.

"If you accept my gift," Darkstalker said, "you never have to worry about him or anyone else like him ever again. Watch." He tapped Vulture's head again. "Enchant this dragon to have the mind of a new-hatched dragonet. You may speak."

Vulture's head slowly lolled sideways and a goofy grin spread across his face. "Urple," he chirruped at Qibli.

It was one of the most horrifying things Qibli had ever seen.

Perhaps reading Qibli's expression, Darkstalker hastily reached over and tapped Vulture again. "Go back to the way you were before the last spell," he said. "Now I enchant this dragon to feel guilt for all the terrible things he's done."

Vulture's face collapsed into grief. "I'm a monster," he whispered. "All those deaths . . . the cruelty to my family . . . how can I ever make up for it all?"

"See how easy it is?" Darkstalker said to Qibli. "Let's see — now be a grandfather who loves Qibli more than anything else in the world," he ordered Vulture.

"Qibli!" Vulture cried, reaching his talons toward his grandson. "Dearest of dragons! Have I ever told you how proud I am of you? An Outclaw! Advisor to Queen Thorn! I missed our games so much when you went away with her. But you've grown into such a fine young dragon."

"Stop it, stop it," Qibli said, covering his ears. "It's not real. It's not *real*."

"Of course it is!" Vulture cried exuberantly.

"Shush," Darkstalker said to him, and Vulture instantly fell silent. "But of course it's real," he said to Qibli. "We just made it real. He really feels that way with all his heart right now."

"Because you put a spell on him," Qibli said. "That's not what real means."

Darkstalker looked skeptical. "If magic can improve a dragon," he said, "I don't see what the problem is. We could turn your grandfather into the kindest dragon in the Scorpion Den. Wouldn't it be fun to watch him give away his entire treasure to orphans and homeless dragons?"

Yes, whispered a small but unavoidable part of Qibli's soul.

"Wouldn't that be the best way to deal with this dragon who has haunted your nightmares your entire life?" Darkstalker asked. "Wouldn't it be better than killing him, or whatever the 'real' alternatives are?"

Yes, Qibli's heart whispered again.

"So . . . why didn't *you* do that?" Qibli asked Darkstalker.

"What do you mean?" Darkstalker asked.

"To the IceWings," Qibli said. "When you first came out of the mountain and you saw visions of them threatening your tribe. Why didn't you enchant them all to want peace with you instead? Or cast a spell to make all IceWings and NightWings forget their ancient hatred and forgive everything that's happened? Why didn't you use your magic to avoid war, instead of trying to kill them all?"

Darkstalker's eyes narrowed. His jaw worked silently for a long moment, as though he was grinding his teeth.

"See?" he finally managed to force out. "Smart. Like I said. Always thinking." He turned his head away and thought for another moment.

"Because I haven't forgiven them," he admitted finally. "For what happened to my mother." He took a deep breath. "All right. I see your point. I thought I was protecting the tribe . . . but it was about revenge, too. I can see that." He spoke as if each word was a tooth being yanked out of his mouth.

"Maybe you need to put a kindness spell on yourself," Qibli suggested.

"This is what I mean," Darkstalker said slowly. "How you can keep me on the better paths. You'll suggest peace spells instead of plagues. You'll help me see these things I don't recognize about myself." He paused, and Qibli could tell that Darkstalker wasn't entirely convinced that that was what he wanted.

Is that what I want? To be Darkstalker's conscience? To spend my life telling him the things he doesn't want to hear?

But . . . . I'd have animus magic.

(And Moon would love me. In this future, he sees me with Moon. She must forgive me for this choice. Maybe it's what she would want — me with magic and a chance to influence a better, kinder Darkstalker.)

(Are the IceWings safe in this future? Where's Winter? Are we still friends? Is Turtle safe? What happens to Anemone? Does she have to hide for the rest of her life?)

No, I could fix all of that. I could keep them all safe.

I'd have ANIMUS MAGIC. I could do everything I've ever wanted to do.

"So what do you think?" Darkstalker asked. "Are you ready to become an animus dragon?" He drew a circle in the air around the floating gemstones, and they all whirled into one another until they became a crown, glowing with gems from all over the world. Darkstalker nudged the crown to set it floating gently toward Qibli.

Who would say no to their secret dream come true?

Why would I ever say no?

Say yes to the magic.

Say yes to the bright future.

Say yes.

Qibli looked up into Darkstalker's eyes and said, "No."

— CHAPTER 29 —

"Oh, that's not the right answer," Darkstalker said, fanning out his wings. The gemstone crown vanished abruptly. "That answer leads to bad, bad, bad futures, Qibli."

"No for a lot of reasons," Qibli said. "Starting with this one: I like you, but I can't trust you. I don't know what you'd put in the spell on me, but if there's a chance it could turn me evil, I don't want to risk it. I don't want to turn into a dragon who plays with other dragons like toys." He nodded at the mute figure of his grandfather, perched awkwardly beside Darkstalker.

"Bad futures," Darkstalker continued, his brows lowering, "because if you don't accept my offer, I have to kill you. Surely you understand that."

Qibli felt full of holes, all the way through his bones. Was he really going to die without seeing Moon again? Without knowing for sure that all his friends were safe?

Darkstalker shook his head. "You're too much trouble if you're not my friend. When I take the NightWing army out again, I can't have you coming up with more clever tricks to stop me. I don't like those futures. I also don't like the futures where I *do* kill you, because Moon never forgives me. And then I have no friends, Qibli. Enchanted friends, who aren't the same. No one to keep me good. Where do *you* think that leads?"

"The fact that you can't be good on your own," said Qibli. "That's part of the problem. You shouldn't need a dragon on your shoulder telling you that killing all the IceWings is wrong, or that taking over your father's mind was an awful thing to do."

"He deserved it!" Darkstalker hissed.

"You don't really want that dragon on your shoulder either." Qibli shook his head. "You wouldn't even have listened to Clearsight if she tried to be that dragon."

"I *can* do it myself," Darkstalker said, abruptly shifting course. "See, here I go. Hey, overlords of dragon morality, I hereby acknowledge that killing Qibli would be something only an *evil* dragon would do. And since I'm not evil, I am not going to do that. I am going to take the high road, rip off his earring, and enchant him to be my best friend instead."

"No, wait," Qibli said, taking a step back into the crawl space. His bag bumped hard against his chest, ricocheting off his pounding heart. "Let's talk about, um, moral gray areas."

Darkstalker froze and cocked his head. "What is that?"

"The last vestiges of your soul trying to cough up a reason to let me go?" Qibli suggested.

"No, that . . . whirring sound." Darkstalker shook his head like there were mosquitoes in his ears.

Qibli went quiet, listening, and for the first time felt the vibrations coming from his bag. Puzzled, he tugged it open and pulled out the old telescope-hourglass contraption he'd found in the Night Palace. To his surprise, the hourglass was spinning frantically on its axis, and it sped up as he turned the end of the telescope toward Darkstalker and Vulture.

"Where did you get that?" Darkstalker asked in a hushed voice.

"I found it in a room in your palace," Qibli said. "What is it? Why is it spinning like that?"

Darkstalker edged forward on his outcropping and stretched his neck down toward it. Qibli held the telescope up to his eye and centered it on Darkstalker's bewildered face.

"I made that," Darkstalker said. "For Fathom. Such a long time ago . . . I mean, it doesn't feel that long to me, but I know it was." He squinted at the hourglass, which was still spinning. "It's a soul reader."

"A soul reader," Qibli echoed.

"I made it to reassure Fathom that we were fine. That we could use our magic safely, without going evil." His expression was curiously affectionate, as if he'd just remembered a version of Fathom he genuinely liked. "It shows how much of your soul is still good."

The hourglass slowed, tipped one way, then the other, and finally stopped. The telescope was pointed at Darkstalker. Inside the hourglass, the bottom half was almost entirely full of white sand. In the bell of the top half, only a few grains of black sand were left.

Darkstalker stared at it, disbelief slowly crawling across his face.

"Well, that makes no sense," he said. "Did you do something to it? Did Turtle put a new spell on it?"

"No," Qibli said, touching the hourglass. It swayed slightly under his claws, the sand shifting but staying where it was. "I didn't even know it was animus-touched. What does this mean?"

Darkstalker snatched the object out of Qibli's talons and flipped it over a few times, as if looking for signs of tampering, before turning it back toward himself and squinting at the hourglass again.

"It must be broken," he muttered. "Starting over." He shook it vigorously for a moment and then held it out in his talons. "When this soul reader is pointed at a dragon, I enchant it to measure the good and evil in that dragon's soul and reveal it in the drifts of sand. Black sand to mark the amount of good, white sand to show the amount of evil or damage to that dragon's soul."

Oh, Qibli thought. *Interesting. The black sand indicates goodness — makes sense for a NightWing.* He wasn't surprised, now that he understood it, by the balance of sand in Darkstalker's hourglass.

Darkstalker pointed the telescope at Vulture and peered through it. The hourglass obligingly began to spin, sending whirlwinds of sand dancing inside it. At last it stopped and settled into equilibrium. In the top half: a tiny sprinkling of black sand, about the same as Darkstalker's. In the bottom half, a correspondingly large pile of glittering white sand.

"Now *that's* logical," Darkstalker muttered. "He's *obviously* terrible. So it's working now." He frowned down at the soul reader, inhaled deeply and pointed the end of the telescope at himself.

Shrum shrum shrum. The hourglass tumbled busily.

It slowed to a stop. As before, the mountain of white sand in the bottom was large, almost large enough to overflow the bulb. And in the top half shone those last few tiny grains of black sand.

"But that's impossible!" Darkstalker exploded. He threw the soul reader away from him violently, and Qibli lunged to catch it before it shattered on the stone floor.

"I protected my soul!" Darkstalker cried. Veins were starting to throb in his neck, writhing like livid snakes under his scales. "First with my scroll, and now with my wristband! I shouldn't have lost any of it!"

"And yet it looks like you've lost almost all of it," Qibli pointed out.

He was shocked to see how much this upset Darkstalker. The ancient NightWing seemed to swell to twice his normal enormous size. His wings were flared and twitching wrathfully.

"No!" Darkstalker slammed his tail into the crevasse wall, unleashing a scamper of loud pebbles. "I'm not like other animus dragons. I'm smarter than they are. My soul is safe from my magic! That *can't* be what it looks like!"

"Safe from your magic, maybe," Qibli said. "But not safe from your actions."

"WHAT?" Darkstalker roared.

Qibli squared his shoulders and held his ground, although the expression on Darkstalker's face kind of made him want to retreat all the way back into the crawl space.

"You didn't lose your soul because magic ate it away slowly," Qibli said. "You lost it because you chose to do terrible things, over and over again. Each terrible thing, each betrayal, each murder, added to this mountain." He tapped the white sand side. "That's not the magic's fault. That's *you*. That's who *you* chose to be."

"But — I had good reasons for everything I did," Darkstalker said. "Visions of a good future. Doesn't that count for something?"

"Yes, sometimes," Qibli agreed. "But not when your choices are so dark and damaging. Not when there were better alternatives you didn't even explore."

"Blah blah blah," Darkstalker muttered, but he was staring into space now. "Who . . . that's not possible . . . is it? Where does that go? How does it end?" He twisted his neck around to look above and behind him. "Can you see what I'm seeing? Come on out; I've obviously known you were there since you crawled down here."

There was a pause, and then a ripple in the rocks

overhead, whorls of yellow and blue suddenly appearing on the gray and spreading into the shape of a dragon who was covering the shape of another dragon clinging to the small claw holds in the wall.

"Huh," said Darkstalker. "Actually, I didn't know *she* was there." He jerked his chin at Kinkajou as she peeled herself off Moon. The RainWing shot a glare at him and fluttered down to sit beside Qibli. A moment later, Moon landed on his other side, and even though this meant the three of them were crowded together in the small space, Qibli was finally able to breathe.

"Hello, Darkstalker," Moon said.

"Can you see this vision?" he asked, reaching down toward her. Qibli shivered as Moon rested her talon in the giant NightWing's palm.

She closed her eyes for a long moment.

"Isn't that strange?" Darkstalker said. "It's so blurred, and it ends in darkness. Is someone going to betray me again? But no one's magic can hurt me anymore. And who? Did you see her? She looks like . . . but she can't be."

"If it was her," said Moon, opening her eyes again, "would you take that path? Even knowing it ends in possible darkness, would you do it to see her again?"

A light was kindling in Darkstalker's eyes. "But — do you —" He stopped, his claws gripping the stone. "Yes. Of course I would."

"Then let's see where this path leads," Moon said, tipping her snout up to the sky.

Darkstalker spread his wings and paused. He leaned over to Vulture, tapped his head, and whispered something. Qibli's grandfather vanished again, as suddenly as he'd appeared.

Then Darkstalker took off, aiming for the crack of sky overhead. Qibli exhaled with relief. This was not his final resting place, after all. He would live to see another sunrise, although he wasn't sure he could count on more than one.

"Come on, we have to keep up," Kinkajou said, leaping aloft. Her wings looked like flower petals on a river as she flashed away across the gray stone.

But Moon stopped one of Qibli's wings with her own before he could follow suit.

"I heard all that," she said, looking at him searchingly. "Why did you say no to his offer?"

"Did you want me to say yes?" he asked. "So I could be more special? Like you? I know, it's what I've wished for a hundred times. I just . . . if I'd been born an animus, that would be one thing. But I couldn't accept it as a gift from him. It wouldn't be safe. And I wouldn't know if I was myself anymore." He glanced down at the soul reader. "That much power . . . it would change me. And I'm not sure it would change me in ways I would like. Or, um . . . ways you would like."

"Qibli," she said so fiercely that he flinched. Was she going to tell him to change his mind? To chase after Darkstalker and beg for the magic, after all?

Moon seized his talons in hers. "How are you so brilliant

and such an idiot at the same time? You *are* special. You *don't* need his poisoned magic, or any magic. You're smart and you're brave and you care and you don't give up and you take all of that and use it to help other dragons instead of yourself. That's better than magic. You did the right thing."

"I did?" he said.

"Hey, swooning friends!" Kinkajou shouted from far overhead. "Am I defeating Darkstalker by myself today? Don't you at least want to come watch?"

Moon laughed and let go of Qibli.

"Time to fly," she said, and they did.

CHAPTER 30

A dragon was waiting for them on one of the peaks of Jade Mountain. The three moons illuminated her silhouette, and Qibli heard Darkstalker inhale sharply. He abruptly looped back in the sky to hover in front of Moon.

"I'm not going to fall for this. Turtle made her, didn't he?" he said. "The way I made Clearsight? This is a plan to mess with my head." But his expression wasn't angry, or suspicious. Qibli thought it was more . . . desperately hopeful.

"No," Moon said. "She's real, Darkstalker. She's been in the Ice Kingdom all these years, trapped in a kind of suspended animation spell. She has only lived for tiny fragments of time here and there, so she is not much older than when you last saw her."

"I thought they killed her," he said, his voice breaking.

Moon hesitated. "It's . . . it's actually worse, what Queen Diamond did to her. But she's all right now. She wants to see you."

Darkstalker wheeled around without further argument and soared down to the dragon on the mountaintop. She turned to face him, her wings whispering across the frozen violets that dotted the grass around her talons. It was the dragon from the palace library, Qibli realized.

Moon beckoned to Qibli and Kinkajou and they landed softly nearby, close enough to hear without intruding.

Neither dragon said anything for a long moment as Darkstalker stepped closer and closer to her, his face still anxious with disbelief, his long neck and vast wings towering over her.

Finally he stopped right in front of her and crouched, making himself as small as he could.

"Mother?" he said.

She opened her wings to him. "Darkstalker," she said. "My beloved disaster."

The two dragons folded into each other. Qibli could hear Darkstalker's quiet sobs carried on the wind.

Huh, he thought. *So Darkstalker has a mother who loves him.*

Oh, very good idea, Qibli, this is an excellent time for some self-pity.

"Where did she come from?" he asked Moon softly.

"She's the NightWing Winter rescued from the Ice Kingdom," Moon whispered. "Foeslayer. She's been hiding in the shadows, watching him and the other NightWings, trying to figure out what was happening and what she should do."

"She didn't want to see him immediately?" Qibli said, surprised.

"Well, she'd heard what he did to his father," Moon said, making her voice even quieter. "And she really loved Arctic, you know? I think she was afraid Darkstalker had lost his mind, and she didn't know if her reappearance would make it worse. She said she was thinking of fleeing the continent instead . . . and then she met you."

"Oh," he said, remembering their conversation in the library — and all the things he *probably* wouldn't have said about Darkstalker if he'd known she was his mother.

"I guess you made her realize she had to try reaching him," said Moon. "She came to us after the battle, when she saw Darkstalker take you. We were chasing after him and she joined us. She said she wanted to help."

"I hope she can," he said. "But I don't know how."

"You'd be surprised what that kind of love can do," Moon said with a wistful look. He wondered if she was thinking about her own mother and her strange upbringing, hidden away in the rainforest, but loved very, very much.

"Mother," Darkstalker said in a sudden rush, sitting up to look at her. "Do you remember the soul reader I made?"

"Yes," she said wryly. "I remember you prowling around the house trying to catch your father with it to read his soul."

He hesitated, perhaps reading on her face that she knew everything about what had happened with Arctic.

"It . . . it says I'm evil," he said to her, sounding centuries younger than he looked. "Like, all the way almost entirely completely evil. Worse than Father ever was. I'm not, though, am I? I'm not *evil*."

"Well," said Foeslayer, "I can't say I entirely approve of your choices lately. Or two thousand years ago, for that matter."

Darkstalker hunched his shoulders, his wings hanging askew. "It was *his* fault you got caught by the IceWings," he said petulantly.

"No. It was my fault for letting a stupid fight make me so mad I took off my protection."

"What did they do to you in the Ice Kingdom?" Darkstalker asked. "I'll make them pay. You can watch while I make them all sorry." His claws jerked open and closed again.

"None of the IceWings alive today did anything to me," Foeslayer said firmly. "Except for one, who freed me from my prison."

"But you were imprisoned," he said, pouncing on that word. "All this time? Wasn't it awful? Don't you want revenge?"

"I was never a vengeful dragon," she said with a sigh. "You get that from your father. Calm down, it's true. But it doesn't make *sense* to punish the IceWing tribe for what happened to us all those centuries ago, Darkstalker. Queen Diamond is long gone. The war should have ended then. Time has moved on without us and we should let it, not drag it back into the blood and fire of our old fight."

"But they —"

"Started it?" she interrupted. "They don't see it that way. I remember what Arctic did during our escape from the Ice Kingdom. I understand why they were so angry, and why he never really recovered. I'm sorry you had to live a life shaped by that anger."

She reached out to trace the lines of his face. "I wish I could start over and give you a happy life instead."

"Maybe you can," Moon said, moving forward into the moonlight.

"That's true," Darkstalker said. "You can help me rule Pyrrhia, Mother. I wouldn't need anyone else then." He touched his forehead. "Why can't I see that future?"

"Because I would never say yes to that," Foeslayer said sadly.

"Wait. Darkstalker," Moon cut in. "I've had a new vision since the moment Jade Mountain didn't fall. I wasn't sure it *was* a vision at first, but it keeps looping back over and over."

"Which one?" Darkstalker asked, his gaze shifting to the faraway look. "Qibli as an animus? I liked that one, although it wasn't strongly probable. The others . . . none of them are perfect. I can see I never get Clearsight right. The Ice Kingdom is a frozen wasteland that's a misery to conquer. The SeaWings never stop popping out of the ocean to fight us, no matter how many times I think I've stamped them out. The RainWings are impossible — it's like trying to fight butterflies. An army of invisible butterflies who can melt your face off the moment you fall asleep." He rubbed his eyes. "Thanks to those wretched earrings, becoming king of the whole continent is a lot harder than it should be. It's exhausting. I'm tired and I haven't even begun yet."

He sat down heavily, resting his chin on the ground in

front of Foeslayer. "And what's the point?" he said sadly. "Clearsight's *gone*. I never have dragonets, I never fall in love again. You're still my only friend, and you and Mother spend the rest of your lives yelling at me." He snapped one of the ice-covered flowers off its stem and crushed it into tiny purple fragments between his claws. "Is that what you see, Moon?"

"Not exactly," she said. "The vision I see — I don't think you'd be able to see it."

He raised his head and looked offended. "Oh, really? You can see a future I can't?"

"I think so," she said. "If I'm right about it. It's a vision of a dragonet. He's growing up in the rainforest. He loves to weave and fish and sing. His favorite fruit is strawberries, which he and his friends fly to the mountains to find. He teaches himself to make jam and pies and he writes a song called 'Strawberries as Big as a Scavenger's Head,' which becomes the anthem for a yearly strawberry festival.

"He lives a peaceful, ordinary life. He marries the tribe's blacksmith and they have two funny little dragonets who steal his strawberries and make him laugh every day. They're with him when he dies quietly in his sleep."

She paused, watching him expectantly.

"Well, I don't know who that is," he said. She kept looking at him and he frowned. "I mean, who loves strawberries that much? I've never tried one. They look like they're full of seeds."

"Really?" Moon said with a little laugh. "They're not at all. You'd like them."

"I saw some over here," Foeslayer said, searching a patch of leaves near her talons. She plucked one of the dark jewel-red fruits and passed it to her son.

He held the green stem between his claws and eyed it suspiciously. "Wait," he said. "You think the dragon in your vision is *me*?"

"You without your powers," said Moon. "You without your memories. A new you, with a chance to start over."

Darkstalker snorted, little puffs of flame shooting out of his nose. "Why would I *ever* give up my powers?" he said. "I'm the most powerful dragon Pyrrhia has ever seen! Everyone wants to be me!"

"I don't," said Qibli.

"Me neither!" said Kinkajou. "Evil and smug and fat-headed and evil, no thank you!"

"I'm not —" Darkstalker started and then, surprisingly, fell silent. Foeslayer settled her tail over his and patted one of his free talons as though it was a lonely sloth.

"You could be happy," she said to him. "You could be loved."

"But you have to choose it," Moon said. "You're the only one who can make it real. Imagine it, Darkstalker. If you turn yourself into a different dragon, you could actually do good things for the world."

He shook his head vigorously. "That's ridiculous. Without my powers? What do I do, make pie? You must be joking. Couldn't I do *more* good things with my powers intact?" he asked. "Like take Pyrrhia into the glorious future I've seen?"

"I'd rather have pie," Kinkajou said.

Moon shook her head. "The future of Pyrrhia is not your own personal scroll, waiting for you to write it, Darkstalker. The only future you control is yours. And you have not brought happiness to the dragon tribes. We don't want that future you see if we have to travel your dark path to get there."

Darkstalker spun the strawberry in his claws for a moment, thinking.

"Do it," Foeslayer said quietly. "Become a dragonet again. I'll take care of you. I *want* to. We'll be happy this time."

"All I see this way is darkness," he said, touching his forehead.

"Darkness is all the rest of us see if you do become king," Moon said. "But this way —"

"No," he said. "I can't. I can't do it. I won't."

Moon blinked, looking bewildered. "But my vision — I'm sure this is the path you choose."

Darkstalker's tail lashed back and forth, throwing off his mother's. "I don't want to lose all my memories! I'd forget Clearsight . . . she'd be even more gone that she is now!" He rose to his feet. "No, I'm going to be king. King of the whole continent. King of all the tribes! That's my future; I've seen it a thousand times!"

"Darkstalker, please," Moon pleaded. "I know there's good in you still. If you listen to it, you'll choose this for yourself, I'm sure you will."

"You are a bunch of small-minded little lizards," he said, rising to his full height and spreading his wings. "What, did you think I'd taste a strawberry and decide, mmm, wow, that's worth giving up my magic for?"

He looked down at the tiny fruit in his claws and ripped off all the green leaves. "Or did you have Turtle enchant this? Or perhaps another secret animus I don't know about? It doesn't matter, you boring, *ordinary* creatures. I can't be enchanted by anyone! I'm smarter now; I've made myself completely safe. *Nobody's* animus magic will work on me. Which means nobody will ever be able to stop me." He threw the strawberry in his mouth and swallowed it, casting a dark look at his mother.

"Actually," said Kinkajou, "there is *one* dragon's magic that will still work on you."

He glowered down at her. "You're wrong."

"I'm right," she snapped back.

"Oh, really? Whose?"

She glared right back, and her scales were the color of burning strawberries. "Your own."

— CHAPTER 31 —

Kinkajou upended her pouch and poured a tiny pile of scraps of paper onto the ground in front of her.

Qibli's mouth dropped open.

The last pieces of Darkstalker's scroll. The ones Chameleon used to transform himself into different dragons.

He could see the dark jagged scrawl of Peril's father's handwriting on them — and then, as Kinkajou carefully flipped them over, he recognized her own awkward lettering on the other side, and he remembered the hours and hours she'd spent practicing so she could be the first RainWing in a century to learn to write.

She used his own magic against him.

"What?" Darkstalker said, choking. "But how — I didn't see —"

"I know," Kinkajou said proudly. "Never saw me coming! Taken down by a ball of fluff! Who's insignificant NOW, frogface!"

Darkstalker collapsed forward — no, he was shrinking, Qibli realized.

"You knew," he gasped to his mother. "You helped her."

"Of course I did," she said. "What else could I do? Send you to your room? Extra chores for a week? Somehow neither of those seemed particularly apt for this situation." She patted his shoulder — he was now about the same size as her. "It was this or leave forever and never see you again. I decided we'd both be happier this way."

"But my powers!" he cried. His voice was higher, less cavernous and booming now, as his lungs shrank. "All my magic . . . can't I keep any of it? The mind reading? Wait —" Darkstalker held up his front talons, watching the claws get smaller.

"Sorry, Darkstalker," Qibli said. "You had more than one chance to use them wisely and well, and you chose not to."

"I really thought he was going to choose this for himself," Moon said, tipping her head at the shrinking dragon.

"Oh, I knew he wouldn't," Kinkajou said. "But I couldn't tell you my awesome plan, obviously."

"You told *her*, though. Why didn't he see it in your mind?" Moon asked Foeslayer.

"You don't raise a mind-reading son without learning a few tricks about how to hide your thoughts," Foeslayer said calmly.

"Didn't I help you?" Darkstalker said in a lost, small voice, looking up at Moon. "Didn't I save dragons, too? I'm not evil . . . I'm not . . ."

"Not anymore," Kinkajou said as a shimmer spread across his scales. Darkstalker was a dragonet now, younger than

Anemone . . . and then younger still, until he appeared to be about one year old. He lifted his wings awkwardly and Qibli noticed that the line of white IceWing scales was gone from under his wings.

But he wasn't entirely black either; underneath his wings, in place of the usual NightWing silver star scales, he had a constellation of rainbow-colored scales — one emerald green here, one parrot blue there, sunrise golds and oranges scattered throughout the black scales, like shining beetles dropped on a dark velvet cloth.

"What in the world?" Moon asked.

"Oh, yeah, I made him half RainWing," Kinkajou said, fighting back a giggle. "I thought that would be good for him. And it turned out so pretty!"

"I'll work it into my backstory," Foeslayer said to Moon. "If the other NightWings ever wonder where I came from."

"You're going to join the tribe?" Qibli asked her. "And live with them?"

"The ones in the rainforest," she said. "It's beautiful there, and I hear good things about our new queen." She smiled at Moon. "I don't know what the others are going to do when Darkstalker never comes back. But I couldn't live in the old Night Kingdom anyway. Too many memories."

The dragonet at her feet had been examining his talons closely for the last few minutes. Now his head popped up and he bonked her leg with it. "Hungry!" he chirped.

"What are your new names going to be?" Qibli asked.

"Oh — I'm not sure," she said.

"You should be Awesomeness," Kinkajou suggested.

"Salvation?" said Moon.

Foeslayer laughed. "That's a little grandiose for me." She picked up the tiny dragonet that used to be Darkstalker. He didn't look like a young Darkstalker; his face was too round and his eyes set too wide, but more than all that, there was a serenity in his expression that Qibli had never glimpsed on Darkstalker's face. *Being bombarded by dragon thoughts all day long from the moment you hatch probably isn't the most peaceful existence,* he guessed.

The dragonet wrapped his arms and legs around his mother's neck and nudged her ear with his snout. "HUNGRY," he said in a loud whisper.

"Here," she said, delving into the patch of leaves next to her again. "Have some strawberries."

He seized them with enormous delight and stuffed two in his mouth at once, dripping berry juice down his neck.

"I think I'll call him Peacemaker," she said. "I wonder if history would have been different if I'd chosen a name like that from the beginning."

Peacemaker. Qibli couldn't help but find the name a bit ironic — but then, this wasn't Darkstalker anymore. He was an entirely new dragon. And the spell wasn't in a piece of jewelry that could be removed; it was inside him once he'd eaten that first, enchanted strawberry, changing him permanently and forever. He'd never remember being Darkstalker. He was Peacemaker now, and for always.

"I have a name for you," Qibli said to Foeslayer. "If you're interested."

"Let's hear it," she said.

He smiled at the little dragon stuffing his face with strawberries. "I was thinking maybe . . . Hope?"

"Hope," she said thoughtfully. "I like that."

EPILOGUE

Moon soared down through the dripping trees, scattering raindrops off the branches and setting yellow and green parakeets aflutter. Below her, she could see the NightWing village spread out along the riverbank.

Nearly all the NightWings who had left with Darkstalker had returned to the rainforest after he disappeared. The ruins of the old kingdom on the Talon Peninsula would be fascinating to study — Queen Glory was setting up a team to do that now — but it turned out they weren't actually a great place to live, especially for dragons who were just starting to get used to the plentiful food of the rainforest.

Glory would have let them stay there and choose a new queen for themselves, if that's what they'd wanted, but despite Fierceteeth's best efforts, most NightWings ended up deciding that a RainWing queen wasn't such a catastrophe after all. Especially in comparison to a king who instantly brainwashed them and took them to war. They were all still pretty shell-shocked by that, and by the experience of seeing into the hearts of the IceWings they were trying to kill.

"You're here again?" Moon's mother teased as Moon swept down to land in the village clearing. "Don't you ever have schoolwork to do?"

"I finished it already!" Moon said, jumping up to hug her mother with her wings. Secretkeeper held her close, and her mind said everything about how much she missed Moon, even though she wouldn't let herself say it out loud.

The hum of background thoughts in the rainforest was so different these days. The NightWings were too busy to be resentful, too well-fed to keep complaining, and too abashed by their instant hero worship of Darkstalker to think about leaving again. They'd discovered that when they stopped grumbling all the time, they actually quite liked it in the rainforest. Queen Glory couldn't hand out superpowers, but she had forged another peace with the new IceWing queen, and most of the NightWings had really lost their taste for war.

"You know, you don't have to stay at school if you miss me so much," Secretkeeper said, nudging Moon's snout.

"No, I still love it," Moon said. "Kinkajou and I got a new clawmate — a MudWing. I like her. I miss the ones who aren't in our winglet anymore, though."

Carnelian. Umber.

Winter.

Qibli.

There was still hope that one of them would come back. She hoped for it every day.

I should go see him . . . I should tell him how I feel. I've certainly thought about it enough, trying to figure out how I feel about each of them. I didn't want to choose . . . but if I want either of them in my life, I know I have to.

Moon sighed and looked around the clearing. She let her mother think these visits were to see her, but really she was checking on Darkstalker — not Darkstalker. Peacemaker. And there he was, close to the river, making mud pies.

"Moon!" he sang happily as he saw her approaching. "Moon moon moon mooooon pies." He scrambled over with a smudge of mud on his snout and hugged her leg.

"How are you today, Peacemaker?" Moon asked. *Feeling even the slightest bit evil? Contemplating the conquest of the world?* She knew Kinkajou had worded the transformation spell very carefully, but there was a part of her that couldn't help worrying all the time.

"Sleepy," he said promptly. "Mommy made me get up SO EARLY."

"Which is not how most dragons would describe noon," Hope pointed out, hopping down from one of the baobab trees overhead. "We're all trying to adjust to some kind of normal NightWing sleep schedule," she said to Moon. Lowering her voice, she added, "These modern dragons have it *all wrong.*"

"I'm sure they'll figure it out eventually," Moon said, smiling. "When is your house going to be ready?"

"Mightyclaws is working on it now," Hope answered. She nodded at the dragonet crouched over a flat rock in the pavilion, drawing intently on a square piece of paper. Queen

Glory sat beside him, her scales all gold and dark purple, watching quietly over his shoulder. Behind her, Deathbringer was eyeing the forest fiercely.

Most NightWings had accepted earrings to free themselves from all of Darkstalker's spells, even the ones that gave them extra powers. But a few had chosen to keep their powers, including Mightyclaws. Half the houses in the village had sprung from his magic in the last month.

It turned out this had been Mightyclaws's secret dream when he asked Darkstalker for the power to bring his drawings to life. All Mightyclaws wanted to do was help build a new, truly wonderful place for his tribe to live. That was why he hadn't returned to school; he was too happy and busy here.

"Hope, I wanted to ask you something," Moon said. "Do you know anything about any legends of a lost continent?"

"A little," Hope said. "It was sort of a joke in my time — like, 'I'm so fed up with all of this I'm moving to the lost continent!' 'Where did these weird plums come from, the lost continent?' That sort of thing."

"But is it real?" Moon asked. "Are there really other tribes out there somewhere?"

"Made you a pie!" Peacemaker chirped, smashing a pile of mud over Hope's talons. "Yum yum yum yum," he sang as he buried her claws, his wings fluttering in the breeze from the river.

"Oh, delightful," Hope said. She shot Moon a curious look. "I have no idea. I guess I always thought yes, probably. I mean —" She broke off, freed one of her talons from the mud, and picked up a cantaloupe from a nearby pile of fruit. "Imagine this is our world, right? According to NightWing calculations, our continent only covers about this much of it." She spread her talons on one side of the melon, covering about a third of the space on the knobbly globe. "So it's well within the realm of possibility that there's more land around this side." She turned the melon around. "And if there's another continent, why wouldn't there be more dragons? But it's too far for any dragon to fly, we believe, so there's no way to know for sure."

"Hmm," Moon said. Her temples were starting to pulse again.

"You had a vision, didn't you?" Hope lowered her voice even more. "I know that look."

"Maybe," Moon said. "But it's . . . mysterious."

"As visions should be," Hope said wryly. "Well, before you go looking for trouble, see if you can find anything on the Legend of the Hive."

"What's that?" Moon asked.

"An old story. I don't remember it well, so read about it if you can. It might give you some ideas about these missing tribes."

"AHA!" Peacemaker suddenly declared. "Have an idea! Super good one! Going to take a NAP! Like a RAINWING! YAY!" He scampered off toward one of the hammocks.

"You've only been up for an hour!" Hope protested. "Peacemaker! What about this mess? Excuse me," she said to Moon, and chased after him.

It was always such a strange feeling, coming to see Peacemaker. Moon kept expecting to find hints of Darkstalker in him. It was both a little sad and an enormous relief that she never did. He was exactly the ordinary dragonet that Kinkajou had promised he would be. Very few dragons knew his secret; he himself certainly never would.

Everyone else thought Darkstalker was back under the mountain again, asleep for good this time. Most of them assumed Anemone had taken care of him with the same spell that ended the battle. Others were sure that Moon and Qibli were involved somehow, or thought perhaps the original dragonets of destiny had saved the world again.

Pretty much nobody guessed that the real mastermind who took him down was Kinkajou.

She didn't mind. She said the "Epic Legend of Kinkajou" was a work in progress, and one day when she and Peacemaker were both long gone, the truth would be revealed and then everyone could sing rousing songs about her for the rest of time. But Kinkajou said that for now, really, it was a lot easier to be a student without an Epic Legend following her around.

Moon's mother thought the whole mess with Darkstalker was proof that powers were a curse and disaster for any dragon who had them. But despite everything that had happened, Moon didn't think so.

I like my powers. I like caring about what other dragons think and feeling their emotions. I'm even glad I have my visions, no matter how much they hurt sometimes.

I think there's a way to use my powers for good, like Qibli always says.

And that starts with taking this new vision . . . and doing something about it.

The forest was full of scuttling noises, from fallen leaves tossed by the wind to squirrels darting up tree trunks. But some of the noises were bigger than others, and Winter was getting better at figuring out which ones were scavengers. They had a way of walking even when they were trying to be quiet, and his sharp IceWing ears could pick out their footsteps from quite a distance.

He crept slowly through the trees. Now he could hear whispered squeaking as well, so there were at least two of them. He wondered if his little net would be able to hold both, or if he should focus on catching just one.

There they were! One was clambering around the branches of an apple tree while the other stood below, holding something that looked almost like a miniature dragon basket. *They can make baskets?* Actually, that wasn't too hard to imagine, with those clever little paws.

He felt a little shiver of excitement through his wings. If he could make his scavenger sanctuary happen, he'd get to study them all day long. He'd be able to *see* them making baskets and maybe even drawings, if Sunny was right that they could do that. He'd seen some of the ones Flower drew, but he personally suspected that she was unusual because of spending so many years around dragons. It would be astonishing to discover that capacity in other scavengers as well. A scientific breakthrough, really.

"Winter!" a voice yelled in the distance. "Winter, where are you?"

Oh, no. The scavengers both shot into alert stances, staring around them like little meerkats. The black fur on their heads fluffed and tufted in the wind.

"WINTER!" Whoever it was crashed closer, making an almighty dragon-sized racket.

The scavenger in the tree made a flying leap to the ground, knocking over the other one as it landed. They both scrambled up and bolted away.

With a frustrated growl, Winter shot after them. But it was too late. The scavengers around here must have some kind of system of bolt-holes or well-concealed tunnels. They managed to vanish within a pair of heartbeats.

"There you are!" The dragonet bounding into the clearing was absolutely bright lemon yellow and beaming all over her face. "Riptide said you were skulking around the forest somewhere!"

"I was being STEALTHY, Kinkajou," Winter grumbled. "I know that's a foreign concept to you."

"Oh, hello to you too, grouchy and ridiculous all at the same time!" she said. "I am the *queen* of stealth. I stealthed my way all around that NightWing palace! I can outstealth you any day of the week!" Her scales became pine trees and shadows, and he had to concentrate to keep his glare on the spot where she had been standing.

Although, actually . . . his frown faded. "Hey, that's true!" he said excitedly. "*You* could catch me a scavenger! They'd never see you coming!"

Kinkajou reappeared, lilac and light blue now, looking somewhat mollified. "I *might* be willing to help you with that," she said. "Depending on what you plan to do with it once you have it."

"Riptide is letting me build a den for them in Sanctuary," he explained. Winter had been living with the Talons of Peace since the battle of Jade Mountain, helping them build another town like Possibility, where dragons from every tribe would be welcome. It was nestled in the foothills of the Claws of the Clouds Mountains, beside a small, very cold lake that Winter was particularly fond of.

"Actually," he added, "that's how Riptide got the name for the town — I mentioned wanting to build a scavenger sanctuary, and he liked the word so much he decided to fly with it. I'm hoping to get about six or seven scavengers to live in there so I can watch what they do."

"Your scavenger obsession is so weird," Kinkajou said. "Although they are pretty cute. Almost as cute as sloths."

"But smarter than sloths," Winter pointed out.

Kinkajou looked skeptical. "I guess we'll find out," she said. "Anyway, I'm sure what you meant to say was HI, Kinkajou, oh my goodness, thanks for coming to visit, I've missed you SO MUCH!"

"Indeed," said Winter. "Sorry. Of course. In those exact words." He hesitated. "Did you . . . come by yourself?"

"Oh, that's nice." Kinkajou wrinkled her nose at him. "Way to make a dragon feel wanted."

"I thought I phrased that very politely!" he protested.

"Yes, but *I* know what you mean," she said. "And no, Moon didn't come with me."

He tried valiantly to keep his wings from drooping.

"*You* could visit *her*," Kinkajou reminded him. "You could even have stayed at school. Sunny and Tsunami would have stuck up for you."

"I know," he said, "but I didn't want to cause any more trouble with Snowfall. I'm not a real IceWing to her anymore, so me taking the place of another IceWing who really wanted it . . . well, it wouldn't have made relations between her and the school any easier."

Winter was still surprised that all the queens had agreed to give Jade Mountain Academy another chance. He knew that Queen Snowfall would have preferred to wall off her tribe and never leave the Ice Kingdom again. But after the spell that ended the war, her palace had been flooded with requests from IceWings who wanted to attend Jade Mountain Academy. Even if she had wanted to shut down communications, her subjects wouldn't have let her. And so two new students had arrived to replace Winter and Icicle, and there was a wait list ready for when the school expanded.

"They really won't let you go home?" Kinkajou asked.

"Even after you fought alongside them? Even though you're totally awesome?"

"No, they're still pretty mad at me," Winter said. "Snowfall said I could come back for visits, like for Icicle's trial, and to visit Hailstorm, as long as I leave again within a few days. But my mother doesn't want to see me, and there's no one else I really want to see there. No one in the Circles, I mean."

He heaped a small pile of needles in front of him and nestled a pinecone into the middle of it. "It's not so bad. I thought a lot about some of the stuff Qibli is always saying to me. There are all these IceWings outside the Circles — outside the palaces. I'd never thought about them before, but I visited as many villages as I could to make sure they all were cured of the plague, and you know what? Apart from being less obsessed with status and Circles, they're not that different from the IceWings inside the palaces."

"That is astonishing news," Kinkajou said gravely.

He made a face at her. "I know, I shouldn't have been surprised. Anyway, I met several who were interested in moving to Sanctuary. So I'm not the only IceWing here, which is great."

"But why is Snowfall so mad at you?" Kinkajou asked.

"Oh, the whole First Circle is furious that I've ruined their Diamond Trial by letting Foeslayer escape. Luckily none of them know what she looks like, except Hailstorm, and I'm sure he won't say anything, even if he happens to run into her in the rainforest." He paused. "Moon's last letter said Foeslayer has changed her name and is settling in with the rest of the tribe. I — I know she had something to do with Darkstalker disappearing, but nobody will tell me exactly what happened."

"That's because you might not be cool about it," Kinkajou pointed out.

"I'm always cool!" he protested. "Oh, that wasn't a pun, stop laughing at me. I'm serious. You guys are acting like you can't trust me."

"We know we can trust you to be a loyal friend and awesome dragon and stand with us when we need you, yes," said Kinkajou. "But to let us handle Darkstalker our own way? We're not so sure."

Winter swept his tail through the pine needles. "He's really not coming back, though? Is he asleep under the mountain again? Are we sure he's definitely gone? He won't be back in another two thousand years or something?"

"Winter, he's gone." Kinkajou put one of her talons on his, looking him straight in the eyes. "He's never coming back. Your tribe is safe."

"All right," Winter said with a sigh. "I hope Moon is willing to tell me the whole story someday."

"Like I said, you could visit her. And you could start by apologizing for all those times you yelled at her and didn't believe in her and were totally mean."

He winced. "Was I awful? I was so angry about her being

friends with Darkstalker . . . I guess I can be a little awful when I'm angry."

"You can keep working on that," Kinkajou assured him. "It, um — it might be too late, though."

"I know," he said. "I knew back in the NightWing palace, when she took Qibli with her to face Darkstalker instead of me. It's my own fault." He traced his claw through the carpet of pine needles, wondering how long it would take his heart to heal.

"But we're all still friends, right?" Kinkajou said hopefully. "Turtle and Moon and I miss you."

"I miss you, too," he said. He didn't want to admit it out loud, but he missed Qibli as well. The letters he got from his former clawmate were not those of a triumphant rival, but a best friend who was worried about him.

Best friends with a SandWing? What is the world coming to? And not just a SandWing, but the one who won Moon's heart.

If only I didn't like him so much.

In his last letter, Qibli had promised to come to Sanctuary soon, and to bring Flower and Smolder, in case they had any ideas for his scavenger project.

He won't let me stop being friends with him. None of them will.

As weird as it is, they're my new family now . . . my new tribe.

And I think I'm going to be OK.

"So what do you say?" Kinkajou asked. Her scales rippled and faded into the background, but he could hear her smile in her voice. "Want to go catch some scavengers together?"

He smiled back. "Absolutely."

Peril still couldn't quite believe that Jade Mountain was really her home now.

She was part of a winglet and everything! Turtle's winglet, no less! She went to CLASSES. And STUDIED. And had HOMEWORK. And did projects with OTHER DRAGONS.

It was SO WEIRD.

She still had her own cave, because of the whole accidentally-setting-your-clawmates-on-fire-while-sleepwalking-would-be-bad thing. And she still needed her friends to read all the scrolls to her. She'd asked Starflight to get to work on inflammable scrolls once he and Tamarin were done with their project of making scrolls that blind dragons could read.

Peril figured if anyone could figure out scrolls that wouldn't burn, it was Starflight. He was certainly motivated to. He got hilariously twitchy whenever he smelled Peril anywhere near his papers.

She padded down the corridor toward the prey center. Not because it was highly likely that Clay would be there at any given time, of course. She actually had a perfectly good all-Peril no-Clay reason to go to the prey center.

But she didn't mind the little bounce her heart gave when she peeked into the center and saw him there.

Act normal! Or at least vaguely as though you have any idea what normal is!

He was curled by the river, chatting with his brother Marsh. Marsh's clawmate, Coconut, was there, too, poking around on the far side of the cave. The RainWing's scales were a honey-colored mix of amber and brown, like a gold-dappled version of Marsh's.

Is he busy? Maybe he's busy. Maybe I should —

Clay turned and smiled at her before she could duck out of sight again. She smiled back sheepishly and he padded across the cave to join her.

"Hey, Peril," he said. She knew he sounded kind no matter who he was talking to, but she hoped she wasn't imagining the extra little bit of sweetness in his smile for her.

"I came down to see if anyone wants their food set on fire," Peril said quickly. "The RainWings like it when I roast their bananas and sweet potatoes, so we're experimenting with other stuff. Siamang and I came up with this cooked mashed-up apple thing that is awesome."

"Applesauce?" Clay asked.

"Oh," Peril said. "Is that what it's called? We didn't invent it? OK, fine, applesauce, then. I bet ours is better than anyone else's, though."

"Probably," he said. "You'd better make it for me sometime." He put one wing around her and she somehow managed not to burst into delighted flames.

"What are you doing here?" she asked. "I mean, not that you shouldn't be here, you can be anywhere you want, of course, and it's just a wild coincidence that you happen to be here, in the place where I also happened to be going. WILD COINCIDENCE."

"Checking on Marsh," Clay said. "I was so worried about him after Umber and Sora left . . . but he seems really happy lately. Doesn't he?"

"I think so," Peril said. "I mean, I'm not *super* great at, like, emotions? On other dragons? But I'm pretty sure when a dragon smiles that much, it means he's happy."

"I think it's Coconut," Clay said. "He's the perfect claw-mate for Marsh. I wish we'd paired everyone else into best friends that well."

"I like the SkyWing that Queen Ruby sent to replace Flame," Peril said. "He's not completely terrified of me. It is pretty weird to have conversations with a SkyWing who isn't terrified of me."

"I hope Flame will be all right," Clay said. The angry SkyWing dragonet had accepted an earring reluctantly, choosing freedom from Darkstalker's spells even though it meant having his scars back. But he couldn't stay at the school after what he did to Stonemover, and he didn't want to anyway, and Peril thought that was for the best because he was an awful grouch to be around. Queen Ruby had taken him back to the Sky Kingdom to work with the healers.

"The queen will sort him out," she said. She glanced around the mostly empty prey center. "It seems so quiet today."

"Everyone's working on independent study projects," he said. "I just saw Ostrich, Thrush, and Barracuda talking about the science of RainWing camouflage in the library. And Tamarin, Pike, and Fearless are doing a presentation about Darkstalker's history later, if you're interested."

She shuddered a little, flicking her tail closer to his. "I don't know. Whenever his name comes up, everyone looks at me like they're remembering it was my fault he got out. I mean, I'm clearly the 'talons of fire' in the prophecy. Which makes me want to be like YEAH, I KNOW and I'M SORRY, OK and I'D LIKE TO SEE *YOU* TRY TO SAVE YOUR FRIENDS FROM AN ANCIENT SCROLL WITH NEBULOUS POWERS."

"You said friends," Clay echoed, bumping her side with a grin.

She scrunched up her snout so she wouldn't smile too much. "I think sometimes maybe they actually like me a little bit?"

"Or a lot," Clay said. "My guess is a lot."

"Even Winter has sent me a couple of letters," she said wonderingly, "like he cares what's going on with me. I got one from Qibli today. Sunny read it to me."

"I can help you write a letter back later, if you want," he said. "Although I can't promise any of the words will be spelled right."

She laughed. "Aren't you a teacher now? I'm *pretty* sure teachers should be able to spell."

"Yeah, I carefully avoid writing anything where my students can see it," he said. "Peril, don't feel bad about

Darkstalker anymore. He would have gotten out of his prison sooner or later. He was too smart to be stuck under there for long. And I think that scroll could have been just as dangerous as he was, if it was left floating around the continent."

"Right," Peril said dubiously. Sometimes she agreed and was all like, GOOD FOR ME YAY PERIL, especially whenever Qibli talked about what the scroll might have done to him if it had stayed in his talons. But a lot of the time she remembered Darkstalker bursting out of the mountain and thanking her for releasing him, and then it was hard not to feel like the dragon who nearly set the whole entire world on fire.

She thought for a moment. "You know," she said, nudging Clay's neck with her snout, "sometimes I think it's a good thing it was my dad who found it. He was a jerk, but he could have done much worse things with it. Another dragon might have done way worse things. Right?"

"Right," Clay reassured her.

Peril looked out at the rain. "I wonder if I'll ever see him again. I think he's going to stay pretty mad at me forever."

"You don't need him," Clay said. "You have friends now." He ducked his head to meet her eyes. "You have me."

Now there was no chance of holding back her smile. "Want to go flying with me?" she said impulsively. "I mean, I know it's raining, but it's kind of cool to fly in the rain, unless you're busy, you're probably busy, you're, like, running a school, so, that's OK if you can't, we —"

"Peril," he said, catching one of her front talons in his. "I'd love to."

Turtle spread the scroll out on a sunlit rock and read it again, humming to himself.

Dear Turtle,

Auklet and I send our love. You must come home for a visit soon so you can see the new palace we're building. We chose the perfect island for it and we're starting with an auditorium that will have wonderful acoustics for my scroll readings, with enough room to host dragons from all the tribes. We're not going to hide this one like the Summer Palace. I'm hoping it'll be a center for diplomacy and trade and art that will help us build relations across Pyrrhia, but especially with Queen Moorhen and Queen Glory, who have such interesting ideas.

Thank you for the spell you sent to get rid of the Albatross ghost Darkstalker conjured. What a strange and malevolent piece of magic. Everyone is quite relieved it's gone!

I hope your sister is doing well! Your brothers seem to think you played an enormously clever practical joke on them the last time you were at the palace. I didn't get all the details, but they're very impressed with you. You'd better carefully check your bed for lobsters the next time you're here.

Sending you all my love, and my newest story,
Mother

He dabbled his tail in the water of the lake below him, smiling. Every letter from Queen Coral felt like a new magic spell, making him stronger and braver and more the hero he hoped to be.

Up in the sky, Anemone was doing flips in the air, flinging out her wings happily. A bracelet of pale pink pearls shone around her wrist, matching her scales. It was the only jewelry she wore anymore, most of the time. She'd sat with Qibli for hours one day, working out the words for a spell that would protect her soul — not just from animus magic, but from the feelings of invincibility and superiority that went along with it. Ever since putting it on, she'd been acting lighter and younger, giggling and teasing Pike, and taking her winglet swimming in the mountain lakes every day.

Turtle wasn't sure if it was the magic of the bracelet or the relief that came from not worrying about her soul anymore. The soul reader had revealed a much higher level of good in the princess's soul than they all had feared — and Turtle's own soul was almost entirely good, too, to his delight.

Now Anemone kept the soul reader in her room, and Turtle suspected she checked it fairly often. He hadn't seen her cast any spells in the last month. She'd been focused on doing good things — like donating half her treasure to help build Sanctuary — and otherwise, she seemed content to be a normal student for now.

He heard splashing in the lake and turned to find Kinkajou wading out of the water toward him.

"I thought we were going swimming!" she said.

"I just wanted to read this letter one more time," Turtle said, rolling it up again.

"Awwww." Kinkajou flicked a spray of water at his tail. "You're so cute about your mom, it almost makes me wish I knew who my parents are."

He tipped his head at her. "I could probably find out for you."

"That's all right," she said. "I know you're trying to use your magic as little as possible. I can figure it out some other way if I ever really want to."

Turtle tapped his skyfire armband. "But I can use it, if you ever need to. Qibli's soul spell is really well-written."

"Speaking of well-written," Kinkajou said as he dove into the water. She waited until he surfaced again to finish her thought. "I loved the story you wrote for class the other day. You should write more of it."

"Really?" he said shyly. "You're not just saying that?"

"I'm not enchanted to say nice things about you anymore," she said with a laugh.

He laughed, too, but a little awkwardly. They'd pretty much avoided the subject of the love spell for the last month. He paddled his webbed talons underneath him for a moment, then blurted, "I still really like you, Kinkajou."

Her scales shimmered rose with flecks of citrus orange and yellow. "Oh," she said. "I mean, I really like you, too, just . . . I'm still . . . it's weird, Turtle! It's weird to wake up suddenly having all these feelings and then find out they're not real and then suddenly they're gone but not really because you remember feeling them, which is awfully close to actually still feeling them, and then there are lots of reasons *to* feel them because you *are* adorable but I'm not *totally* sure how much I feel them and so it's *very confusing.*"

"Sure, yeah, OK," he said. "Never mind."

"No, not never mind!" she said, splashing water over his head. "More like, let's keep hanging out and see what happens? And I'll try to figure out which feelings are real after a little more time has passed? That's what I think we should do."

"That's all right with me," he said. "I mean, it's great. Totally great with me." He felt a fish swim right between his claws, but it wiggled away when he tried to grab it. "You really think I'm adorable?"

"Yes," said Kinkajou, "but I think lots of things are adorable, so don't get too excited. I mean, you're somewhere between baby sloths and Anemone's crush on Tamarin on the adorableness scale."

He dunked his head underwater, hiding his smile. A moment later, he popped out again. "Wait, what? Anemone has a crush on someone?"

"Oh my gosh, yes," Kinkajou said with a giggle. "You haven't noticed? She's been casually showing up everywhere Tamarin is, offering to read her scrolls, leaving her little gifts of flowers or unusual fruit. It's almost cute enough to make me forgive her, but I told Tamarin she better be careful. I am watching VERY CLOSELY to make sure Anemone doesn't use any magic on my friend."

"She won't," Turtle said confidently. "Our soul spells stipulate that we can only do magic that doesn't affect another dragon's free will. And that we can't do any magic that's selfishly motivated. Both of those should keep Anemone from doing any more love spells."

"Hmmmph," said Kinkajou. "Well, I'm keeping an eye on her anyway. She's going to have to be pretty super awesome to ever be worthy of Tamarin."

I'm going to work hard to be super awesome, too, Turtle promised himself. *I've read enough romance scrolls; I should have some idea of what to do. It'll be crazy if I actually end up in one of those stories myself.*

Save the world, check. Stop being afraid of my magic, check. Figure out a way to protect my soul, check.

Become the kind of dragon I'd want to read about — working on it. Probably working on it for the rest of my life. But I think I'm getting there.

A gust of wind lifted a spray of sand and danced it across the dunes. Qibli set the stone he was carrying into its place in the wall and checked the sky. Dark blue and cloudless, as usual, as afternoon faded into evening. A few stars were already shining over the horizon and the moons were rising in the distance. Everything was calm. Nothing to worry about.

"Time for a break," Six-Claws called from the roof of the treasury.

The SandWings around Qibli stretched and wandered off in search of water. The reconstruction work was almost done; everything Vulture, the Talons of Power, and Qibli's sandstorm had done to the palace was nearly fixed.

Qibli spotted Queen Thorn standing next to Six-Claws, as though she'd been there watching for a while. She said something to her general and then flew down to land beside Qibli.

"Six-Claws says you've been working hard," she said, handing him a flask of water.

"Thank you, Your Majesty," he said.

"OK, enough of that," she said. "Your talents are completely wasted on building walls. When are you going back to school?"

"Don't you need me here?" he said.

"There will still be plenty to do after you are done with school," she said firmly. "Are you hiding from someone?"

That was a little too perceptive for Qibli to handle. "No!" he said quickly.

"Oh, good," she said. "Because the someone you've not been hiding from is here to see you."

"She is?" he said, flaring his wings. Queen Thorn gave him an amused glance and he realized he'd given himself away. "I mean, who? What? I have no idea what you're talking about."

"I told her to wait for you in the observatory," Thorn said, nodding at the domed tower that was open to the sky. "If she can talk you into going back to school, I'll give her some kind of SandWing medal of honor."

Qibli's wings were trembling so much he wasn't sure he'd make it all the way up to the tower. He took a few deep breaths, poured the water over his head to clean off the sand, and shook himself dry.

Moon was peering into the telescope as he came through the hole in the roof.

"This is amazing," she said, turning to him with the brightest of smiles. "I can see craters on that moon! Are there any SandWing astronomy scrolls? Does this palace have a library? It must, right?"

"It does," Qibli said. "I can take you there if, um . . . if that's why you're here."

"No, no, it's not," she said. She crossed the room and was suddenly right in front of him, like he'd been imagining for weeks. What were all the clever things he was going to say? Why had they all flown out of his brain?

"Please come back to school, Qibli," she said. She took his front talons in hers. "We miss you. *I* miss you."

"Moon," he said, looking down at the floor. "You should be saying this to Winter."

She paused. "Winter," she said cautiously. "Why?"

This part he'd prepared for. That didn't make this any easier to say, but he was determined to try. "Because he needs you. He'd go back to school if you asked him. You make him a better dragon and I . . . I don't know if he can live without you."

She studied his face. "I don't know if that's true, Qibli. I think he'll be all right no matter what happens — he's strong and smart and he's going to do great things with his life. But I do know *I* need *you*."

That wasn't in any of the possible scripts Qibli had practiced. He was startled into meeting her eyes. When she smiled, her teardrop scales became little rivulets of silver.

"I want to be with someone who's kind and makes me laugh and listens to me. That's you. When I think about the future and everything I want to do with my life, I think about you. That's what I know."

Qibli wasn't sure his lungs were working properly, or maybe that was his heart trying to escape from his chest to fly around the room.

"But —" he started.

"No, no," she said. She touched her claws to his temples. "I know your brain is shooting like a comet right now. Stop thinking about all the problems and scenarios and ways out. Just take a breath and look at me."

He did. Her eyes looked into him, and even with the sky-fire hiding his thoughts, he knew she saw his whole self. And that was what she wanted, somehow, miraculously.

"Can we try being together?" she asked. "Without a prophecy or a scroll or a catastrophe or a war or anything else crazy going on? Don't overthink. Say yes."

"Yes," he said.

A smile spread across her face like a sunrise. "Awesome," she said.

"Awesome," he agreed, smiling back.

They stood there, smiling and feeling very silly, for a long quiet moment.

"So," she said, "I know I literally just said 'without a prophecy or catastrophe or anything crazy,' but . . . I've kind of been having a vision lately."

"Oh no," he said with a laugh. "Another mysterious prophecy?"

"Not exactly," she said. "But there's something I need to check out. I was hoping you'd come with me?"

"Anywhere," he said. "Always."

They said good-bye to Queen Thorn, flew west through the night, and reached the coast before morning. Qibli had never been this far west; he'd never seen this edge of the Kingdom of Sand. He hadn't quite thought about the surging ocean right at their doorstep, although he knew there were a few SandWing settlements along the water. But Moon didn't take them in that direction; she turned north instead, toward the border with the Ice Kingdom.

In a little cove north of the farthest northern oasis, they found what she was looking for: a small hut on the beach, roofed with palm fronds.

Qibli glanced at Moon in confusion as they landed on the damp sand in front of it. "Who lives here?"

"Someone I saw in my vision, I think," she said. "If I'm right, Turtle saw her, too, just for a moment, in Darkstalker's throne room. He told me about it — but he said he wasn't sure she was real. I think she is, and I think we'll find her here."

As she said that, the door opened and a SandWing emerged. She was tall and long-necked and graceful, with wide black eyes and a dappled brown triangle pattern on her wings. She watched them gravely as they climbed the beach toward her.

"Hello," Moon said, dipping her head to the stranger. "My name is Moon and this is Qibli. Did you know we were coming?"

"I knew someone would come," she said in a quiet voice. "I guessed it would be soon."

"What's your name?" Moon asked. "I saw you in a vision, but I don't really know why."

"I'm Jerboa," said the SandWing.

Qibli's eyes widened, and she noticed and shook her head. "Not the original Jerboa," she said. "Her daughter."

"From way back in Darkstalker's time?" Qibli asked.

"Yes. My mother cast a spell to make sure nothing could ever harm me." Jerboa shrugged. "I've been waiting a long time to fulfill my purpose."

"Your purpose?" Moon asked.

"Yes," Jerboa said again. She spread one wing to invite them into the hut. "I believe the first step is introducing you."

"To who?" Qibli asked, stepping inside. He edged sideways to make room for Moon to enter, too, and his eyes took a moment to adjust to the dark interior.

There was an injured dragon in there, lying on a bed of palm fronds. She sat up as they entered and eyed them warily.

And then Qibli saw the shape of her wings, and her face, and the color of her scales, and he realized this dragon was no hybrid. She was not from any tribe he'd ever seen before.

She was something completely different.

"What —" Moon whispered. "How —?"

"I believe this," said Jerboa, "is our first visitor from the lost continent."

WINGS
OF
FIRE

will continue . . .

Blue dug in his claws as Io tried to throw him out the door. "Wait, wait! Run *where*?"

"Anywhere!" she said. "Listen, Blue. Stop trusting the HiveWings *right now*. They've let you go about your ordinary life so far, but now you look dangerous to them, and they're not going to let you have that life back. It's gone."

"But if I'm good, if I do what I'm told — I mean, I'm *not* dangerous. I could *never* be dangerous."

"I know," Io said. "But they don't care. Please promise me you'll hide from them, Blue. Don't let them catch you."

"For how long?" Blue said. "Where can I go? What about my Metamorphosis? It's really soon and then I'll have to come back here."

Io sighed. "Let's hide you first and then figure that out," she said. She shoved open the door, flung him outside, and bolted after him. Blue found himself running even though his brain was shouting at him to go back, to ask the guards for help, to make sure Luna was all right.

Was she still terrified? What had the guards done to Swordtail? Was he lying beside Luna on the sand now, bleeding and swollen with venom?

Blue shuddered, his claws wobbling underneath him.

They had just reached the edge of the outer courtyard when he heard shouts behind them. "Stop! You there! SilkWings! Stop at once!"

His feet obeyed instinctively. Guards were talking to him;

guards were to be listened to. You never argued with HiveWing guards.

But Io didn't stop. Io threw her talons around his chest and hurled them up into the air, her spectacular wings pumping desperately.

"Io!" Blue yelped with fear as his claws left the ground. Suddenly they were flying along the narrow streets, flashes of startled faces peering out of windows at them.

"Stop! Queen Wasp orders you to stop at once!"

Where did Io think they were going? Nobody ran from the queen's guards. And she would surely kill them both for disobeying her orders.

Io let out a small roar of frustration. They were nearly at the exit that led to the tunnels spiraling up — but guards were closing rank in front of it, spears crossed, teeth gleaming.

That's the only exit, Blue thought frantically. There weren't even any windows or ledges to the open sky on this level of the Hive.

Oh, he realized with a fresh burst of terror. *That's probably intentional.*

So there's no way for a flamesilk to escape.

THE DRAGONS ARE READY TO MEET THEIR DESTINY!